Hiram Corson, Decimus Juvenal

The Satires of Decimus Junius Juvenalis

with a literal interlineal translation on the Hamiltonian system. With the life of

Juvenal, by William Gifford

Hiram Corson, Decimus Juvenal

The Satires of Decimus Junius Juvenalis
with a literal interlineal translation on the Hamiltonian system. With the life of Juvenal, by William Gifford

ISBN/EAN: 9783337367602

Printed in Europe, USA, Canada, Australia, Japan

Cover: Foto ©Andreas Hilbeck / pixelio.de

More available books at **www.hansebooks.com**

THE SATIRES

OF

DECIMUS JUNIUS JUVENALIS,

WITH

A LITERAL INTERLINEAL TRANSLATION,

ON THE

HAMILTONIAN SYSTEM.

WITH THE LIFE OF JUVENAL,

By WILLIAM GIFFORD, Esq.

For the Use of Schools and Private Learners.

BY

HIRAM CORSON, A. M.,

EDITOR OF "CHAUCER'S LEGENDE OF GOODE WOMEN;" PROFESSOR OF
RHETORIC AND OF THE ENGLISH LANGUAGE AND LITERATURE
IN ST. JOHN'S COLLEGE, ANNAPOLIS; LATE PROFESSOR
OF MORAL SCIENCE, HISTORY, AND RHETORIC,
IN GIRARD COLLEGE, PHILADELPHIA.

PHILADELPHIA:
CHARLES DESILVER;
CLAXTON, REMSEN & HAFFELFINGER;
J. B. LIPPINCOTT & CO.
New York: D. APPLETON & CO. Boston: NICHOLS & HALL.
Cincinnati: ROBERT CLARKE & CO; WILSON, HINKLE & CO
San Francisco: A. L. BANCROFT & CO.
Chicago: S. C. Griggs & Co.—Charleston, S. C.: J. M. Greer & Son; Edward Perry
& Son.—Raleigh, N. C.: Williams & Lambeth.—Baltimore, Md.: Cushings
& Bailey; W. J. C. Dulaney & Co.—New Orleans, La.: Stevens &
Seymour.—Savannah, Ga.: J. M. Cooper & Co.—Macon, Ga.:
J. M. Boardman.—Augusta, Ga.: Thos. Richards &
Son.—Richmond, Va.: Woodhouse & Parham.
1874.

PREFACE.

The present translation of Juvenal differs from the other translations in the series of interlinears published by Mr. DESILVER, in the following respect :—The order of the original has been preserved, and the order in which the words of the translation should be read, when it departs from the English order, is indicated by numerals. This has been thought an improvement which will be recognized by all educators and students, and by all who may have occasion to consult the original.

The arguments of the Satires have been taken from the excellent translation of Juvenal by Evans, published in Bohn's series. H. C.

THE LIFE OF JUVENAL.

BY WILLIAM GIFFORD, ESQ.

DECIMUS JUNIUS JUVENALIS, the author of the following Satires, was born at Aquinum, an inconsiderable town
of the Volsci, about the year of Christ 38. He was either
the son, or the foster-son, of a wealthy freedman, who gave
him a liberal education. From the period of his birth, till
he had attained the age of forty, nothing more is known
of him than that he continued to perfect himself in the
study of eloquence, by declaiming, according to the practice of those days; yet more for his own amusement, than
from any intention to prepare himself either for the schools
or the courts of law. About this time he seems to have
discovered his true bent, and betaken' himself to poetry.
Domitian was now at the head of the government, and
showed symptoms of reviving that system of favoritism
which had nearly ruined the empire under Claudius, by
his unbounded partiality for a young pantomime dancer
of the name of Paris Against this minion, Juvenal seems
to have directed the first shafts of that satire which was
destined to make the most powerful vices tremble, and
shake the masters of the world on their thrones. He composed a few lines on the influence of Paris, with considerable success, which encouraged him to cultivate this kind
of poetry : He had the prudence, however, not to trust
himself to an auditory, in a reign which swarmed with

informers; and his compositions were, therefore, secretly
handed about amongst his friends. By degrees he grew
bolder; and, having made many large additions to his first
sketch, or perhaps re-cast it, produced what is now called
his seventh Satire, which he recited to numerous as-
semblages. The consequences were such as he had
probably anticipated: Paris, informed of the part which
he bore in it, was seriously offended, and complained to
the emperor, who, as the old account has it, sent the author
by an easy kind of punishment, into Egypt with a military
command. To remove such a man from his court must
undoubtedly have been desirable to Domitian; and, as he
was spoken of with kindness in the same Satire, which is
entirely free from political allusions, the "facetiousness"
of the punishment (though Domitian's was not a facetious
reign) renders the fact not altogether improbable. Yet,
when we consider that these reflections on Paris could
scarcely have been published before LXXXIV., and that the
favorite was disgraced and put to death almost immediately
after, we shall be inclined to doubt whether his banish-
ment actually took place; or, if it did, whether it was of
any long duration. That Juvenal was in Egypt is certain; but he might have gone there from motives of personal safety, or, as Salmasius has it, of curiosity. However this may be, it does not appear that he was ever long
absent from Rome, where a thousand internal marks clearly
show that all his Satires were written. But whatever
punishment might have followed the complaint of Paris,
it had no other effect on our author, than that of increasing his hatred of tyranny, and turning his indignation
upon the emperor himself, whose hypocrisy, cruelty, and
licentiousness, became, from that period, the object of his
keenest reprobation. He profited, indeed, so far by his
danger or his punishment, as to recite no more in public;

but he continued to write during the remainder of Domitian's reign, in which he finished, as I conceive, his second,
third, fifth, sixth, and perhaps thirteenth satires; the
eighth, I have always looked upon as his first.

In xcv., when Juvenal was in his 54th year, Domitian
banished the philosophers from Rome, and soon after from
Italy, with many circumstances of cruelty; an action, for
which, I am sorry to observe, he is covertly praised by
Quintilian. Though Juvenal, strictly speaking, did not
come under the description of a philosopher, yet, like the
hare in the fable, he might not unreasonably entertain some
apprehensions for his safety, and, with many other persons
eminent for learning and virtue, judge it prudent to with-
draw from the city. To this period I have always inclined
to fix his journey to Egypt. Two years afterwards the
world was happily relieved from the tyranny of Domitian; and Nerva, who succeeded him, recalled the exiles.
From this time there remains little doubt of Juvenal's being at Rome, where he continued his studies in tranquility.

His first Satire, after the death of Domitian, seems to
have been what is now called the fourth. About this
time, too, he probably though, of revising and publishing
those which he had already written; and composed or
completed that introductory piece, which now stands at
the head of his works. As the order is everywhere broken
in upon, it is utterly impossible to arrange them chronologi-
cally; but I am inclined to think that the eleventh Satire
closed his poetical career. All else is conjecture; but in
this he speaks of himself as an old man,

" Nostra bibat vernum contracta cuticula solem ;"

and indeed he had now passed his grand climacteric.

This is all that can be collected of the life of Juvenal;
and how much of this is built upon uncertainties? I hope,
however, that it bears the stamp of probability, which is

all I contend for; and which, indeed, if I do not deceive myself, is somewhat more that can be affirmed of what has been hitherto delivered on the subject.

Little is known of Juvenal's circumstances; but, happily, that little is authentic, as it comes from himself. He had a competence. The dignity of poetry is never disgraced in him, as it is in some of his contemporaries, by fretful complaints of poverty, or clamorous whinings for meat and clothes: the little patrimony which his foster-father left him, he never diminished, and probably never increased. It seems to have equalled all his wants, and, as far as appears, all his wishes. Once only he regrets the narrowness of his fortune; but the occasion does him honor; it is solely because he cannot afford a more costly sacrifice to express his pious gratitude for the preservation of his friend: yet "two lambs and a youthful steer" bespeak the affluence of a philosopher; which is not belied by the entertainment provided for his friend Persius, in that beautiful Satire which is here called the last of his works. Further it is useless to seek; from pride or modesty, he has left no other notices of himself; or they have perished. Horace and Persius, his immediate predecessors, are never weary of speaking of themselves. The life of the former might be written, from his own materials, with all the minuteness of a contemporary history; and the latter, who attained to little more than a third of Juvenal's age, has left nothing to be desired on the only topics which could interest posterity—his parent, his preceptor, and his course of studies.

SATIRE I.

ARGUMENT.

THIS Satire seems, from several incidental circumstances, to have been produced subsequently to most
of them ; and was probably drawn up after the author
had determined to collect and publish his works, as a
kind of Introduction.

He abruptly breaks silence with an impassioned complaint of the importunity of bad writers, and a resolution of retaliating upon them ; and after ridiculing their
frivolous taste in the choice of their subjects, declares his
own intentions to devote himself to Satire. After ex-
posing the corruption of men, the profligacy of women,
the luxury of courtiers, the baseness of informers and
fortune-hunters, the treachery of guardians, and the
peculation of officers of state, he censures the general
passion for gambling, the servile rapacity of the patricians, the avarice and gluttony of the rich, and the miserable poverty and subjection of their dependents ; and after
some bitter reflections on the danger of satirizing living
villany, concludes with a resolution to attack it under
the mask of departed names.

Semper   ego   auditor   tantum?   nunquamne repo-
Always   I   a-hearer   only?   never   shall-

nam,   Vexatus   toties   rauci   Theseide   Codri?
I-repay,   vexed   so-often of-hoarse with-the-Theseis Codrus?
                                           2   1   3

Impunè   ergo   mihi   recitaverit   ilſe   toga-
With-impunity therefore to-me   shall recite   that (poet) (his)
                                      2   1

tas,   Hic   Elegos?   impunè   diem   consumpserit
comedies, This, (his)-Elegies? with-impunity a-day   shall consume
                                                          3

9

ingens Telephus? aut summi plenâ jam
huge   Telephus? or   of-the-whole full already
1   2   3   6   5

margine libri Scriptus, et in tergo, necdum
the-margin book written and on the-back nor-as-yet
2   4   8   7   9   10

finitus Orestes? Nota magis nulli domus est
finished Orestes? Known more to-no-one house is
11   1   2   more 3   1

sua, quam mihi lucus Martis, et Æoliis
his-own than to-me the-grove of-Mars and to-the-Eolian
2   4

vicinum rupibus antrum Vulcani. Quid agant
near   rocks   the-cave of-Vulcan. What can-do
3   5   1   2

venti; quas torqueat umbras Æacus; unde alius
the-winds; what may-torment shades Æacus; whence another
1   1   4   2   3

furtivæ devehat aurum Pelliculæ; quantas jacu-
of-the-stolen may-convey the-gold fleece: how-great may
3   1   2   4   1

letur Monychus ornos; Frontonis platani, convul-
hurl   Monychus ash-trees; of-Fronto the-plane-trees and-the
4   3   2   of-Fronto 1

saque marmora clamant Semper, et assiduo
convulsed marbles complain always, and with-the-assiduous
                                              3

ruptæ lectore columnæ. Expectes eadem à
broken reader the-columns. You-may-expect the-same (things) from
2   4   1

summo minimoque poëtâ. Et nos ergo ma-
the-highest, and-the-least poet. And we therefore (our)

num ferulæ subduximus, et nos Consilium
hand from-the-ferule have-withdrawn: and we counsel

dedimus Syllæ, privatus ut altum Dormiret.
have-given to-Sylla, a-private (man) that soundly he-should-sleep.
                                   2   1

Stulta est clementia, cum tot ubique Vatibus
Foolish is the-clemency, when so-many everwhere poets
                                 2   1   3

occurras, perituræ parcere chartæ. Cur tamen
you-may-meet, destined-to-perish to-spare paper. Why yet
           3   1   2   2   1

hoc libeat potius decurrere campo, Per quem
this it-should-please (me) rather to-run-along field, through which
4   1   2   3   5

magnus equos Auruncæ flexit alumnus; Si va-
(the) great (his) horses of-Aurunca drove pupil; if there
1   5   3   4   2

eat, et placidi rationem admittitis, edam. Cum
is-leisure, and composed the-reason you-admit I-will-tell. When
       2   4   1   3

tener   uxorem   ducat   spado :   Mævia   Tuscum   Fi-
a-tender   a-wife   can-marry   eunuch :   Mævia   a-Tuscan   can
1   4   3   2   2   1

gat aprum,   et   nudâ   teneat   venabula   mammâ :
stick   boar   and   with-a-naked   can-hold   hunting-spears   breast :
      3   1   2   4

Patricios   omnes   opibus   cum   provocet   unus,
patricians   all   with-riches   when   can-challenge   one
5   4   6   1   3   2

Quo   tondente   gravis   juveni   mihi   barba   sonabat :
who   clipping,   troublesome   a-youth   to-me   (my) beard   sounded :
      2   4   3   1

Cum   pars   Niliacæ   plebis,   cum   verna   Canopi
When   a-part   of-the-Nilian   commonalty,   when   a-slave   of-Canopus,

Crispinus,   Tyrias   humero   revocante   lacernas,
Crispinus,   the-Tyrian   (his)-shoulder   recalling   cloaks,
      3   1   2   4

Ventilet   æstivum   digitis   sudantibus   aurum,
can-ventilate   the-summer   on-(his)-fingers   sweating   gold,
      3   2   1

Nec   sufferre   queat   majoris   pondera   gemmæ :
nor   bear   can-he   of-a-larger   the-weight   gem ;
      2   1   3

Difficile   est   Satiram   non   scribere.   Nam   quis
difficult   it-is   satire   not   to-write.   For   who

iniquæ   Tam   patiens   urbis,   tam   ferreus,
of-the-iniquitous   so   enduring   city,   so   hardened,
3   1   2   4

ut   teneat   se ?   Causidici   nova   cum   veniat
that   he-may-contain   himself ?   of-lawyer   the-new   when   comes
      4   2   1   6

lectica   Mathonis   Plena   ipso ;   et   post   hunc
litter   Matho   full-of   himself ;   and   after   him
3   5

magni   delator   amici,   Et   citó   rapturus   de
of-a-great   the-accuser   friend,   and   soon   about-to- seize   from
2   1   3

nobilitate   comesâ   Quod   superest :   quem
nobility   the-devoured   what   remains :   whom
2   1

Massa   timet ;   quem   munere   palpat   Carus ;   et
Massa   fears :   whom   with-a-gift   soothes   Carus ;   and
                  2   1

a   trepido   Thymele   summissa   Latino.   Cum te
from   trembling   Thymele   sent-privately   Latinus.   When   thee
3   4   1   2   5

summoveant,   qui   testamenta   merentur   Noctibus,
they-can-removo   who   wills   merit   by-nights,
            2   1

In cœlum quos evehit optima summi Nunc
into heaven whom exalts (the-best of-the-highest now
2   3   1   7   2   4   1

via processûs,) vetulæ vesica beatæ. Unciolam
way success,) old-woman the-lust of-a-rich. A-little-ounce
3   5   6   4   5

Proculeius habet, sed Gillo deuncem : Partes
Proculeius has, but Gillo eleven-ounces : portions
3

quisque suas, ad mensuram inguinis hæres:
every-one his, according-to the-measure of-his—— heir :
1   2   5   6   7   4

Accipiat sané mercedem sanguinis, et sic Palleat,
let-him-receive well the-reward of-his-blood, and so grow-pale
2   1

ut nudis pressit qui calcibus anguem, Aut
as with-naked has-pressed (one)-who heels a-snake, or
2   4   1   3

Lugdunensem rhetor dicturus ad aram. Quid
of-Lyons a-rhetorician about-to-speak at the-altar. What
5   1   2   3   4

referam? quantâ siccum jecur ardeat irâ, Cum
shall-I-say? with-how-great (my)-dry liver burns anger, when
2   3   4   1

populum gregibus comitum premat hic spoliator
the-people with-flocks of-companions presses-on here, a-spoiler
6   7   8   5   1   2

Pupilli prostantis? et hic damnatus
of-his-pupil standing-exposed-(to-hire)? and here, condemned
3   4

inani Judicio (quid enim salvis infamia
by-an-empty judgment (what (is) for (being) safe infamy
2   1   5   3

nummis?) Exul ab octavâ Marius bibit, et
money?) the-exile from the-eighth-(hour) Marius drinks, and
4   3   4   1   2

fruitur Dis Iratis: at tu victrix provincia
enjoys Gods the-angry: but thou, victorious province,
2   1

ploras! Hæc ego non credam Venusinâ
wailest! These-(things) I not shall-believe of-the-Venusinian
2   3   1   4   2

digna lucernâ? Hæc ego non agitem? sed quid
worthy lamp? These-(subjects) I not must-agitate? but why
1   3   2   1   4

magis Heracleas, Aut Diomedeas, aut mugitum
rather Heracleans, or Diomedeans or the lowing

labyrinthi, Et mare percussum puero, fabrumque
of-the-labyrinth, and-the-sea stricken by-a-boy, and-the-artificer
2

volantem? Cum leno accipiat mœchi
flying? when the-pander can-accept of-the-adulterer
1 2

bona, si capiendi Jus nullum uxori,
the-goods, if of-taking (there-is) right no to-the-wife,
1 2 1

doctus spectare lacunar, Doctus et ad calicem
taught to-look-at the-ceiling, taught also at a-cup

vigilanti stertere naso: Cum fas esse
with-a-vigilant to-snore nose. When right (it) to-be
2 1 3 3 2

putet curam sperare cohortis, Qui bona
he-can-think the-care to-hope-for of-a-cohort, who (his) goods
1 2 1 3

donavit præsepibus, et caret omni majorum
has-given to-stables, and lacks all of-his-ancestors
2

censu, dum pervolat axe citato Flaminiam:
the-estate, while he-flies-over with-axle swift the-Flaminian(way):
1

puer Automedon nam lora tenebat, Ipse
the-boy Automedon for the-reins was-holding, he-himself
2 3 1 2

lacernatæ cum se jactaret amicæ. Nonne
to (his) cloaked when himself boasted mistress. Doth-it-not
5 1 4 3 6

libet medio ceras implere capaces
please in-the-middle-of waxen-tablets to-fill capacious
4 3 1 2

Quadrivio — cum jam sextâ cervice feratur
a-cross-way — when now on-a-sixth neck can-be-borne
5

(Hinc atque inde patens, ac nudâ pene
(here and there exposed, and in-a-naked almost
2 1

cathedrâ, Et multum referens de Mæcenate
chair and much reminding of Mæcenas
3 2

supino) Signator falso, qui se lautum, atque
the-supine) a-signer to-the-false, who himself splendid and
1

beatum Exiguis tabulis, et gemmâ fecerat
happy with-small tables, and with-a-gem had-made
2 3 4 5 6 8 1

udâ? Occurrit matrona potens, quæ molle
wet? Occurs a-matron potent, who soft
7

Calenum Porrectura viro micet sitiente
Calenian-(wine) about-to-reach-forth, (her)-husband mixes thirsting
2 1

rubetam,   Instituitque   rudes   melior   Locusta
a-toad,   instructs-and   (her) rude   a-better   Locusta
         4   1   5   2   3

propinquas,   Per   famam,   et   populum,   nigros
neighbors,   through   fame   and   the-people   (their) black
   6   2

efferre   maritos.   Aude   aliquid   brevibus
to-bring-forth   husbands.   Dare   something   the-small
   1   3   2

Gyaris,   et carcere   dignum,   Si   vis   esse   aliquis.
Gyaræ,   and a-prison   worthy,   if   you-wish   to-be   somebody.
   3   4   5   1

PROBITAS   LAUDATUR,   ET   ALGET.   Criminibus   debent
Probity   is-praised   and   starves.   To-crimes   they-owe

hortos,   prætoria,   mensas,   Argentum   vetus,   et
gardens,   palaces,   tables,   silver   old,   and

stantem   extra   pocula caprum.   Quem   patitur
standing   on-the-outside-of   cups   a-goat.   Whom   does-suffer
   2   3   4   1   1   5

dormire   nurûs   corruptor   avaræ?   Quem
to-sleep   daughter-in-law   the-corrupter   of-a-covetous?   Whom
   6   4   2   3

sponsæ   turpes,   et   prætextatus   adulter?   Si
wives   lewd   and   the-young   adulterer?   If

natura negat, facit indignatio versum, Qualemcunque
nature   refuses, makes   indignation   verse,   such-as
                  2   1

potest: quales · ego,   vel   Cluvienus.   Ex   quo
it-can: such-as   I,   or   Cluvienus.   From what-(time,)

Deucalion,   nimbis   tollentibus   aequor,
Deucalion,   (the-rain-storms   raising   · the-sea,)

Navigio   montem   ascendit,   sortesque
with-his-bark   the-mountain   ascended,   lots   and
                                           3   1

poposcit,   Paulatimque   animâ caluerunt   mollia
asked-for,   by-little-and-little-and   with-life   grew-warm   the-soft
   2   2   1   3   1

saxa, Et   maribus   nudas   ostendit   Pyrrha   puellas:
stones,   and   to-males   naked   showed   Pyrrha   damsels:
   2   3   2   1   4

Quicquid   agunt   homines,   votum,   timor,   ira,
whatever   do   men,   a-vow,   fear,   anger,
              2   1

voluptas,   Gaudia,   discursus,   nostri   est   farrago
pleasure,   joys,   discourse,   of-our   is   the-mixed-subject
                                 3   1   2

libelli.   Et   quando   uberior   vitiorum copia?
little-book. And   when (was-there)-a-more-fruitful of-vices abundance
   4   2   1

quando   Major   avaritiæ   patuit   sinus?   alea
when   a-greater   of-avarice   has-lain open   bosom?   the-dice
       2   3   1   2   2

quando   Hos   animos?   neque   enim   loculis
when   these   spirits?   not   for   purses
  1   3   1   5

comitantibus   itur   Ad   casum   tabulæ,   positâ
accompanying   it-is-gone   to   the-chance   of-the-table,   being-staked
  6   1 2   4   4

sed   luditur   arcû.   Prælia   quanta   illic   dispensatore
but   it-is-played   a-chest.   Battles   how-many   there   the-steward
 1   2   3   2   1   4   5

videbis   Armigero!   simplexne   furor   sestertia
will-you-see   (being)-armour-bearer!   (is-it)-simple   madness   sestertia
   3   6   3

centum   Perdere,   et   horrenti   tunicam   non   reddere
a-hundred   to-lose,   and   to-a-ragged   a-coat   not   to-give
  2   1   4   3   1   2

servo?   Quis   totidem   erexit   villas?   quis   fer-
servant?   Who   so-many   has-erected   villas?   what   courses-
  5   2   1   3

cula   septem   Secretó   cœnavit   avus?   nunc   sportula
of-dishes   seven   in-secret   dined-on   ancestor?   now   basket
  4   3   5   2   1   2

primo   Limine   parva   sedet,   turbæ   rapienda
on-the-first   threshold   a-little   sits,   crowd   to-be-snatched-by
   3   4   1   3   1

togatæ.   Ille   tamen   faciem   prius   inspicit,   et
the-gowned.   He   but   the-face   first   inspects   and
   2   2   1

trepidat   ne   Suppositus   venias,   ac
trembles   lest   put-in-the-place-of-another   you-come   and

falso   nomine   poscas: Agnitus   accipies.   Ju-
in-a-false   name   ask: acknowledged   you-will-receive.   He-
  2   3   1

bet   a   præcone   vocari   Ipsos   Trojugenas:
commands   by   the-crier   to-be-called   the-very   descendants-of-the-Trojans:
            2   1

nam   vexant   limen   et   ipsi   Nobiscum: da
for   molest   the-threshold   also   they-themselves   with-us: "give
      3   4   2   1

Prætori,   da   deinde   Tribuno.   Sed   libertinus
to-the-Prætor.   give   then   to-the-Tribune."   But   the-freedman

prior   est: prior,   inquit,   ego   adsum: Cur   timeam,
first   is: the-first,   says-he,   I   am-present.   Why   should-I-fear,
 2   1   2   3   1

dubitemve,   locum   defendere?   quamvis   Natus   ad
or-hesitate   my-place   to-defend?   although   born   at

Euphratem,   molles   quod   in   aure   fenestræ
the-Euphrates   the-soft   which   in   my-ear   holes
              2   1   4   3

Arguerint, licet ipse　　negem:　sed quinque tabernæ
prove,　　though I-myself should-deny-it: but　five　houses
5

Quadringenta　　parant:　quid　confert　purpura
four-hundred-(sestertia)　procure,　what　confers　the-purple

majus Optandum, si Laurenti custodit in agro
more　to-be-wished for, if, of-Laurentum keeps　in the-field
2　　　　4　　　　1

Conductas Corvinus oves? Ego possideo plus
hired　Corvinus　sheep? I　possess　more
5　　3　　　6

Pallante et Licinis; expectent ergo Tribuni. Vin-
than-Pallas and the-Licini: let wait therefore the-Tribunes. Let-
3　　　2　　　1

cant divitiae: sacro nec cedat honori Nuper in hanc
prevail riches : to-sacred nor let-him-yield honor lately into this
3　　1　　2　　4　　2　4　5

urbem pedibus qui venerat albis: Quandoquidem
city　with-feet who came　white:　since
6　　7　9　1　3　8

inter nos sanctissima divitiárum Majestas: etsi,
among us　most-sacred　of-riches-(is)　the-majesty : although,
3　　　2　　1

funesta Pecunia, templo Nondum habitas, nullas
O-baneful money! in-a-temple not-as-yet thou-dost-dwell, no
2

nummorum ereximus aras, ut colitur Pax,
of-money　we-have-erected altars as is-worshipped Peace
4　　1　　3　　2　　1

atque Fides, Victoria, Virtus, Quæque salutato
and　Faith,　Victory,　Virtue, which-and with-a-visited
3　1　　5

crepitat Concordia nido. Sed cum summus honor
chatters　Concord　nest. But when the-highest honor
4　　2　　6

finito computet anno, Sportula quid referat,
being-finished can-compute the-year the-sportula what brings-in
3　　1　　2　　2　　1　　3

quantum rationibus addat, Quid facient comites,
how-much to-(its)-accounts it-adds, what will do the-attendants
2　　1　　2　1

quibus hinc toga, calceus hinc est, Et panis,
to-whom from-hence a-gown, a-shoe from-hence, is, and bread,

fumusque domi? densissima centum Quadrantes
and-smoke of-the-house ? a-very-dense a-hundred farthings
3　　4

lectica petit, sequiturque maritum Languida, vel
litter　seeks, · follows-and the-husband　sick　or
1　　2　　3　1　　4　　6　7

prægnans, et circumducitur uxor. Hic petit
pregnant,　and is-led-about the-wife. This asks-for
8　　5　　9　　2

absenti,   notâ   jam   callidus   arte,   Ostendens
the-absent,   in-a-known   now   cunning   art,   showing
   3   1   2   4

vacuam,   et   clausam   pro conjuge   sellam :   Galla
the-empty,   and   shut-up   instead-of-the-wife   sedan :   Galla
         2   1   3

mea   est,   inquit,   citius   dimitte;   moraris?
my   it-is,   says-he,   quickly   dismiss (her):   do-you-delay ?
2   1

Profer,   Galla,   caput.   Noli vexare, quiescit.
put-out,   Galla,   (your) head.   Do-not-vex-(her), she-is-asleep.

Ipse   dies   pulchro   distinguitur   ordine
itself   the-day   by-a-beautiful   is-distinguished   order
2   1   3   5   6   4

rerum ;   Sportula,   deinde   forum,   jurisque
of-things ;   the-sportula,   then   the-forum,   the-law and
5   4   1

peritus   Apollo, Atque   triumphales,   inter   quas
skilled-in   Apollo,   and   the-triumphals,   among   which
3   2

ausus   habere   Nescio   quis   titulos   Ægyptius
has-dared   to-have   I-know-not   who   titles   an-Egyptian,
3   4   2   5   1

atque   Arabarches ;   Cujus   ad   effigiem   non
and   an-Arabian-prefect ;   whose   at   image   not
         2   1   3   2

tantum   mejere   fas   est.   Vestibulis
so-much-as   to-make-water   right   it-is.   from-the-vestibules
        3   1

abeunt   veteres,   lassique   clientes,   Votaque
go-away   the-old   and-tired   clients,   and-(their)-wishes

deponunt,   quanquam   longissima   cœnæ   Spes
lay-aside,   although   a-very-long   of-a-dinner   expectation
         2   1

homini :   caules   miseris,   atque
(has-been)-to-the-man :   pot-herbs   for-the-wretches,   and

ignis   emendus.   Optima   sylvarum
fire   (is)-to-be-bought.   The-best-(things)   of-the-woods

interea,   pelagique-   vorabit   Rex   horum,
meanwhile,   and-of-the-sea,   will-devour   lord   their,
        3   2   1

vacuisque   toris   tantum   ipse   jacebit ; Nam
and-on-the-empty   beds   only   himself   will-lie ;   for
do   tot   pulchris,   et   latis   orbibus,   et
from   so-many   beautiful,   and   wide   dishes,   and
tam   Antiquis,   unâ   comedunt   patrimonia   mensâ.
so   ancient,   at-one   they-devour   patrimonies   meal.
  1   2

Nullus jam parasitus erit: sed quis feret istas
no now parasite there-will-be: but who will-bear that
3 2 1

Luxuriæ sordes? quanta est gula, quæ sibi
of-luxury mean-nastiness? how-great is the-gullet, which for-itself
2 1

totos Ponit apros, animal propter convivia
whole puts-(on-the-table) boars, an-animal for feasts
2 1 2

natum? Pœna tamen præsens, cum tu deponis
born? Punishment yet-(there-is) a-present when you put-off
1 3 1 2

amictus Turgidus, et crudum pavonem in bal
(your)-clothes turgid, and an-indigested peacock into the-
2

nea portas: Hinc subitæ mortes, atque intestata
baths carry: hence sudden deaths, and intestate
1

senectus. It nova, nec tristis per cunctas
old-age. goes a-new nor-(is-it) a-sorrowful-(one) through all
5 1 3 4 6 7

fabula cœnas; Ducitur iratis plaudendum funus
story dinner-parties; is-lead-forth by-angry to-be-applauded a-corpse
2 8 5 3 2 1

amicis. Nil erit ulterius, quod nostris moribus
friends. Nothing will-(there)-be further which to-our morals
4

addat Posteritas: eadem cupient, facientque
can-add Posterity: the-same-(things) will-desire and-do
2 1 4 2 3

minores. OMNE IN PRÆCIPITI VITIUM STETIT;
(our)-descendants. all on the-highest-(point) vice has-taken-a-stand,
1 1 4 2 3

utere velis, Totos pande sinus: dicas hic
use sails, (their)-whole spread-open bosoms; you-may-say here
2 1

forsitan, "unde Ingenium par materiæ? unde
perhaps,— "whence-(is-there) genius equal to-the-matter? whence

illa priorum Scribendi quodcunque animo
that of-former-(writers) of-writing whatever, with-a-mind
2

flagrante liberet Simplicitas, cujus non audeo
burning, it-might-please-(them) simplicity, of-which not I-dare
1 2 1

dicere nomen? Quid refert dictis ignoscat Mutius,
speak the-name? what signifies (things)-said would-forgive Mutius,
4 3 2

an non? Pone Tigellinum: tædâ lucebis in
whether-or-not? Set-down Tigellinus: torch you-will-shine in
1 3 1

illâ, Quâ stantes ardent, qui fixo gutture fumant,
that, in-which standing they-burn, who with-fixed throat smoke,
2

Et latum mediâ sulcum diducis arenâ. Qui dedit
and a-wide in-the-midst-of furrow you-draw-out sand. Who gave
2 4 3 1 5

ergo tribus patruis aconita, vehetur Pensilibus
therefore to-three uncles, wolf's-bane, shall-he-be-carried with-pensile

plumis, atque illinc despiciet nos? Cûm veniet
feathers and thence look-down-on us? when he-shall-come

contrà, digito compesce labellum: Accusator
opposite, with-finger restrain the-lip an-accuser

erit, qui verbum dixerit, hic est.
(there)-will-be-(of-him) who the-word shall-say, that is-he

Securus licet Æneam, Rutilumque ferocem Com-
Secure though Æneas, and Rutilian the-fierce you-
2 1 2 1

mittas: nulli gravis est percussus Achilles:
match: to-no-one grievous is smitten Achilles:

Aut multum quæsitus Hylas, urnamque secu-
or much sought Hylas, and-(his)-pitcher having-

tus. Ense velut stricto, quoties Lucilius
followed. With-a-sword as drawn, as-often-as Lucilius
2 1

ardens Infremuit, rubet auditor, cui
ardent raged, reddens the-hearer, to-whom
2 1

frigida mens est Criminibus, tacitâ sudant
frigid a-mind is with-crimes, with-silent sweat
3 2 1 3 2

præcordia culpâ. Inde iræ, et lachrymæ.
the-præcordia guilt. thence anger and tears.
1

Tecum priûs ergo voluta Hæc
with-thyself first therefore revolve these (things)

animo ante tubas; galeatum serò
in-the-mind before the-trumpets; the-helmeted late

duelli Pœnitet" Experiar quid concedatur
of-a-fight it-repents" I-shall-try what may-be-allowed

in illos, Quorum Flaminiâ tegitur cinis
towards those whose in-the-Flaminian is-covered ashes,
3 2 1

atque Latina.
and Latin (way).

SATIRE II.

ARGUMENT.

This Satire contains an animated attack upon the hypocrisy of the philosophers and reformers of the day, whose ignorance, profligacy, and impiety it exposes with just severity.

Domitian is here the object; his vices are alluded to under every different name ; and it gives us a high opinion of the intrepid spirit of the man who could venture to circulate, even in private, so faithful a representation of that blood-thirsty tyrant.

Ultra | Sauromatas | fugere | hinc | libet | et
Beyond | the-Sauromatæ | to-flee | hence | it-would-please (me) | and

glacialem | Oceanum, | quoties | aliquid | de | moribus
the-icy | Ocean, | as-often-as | anything | concerning | morals

audent | Qui Curios | simulant | et Bacchanalia
they-dare | who Curii | feign (themselves) | and (like) Bacchanals

vivunt. | Indocti | primûm: | quanquam | plena | omnia
live. | (they-are) unlearned | first: | though | filled | all-things
 | | 2 | 1 | | 2 | 1

gypso | Chrysippi | invenias: | nam | perfectiss
with-plaster | of-Chrysippus | you-may-find : | for | the-most-

imus | horum | est, | Si | quis | Aristotelem | similem | vel
perfect | of-these | is, | if | anyone | Aristotle | like | or

Pittacon | emit, | Et | jubet | archetypos | pluteum
Pittacus | buys, | and | commands | original-images | a-book-case
 | | | | 3 | 1

servare | Cleanthis. | Fronti | nulla | fides: | quis
to-keep | of-Cleanthes. | to-countenance (there-is) no | faith : | what
2 | | | | | 2

enim | non | vicus | abundat | Tristibus | obscœnis ?
for | not | street | abounds | with-grave | obscenes ?
1 | 5 | 3 | 4

castigas | turpia, | cum | sis | Inter
dost-thou-reprove | base-(things) | when | thou-art | among
 | | | | 3

Socraticos | notissima | fossa | cinædos ? | Hispida
the-Socratic | a-most-noted | ditch | catamites ? | Rough
4 | 1 | 2 | 5

membra | quidem, | et | duræ | per | brachia | setæ
limbs | indeed | and | hard | on | the-arms | bristles
 | | | 2 | | 3 | 1

Promittunt | atrocem | animum: | sed | podice
Promise | a-fierce | mind : | but | on-the-podex
 | | | | 3

lœvi   Cæduntur   tumidæ,   medico
of-the-unlucky (one)   are-lanced   the-swollen   the-physician
    4   5   1   6

ridente,   mariscæ.   Rarus   sermo   illis,   et
laughing   caricous-tumors.   Raro (is) talk   to-them   and
    7   2

magna   libido   tacendi,   Atque   supercilio
great   the-desire   of-keeping-silence,   and   than-the-eyebrow
                                              3

brevior   coma;   verius   ergo,   Et   magis
shorter   hair;   more-truly   therefore   and   more
    2   1

ingenuè   Peribonius: hunc   ego   fatis   Imputo,
ingenuously,   Peribonius: him   I   to-the-fates   Impute,

qui   vultu   morbum,   incessuque   fatetur.   Horum
who   in-look   (his)-disease   and-gait   confesses.   Of-these
                        3   1   2

simplicitas   miserabilis,   his   furor   ipse
the-simplicity (is)   pitiable,   to these   madness   itself

Dat   veniam: sed   pejores,   qui   talia   verbis
gives   pardon: but   worse (they)   who   such (things)   with-words

Herculis   invadunt   et   de   virtute   locuti   Clunem
of-Hercules   attack   and   of   virtue   having spoken   the tail
                                                                      2

agitant: ego   te   ceventem,   Sexte,   verebor,
agitate: I   thee   lecherous,   Sextus,   shall fear
    1   2   1   3

Infamis   Varillus   ait?   quo   deterior   te?
infamous   Varillus   says,?   in-what (am-I) worse-than   thee?
    2   1

Loripedem   rectus   derideat,   Æthiopem   albus.
the-bandy-legged   the-straight   let deride,   the-Æthiopian   the-white.
    4   2   1   3   2   1

Quis   tulerit   Gracchos   de   seditione
Who   could-have-borne   the-Gracchi   about   sedition
                                                      2   3

querentes?   Quis   cœlum   terris   non   misceat,
complaining?   Who   heaven   with-earth   not   would mix
    1   2   1

et   mare   cœlo,   Si   fur   displiceat   Verri,
and   the-sea   with-heaven,   if   a-thief   should-displease   Verres,

aut   homicida   Miloni?   Clodius   accuset   mœchos,
or   a-homicide,   Milo?   (if) Clodius   should-accuse   adulterers

Catilina   Cethegum?   In   tabulam   Syllae   si
Cataline,   Cethegus?   Against   the-table   of-Sylla   if

dicant   discipuli   tres?   Qualis   erat   nuper
should-speak   disciples   three?   Such   was   lately
    3   2   1   2

tragico   pollutus   adulter   Concubitu :   qui   tunc
with-a-tragical   polluted   the-adulterer   intrigue: who   then
4   3   1   5

leges   revocabat   amaras   Omnibus,   atque   ipsis
laws   was-recalling   bitter   to-all,   and   themselves
4

Veneri,   Martique   timendas :   Cum   tot   abortivis
by-Venus   and-Mars   to-be-feared: when   from-so-many   abortives
2   3   1

fœcundam   Julia   vulvam   Solveret,   et   patruo
(her) fruitful   Julia   womb   released,   and   to-(her)-uncle
3   1   4   2   4

similes   effunderet   offas.   Nonne   igitur   jure,   ac
like   poured-forth   lumps.   Do-not   therefore,   justly,   and
3   1   2

meritò,   vitia   ultima   fictos   Contemnunt   Scauros,
deservedly,   vices   extreme   the-feigned   despise   Scauri,
   2   1   2   1

et   castigata   remordent?   Non   tulit   ex
and,   being-reproved,   bite-back?   Not   endured   from-among
       3   2   6

illis   torvum   Laronia   quendam   Clamantem   toties,
them   grim-(one)   Laronia   a-certain   crying-out   so-often,
   5   1   4

ubi   nunc   lex   Julia ?   dormis ?   Atque   ita
where (is)   now   law   the-Julian ?   dost-thou-sleep ?   And   thus
      2   1

subridens :   felicia   tempora !   quæ   te   moribus
smiling :   happy   times !   which   thee   to-manners
                                 2

opponunt :   habeat   jam   Roma   pudorem ;   Tertius   è
oppose :   may-have   now   Rome   shame ;   a-third   from
1   3   1   2   3

cœlo   cecidit   Cato.   Sed   tamen   unde   Hæc
heaven   has-fallen   Cato.   But   yet   whence   these
4   2   1   2

emis,   hirsuto   spirant   opobalsama   collo   quæ
dost-thou-buy   from-the-rough   breathe   perfumes   neck   which
1   6   5   3   7   4

tibi?   ne   pudeat   dominum   monstrare   tabernæ.
to-thee?   let-it-not shame (thee)   the-master   to-show   of-the-shop
8   2   1

Quod   si   vexantur   leges,   ac   jura,   citari
But · ·   if   are-disturbed   the-statutes   and   laws,   to-be-aroused
            4   1   2   3   3

Ante   omnes   debet   Scantinia ;   respice   primum
before   all   ought   the-Scantinian ;   consider   first
            2   1

Et   scrutare   viros :   faciunt   hi   plura ;   sed
and   examine   the-men :   do   these   more-things   but
                2   1

illos   Defendit   numerus,   junctæque   umbone
those   defends   number,   and joined   with-a-buckler
   2   1   2

phalanges.   Magna   inter   molles   concordia :
phalanxes.   (There-is) great   among   the-effeminate   concord:
1   2   1

non erit   ullum   Exemplum   in   nostro   tam
There-will-not-be   any   example   in   our   so
2

detestabile ˙ sexu :   Tædia   non   lambit   Cluviam,
detestable   sex :   Tædia   not   licks   Cluvia,
3   1   2   1

nec   Flora   Catullam :   Hippo   subit   juvenes,   et
nor   Flora   Catulla :   Hippo   sustains   youths,   and

morbo   pallet   utr. que.   Nunquid   nos   agimus
disease   pales   with-each.   Do   we   plead
3   1   2

causas ?   civilia   jura   Novimus ?   aut   ullo
causes ?   the-civil   laws   do-we-know ?   or   with-any

strepitu   fora   vestra   movemus ?   Luctantur
noise   courts   your   do-we-move ?   wrestle
2   1   2

paucæ,   comedunt   coliphia   paucæ ;   Vos   lanam
a few,   eat   wrestlers'-diet   a-few ;   you   wool
1   2   3   1   2

trahitis,   calathisque   peracta   refertis   Vellera :
card   and-in-baskets   the-finished   carry-back   fleeces :
1   2   1

Vos   tenui   prægnantem   stamine   fusum   Pene-
you   with-slender   big   thread   the-spindle   than-
3   2   4   1

lope   melius,   levius   torquetis   Arachne,
Penelope   better   finer   do-twist   than-Arachne,
6   5   8   7   9

Horrida   quale   facit   residens   in   codice   pellex.
the horrid   as   does   sitting   on   a-log   harlot.
3   1   2   4

Notum   est   cur   solo   tabulas   impleverit
Known   it-is   why   with-only   (his) will   filled
4   3   2

Hister   Liberto ;   dederit   vivus   cur   multa
Hister   (his) freedman;   he-gave   alive   why   . much
1   5   3   2   1

puellæ :   Dives   erit,   magno   quæ   dormit
to-a-wench;   rich   she-will-be   in-a-largo   who   sleeps
4   1

tertia   lecto.   Tu   nube,   atque   tace :   donant
third   bed.   Do thou   marry   and   be-silent: bestow
3   5

arcana   cylindros.   Do   nobis   post   hæc   tristis
secrets   gems.   On   us   after (all)   these (things)   a-sad
1

sententia	fertur :	Dat	veniam	corvis,	vexat
sentence	is-passed:	grants	pardon	to ravens,	vexes
	2		3	4	5

censura	columbas.	Fugerunt	trepidi,	vera	ac
censure	doves.	Fled	trembling	(things) true	and
1	6	5	4		2

manifesta	canentem	Stoicidæ:	quid	enim	falsi
manifest	(her) proclaiming	the Stoicides :	what	for	of-false
3	1	5	2	1	

Laronia?——Sed	quîd	Non	facient	alii,
(had) Laronia (uttered)—But	what	will not	do	others
			2	1

cum	tu	multicia	sumas,	Cretice,	et
when	thou	transparent (garments)	assumest,	O-Creticus,	and

hanc	vestem	populo	mirante	perores	In
this	apparel	the-people	wondering-at	thou-declaimest	against
3	4	1	2		

Proculas,	et	Pollineas?	est	mœcha	Fabulla .
the-Proculæ	and	Pollineæ ?	is	an-adultress	Fabulla :
			2		1

Damnetur	si	vis,	etiam	Carfinia :	talem	Non
Let be-condemned	if	you-please,	also	Carfinia :	such	sho'll-
1		4	3	2		

sumet	damnata	togam.	Sed	Julius	ardet,	Æstuo ;
not-put-on	condemned	a-gown.	"But	July	burns,	I-roast ;"
8	2	1				

nudus	agas ;	minus est insania turpis. En habitum,
naked	administer-justice ;	less is madness shameful. Lo the-habit,

quo	te	leges,	ac	jura	ferentem	Vulneribus
in-which	thee	statutes	and	laws	bearing	with-wounds
		2		3	1	2

crudis	populus	modò	victor,	et illud	Montanum
raw	the-people	just-now	victorious	and that	mountain
2	1				1

positis	audiret	vulgus	aratris.	Quid	non pro-
laid-by	might-hear	vulgar	ploughs.	What	would you-
4	5	2	3		

clames,	in	corpore	Judicis	ista	Si	videas ?
not-proclaim	on	the-body	of-a-judge	those (things)	if,	you-should-see?
		2	3	4	1	5

quæro	an	deceant	multicia	testem ?
I-ask	whether	would-become	transparent (garments)	a-witness ?
		2	1	

Acer	et indomitus,	libertatisque	magister,	Cretice
Severe	and unsubdued,	and of-liberty	master,	O-Creticus
		2		1

pelluces!	Dedit	hanc	contagio	labem,	Et
you-are-transparent!	gave	this	contagion	stain,	and
	2		1		

dabit in plures : sicut grex totus in agris Unius
will-give (it) to more : as a herd whole in the-fields of-one
2   1   4

scabie   cadit,   et   porrigine   porci ;   Uvaque
by-the-scab falls and measles swine ; and a grape
2   1   3   5

conspectâ livorem ducit ab uvâ.   Fœdius   hoc
beheld   a-blueness derives from a-grape. More-shameful than-this
4   2   1   3   2   3

aliquid quandoque audebis amictu ; Nemo repentè
something sometime you-will-dare dress ; No-one suddenly
1   5   6   4

fuit turpissimus. Accipient te   Paulatim,   qui
was most-base. They-will-receive thee by-little-and-little, who

longa domi redimicula sumunt Frontibus,   et
long at-home fillets place on-their-brows and
3   1   4   2   5

toto   posuére monilia collo, Atque Bonam
over-the-whole have-placed ornaments neck, and the-good
3   1   2   · 4   2

tenerœ placant abdomine porcœ, Et magno
of-a-tender appease with-the-belly sow and with-a-large
5   1   4   6

cratere Deam : sed more sinistro Exagitata procul
goblet Goddess ; but by a custom perverted, driven away far
3   2   1   2   4   3

non intrat fœmina limen. Solis ara Deœ
not enters woman the-threshold. alone the-altar of-the-goddess
6   5   1   5   1   2

maribus patet : ite profanœ, Clamatur : nullo
to-males is-open : " Go ye-profane " is-cried-aloud : with-no
4   3

gemit hic tibicina cornu. Talia secretâ co-
moans here the-female-flutist horn. Such with-a-secret
4   2   3   1   2

luerunt Orgia tœdâ Cecropiam soliti Baptœ
used Orgies torch the-Cecropian accustomed the-Baptœ
4   1   3   8   6   5

lassare Cotytto. Ille surpercilium madidâ fuligine
to-weary Cotytto. One (his) eyebrow with-wet soot
7   9

tactum Obliquâ producit acu, pingitque trementes
touched, with-oblique lengthens needle, and-paints (his) trembling
2   1   2

Attollens oculos ; vitreo bibit ille Priapo,
lifting-(them)-up eyes ; out-of-a-glass drinks another Priapus,
1   3   3   2   1   4

Reticulumque comis auratum ingentibus implet,
and-a-little net with hair golden much fills,
2   8   5   4   4   6

Cærulea   indutus   scutulata,   aut galbana rasa;
blue   having-put-on   female-garments or white-vests smooth
2   1   2   1

Et per Junonem domini jurante ministro. Ille
and by the-Juno of-(his)-master swearing the-servant. Another
   3   4   2   1

tenet speculum, pathici gestamen Othonis Actoris
holds a-looking-glass, of-pathic the-bearing Otho of-Actor
                  2   1   2 4

Aurunci spolium, quo se ille videbat Armatum,
Auruncian the-spoil in-which himself he viewed armed
   3   1

cum jam tolli vexilla juberet. Res
when now to-be-taken-up the-banners he-commanded. a-thing
              3   2   1

memoranda novis annalibus, atque recenti His-
to-be-commemorated in-new annals, and in-recent

toriâ; speculum civilis sarcina belli! Nimirum
history, a-looking-glass of-civil the-baggage war! Doubtless
                  2   1   3

summi ducis est occidere Galbam, Et
of-the-greatest general it is (the-part) to-kill Galba, and
    2   3   1

curare cutem summi constantia civis;
to-care-for the-skin of-the-highest the-perseverance citizen;
                    2   1

Bedriaci in campo spolium affectare Palati,
of-Bedriacum in the-field the-spoil to-affect of-the-palace,
   2   1   2   1

Et pressum in faciem digtis extendere
and pressed over the-face with-the-fingers to-extend
      4   2   5   1

panem: Quod nec in Assyrio pharetrata
bread which neither in the-Assyrian the-quivered
  3   3   4   1

Semiramis orbe, Mœsta nec Actiacâ fecit
Semiramis world, sad nor In-(her)-Actiacan did
  2   5   2   1   5   4

Cleopatra carinâ. Hic nullus verbis pudor, aut
Cleopatra gally. Here (is) no in-words modesty or
  3   2   1

reverentia mensæ: Hic turpis Cybeles, et
reverence of-the-table: hero of-filthy Cybele, and

fracrâ voce loquendi Libertas, et crine
with-broken voice of-speaking the-liberty, and with-hair
  2   3   1   3 5

senex fanaticus albo Sacrorum antistes rarum
an-old fanatic white of-sacred-things chief-priest a-rare
  1   2   4   2   1

ac memorabile magni Gutturis exemplum,
and memorable of-a-great throat example,
                    2   3   1

con lucondusque   magister.   Quid   tamen   expectant,
and to-be-hired   a-master   What   yet   do-they-wait-for,
2   1   2   1

Phrygio   queis   tempus   erat   jam   More
in-the-Phrygian   for-whom   time   it-was   now   manner
5   1   4   2   3   6

supervacuam   cultris   abrumpere   carnem?   Quad-
the-superfluous   with-knives   to-cut-away   flesh?   Four-
9   8   7   10

ringenta   dedit   Gracchus   sestertia,   dotem
hundred   gave   Gracchus   sestertia   a-dower
3   2   1   4

Cornicini: sive   hic   recto   cantaverat   aere;
to-a-horn-blower   or   he   with-straight   had-sounded   brass;
2   1

Signatæ   tabulæ: dictum   feliciter!   ingens   Cœna
signed (were) the-writings: said   "Happily"   a-great   supper
2   1

sedet: gremio   jacuit   nova   nupta   mariti.
is-set   in-the-bosom   lay   the-new'   married   of-the-husband.
2   3   1

O Proceres,   censore   opus   est,   an   haruspice
O ye-nobles,   for-a-censor   need   is-(there)   or   for-a-sooth-sayer
4   2   1   5   6

nobis?   Scilicet   horreres,   majoraque   monstra
to-us?   What!   would-you-dread,   and-greater   prodigies
3

putares,   Si   mulier   vitulum,   vel   si   bos
think-(them)   if   a-woman   a-calf,   or   if   a cow

ederet   agnum?   Segmenta,   et   longos   habitus,
should-bring-forth   a-lamb?   collars   and   long   habits

et   flammea   sumit,   Arcano   qui   sacra
and   wedding-veils   he-takes   with-a-secret   who   sacred-(things)
5   1   3

ferens   nutantia   loro   Sudavit   clypeis   ancilibus.
carrying   nodding   rein   sweated   with-the-shields   ancilian.
2   4   6

O pater   urbis!   Unde   nefas   tantum   Latiis
O father   of-the-city!   Whence   wickedness   so-great   to-Latin

pastoribus?   unde   Hæc   tetigit,   Gradive,   tuos
shepherds?   whence   this   has-touched   O-Gradivus,   thy
2   1   5   4   6

urtica   nepotes?   Traditur   ecce   viro   clarus
nettle   descendants?   is-consigned   behold   to-a-man   illustrious
3   7   6   1   3

genere,   atque   opibus   vir: Nec   galeam   quassas,
by-family,   and   wealth   a-man   Neither (your) helmet   you-shake,
4   5   2

nec   terram   cuspide   pulsas,   Nec   quereris
nor   the-earth   with-(your)-spear   smite,   nor   complain

patri!   Vade   ergo,   et   cede   severi   Jugeribus
to-the-father!   Go   therefore   and   depart   of-the-severe   from-the-acres
2   1

campi, quem negligis. Officium cras Primo
field which you-neglect a-business to-morrow at-the-first
3

sole mihi peragendum in valle Quirini. Quæ
sun by-me (is)-to-be-dispatched in the-vale of-Quirinus. What

causa officii? quid quæris? nubit amicus,
the-cause of-the-business? what do-you-ask? marries a-friend
2 1

Nec multos adhibet. Liceat modo vivere:
Nor many does-he-admit. Let-it-be-permitted only to-live,

fient, Fient ista palam, cupient et
will-be-done, will-be-done these-(things) openly, will-desire and
2 3 1 4 2 1

in acta referri. Interea tormentum
into the-public-registers to-be-borne Meanwhile torment
4 5 3 2

ingens nubentibus hæret, Quòd nequeunt
a great to-(those-thus)-marrying sticks that they-cannot
1 4 3

parere, et partu retinere maritos. Sed
bring-forth and by-birth retain (their)-husbands. But

melius, quod nil animis in corpora
(it-is)-better that nothing to-(their)-minds over (their)bodies
2 1 4

juris Natura indulget; steriles moriuntur, et
of-right Nature indulges; barren they-die, and
3

illis Turgida non prodest conditâ pyxide
them turgid not profits with-medicated box
5 4 2 3

Lyde, Nec prodest agili palmas præbere
Lyde, nor does-it-profit to-the-nimble (their)-palms to-present
1 3 2 1

Luperco. Vicit et hoc monstrum tunicati fuscina
Lupercus. Outdid yet this prodigy of-the-coated the-fork
4 5 1 6 3 2

Gracchi, Lustravitque fugâ mediam gladiator
Gracchus, and-he-traveled in-flight the-middle-of a-gladiator
4 2 1

arenam, Et Capitolinis generosior, et
the-arena-stage, and than-the-Capitolini more-nobly-born, and·
3 2 1

Marcellis, Et Catulis, Paulique minoribus, et
the-Marcelli, and the-Catuli, and of-Paulus the-posterity, and
2 1

Fabiis, et Omnibus ad podium spectantibus:
the-Fabii, and all at the-podium the-spectators:
2 1

his licèt ipsum Admoveas, cujus tunc
to-these though him you-should-add whose then
2 1 2 5

munere retia misit. Esse aliquos manes et
at-expense the-net he-threw. to-be any ghosts and
1 8 7 4 6 3 1 2

subterranea   regna,   Et   contum,   et   Stygio
subterranean   realms,   and   a-boat-pole   and   the-Stygian
                                                         4

ranas in gurgite   nigras,   Atque   unâ   transire
frogs in gulf   black,   and   in-one to-pass-over
2   3   5   1   5

vadum   tot   millia   cymbâ,   Nec   pueri   credunt,
the-ford so-many thousands boat, not-even boys believe
     4   1   2   6

nisi   qui   nondum   ære   lavantur :   Sed
unless (those)-who not-yet for-money are-washed : But

tu   vera   puta.   Curius   quid   sentit,   et
thou (them-to-be) true think. Curius what   thinks   and
                                    3   1   2

ambo   Scipiadæ?   quid   Fabricius,   manesque
both   the-Scipios? what Fabricius,   and-the-manes

Camilli?   Quid   Cremeræ   legio,   et   Cannis
of-Camillus? What of-Cremera the-legion, and at-Cannae
                   2   1

consumpta   juventus,   Tot   bellorum   animæ,
consumed   the-youth of-so-many wars   the souls,
2   1

quoties   hinc   talis   ad illos   Umbra
as-often-as from hence such to them   a shade
                             2   1

venit?   Cuperent   lustrari,   si   qua   darentur
comes?   They-would-desire to-be-purified, if any c'd-be-supplied
                                                        2

sulfura   cum   tædis,   et   si   foret
sulphur   with pine-torches, and if (there) could-bo
1

humida   laurus.   Illuc,   heu!   miseri
a-wet   laurel.   Thither, alas! we-wretches

traducimur :   Arma   quidem   ultra   Litora
are conveyed (our) arms, indeed, beyond the-shores

Juvernæ   promovimus, et   modo   captas   Orcadas,
of-Juverna we-have-advanced and lately captured Orcades,

ac   minimâ   contentos   nocte   Britannos.
and   with-very-little content night   the-Britons.
3   2   1

Sed   quæ nunc   populi   fiunt   victoris
But (the things) which now people are-done of the-victorious
                           5   1   4

in   urbe,   Non   faciunt   illi,   quos   vicimus.
in   the city, not   do   those   whom   we-have-conquered.
2   3   5   4   1   2   3

Et   tamen   unus   Armenius   Zalates   cunctis
And   yet   one   an-Armenian Zalates   (than) all
                     2   1   2

narratur   ephebis   Mollior   ardenti   sese
is-related (our) striplings more-soft to-a-burning himself
4   3   1   3   2

indulsisse   Tribuno.   Adspice,   quid   faciant
to-have-yielded tribune. Behold,   what   may-do
1   2

commercia !   venerat   obses.   Hic   fiunt   homines.
commerce !   ho-had-come   a-hostage.   Here they-become   men.
             1

Nam   si   mora   longior   urbem   Indulsit
For   if   stay   a-longer   the-city   has-indulged
                 2   1   4   3

pueris,   non umquam   deerit   amator :
to-boys,   never   will-be-wanting   a lover :

Mittentur   bracæ,   cultelli,   frena,   flagellum.
will-be-laid-aside   trowsers,   knives,   bridles,   whip.
    2   1

Sic   prætextatos   referunt   Artaxata   mores.
Thus   prætextate they-carry-back to-Artaxata   morals.
          2   1   4   3

SATIRE III.

ARGUMENT.

Umbritius, an Aruspex and friend of the author, disgusted at the prevalence of vice and the disregard of unassuming virtue, is on the point of quitting Rome; and when a little way from the city, stops short to acquaint the poet, who has accompanied him, with the causes of his retirement. These may be arranged under the following heads:—That Flattery and Vice are the only thriving arts at Rome; in these, especially the first, foreigners have a manifest superiority over the natives, and consequently engross all favour—that the poor are universally exposed to scorn and insult—that the general habits of extravagance render it difficult for them to subsist—that the want of a well regulated police subjects them to numberless miseries and inconveniences, aggravated by the crowded state of the capital, from all which a country life is happily free, on the tranquility and security of which he dilates with great beauty.

Quamvis	digressu	veteris	confusus	amici,
although	at-the-departure	of-an-old	much-troubled	friend,
	2		1	

Laudo	tamen,	vacuis	quod	sedem	figere
I-commend (him)	yet,	at-empty	because	(his) abode	to-fix
2	1	7	3	6	5

Cumis	Destinet,	atque	unum	civem	donaro
Cumæ	he-intends	and	one	citizen	to-give
8	4				

Sibyllae.	Janua	Baiarum	est,	et	gratum
to-the-Sibyl.	The-gate	of-Baiæ	it-is,	and	a-grateful

litus	amœni	Secessûs.	Ego	vel	Prochytam	præpono
shore	of-pleasant	retirement.	I	even	Prochyta	prefer

Suburæ.	Nam	quid	tam	miserum,	tam
to-the-Subura.	For	what	so	wretched,	so
solum	vidimus,	ut	non	Deterius	credas
solitary	have-we-seen,	that	not	worse	you-w'd deem (it)

horrere   incendia, lapsus   Tectorum   assiduos,
to dread   fires,   falling   of-houses   the constant,
                       2   1

ac   mille   pericula   sævæ   Urbis,   et
and   the thousand   perils   of the cruel   City,   and

Augusto   recitantes   mense   poetas ?   Sed
in-August   reciting   month   poets ?   But
3   2   1

dum   tota   domus   rhedâ   componitur
while   (his) whole   household   waggon   is-being-stowed
                           3   1

unâ,   Substitit ad   veteres   arcus   madidamque
in one   he-has-stopped at   the-old   arches   and the moist
2

Capenam;   Hic,   ubi   nocturnæ   Numa
Capena;   here,   where   (his) nocturnal   Numa
                              3   1

constituebat   amicæ,   Nunc   sacri   fontis
was-wont-to-appoint-with   mistress,   now   of-the-sacred   fountain
2   2

nemus   et   delubra   locantur   Judæis,
the-grove   and   the-shrines   are-let-out   to-Jews,
1

quorum   cophinus   fœnumque   supellex.
of-whom   a basket   and hay   (are) the-household-stuff.

Omnis   enim   populo   mercedem   pendere
every   for   to-the-people   a rent   to-pay
2   1   7   6   5

jussa   est   Arbor,   et   ejectis   mendicat
is-commanded   tree,   and   having-been-ejected   bogs
4   3   2   4

silva   Camenis.   In   vallem   Egeriæ
the wood   the-Camenæ.   Into   the vale   of-Egeria
3   1

descendimus   et   speluncas   Dissimiles
we-descend   and   caves   unlike

veris.   Quanto   præstantius   esset   Numen
the-true.   How-much   nearer-in-influence   would be   the deity

aquæ,   viridi   si   margine   clauderet
of-the water,   with-its-green   of   margin   enclosed
              2   1   2

undas   Herba,   nec   ingenuum   violarent
the waves   the-turf,   nor   the native   violated
              1   3   2

marmora   tophum?   Hic   tunc   Umbritius:
marbles   limestone?   Here   then   Umbritius:
1

Quando   artibus,   inquit,   honestis   Nullus
Since   arts,   says-he,   for-honest   (there is) no
              2   3   1

in   Urbe   locus,   nulla   emolumenta   laborum,
in   the City   place,   no   emoluments   of labors,
2   1

Res hodie minor est, here quam fuit,
(one's) substance to-day less is yeste day than it-was,
3 1 2

atque eadem cras Deteret exiguis aliquid :
and the same, to-morrow will-rub-away from-the-little something :
2 1

proponimus illuc Ire, fatigatas ubi Dædalus
we propose thither to-go, (his) wearied where Dædalus
4 1 2

exuit alas, Dum nova canities, dum
put-off wings, while new greyness (is), while
3 2 1

prima et recta senectus, Dum superest
fresh and erect old-age (is), while (there) remains
2 1

Lachesi, quod torqueat, et pedibus me , Porto
to-Lachesis, what she-may-spin, and feet myself I carry
2

meis, nullo dextram subeunte bacillo. Cedamus
on-my, no (my) right-hand supporting staff. let-us-withdraw
1 3 2 1

patriâ: vivant Arturius istic, et Catulus ; maneant
(our) native soil: let live Arturius there and Catulus ; let (those) stay
2 1

qui nigra in candida vertunt, Queis facile
who black into white turn, to-whom easy
est ædem conducere, flumina, portus,
it is a-building to hire, ·· rivers, ports,
2 1

Siccandam eluviem, portandum ad busta
to-be-dried a sewer to be carried to the pile
2 1 2

cadaver, Et præbere caput dominâ venale
a corpse, and to expose a head the mistress venal
1 2 4 1

sub hastâ. Quondam hi cornicines et
under spear. Quondam these horn-blowers and
3 5 2 1

municipalis arenæ Perpetui comites, notæque
of a municipal theatre constant attendants, and known
2

per oppida buccae, Munera nunc edunt
through towns cheeks, public shows, now set forth
1 3 1 2

et verso pollice vulgi Quemlibet occidunt
and being turned thumb the people's, whom they will kill
3 2 1

populariter : inde reversi conducunt foricas :
as the people please: thence returned they hire jakes:
et cur non omnia ? cum sint Quales
and why not all things ? since they are such as
ex humili magna ad fastigia rerum
from low-(estate) great to, heights of circumstances
2 1

Extollit,   quoties   voluit   Fortuna   j)cari.
raises up,   as often as   she has a mind   Fortune   to joke.
2   3   4   1   5

Quid   Romæ   faciam?   mentiri   sencio:
What   at Rome   can I do?   to lie   I know not

librum,   Si   malus   est,   nequeo   laudare,   et
a book   if   bad   it is   I cannot   praise   and
        2   1

poscere: motus   Astrorum   ignoro: funus
ask for: the motions   of the stars   I am ignorant of: the funeral

promittere   patris   Nec   volo   nec   possum:
promise   of a father   I neither   will   nor   can:
2   1

ranarum   viscera   nunquam   Inspexi: ferre
of toads   the entrails   never   have I inspected: to bear
2   1

ad   nuptam   quæ   mittit   adulter,   Quæ
to   a married (woman)   what   sends   an adulterer,   what
                2   1

mandat,   nôrint   alii: me   nemo   ministro   Fur
he commits   to charge let know   others: I   no one   assistant   a thief
        2   1   2   1   3   5

erit;   atque   ideo   nulli   comes   exeo,
shall be   and   therefore   to no one   a companion   I go forth,
4   3   2   1

tanquam   Mancus   et   extinctæ   corpus   non utile
as   maimed   and   of an extinct   body   a useless
                3   2   1

dextræ.   Quis   nunc   deligitur,   nisi   conscius,
right hand.   who   now   is loved   unless   conscious,
4

et   cui   fervens   Æstuat   occultis   animus
and   whose   fervent   boils   with (things) hidden   mind,
                    2   3   1

semperque   tacendis?   Nil   tibi   se   debere
and ever   to be kept silent?   nothing   to you   himself   to owe

putat,   nil   conferet   unquam,   Participem   qui
he thinks,   nothing   will he bestow   ever,   partaker,   who
            2   1   4   1

te   secreti   fecit   honesti.   Carus   erit
you   secret   has made   of an honest.   Dear   he will be
3   6   2   5

Verri,   qui   Verrem   tempore,   quo   vult,
to Verres   who   Verres   at time   any   he wishes,
                    2   1

Accusare   potest.   Tanti   tibi   non   sit
accuse   can.   of so much (value)   to you   not   let be
                    2   1   7

opaci   Omnis   arena   Tagi,   quod-
of dark   all   the sand   Tagus,   which
5   3   4   6

que   in   mare   volvitur   aurum,   Ut
and   into   the sea   is rolled   the gold   that
1   2

somno carcas, ponendaque³ præmia²
sleep *yon sh'd want,* *and to be rejected* *rewards*

sumas¹ Tristis, et a⁴ magno⁵ semper² timearis¹ ³
sh'd take *sorrowful, and* *by* *a great* *always* *be feared*

amico.⁶ Quæ nunc² divitibus⁵ gens¹ acceptissima³
friend *What* *now* *rich men* *nation (is)* *most acceptable*

nostris,⁴ Et quos præcipue fugiam, properabo
to our, *and* *whom* *especially* *I w'd avoid,* *I will hasten*

fateri; Nec pudor obstabit. Non possum ferre,
to confess; *nor* *shall shame* *hinder.* *I cannot* *bear,*

Quirites, Græcam urbem: quamvis quota portio
O Romans, *a Grecian* *city:* *though* *what (is)* *the portion*

fæcis² Achææ?¹ Jampridem Syrus in² Tiberim³
dregs *of Achæan?* *Some while since* *Syrian* *into* *the Tiber*

defluxit⁴ Orontes,¹ Et linguam, et mores, et cum
has flown *Orontes* *and (its) language, and* *morals,* *and* *with*

tibicine chordas Obliquas, necnor gentilia tympana
the piper *harps* *oblique,* *also* *(its) national* *timbrels*

secum Vexit, et ad⁴ Circum⁵ jussas² prostare³
with itself *has brought, and* *at* *the Circus* *bidden* *to expose (themselves)*

puellas.¹ Ite, quibus grata est pictâ³ lupa²
girls. *Go ye,* *to whom* *pleasing* *is* *with a painted* *strumpet*

Barbara¹ mitrâ.⁴ Rusticus² ille¹ tuus sumit
a-barbarian *mitre.* *rustic* *that* *of thine* *assumes*

trechedipna, Quirine, Et ceromatico fert
the trechedipna, *O Quirinus,* *and* *on his perfumed* *wears*

nicteria³ collo.¹ Hic altâ Sicyone, ast hic Amydone
the nicteria *neck.* *This (one)* *high* *Sicyon* *but this (one)* *Amydon*

relictâ, Hic Andro, ille Samo, hic Trallibus,
having been left, *this (one)* *from Andros,* *that from Samo,* *this from Tralles,*

aut Alabandis, Esquilias,² dictumque³ petunt¹ a⁶
or *Alobanda,* *the Esquiliæ* *and named* *seek* *from*

vimine⁷ collem;⁴ Viscera magnarum⁵ domuum,
an osier *the hill;* *the bowels* *of great* *houses,*

dominique² futuri.¹ Ingenium² velox,¹ audacia²
and lords *futuro* *Wit* *quick,* *impudence*

perdita,¹ sermo Promptus, et Isæo³
desperate, *speech* *ready,* *and* *than Isæus*

torrentior :   edo   quid   illum   Esse   putes ?
more rapid :   say   what   him   to be   do you think ?
1   2   3   1

quemvis   hominem   secum   attulit   ad   nos:
what man   you please   with himself   he has brought   to   us :

Grammaticus,   Rhetor,   Geometres,   Pictor,
Grammarian,   Rhetorician,   Geometrician,   Painter,

Alæptes,   Augur,   Schœnobates,   Medicus,   Magus :
Anointer,   Augur,   Rope-dancer,   Physician,   Wizard :

omnia   novit.   Grœculus   esuriens   in   coelum,
all (things)   he knows.   a Greekling   hungry   into   heaven,
                           2   1

jusseris,   ibit.   Ad   summum   non   Maurus
sh'd you command,   will go.   In   fine   not   a Moor
2   1   2   3

erat,   nec   Sarmata,   nec   Thrax,   Qui
he was,   nor   Sarmatian,   nor   Thracian,   who
1

sumpsit   pennas,   mediis   sed   natus
put on   wings,   in the midst of   but   born
                    3   1   2

Atheuis.   Horum   ego   non   fugiam   conchylia ?
Athens   Of these   shall I   not   flee   the purple finery ?
4

me   prior   ille   Signabit ?   fultusque
than me   sooner   shall he   sign ?   and supported
2   1

toro   meliore   recumbet,   Advectus   Romam,
by a conch   better   shall he recline at table   brought   to Rome
        2   1

quo   pruna   et   coctona   vento ?   Usque   adeo
by which   plums   and   figs   wind ?   even   so
        2   1

nihil   est,   quod   nostra   infantia   coelum
nothing   is it,   that   our   infancy   the air
                                            2

Hausit,   Aventini,   baccâ   nutrita   Sabinâ ?
drank   of Aventinus   berry   nourished   by the Sabine?
1   3   1   2

Quid !—quod   adulandi   gens   prudentissima   laudat
What !—   because   in flattering   a nation   most expert   praises

Sermonem   indocti,   faciem   deformis   amici,
the speech   of an unlearned,   the face   of a deformed   friend

Et   longum   invalidi   collum   cervicibus
and   the long   of the feeble   neck   to the neck
        2   4   3   5

æquat   Herculis,   Antæum   procul   a   tellure
equals   of Hercules   Antaeus   far   from   the earth
1   6   2

tenentis—miratur   vocem angustam,   quâ   deterius
holding—admires   a voice   squeaking   than which   worse
1   2   1   3   2

nec   Ille   sonat,   quo   mordetur   gallina
not   he   utters   who   is bitten   the hen
1   3   2

   marito!   Hæc   eadem   licet   et   nobis
(being) a husband! These same (things) it is allowed   also   us
   1

laudare : sed   illis   Creditur.   An   melior cum
to praise but to them (alone) credit is given. Whether (is he) better when

Thäida ., sustinet,   aut   cum   uxorem   comœdus
Thais he sustains (the part of) or when a wife   the comedian
2   1   3   1

agit,   vel Dorida nullo   Cultam   palliolo?   mulier
acts,   or   Doris   with no dressed   cloak?   a woman
2-   2   1   2

nempe   ipsa   videtur,   Non persona   loqui :   vacua
truly   herself seems,   not the actor, to speak: bare
1   2   1   3

et   plana   omnia   dicas   Infrà   ventriculum,
and plain   all   you w'd declare below   the belly
     4   2

et   tenui   distantia   rimâ.   Nec   tamen   Antiochus,
and with a thin differing slit.   Neither yet   Antiochus,
     2   1   2   1   1

nec   erit   mirabilis   illic   aut   Stratocles,   aut
nor   will be admirable   there   either Stratocles,   or
2   4 6   3   5

cum   molli   Demetrius   Hæmo: Natio   comœda
with soft   Demetrius   Hæmus;   the Nation comic
2   3   1   4   2

est: rides?   majore   cachinno   Concutitur :
is   do you laugh?   with greater   laughter   is he shaken:
1

flet,   si   lachrymas   conspexit   amici,   Nec dolet ;
he weeps if the tears   he has seen of a friend, not that he grieves;
             2 ,   1

igniculum   brumæ   si   tempore   poscas,   Accipit
a little fire of winter if   in time   you ask for, he puts on
5   3   1   2   4

endromidem;   si   dixeris,   aestuo,   sudat. Non
a great coat; if   you sh'd say,   I am hot, he sweats. we are

sumus   ergo   pares :   melior   qui   semper,
not   therefore equals: better (is he) who   always,

et   omni   Nocte   dieque   potest   alienum   sumere
and all   night   and day   is able   another's   to assume
                                           2   1

vultum ;   A   facie   jactare   manus,   laudare
countenance, from the face   to cast   the hands, to praise
                    2   1   2

paratus,   Si   bene   ructavit,   si   rectum   minxit
prepared   if   well   has belched if   rightly   made water
1   3   2   4   5   6

amicus,   Si   trulla   inverso   crepitum
(his) friend, if   the cup   from the inverted a crack
1   2   5   4

dedit *has given* 3 — aurea *golden* 1 — fundo. *bottom.* 6 — Præterea *moreover*

sanctum *sacred* — nihil *nothing* — est, *is,* — et *and* — ab *from*

inguine *(their) lust* — tutum : *safe:* — Non *not* — matrona *the matron* — laris, *of a household,*

non *not* — filia *a daughter* 2 — virgo, *virgin,* 1 — neque *nor* — ipse *himself* 2 — Sponsus *the wooer* 1

lævis *smooth* — adhuc, *as yet,* — non *not* — filius *the son* — ante *before* — pudicus. *chaste.*

Horum *of these* 4 — si *if* 1 — nihil *nothing* 3 — est, *there is,* 2 — aulam, *the house* — resupinat *he turns upside down*

amici : *of (his) friend* — Scire *know* — volunt *they will* — secreta *the secrets* — domûs, *of the family*

atque *and* — inde *thence* — timeri. *be feared* — Et *and* — quoniam *since* — cœpit *has begun* 3

Græcorum *of the Greeks* 2 — mentio, *mention* — 1 — transi *pass over* — Gymnasia, *the schools* — atque *and*

audi *hear* — facinus *a villainous deed* — majoris *of the greater* — abollæ. *abolla.* — Stoicus *a stoic*

occidit *killed* — Baream, *Bareas,* — delator *an informer* — amicum, *(his) friend*

Discipulumque *and (his) disciple* 2 — senex, *an old man,* 1 — ripâ *bank* 4 — nutritus *nourished* 1 — in *on* 2

illà, *that* 3 — Ad *at* — quam *which* — Gorgonei *of the Gorgonean* 2 — delapsa *dropt down* 4 — est — penna *a feather* 1

caballi. *pack-horse* 3 — Non *Not* 3 — est *is* 2 — Romano *Roman* 5 — cuiquam *for any* 4 — locus *a place* 1 — hic, *here* 4

ubi *where* — regnat *reigns* — Protogenes *Protogenes* 2 — aliquis, *some* 1 — vel *or* — Diphilus, *Diphilus,* — aut *or*

Erimanthus, *Erimanthus,* — Qui *who* — gentis *of (his) nation* 2 — vitio *from the vice* 1 — nunquam *never*

partitur *shares* — amicum ; *a friend;* — Solus *he alone* — habet. *has (him)* — Nam *for,* — cùm *when*

facilem *(his) easy* 3 — stillavit *he has dropt* 1 — in *into* 2 — aurem *ear* 4 — Exiguum *a little from* — de *of (his)* — naturæ *nature* 2

patriæque *and of (his) country* 3 — veneno, *the poison,* 1 — Limine, *from the threshold* — summoveor : *I am removed*

perièrunt *have perished* — tempora *times* 1 — longi *of long* — Servitii : *service:* 2 — nusquam *nowhere* — minor *less*

est   jactura   clientis.   Quod   porrò   officium
is   the loss   of a client. What   moreover (is) the office

(ne   nobis   blandiar)   aut   quod   Pauperis   hic
(lest   ourselves   I flatter)   or   what   of a poor man here
                                                        2   3

meritum,   si   curet   nocte   togatus   Currere,
the merit   if   takes care   by night   a client   to run
   1   2   3   1

cùm   Prætor   lictorem   impellat,   et   ire   Præcipitem
when   the prætor the lictor   drives on   and   to go   precipitate
                        2   1

jubeat,   '   dudum   vigilantibus   orbis,   Ne   prior
commands (him)   long since   awake   the childless lest   first
                    2   3   1

Albinam,   aut   Modiam   collega   salutet?   Divitis
Albina   or   Modia   his colleague sh'd salute? of a rich
   3   4   5   1   2   3

hic   servi   claudit   latus   ingenuorum   Filius:
here   slave   closes   the side   of the-free-born the son
  1   4   5   2

alter   enim   quantum   in   legione   Tribuni   Accipiunt,
another   but   as much as   in   a legion   tribunes receive,
   2   1

donat   Calvinæ,   vel   Catienæ,   Ut   semel   atque
presents   to Calvina   or   Catiena,   that   once   and

iterùm   super   illam   palpitet: at   tu   Cùm
again   over   her   he may palpitate: but   thou,   when

tibi   vestiti   facies   scorti   placet,   hæres,   Et
thee   of a well dressed   the face   harlot   pleases, dost hesitate, and
  5   2   1   3   4

dubitas   altâ   Chionem   deducere   sellâ.   Da
doubtest   from (her) high Chione to lead down   chair.   Produce
   3   2   1   4

testem   Romæ   tam   sanctum,   quam   fuit   hospes
a witness at Rome   as   just   as   was   the host

Numinis   Idæi: procedat   vel   Numa,   vel
divinity   of the Idean: let come forth   even   Numa,   or (he)
   2   1

qui   servavit   trepidam   flagranti   ex æde   Minervam:
who   preserved   trembling   the burning   from temple   Minerva:
                        3   2   4   1

Protinus   ad   censum;   de   moribus
Immediately   as to   income   concerning   morals

ultima   fiet   Quæstio: quot   pascit   servos?
the last   will be made   Inquiry: how many   he maintains   servants?
              2   1   2   1

quot   possidet   agri   Jugera?   quam   multâ
how many   he possesses   of land   acres   in how   many
              3   2   1

magnâque   paropside   cœnat?   Quantum
aud great   a dish   ho sups?   as much as
                                                       1   3

quisque   sua   nummorum   servat   in   arca,
every ono   his   of money   keeps   in   chest
4   7   2   5   6   8

Tantum   habet   et   fidei.   Jures   licèt
so much   has ho   also   of crodit.   you sh'd swear by   though
                                                     2   1

et   Samothracum,   Et   nostrorum   aras,
both   of tho Samothracian   aud   of our (gods)   the altars,
                      2   3   1

contemnere   fulmina   pauper   Creditur,   atque
to contemn   thunders   a poor (man)   is believed,   and
3   4   1   2

Deos,   Dis   ignoscentibus   ipsis.   Quid,   quòd
the gods,   the gods   forgiving (him)   themselves: What,   because
                                         2   1

materian   præbet   causasque   jocorum   Omnibus
matter   affords   and causes   of jests   to all
4   3

hic   idem,   si   fœda   et   scissa   lacerna,
this   same (poor fellow) if   dirty   and   rent   (his) cloak,
1   2

Si   toga   sordidula   est   et   ruptâ   calceus
if (his) toga   some what soiled   is,   aud   with-burst   shoo
                                                  4   2

alter   Pelle   patet: vel   si   consuto   vulnere
one or other   upper leather gapes: or   if   in the stitched up   rupture
1   6   3   8   9

crassum   Atque   recens   linum   ostendit   non
tho coarse   and   receut   thread   shows   not
5   6   7   4   1

una   cicatrix?   Nil   habet   infelix   paupertas
one   patch (only)?   nothing   has   unhappy   poverty
2   3

durius   in   se,   Quam   quod   ridiculos   homines
harder   in   itself,   than   that   ridiculous   men
                                               3   2

facit.   Exeat,   inquit,   si   pudor   est,   et   de
it makes.   Let him go out,   says he,   if   (to him) shame   is,   and   from
1   2

pulvino   surgat   equestri,   Cujus   res   legi
cushion   let him rise   tho equestrian,   whoso   estate   the law
4   1   3   3

non   sufficit,   et   sedeant   hìc   Lenonum   pueri
not   suffices.   and   let thero sit   here   of pimps   tho sons
1   2   2   1

quocunque   in   fornice   nati.   Hic   plaudat
whatever   in   brothel   born.   Here   lot applaud
2   1   4

nitidi — of a spruce — 2
præconis — crier — 3
filius — the son — 1
inter — among
Pinnirapi — of a sword-player — 3
cultos — smart — 1

juvenes, — youths — 2
juvenesque — and the youths
lanistæ : — of a fencer :
Sic — thus
libitum — it pleased

vano, — vain
qui — who — 2
nos — us — 4
distinxit, — distinguished, — 3
Othoni. — Otho. — 1
Quis — what

gener — son-in-law
hic — here
placuit — hath pleased — 3
censu — in estate — 2
minor, — inferior, — 1
atque — and

puellæ — of a girl — 3
Sarcinulis — to the money-bags — 2
impar ? — unequal? — 1
quis — what
pauper — poor (man)

scribitur — is written down
hæres ? — heir ?
Quando — When
in — in
consilio — counsel
est — is he

Ædilibus ? — with Ædiles?
agmine — In a body — 2
facto — formed — 1
Debuerant — ought — 3
olim — long ago — 4

tenues — the poor — 1
migrâsse — to have migrated — 5
Quirites. — Romans. — 2
Haud — not
facile — easily

emergunt, — do they emerge,
quorum — whose
virtutibus — virtues
obstat — opposes — 4
res — means — 2

angusta — narrow — 1
domi : — at home : — 3
sed — but
Romæ — at-Rome
durior — more hard
illis — to them

Conatus : — the endeavor :
magno — at a great (price) — 3
hospitium — lodging — 2
miserabile, — a miserable, — 1

magno — at a great (price) — 2
Servorum — of servants
ventres, — the bellies, — 1
et — and
frugi — a frugal

cœnula — little supper
magno. — at a great (price).
Fictilibus — in earthen vessels
cœnare — to sup

pudet, — it shames
quod — which
turpe — disgraceful
negavit — he denied (to be)
Translatus — (who was) translated

subitò — suddenly
ad — to
Marsos, — the Marsi
mensamque — and the table — 2
Sabellam, — Sabellan — 1

Contentusque — and content
illic — there
Veneto, — with a Venetian
duroque — and coarse
cucullo. — hood.

Pars — a part
magna — great
Italiæ — of Italy
est, — there is,
si — if
verum — the truth
admittimus, — we admit,

in — in
quâ — which
Nemo — nobody
togam — the gown
sumit, — takes
nisi — unless
mortuus. — dead.
Ipsa — itself — 2

dierum   Festorum   herboso   colitur   si   quando
days   of festal   in a grassy   it is celebrated   if   at any time
4   3   8   7   5   6

theatro   majestas,   tandèmque   redit   ad
theatro   the solemnity   and at length   returns   to
9   1   3

pulpita   notum   Exodium,   cùm   personæ   pallentis
the stage   a known   farce,   when   of the mask   pale-looking
4   1   2   2   4   3

hiatum   In   gremio   matris   formidat   rusticus
the gaping   In   the lap   of the mother   dreads   the rustic
1   3   4   5   1

infans :   Æquales   habitus   illic,   similemque   videbis
infant: equal (are)   habits   there,   and alike   you will see
2

Orchestram,   et   populum :   clari   velamen
the orchestra   and   people: of bright   the clothing
2   1

honoris,   sufficiunt   tunicæ   summis
honor,   suffice   tunics   for the chief
3   2   4

Ædilibus   albæ.   Hic   ultro   vires   habitûs
Ædiles   white.   Here   beyond   ability   (is) of dress
5   1   2

nitor :   hic   aliquid   plus   Quam   satis   est ;   interdum
a finery: here   something more   than   enough   is ;   sometimes
1   2   1

aliena   sumitur   arcâ.   Commune   id   vitium
from another's   it is taken   chest.   common   that   vice
2   1

est :   hic   vivimus   ambitiosâ   Paupertate   omnes:
is: here   we live   in ambitious   poverty   all

quid   te   moror ?   Omnia   Romæ   Cum
why   you   do I delay ?   all (things)   at Rome   (are) with

pretio.   Quid   das,   ut   Cossum   aliquando
a price.   What   give you,   that   Cossus   sometimes

salutes ?   Ut   te   respiciat   clauso   Veiento
you may salute?   that   on you   may look   with closed   Veiento
2   3   1

labello ?   Ille   metit   barbam,   crinem   hic
lip?   That (one)   shaves   the beard,   the hair   this (one)
4

deponit   amati :   Plena   domus libis   venalibus:
deposits   of a favorite;   full   the house of cakes   venal:

accipe,   et   illud   Fermentum   tibi   habe ;   præstare
take,   and   that   leaven   to thyself   have;   to pay

tributa   clientes   Cogimur,   et   cultis   augere   peculia
tributes   we clients   are compelled,   and of spruce   to augment the wealth
3   1   2

servis. Quis timet, aut timuit gelidâ Prænesto
servants. who fears ~~or~~ ~~is~~ the feared in cold Prænesto
4

ruinam ; Aut positis nemorosa inter
the fall of a house; or placed shady among
2 4 3

Juga Volsiniïs, aut simplicibus Gabiis
hills at Volsinium, or at simple Gabii
5 1

aut proni Tiburis arce ? Nos
or of prone Tibur at the tower? wo
2 3 1

urbem colimus tenui tibicine fultam
a city inhabit by a slender prop supported

magna parte sui : nam sic labentibus obstat
in a great part of itself: for thus (what is) falling hinders
2

villicus, et veteris rimæ contexit hiatum ;
the steward, and of an old chink has covered the gaping;
1 3 4 1 2

Securos pendente jubet dormire ruinâ. Vivendum
securo impending he bids (us) to sleep ruin. one should
3 5 1 2 4

est illic, ubi nulla incendia, nulli Nocte
live there where (there are) no burnings, no in the night
2

metus: jam poscit aquam, jam frivola
fears: already asks for water, already (his) lumber
1 2

transfert Ucalegon : tabulata tibi jam tertia
removes Ucalegon: floors your already third
1 3 1 2

fumant: Tu nescis ; nam si gradibus
smoke: thou knowest not; for if steps
3

trepidatur ab imis, Ultimus ardebit, quem
they are alarmed from the lowest, the highest will burn, which
1 2

tegula sola tuetur A pluviâ: molles ubi
the roof alone defends from rain: the soft where
2 1

reddunt ova columbæ. Lectus erat Codro
lay (their) eggs pigeons. a bed was to Codrus
4 5 3

Proculâ minor : urceoli sex Ornamentum abaci ;
than Procula less: little pitchers six the ornament of the cupboard;

necnon et parvulus infra Cantharus, et
also both a small underneath jug and
2 1

recubans (reclining) sub (under) eodem (the same) marmore (marble) Chiron; (a Chiron;)

Jamque (and now) vetus (an old) Græcos (his Greek) [3] servabat (preserved) [2] cista (chest) [1]

libellos, (books,) [4] Et (and) divina (divine) [4] Opici (barbarous) [1] rodebant (wore gnawing) [3] carmina (verses) [5]

mures. (mice.) [2] Nil (nothing) habuit (had) Codrus: (Codrus:) quis (who) enim (forsooth)

negat? (denies (it)?) et (and) tamen (yet) illud (that) Perdidit (he lost) [4 5] infelix (unhappy) [3]

totum (whole) [1] nil: (nothing:) [2] ultimus (the utmost) [2] autem (but) [1] Ærumnæ (to his affliction) [4] cumulus (addition) [3]

quòd (was) that nudum, (naked) et (and) frusta (scraps) [2] rogantem (begging) [1] Nemo (nobody) cibo (with food)

nemo (nobody) hospitio, (with entertainment) tectoque (and a roof) juvabit. (will help (him.)) Si (if) magna (the great)

Asturii (of Asturius) [2] cecidit (has fallen) [3] domus: (house:) [1] horrida (ghastly (is)) mater, (the mother,)

Pullati (sadly clothed (are) the nobles,) proceres, differt (defers) [2] vadimonia (recognizances) [3] Prætor: (the Prætor:) [1]

Tunc (then) gemimus (we lament) casus (the misfortunes) urbis, (of the city,) tunc (then) odimus (we hate)

ignem: (fire:) Ardet (it burns) adhuc— (yet—) et jam (and now) accurrit. (runs (one)) qui (who)

marmora (marbles) donet, (can present,) Conferat (can contribute) impensas: (expenses:) hic (this (one))

nuda (naked) et (and) candida (white) signa; (statues;) Hic (this (one)) aliquid (something)

præclarum (famous) Euphranoris, (of Euphranor) et (and) Polycleti; (Polycletus;)

Phæcasianorum (of Phæcasian) [3] vetera (ancient) [1] ornamenta (ornaments) [2]

deorum; (gods;) [4] Hic (this (one)) libros (books) dabit (will give) et (and) forulos, (book-cases,)

mediamque (and middle) Minervam; (Minerva;) Hic (this (one)) modium (a bushel) argenti: (of silver;)

meliora, (better,) ac (and) plura (more (things)) reponit (lays up) Persicus (the Persian,) orborum (of destitutes)

lautissimus,   et   merito   jam   Suspectus,   tan-
the most splendid,   and   deservedly   now   suspected,   as
                                 2   1

quam   ipse   suas   incenderet   ædes.   Si
if   he himself   his own   set fire to   house.   If
                      2   1   3

potes   avelli   Circensibus,   optima,   Soræ   Aut
you c'd be plucked away   from the Circenses,   a most excellent   at Sora,   or
                                                                 2

Fabrateriæ   domus,   aut   Frusinone   paratur,
Fabrateria   house,   or   Frusino   is got
3   1   -

Quanti   nunc   tenebras   unum   conducis   in
at the price for which now   darkness   one   you hire   for
                                   3   1   2

annum :   Hortulus   hic,   puteusque   brevis,
year :   a little garden   here,   and a well   shallow,
4   2   1

nec   reste   movendus,   In   tenues   plantas
not   by a rope   to be drawn,   upon   the small   plants
                                   4   5   6

facili   diffunditur   haustu.   Vivo   bidentis
with an easy   it is poured   draught.   live   of the fork
2   1   3   2

amans,   et   culti   villicus   horti,   Unde
fond   and   of a cultivated the farmer   garden   whence
1   2   1   3

epulum   possis   centum   dare   Pythagoræis
a feast   you can   to a hundred   give   Pythagoreans
                      2   1   3

Est   aliquid   quocunque   loco,   quocunque
It is   something   in whatsoever   place,   in whatsoever

recessu,   Unius   seso   dominum   fecisse
retirement,   of one   oneself   master   to have made
                4   2   3   1

lacertæ.   Plurimus   hic   æger   moritur
lizard.   many a   here   sick (man)   dies
5   2   1   3

vigilando   (sed   illum   Languorem   peperit
from watching   (but   that   languor   hath produced
                                                              2

cibus   imperfectus,   et   hærens   Ardenti
food   imperfect,   and   sticking   to the burning
1

stomacho)   nam   quæ   meritoria   somnum
stomach)   for   what   hired lodgings   sleep
                                                              2

Admittunt?   magnis   opibus   dormitur   in
admit ?   with great   wealth   one sleeps   in the
1

urbe.   Inde   caput   morbi,   rhedarum   transitus
city.   There   the source   of the disease,   of carriages   the passing
      2   1

arcto   Vicorum   inflexu,   et   stantis   convicia
in the narrow   of the streets   turning,   and   of the standing   the foul language
      2   1   2   1

mandræ   Eripiunt   somnum   Druso,   vitulisque
team   take away   sleep   from Drusus,   and calves
3   2

marinis.   Si   vocat   officium,   turbâ   cedente
marine.   if   calls   business,   the crowd   giving away,
1   2   1

vehetur   Dives,   et   ingenti   curret   super
will be carried along   the rich man   and   with a large   will pass swiftly   above
      2   1   2

ora   Liburno,   Atque   obiter   leget,   aut   scribet,
their faces   Liburnian,   and   in the way   he will read, or   write,
3   1

aut   dormiet   intus;   Namque   facit   somnum
or   sleep   within;   for   causes   sleep
                                4   5

clausâ   lectica   fenestrâ.   Ante   tamen
shut   a litter   with the window.   Before   but
3   1   2   3   1

veniet: nobis   properantibus   obstat   Unda
he will come: us   hastening   obstructs   the crowd
2   3   1

prior,   magno   populus   premit   agmine   lumbos
before,   with a great   the people   press   concourse   the loins
2   4   2   5   3

Qui   sequitur: ferit   hic   cubito,   ferit
who   follow   strikes   this (one)   with the elbow,   strikes
1   2   1   2

assere   duro   Alter;   at   hic   tignum   capiti
joist   with a hard   another;   but   this (one)   a beam   against the head
4   3   1   2   3

incutit,   ille   metretam.   Pinguia   crura
drives,   that (one)   a tub.   thick   the legs
1   2   1

luto: plantâ   mox   undique   magnâ   Calcor,
with mud: with a foot   presently   on all sides   great   I am trodden on
      3   5   1   2   4

et   in   digito   clavus   mihi   militis   hæret.
and   in   the toe   the nail   to me   of a soldier   sticks
      4   5   1   6   2   3

Nonne   vides   quanto   celebretur   sportula
do you   not see   with how much   is frequented   the sportula
                                 3   2

fumo?   Centum   convivæ;   sequitur   sua   quemque
smoke?   a hundred   guests;   follows   his own   every one
1   3   1   4

culina;   Corbulo   vix   ferret   tot   vasa   ingentia,
kitchen   Corbulo   hardly   c'd bear   so many   vessels   great
2   2   1

tot   res   Impositas   capiti   quot
so many   things   put on   (his) head   as

recto   vertice   portat   Servulus   infelix;
with an upright   top   carries   little slave   an unhappy

et   cursu   ventilat   ignem.
and   in running   ventilates   the fire.

Scinduntur   tunicæ   sartæ :   modo   longa   coruscat
are torn   tunics   tho patched: now   a long   brandishes,
3   2   1   2

Sarraco   veniente   abies,   atque   altera   pinum
the wagon   coming   fir tree   and   other   a pine
3   4   1   2   1

Plaustra   vehunt,   nutant   alte,   populoque
carts   carry,   they nod   on high   and the people
                2

minantur.   Nam   si   procubuit,   qui   saxa
threaten   but   if   has fallen down   which   stones
1   6   2   5

Ligustica   portat   Axis,   et   eversum   fudit
Ligustian   carries   the axle   and   the overturned has   poured
4   3   1   2   1

super   agmina   montem,   Quid   superest   de
upon   tho crowd   mountain,   what   remains   of
        3

corporibus?   quis   membra,   quis   ossa   Invenit ?
(their) bodies?   who   members,   who   bones   finds ?

obtritum   vulgi   perit   omne   cadaver   more
ground to pieces   of the vulgar   perishes   every   carcass   in the manner
4   3   1   2

animæ.   Domus   interea   secura   patellas
of the soul.   the family   meanwhile   unconcerned   the dishes

jam   lavat   et   buccâ   foculum   excitat,
now   washes   and   with the cheek   a little fire   arouses

et   sonat   unctis   strigilibus,   pleno   et
and   makes a sound   with anointed   scrapers   with a full   and
                4   1

componit   lintea   gutto.   Hæc   inter
puts together   the napkins   cruse   These (things)   among
2   3   5

pueros   varie   properantur :   at   illo   jam   sedet
the servants   variously   are hastened: but   he   now   sits
    2   1

in   ripâ,   tetrumque   novitius   horret
on   the bank,   and tho black   a novice   dreads
1   4   2   3

Porthmea;   nec   sperat   cœnosi   gurgitis
ferryman;   nor   does he hope for   of the muddy   pool
5   2   3

alnum   Infelix,   nec   habet   quem   porrigat
the boat   unhappy,   nor   has he   which   he can reach forth
1   2

ore   trientem.   Respice   nunc   alia,   ac
from his mouth   a farthing.   Consider   now   other,   and
1

diversa   pericula   noctis: Quod   spatium
different   dangers   of the night: what   space

tectis   sublimibus,   unde   cerebrum   Testa
from roofs   high   whence   the brain   a potsherd
2   1

ferit,   quoties   rimosa   et   curta   fenestris
strikes,   as often as   cracked   and   broken   from the windows
2   3   1

Vasa   cadunt,   quanto   percussum   pondere
vessels   fall,   with how great   the stricken   weight
                                    4   1

signent,   Et   lædant   silicem: possis   ignavus
they mark,   and   wound   flint: you may   idle
2   3   2

haberi,   Et   subiti   casûs   improvidus,   ad
be accounted,   and   of sudden   accident   improvident,   to
1   2   1

cœnam   si   Intestatus   eas;   adeo   tot
supper   if   intestate   you go;   as   many

fata   quot   illâ   Nocte   patent   vigiles,
fates   (there are) as   in that   night   there are open   watchful
                                        there are open

te   prætereunte,   fenestræ.   Ergo   optes   votumque
you passing by,   windows.   therefore   you sh'd desire   and wish
2   3   1   4

feras   miserabile   tecum,   Ut   sint   contentæ
sh'd carry   a miserable   with you'   that   they may be   content
1   3   2

patulas   effundere   pelves.   Ebrius,   ac
broad   to pour forth   basins.   (one) drunken,   and
2   1

petulans,   qui   nullum   forte   cecidit,   Dat
petulant,   who   nobody   haply   has felled   suffers

pœnas,   noctem   patitur   lugentis   amicum
punishment,   the night   suffers   mourning   (his) friend
            2   1   2

Pelidæ;   cubat   in   faciem   mox   deinde
of Pelides;   he lies   on   (his) face   presently   then
1   2   1

supinus: Ergo   non   aliter   poterit   dormire:
on his back: for   not   otherwise   c'd he   sleep:

Quibusdam Somnum rixa facit: sed
to some sleep a quarrel causes: but
              3 1 2

quamvis improbus annis, Atque mero
though wicked from years, and with wine
                                           2

fervens, cavet hunc, quem coccina læna
heated, he is aware of him, whom a scarlet cloak
1

Vitari jubet, et comitum longissimus ordo;
to avoid commands, and of attendants a very long train

Multum præterea flammarum, atque ænea
a great number besides of lights, and a brazen
2 1

lampas. Me quem Luna solet deducere,
lamp. Me whom the moon is wont to attend,

vel breve lumen Candelæ, cujus dispenso
or the short light of a candle, whose I dispose
                                                              2

et tempero filum, Contemnit: miseræ
and regulate wick, he despises: of a wretched
              1 3

cognosce prooemia rixæ, Si rixa est,
know the preludes quarrel, if a quarrel it is
1 2 4

ubi tu pulsas ego vapulo tantùm.
where you strike (and) I am beaten only.
                                 2 1

Stat contrà, stariquc jubet; parere necesse
He stands opposite and to stand bids (you); to obey necessary

est; Nam quid agas, cùm te furiosus
it is; for what can you do, when you a madman

cogat, et idem Fortior? unde venis?
compels, and the same the stronger? whence come you?

exclamat: cujus aceto, Cujus
he exclaims: with whose vinegar, whose

conche tumes? quis tecum sectile porrum
bean swell you? what with you sliced leek
                                        2

Sutor, et elixi vervecis labra comedit?
cobbler and a boiled sheep's head has eaten?
1

Nil mihi respondes? aut dic, aut accipe
Nothing to me do you respond? either tell, or take

calcem: Ede ubi consistas: in quâ te
a kick: tell where you abide: in what you
                                                                 3

quæro puesenchâ? Dicere si tentes aliquid,
do I seek begging-place? to say if you sh'd attempt anything
2 1 3 1 2 4

tacitusve recedas, Tantundem est: feriunt
or silent retire, all the same it is: they strike

pariter : vadimonia deinde Irati faciunt. Libertas
equally bails then they angry make (you give). The liberty
3

pauperis hæc est: Pulsatus rogat, et pugnis
of a poor man this is: beaten he asks, and with fists
4 1 2

concisus adorat, Ut liceat paucis cum dentibus
bruised he entreats that he may a few with teeth
4 3 5

inde reverti. Nec tamen hoc tantum metuas :
thence return. Nor yet this only may you fear
2 1

nam qui spoliet te Non deerit: clausis
for (one) who will rob you will not be wanting, being shut
2

domibus, postquam omnis ubique Fixa catenatæ
the houses, after every everywhere fixed of the chained
1 2 1 3 5

siluit compago tabernæ. Interdum et ferro
has been silent fastening shop. Sometimes and with a sword
7 4 6 2 1

subitus grassator agit rem, Armato quoties
the sudden foot-pad does the thing, with an armed as often as
2 1

tutæ custode tenentur Et Pontina palus,
safe guard are kept both the Pontine marsh
4 3

et Gallinaria pinus. Sic inde huc omnes
and the Gallinarian pine. Thus thence hither all

tanquam ad vivaria currunt. Quâ fornace
as to vivaries run. in what furnace

graves, quâ non incude catenæ? Maximus
heavy on what (are) not anvil chains? the greatest
4 1 3 2 5

in vinclis ferri modus, ut timeas, ne
in fetters of iron quantity (is used), so that you may fear lest
3 2 1

Vomer deficiat, ne marræ et sarcula desint.
the ploughshare may fail, lest hoes and spades may be wanting.

Felices proavorum atavos, felicia dicas, Secula,
Happy of early times (our) forefathers, happy you may call the ages,
2 1

quæ quondam sub regibus atque tribunis Viderunt
which formerly under kings and tribunes saw

uno contentam carcere Romam. His alias
with one content prison Rome. to these other
3 2 4 1

poteram, et plures subnectere causas;
1 could   and   more   subjoin   causes
4   1   2   5   3

Sed jumenta vocant, et sol inclinat; eundum
but (my) cattle call and the sun inclines; I must

est : Nam mihi commotâ jamdudum mulio
go;   for to me with his shaken long since the muleteer
            6   3   1   2

virgâ Innuit: ergo vale nostri memor;
whip has hinted: therefore farewell of us mindful;
4   5   4

et quoties te Roma tuo refici properantem
and as often as you Rome to your to be refreshed hastening
                3   1   6   5   4

reddet Aquino, Me quoque ad Helvinam Cererem
shall restore Aquinum me also to Helvina Ceres
2   7

vestramque Dianam convelle â Cumis ; Satirarum
and your   Diana   rend from Cumæ   of-your-satires
                                                2

ego (ni pudet illas) Adjutor gelidos
I   (unless it shames them) a helper (your) cold
                                                4

veniam caligatus in agros.
will come armed into fields.
1   2   8   5

SATIRE IV.

ARGUMENT.

In this Satire Juvenal indulges his honest spleen against Crispinus, already noticed, and Domitian, the constant object of his scorn and abhorrence. The introduction of the tyrant is excellent; the mock solemnity with which the anecdote of the Turbot is introduced, the procession of the affrighted counsellors to the palace, and the ridiculous debate which terminates as ridiculous a decision, show a masterly hand. The whole concludes with an indignant and high-spirited apostrophe.

Ecco	iterum	Crispinus;	et	est	mihi	sæpe
Behold	again	Crispinus;	and	he is	by me	often

vocandus	Ad	partes;	monstrum	nullâ	virtute
to be called	to (his)	parts;	a monster	by no	virtue

redemptum	A	vitiis,	æger,	soláque	libidine
redeemed	from	vices,	sick	and alone 2	in lust 1

fortis :	Delicias	viduæ	tantum	aspernatur
strong:	the charms	of a widow	only	despises 2

adulter.	Quid	refert	igitur	quantis	jumenta
the adulterer. 1	what	signifies it	therefore	in how great	(his) cattle 3

fatiget	Porticibus,	quantâ	nemorum	vectetur
he fatigues 2	porches, 1	how great 2	of groves 4	he will be carried 5

in	umbrâ,	Jugera	quot	vicina	foro,	quas
in 1	a shade, 3	acres	how many	near	the forum,	what

emerit	ædes?	Nemo	malus	felix;	minime
he may have bought houses? 2	No one 1		bad	(is) happy:	least (of all)

corruptor,	et	idem	Incestus,	cum	quo
a corrupter,	and	the same	incestuous,	with	whom

nuper	vittata	jacebat	Sanguine	adhuc	vivo
lately	a filletted	lay	with blood	as yet	alive
	2	1	6	7	8

terram	subitura	sacerdos.	Sed	nunc	de
ground	about-to go under	priestess.	But	now	conc rning
5	4	3			

factis	levioribus;	et	tamen	alter	Si
deeds	lighter;	and	yet	another	if

fecisset	idem,	caderet	sub	judice	morum.
h had done	the same,	w'd fall	un ler	the judge	of morals.

Nam	quod	turpe	bonis,	Titio,	Seioque,
for	what(w'd be)	base	in good (men),	Titius,	and Seius

decebat	Crispinum;	quid	agas,	cûm	dira,
b came	Crispinus;	what	can you do,	sin e	dire,

et	fœdior	omni	Crimine	persona	est?
and	fouler	than every	crime	(his) person	is?

nullum	sex	millibus	emit,	Æquantem	sane
a mullet	for six	thousand (sestertia)	he bought,	equalling	truly
				2	1

paribus	sestertia	libris,	Ut	perhibent,	qui
to a like number	the sestertia	pounds,	as	they report,	who
4	3	5			

de	magnis	majora	loquuntur.		Consilum
of	great (things)	greater	speak.		the device

laudo	artificis,	si	munere	tanto	Præcipuam
I praise	of the contriver,	if	with a gift	so large	the chief
					2

in	tabulis	ceram	senis	abstulit	orbi.
on	the will	wax	old man	he has obtained	of a childless.
	4	3	6	1	5

Est	ratio	ulterior,	magnæ	si	misit
There is	reason	further,	to a great	if	he sent (it)
	2	1	3	1	2

amicæ,	Quæ	vehitur	clauso	latis	specularibus
mistress,	who	is carried	in a close	with broad	windows
4				2	3

antro.	Nil	tale	expectes:	emit	sibi:
litt r.	Nothing	such	look for:	he bought (it)	for himself:
1					

multa	videmus,	Quæ	miser	et	frugi	non
many (things) we see,		which	the wretched	and	frugal	not
						3

fecit	Apicius:	hoc	tu	Succinctus	patriâ
did	Apicius:	this	thou	(with your) girt	country's
2	1	this thou (didst)		3	4

quondam,	Crispine,	papyro.	Hoc	pretium
formerly,	Crispinus,	papyrus.	(Is) this	the price
2	1	5		

squamæ?   potuit   fortasse   minoris   Piscator,
of a scale?   might   perhaps   at-less   the fisherman
        3   1   2

quàm   piscis,   emi.   Provincia   tanti   Vendit
than   the fish,   be bought.   A province   at so much   sells

agros: sed   majores   Appulia   vendit.   Quales
fields: but   greater (fields)   Appulia _   sells.   What

tunc   epulas   ipsum   glutisse   putemus
then   dainties   himself   to have gorged   can we think
 2   1   3   4   1

Induperatorem,   cùm   tot   sestertia,   partem
the emperor,   when   so many   sestertia,   part
   2   2

Exiguam,   et   modicæ   sumptam   de   margine
a small,   and   of a moderate   taken   from   the margin
  1   3   1   2

cœnæ   Purpureus   magni   ructârit   scurra
supper   a purple   of a great   belched   buffoon
                   2   4   1

palati,   Jam   princeps   equitum,   magnâ   qui
palace,   now   chief   of knights,   with a loud   who
  3   3   1

voce   solebat   Vendere   municipes   pactâ
voice   used   to sell   (his) countrymen   for bargained
 4   2   2   3

mercede   siluros?   Incipe   Calliope,   licet
wages   siluri?   Begin   Calliope,   it is permitted
  4   1

hic   considere: non   est   Cantandum,
(you) here   to dwell: not   is it   to be sung (by you),

res vera   agitur: narrate   puellæ   Pierides;
a matter true   is treated: relate   (it) ye maids   Pierian;

prosit   mihi   vos   dixisse   puellas.   Cùm
let it avail   me   you   to have called   maids.   when

jam   semianimum   laceraret   Flavius   orbem
now   the half dead   had torn   Flavius   world
        4   3   2   5

Ultimus,   et   calvo   serviret   Roma   Neroni
the last,   and   a bald   served   Rome   Nero
  1   3   2   1   4

Incidit   Adriaci   spatium   admirabile   rhombi,
there fell (into a net)   of an Adriatic   size   a wondrous   turbot,
                 3   2   1   4

Ante   domum   Veneris,   quam   Dorica   sustinet
before   the house   of Venus,   which   Doric   sustains
                                 2

Ancon,   Implevitque   sinus: neque   enim
Ancon,   and filled   (its) folds: not   for
  1   4   1

minor   hæserat   illis,   Quos   operit   glacies
a less   had   stuck   than those,   which   covers   ice
2   3   5   3   2

Mæotica,   ruptaque   tandem   Solibus   effundit
the Mæotic,   and broken   at length   by the suns   pours forth
1   2   1

torpentis   ad ostia   Ponti,   Desidiâ   tardos,
of the dull   at the mouths   Pontic,   by idleness   slow
2   1   3

et   longo   frigore   pingues.   Destinat   hoc
and   by long   cold   fat.   Destines   this
                    4   5

monstrum   cymbæ   linique   magister   Pontifici
monster   of the boat   and net   the master   for the Pontiff
6   2   3   1   2

summo :   quis   enim   proponere   talem,   Aut
chief :   who   for   to offer (for sale)   such (a one)   or
1   2   1

emere   auderet ?   cùm   plena   et   littora
to buy (it)   would dare ?   since   full   too   the shores
                6   2   1

multo   Delatore   forent :   dispersi   protinus
with many   an informer   might be :   the dispersed   forthwith
3   4   5   3

algæ   Inquisitores   agerent   cum   remige
of sea-weed   inquisitors   would contend   with   the boatman
2   1   2

nudo ;   Non   dubitaturi   fugitivum   dicere
naked ;   not   hesitating   a fugitive   to say
1   3   1

piscem,   Depastumque   diu   vivaria   Cæsaris
(that) the fish, (was) and (had) fed in   long   the ponds   of Cæsar,
2   2   1

inde   Elapsum,   veterem   ad   dominum   debere
thence   escaped,   (its)   old   to   master   ought
                    4   3   5   1

reverti.   Si   quid   Palphurio,   si   credimus
to return.   If   at all   Palphurius,   if   we believe
2

Armillato,   Quicquid   conspicuum   pulchrumque
Armillatus,   whatever   remarkable,   and beautiful
                    2

est   æquore   toto,   Res   fisci   est,   ubicunque
is   sea   in the whole,   a matter of revenue is,   wherever
1

natat.   Donabitur   ergo,   Ne   pereat.   Jam
it swims.   It shall be presented,   therefore,   lest   it sh'd perish.   now
                                      3

lethifero   cedente   pruinis   Autumno,   Jam
deadly   yielding   to hoar-frosts   Autumn   now
1   4   5   2   2

quartanam	sperantibus	ægris,	Stridebat	deformis
a quartan	expecting	the sick,	howled	deformed
4	3	1	3	1

hyems,	prædamque	recentem	Servabat:	tamen
winter,	and the prey	recent	preserved:	yet
2		2	1	

hic	properat,	velut	urgeat	Auster	Utque
he	hastens,	as if	urged	the South wind,	and as soon as
			2	1	

lacus	suberant,	ubi,	quanquam	diruta	servat
the lakes	they had got to	where,	though	demolished	preserves
2	1				2

Ignem	Trojanum,	et	Vestam	colit	Alba
fire	the Trojan,	and	Vesta	worships	Alba
4	3	5	7	6	1

minorem,	Obstitit	intranti	miratrix	turba
the less,	opposed	(him) entering	a wondering	crowd
8	4	5	1	2

parumper:	Ut	cessit,	facili	patuerunt
for a while:	as	it yielded,	with an easy	opened
3			1	2

cardine	valvæ:	Exclusi	spectant	admissa
hinge	the gates:	shut out	behold	let in
4	1	2	3	5

opsonia	patres.	Itur	ad	Atridem:	tum
the dainties	the fathers.	It is gone	to	Atrides:	then
4	1				

Picens,	accipe,	dixit,	Privatis	majora	focis;
the Picenian,	accept,	said,	for private	things too great	fire-places;
	2	1	2	1	3

genialis	agatur	Iste	dies;	propera
as a festival	let be passed	this	day;	hasten

stomachum	laxare	saginis,	Et	tua	servatum
the stomach	to relieve	from (its) crammings,	and	thy	reserved
				5	3

consume	in	sæcula	rhombum,	Ipse	capi
consume	for	times	a turbot,	itself	be taken
1	4	6	2		

voluit.	quid	apertius?	et	tamen	illi
would.	what	(could be) more open?	and	yet	his
					1

surgebant	cristæ;	nihil	est,	Quod	credere
arose	crest;	nothing	there is,	which	to believe
3	2				3

de	se	non	possit,	cum	laudatur	Dis
of	itself	it may	not be able,	when	is praised	to the gods
1	2				4	3

æqua	protestas.	Sed	deerat	pisci	patinæ
equal	a power.	But	there was wanting	for the fish	of pot
2	1				2

mensura:	vocantur	Ergo	in	concilium	proceres
a size:	are called	therefore	into	council	the nobles
1	3	1		4	2

quos   oderat   ille ;   in   quorum   facie   miserœ,
whom   hated   he ;   in   whose   face   of a miserable
                                                                    3

magnæque   sedebat   Pallor   amicitiæ.   Primus,
and great   was sitting   the paleness   friendship.   First,
    4   1   2   5

clamante   Liburno,   Currite, jam   sedit;   raptâ
crying out   a Liburnian   Run,   already   he is seated;   with   a snatched up
    2   1

properabat   abollâ   Pegasus,   attonitœ   positus
hastened   gown   Pegasus,   to the astonished   appointed
    2   1   4   2

modò   villicus   urbi ;   Anne   aliud   tunc   Præfecti?
lately   bailiff   city ;   Were   anything else   then   the Præfects?
    1   3   5   3   2   1

quorum   optimus,   atque   Interpres   legum
of whom   (he was) the best,   and   interpreter   of the laws
                                             2   3

sanctissimus ;   omnia   quanquam   Temporibus
the most upright;   all (things)   though   in times
    1   2   1   ,   2

diris   tractanda   putabat   inermi   Justitiâ.
dire   (were) to be handled   he thought   with unarmed   justice.
    1

Venit   et   Crispi   jucunda   senectus,   Cujus
came   also   of Crispus   the pleasant   old age,   whoso
    5   4   3   1   2

erant   mores,   qualis   facundia,   mite   Ingenium:
were   manners,   as   (his) eloquence,   a gentle   disposition :
    2   1

maria,   ac   terras,   populosque   regenti   Quis
seas,   and   lands,   and peoples   (to one) governing   who
    2   3   4   1

comes   utilior,   si   clade   et   peste   sub   illâ
a companion   more useful,   if   slaughter   and   pestilence   under   that
    2   1   3   4   1   2

Sævitiam   damnare,   et   honestum   afferre   liceret
cruelty   to condemn,   and   honest   to give   it were permitted
    3   2   4   6   5   1

Consilium ?   sed   quid   violentius   aure
counsel?   but   what   more violent   than the ear
    7

tyranni,   Cum   quo   de   nimbis,   aut   æstibus,
of a tyrant,   with   whom   of   showers,   or   heats,
                         4   5   6   7

aut   pluvioso   Vero   locuturi   fatum   pendebat
or   a rainy   spring (though only) going to speak   the fato   depended
    8   9   10   3   1   11

amici ?   Ille   igitur   nunquam   direxit   brachia
of a friend?   He   therefore   never   directed   (his) arms
    2

contra   Torrentem ;   nec   civis   erat, qui   libera
against   the torrent   nor   a citizen   was he, who   the free
                                           2   1   3

posset   Verba   animi   proferre,   et vitam   impendere
could   words   of his mind   utter,   and [his] life   spend
1   4   5   2

vero.   Sic   multas   hyemes,   atque   octogesima
for the truth. Thus   many   winters,   and   the eightieth
            2   3   4   5

vidit   Solstitia: his armis,   illâ   quoque   tutus
he saw   Solstices: with these arms,   that   also   safe
1   4   2   1

in   aulâ.   Proximus   ejusdem   properabat   Acilius
in   court.   next   of the same   hurried·   Acilius
3   5   2   3

ævi   cum   juvene   indigno   quem   mors
age   with   a youth   unworthy   whom   a death
1

tam   sæva   maneret   Et   domini   gladiis   jam
so   cruel   sh'd await   and   of the tyrant   by the swords   now
so   cruel   4   3   1

festinata :   sed   olim   Prodigio   par   est   in
hastened: but   long since   to a prodigy   equal   is   in
2   5   4   3

nobilitate   senectus :   unde   fit,   ut   malim
nobility   old age   whence   it is   that   I w'd rather
2   1

fraterculus   esse   gigantum.   Profuit   ergo   nihil
a little brother   be   of the giants   It availed   therefore   nothing
                                                       2   3

misero,   quòd   cominus   ursos   Figebat   Numidas,
the wretch,   that   in close fight   bears   he pierced   Numidian
1   3   1   2

Albanâ   nudus   arenâ   Venator :   quis   enim
in the Alban   a naked   theatre   hunter   who   for
3   1   4   2   2   1

jam   non   intelligat   artes   Patricias ?   quis   priscum
now   not   can understand   the arts   patrician?   who   old
              2   1   3

illud   miretur   acumen   Brute   tuum?   facile   est
that   can wonder at   subtlety   O Brutus   of thine?   easy   it is
2   1   4

barbato   imponere   regi.   Nec   melior   vultu,
on a bearded   to impose   king·   Nor   better   in countenance,
      2   1·

quamvis   ignobilis   ibat   Rubrius,   offensæ   veteris
though   ignoble   went   Rubrius,   offence   of an old
                                        3   2

reus,   atque   tacendæ;   Et   tamen   improbior
guilty,   and   to be kept silent;   and   yet   more wicked
1

Satiram scribente cinædo. Montani quoque venter
satire writing than the pathic. of Montanus too the belly
3 2 1 2 3 1

adest abdomine tardus: Et matutino sudans
is present, from his paunch slow: and with morning sweating
2 1 3 2

Crispinus amomo; Quantum vix redolent duo
Crispinus perfume as much scarcely smell two
1 4

funera : sævior illo Pompeius tenui jugulos
corpses: more cruel than he Pompeius with a thin throats
3

aperire susurro : Et qui vulturibus servabat
to cut whisper: and who vultures was preserving
2 1 2 6 3

viscera Dacis, Fuscus, marmoreâ meditatus
(his) bowels for the Dacian Fuscus, in (his) marble having meditated
4 5 1 3 1

prælia villâ : Et cum mortifero prudens
wars villa: and with deadly prudent
2 4 3 4 1

Veiento Catullo, qui nunquam visæ flagrabat
Veiento Catullus, who never seen burned
2 5 4 5 1

amore puellæ, Grande, et conspicuum nostro
with the love of a girl, a great, and a conspicuous in our
2 3 4 2

quoque tempore monstrum! Cæcus adulator,
also time monster! a blind flatterer,
1 3 5

dirusque a ponte satelles Dignus Aricinos qui
and a dire from the bridge attendant worthy the Aricinian that he
2 1 4 1

mendicaret ad axes, Blandaque devexæ jactaret
sh'd beg at axles, and kind to the descending throw
2 3 5 2 4 1

basia rhedæ. Nemo magis rhombum stupuit:
kisses carriage. nobody more the turbot wondered at
3 5 2 1

nam plurima dixit In lævum conversus;
for very many (things) he said to the left turned
2 1

at illi dextra jacebat Bellua; sic pugnas
but on his right hand lay the beast; thus the battles
2

Cilicis laudabat, et ictus ; Et perma,
of the Cilician he praised, and strokes; and the machine,
5 1 3 4

et pueros inde ad velaria
and the boys thence to the coverings

raptos. Non cedit Veiento, sed
snatched up. Not yields Veiento, but
3 2 1

ut fanaticus œstro Percussus,
as a fanatic gad-fly stung
3 1

Bellona,   tuo   divinat;   et   ingens   Omen
OBellona,   with thy   divines;   and   a great   Omen
           2

habes,   inquit,   magni   clarique   triumphi :
you have,   says,   of a great   and illustrious   triumph:

Regem   aliquem   capies,   aut   de   temone
King   some   you will take,   or   from   chariot

Britanno   Excidet   Arviragus :   peregrina   est
a British   will fall   Arviragus: foreign   is

bellua,   cernis   Erectas   in   terga   sudes ?
the beast,   do you perceive   erect   on (his) back   the spears ?

hoc   defuit   unum   Fabricio,   patriam   ut
this   was wanting   one (thing)   to Fabricius,   the country   that

rhombi   memoraret,   et   annos.   Quidnam
of the turbot   he sh'd tell,   and   (its) years.   What

igitur   censes ?   conciditur?   absit   ab   illo
then   thinkest thou ?   is it to be cut up ?   absent be   from   it

Dedecus   hoc,   Montanus   ait;   testa   alta
disgrace   this,   Montanus   says;   a pot   deep
  2   1

paretur,   Quæ   tenui   muro   spatiosum
let be prepared,   which   with (its) thin   wall   the spacious
                      2

colligat   orbem ;   Debetur   magnus   patinæ
may collect   orb;   is due   a great   to the dish
  1

subitusque   Prometheus :   Argillam,   atque   rotam
and sudden   Prometheus :   the clay,   and   the wheel

citius   properate :   sed   ex   hoc   Tempore
quickly   hasten :   but   from   this   time

jam,   Cæsar,   figuli   tua   castra   sequantur.
now,   Cæsar,   let potters   your   camp   follow.

Vicit   digna   viro   sententia :   noverat   ille
prevailed   worthy   the man   the opinion :   had known   he
  4   2   3   1   2   1

Luxuriam   imperii   veterem,   noctesque   Neronis
luxury   of the empire   the old,   and the nights   of Nero
  2   1

jam   medias,   aliamque   famem,   cùm   pulmo
now   half spent,   and another   hunger,   when   the lungs

Falerno   Arderet :   nulli   major   fuit   usus
with Falernan   burned :   to none   a greater   was there   experience

edendi   Tempestate   meâ.   Circeis   nata   forent
of eating   in time   my   (whether) at Circæi   were   bred
           2   1   1   3

an   Lucrinum   ad   saxum,   Rutupinove   edita
or   the Lucrine   at   rock,   or from the Rutupian   sent forth
4   6   5   7 8   10   9

fundo,	Ostrea,	callebat	primo	deprendere
bottom,	oysters,	he knew well	at the first	to discover
11	2		2	1

morsu ;	Et	semel	aspecti	littus	dicebat
bite ;	and	once	looked at	the shore	told
		4	5	2	1

echini.	Surgitur,	et	misso	Proceres	exire
of a sea-urchin.	They rise,	and	for the dismissed	the nobles	to depart
3			4	1	3

jubentur	Concilio,	quos	Albanam	dux
are commanded	council,	whom	the Alban	general
2	5		4	2

magnus	in	arcem	Traxerat	attonitos,	et
the great	into	tower	had drawn	astonished,	and
1	3	5	6	7	

festinare	coactos,	Tanquam	de	Cattis
to hasten	compelled,	as if	concerning	the Catti
2	1		3	4

aliquid,	torvisque	Sicambris	Dieturus ;	tanquam
something,	and the fierce	Sicambri	about to say ;	as if
2	5	6	1	

diversis	partibus	orbis	Anxia	præcipiti
from different	parts	of the world	an alarming	on hurried
				3

venisset	epistola	pennâ.	Atque	utinam
had come	epistle	wing.	And	would that
2	1			

his	potius	nugis	tota	illa	dedisset
to these	rather	trifles	all	those	he had given
2	1		2	3	1

Tempora	sævitiæ,	claras	quibus	abstulit
times	of cruelty,	renowned	in which	he took from
		4	1	2

urbi	Illustresque	animas	impunè,	et	vindice
the city	and illustrious	souls	with impunity,	and	an avenger
3					2

nullo.	Sed	periit,	postquam	cerdonibus
no one.	But	he perished	after that	by cobblers
1				3

esse	timendus	Cœperat :	hoc	nocuit
to be	feared	he had begun :	this	hurt (him)
2		1		

Lamiarum	cæde	madenti.
of the Lamiæ	with slaughter	reeking.
3	2	1

SATIRE V.

ARGUMENT.

Under pretence of advising one Trebius to abstain from the table of Virro, a man of rank and fortune, Juvenal takes occasion to give a spirited detail of the insults and mortifications to which the poor were subjected by the rich, at those entertainments to which, on account of the political connexion subsisting between patrons and clients, it was sometimes thought necessary to invite them.

Si	te	propositi	nondûm	pudet,	atque
If	you	of (your) purpose	not yet	it shames,	and

eadem	est	mens,	Ut	bona	summa
the same	is	(your) mind,	that	good	the highest

putes	alienâ	vivere	quadrâ ;	Si	potes
you can think (it)	from another's	to live	trencher ;	if	you can

illa	pati,	quæ	nec	Sarmentus	iniquas
those (things)	suffer	which	neither	Sarmentus	the unequal

Cæsaris	ad	mensas,	nec	vilis	Galba
of Cæsar	at	tables,	nor	vile	Galba

tulisset,	Quamvis	jurato	metuam	tibi
e'd have borne,	though	upon oath	I sh'd fear	you

credere	testi.	Ventre	nihil	novi
to believe	(as) a witness.	Than the belly	nothing	I know

frugalius :	hoc	tamen	ipsum	Defecisse
more frugal :	that	yet	itself	to have failed

puta,	quod	inani	sufficit	alvo :	Nulla
suppose	which	for an empty	suffices	stomach,	no

crepido	vacat ?	nusquam	pons,	et	tegetis
hole	is there vacant ?	no where	a bridge,	and	of a rug

pars	Dimidiâ	brevior ?	tantine	injuria
part	by the half	shorter ?	of so great (value is)	the injury

cœnæ?   Tam   jejuna   fames;   cum   possis
of a supper?   so   craving (is)   hunger;   when   you might

honestius   illic   Et   tremere,   et   sordes
more honorably   there   both   tremble,   and   the filth [2]

farris   mordere   canini?   Primo   fige   loco,
meat [4]   gnaw [1]   of dog's? [3]   In the first [2]   fix [1]   place,

quod   tu   discumbere   jussus   Mercedem   solidam
that   you   to recline at table [2]   bidden [1]   reward [3]   solid [2]

veterum   capis   officiorum;   Fructus   amicitiæ
of old [4]   receive [1]   services; [5]   The fruit   of friendship [2]

magnæ   cibus;   imputat   hunc   Rex,   Et
great (is) [1]   food: reckons [3]   this [1]   the great man, and [2]

quamvis   rarum,   tamen   imputat.   Ergo
though   rare   yet   he reckons (it)   Therefore

duos   post   Si   libuit   menses   neglectum
two [3]   after [2]   if, [1]   it has pleased (him) [5]   months [4]   a neglected [2]

adhibere   clientem,   Tertia   ne   vacuo   cessaret
to invite [1]   client,   the third [2]   lest [1]   on an empty [5]   sh'd be idle [4]

culcitra   lecto,   Una   simus,   ait;   votorum
pillow [3]   bed, [6]   "together [2]   let us be," [1]   says he: of your wishes

summa;   quid   ultra   Quæris?   habet   Trebius,
(it is) the sum;   what   beyond   do you seek?   has (that) [2]   Trebius, [1]

propter   quod   rumpere   somnum   Debeat,
for   which   to break   his sleep   he ought,

et   ligulas   dimittere;   sollicitus,   ne   Tota
and (his)   shoe-ties   to leave loose;   solicitous   lest   the whole

salutatrix   jam   turba   peregerit   orbem   Sideribus
saluting   already [2]   crowd [1]   sh'd have finished   the circle,   the stars

dubiis,   aut   illo   tempore,   quo   se   Frigida
dubious,   or   at that   time .   in which [6]   themselves   the cold [1]

circumagunt   pigri   sarraca   Boötæ.   Qualis
turn round [5] [7]   of slow [3]   wains [2]   Bootes. [4]   What sort of [2]

cœna   tamen?   Vinum,   quod   succida   nolit
a supper   yet? [1]   Wine   which   moist   would not [2]

Lana   pati: de   convivâ   Corybanta   videbis.
wool [1]   endure: from   a guest   a Corybant   you will see.

Jurgia   proludunt;   sed   mox   et   pocula   torques
Brawls   they begin;   but   presently   both   cups   you throw

Saucius,   et   rubrâ   detergcs   vulnera   mappâ:
wounded,   and   with a red   wipe   wounds   napkin
   3   1   2   4

Inter   vos   quoties,   libertoramque   cohortem
between   you   how often   and of freedmen   a troop
   2   1   2   1

Pugna   Saguntinâ   fervet   commissa   lagenâ?
the battle   with a Saguntine   glows   fought   pot?
   2   4   1   3

Ipse   capillato   diffusum   Consule   potat,
He himself   long haired   (what was) racked off   the Consul   drinks,
   4   2   3   1

Culcatamque   tenet   bellis   socialibus   uvam,   Cardiaco
and trodden   possesses   in wars   the social   the grape,   to a cholicky
   3   1   4   6   5   2   4

nunquam   cyathum   missurus   amico.   Cras
never   a cup (of it)   about to send   friend.   To morrow
   1   3   2   5

bibet   Albanis   aliquid   de   montibus,   aut   de
he'll drink   the Alban   something from   mountains,   or   from
       3   1   2   4

Setinis,   cujus   patriam,   titulumque   senectus
the Setine,   whose   country,   and title   old age

Delevit   multâ   veteris   fuligine   testæ.   Quale,
has destroyed   by the much   of the old   mouldiness   cask.   Such,
          2   1

coronati,   Thrasea,   Helvidiusque   bibebant,   Brutorum
crowned,   Thraseas,   and Helvidius   drank,   of the Bruti
                                     2

et   Cassi   natalibus.   Ipse   capaces   Heliadum
and   Cassius   on the birth-day.   Himself   capacious   of the Heliades
                 1   2   4   6

crustas,   et   inæquales   beryllo   Virro   tenet
pieces,   and   unequal   with beryl   Virro   holds
   5   7   10   9   1   3

phialas: tibi   non   committitur   aurum;   Vel
cups: to you   not   is committed   gold;   or
   8

si   quando   datur,   custos   affixus   ibidem,
if   at any time   it is given,   a guard (is)   fixed   there,

Qui   numeret   gemmas,   unguesque   observet
who   may count   the gems,   and (your) nails   observe
                                 1   5

acutos: Da   veniam,   præclara   illic   laudatur
sharp: Grant   pardon,   a very bright   there   is commended
   4   2   1   4

iaspis;   Nam   Virro   (ut multi)   gemmas
jasper;   for   Virro   (as many do)   his gems
   3   2

ad   pocula   transfert   A   digitis;   quas   in
to   the cups   transfers   from (his) fingers;   which   in
          3   1

vaginæ   fronte   solebat   Ponere   zelotypo
of (his) scabbard   the front   used   to put   to jealous
   2   1   3

juvenis prælatus Hiarbæ. Tu Beneventane
the youth preferred Hiarbas. You of the Beneventano
1 2 4 7

sutoris nomen habentem Siccabis calicem
cobler the name having shall drain a pot
8 6 5 1 2

nasorum quatuor, ac jam Quassatum, et
handles of four, and now shattered, and
4 3

rupto poscentem sulphura vitro. Si
for the broken requiring sulphur glass. If
3 1 2

stomachus · domini fervet vinove cibove,
the stomach of the master is hot either with wine or meat,

Frigidior Geticis petitur decocta pruinis.
col ler than Getic is so ight boiled [water] hoar-frosts.
3 4 2 1

Non eadem vobis poni modo vina
not the same before you to be set just now wines
5 3 7 6 2 4

querebar? Vos aliam potatis aquam. Tibi
was I complaining? you other drink water. To you
1 2 1

pocula cursor Gætulus dabit, aut nigri
the cups lackey a Getulian will give, or of a black
2 1 3

manus ossea Mauri, Et cui per midiam
hand the bony Moor, and whom at mid
2 1 3 4

nolis occurrere noctem, Clivosæ veheris
you w'd be unwilling to meet night, of the hilly you are carried
1 5 5 2

dum per monimenta. Latinæ. Flos Asiæ
while thro' the monuments. Latin way. A flower of Asia
1 3 4

ante ipsum, pretio majore, paratus Quam
(is) before him, at a price greater purchased than

fuit et Tulli census pugnacis, et Anci :
was both Tul'us the estate of warlike, and of Ancus
2 4 1 3

Et, ne te teneam, Romanorum omnia
and, lest you I may detain, of the Roman all
3 1

regum Frivola. Quod cùm ita sit, tu
kings the trifles. Which since so it is, thou
2

Gætulum Ganymedem Respice, cùm sities:
the Getulian Ganymede look back upon, when you are thirsty:

nescit tot millibus emptus Pauperibus
knows not for so many thousands bought for the poor
5 3 4 2 7

miscere   puer: sed   forma,   sed   ætas
to mix (wine) a boy: but (his) form,   but (his) age
6   1

Digna   supercilio.   Quando   ad   te   pervenit
(are) worthy disdain.   when   to   you   comes

ille?   Quando,   vocatus   adest   calidæ,
he?   When,   being called does he attend of hot,
                                        2

gelidæve   minister?   Quippe   indignatur   veteri
or cold (water) (as) the minister? Since   he scorns   an old
3   1   2

parere   clienti;   Quodque   aliquid   poscas,
to obey   client;   and that   anything   you sh'd ask for,
1   2   1

et   quòd   se   stante   recumbas.   MAXIMA
and   that   himself standing you sh'd recline. VERY GREAT
                                                    2

QUAEQUE   DOMUS   SERVIS   EST   PLENA   SUPERBIS.
EVERY   HOUSE   SERVANTS IS   FULL   OF INSOLENT.
1   4   1   2   3

Ecce   alius   quanto   porrexit   murmure
Behold another with what has reached grumbling
3   1   2

panem   Vix   fractum,   solidæ   jam   mucida
the bread Scarcely broken,   of solid already musty
                              2

frusta   farinæ,   Quæ   genuinum   agitent,   non
pieces   meal,   which   a grinder   may shake,   not
1   3   2   1

admittentia   morsum.   Sed   tener,   et   niveus,
admitting   a bite.   But   the tender, and white,

mollique   siligine   factus,   Servatur   domino:
and with soft flour   made,   is kept   for the master:

dextram   cohibere   memento;   Salva   sit
(your) right hand to restrain remember;   safe   let be

artoptæ   reverentia: finge   tamen   te
of the butler the reverence: suppose yet   yourself
2   1   1

Improbulum;   superest   illic   qui   ponere
a little impudent; remains   there (one) who to lay it down
                   2   1   2

cogat.   Vis   tu   consuetis,   audax   conviva,
can compel (you) "Will you from the accustomed, impudent guest,
                        3   1   2

canistris,   Impleri,   panisque   tui   novisse
baskets,   fill yourself, and of bread your own know
4   5   1 4 6   5   2

colorem?   Scilicet   hoc   fuerat,   propter   quod
the color? "So then   this   it was,   for   which
3

Sæpe relictâ Conjuge, per montem adversum,
ofton left my wife, over the mount adverse
    2   1   2   4   3

gelida-que cucurri Esquilias, fremeret sævâ
and the cold I have run Æsquiliæ, rattled with cruel
    5   1   6   4   5

cùm grandine vernus Jupiter, et multo
when hail the vernal air, and with much
 1   6   2   3

si llaret penula nimbo. Aspice, quam longo
dropped my clock rain." See, with how long
        1   4

dis endat pectore lancem, Quæ fertur domino,
distends a breast the dish, which is brought to the master
  6   1   7   3   4   5

squilla: et quibus undique septa Asparagis,
a lobster: and with what on all sides surrounded asparagus,
   2   2   3   1

quâ despiciat convivia caudâ, cum venit
with what he can look down on the banquet a tail, when he comes
        2   3   1

excelsi manibus sublata ministri. Sed tibi
of a tall by the hands borne aloft attendant. But to you
  3   1

dimid'o constrictus Cammarus ovo Ponitur,
with half hemmed-in a common crab an egg is set,
  4   3   5   1

exiguâ feralis cœna pateilâ. Ipse Venafrano
in a tiny a funeral supper little platter. He himself with Venafran oil
  3   1   2   3

piscem perfundit; at hic, qui Pallidus offertur
(his) fish covers; but this, which pale is offered
 2   1   3   1   4

misero tibi caulis, olebit Laternam; illud
to miserable you cabbage, will smell of a lamp, that (oil)
         2   2

enim vestris datur alveolis, quod Canna
for to your is given sauce-boats, which a reed-boat
 1   4   3

Micipsarum prorâ subvexit acutâ; Propter
of the Micipsæ prow brought over in (its) sharp; on account of
           3   1   2

quod Romæ cum Bocchare nemo
which at Rome with a Bocchar nobody

lavatur; Quod tutos etiam facit
bathes; which safe also makes

à serpentibus Afros. Mullus erit
from serpents the Africans. A mullet will be

domino, quem misit Corsica, vel
for the master, which sent Corsica, or
                    2   1

quem Taurominitanæ rupes, quando omne
which the Tauromenian rocks, since all

peractum   est,   Et   jam   defecit   nostrum
has been dragged through, and   now   has failed   our
3   1

mare;   dum   gula   sævit,   Retibus   assiduis
sea;   while   gluttony   rages,   with nets   assiduous
2

penitus   scrutante   macello   Proxima;   nec
thoroughly   searching   the market   the neighbouring (seas);   nor
2   3   1

patitur   Tyrrhenum   crescere   piscem;   Instruit
suffers it   a Tyrrhene   to grow   fish;   supplies
2   1   3

ergo   focum   provincia;   sumitur   illinc   Quod
therefore   the kitchen   a province: is taken   thence   what
2   1   2   1

captator   emat   Lenas,   Aurelia   vendat.
the legacy-hunter may buy   Lenas,   Aurelia   sell.
2   1

Virroni   muræna   datur,   quæ   maxima   venit
To Virro   a lamprey   is given,   which   the largest   came
2   1

gurgite   de   Siculo: nam   dum   se   continet
whirlpool   from   the Sicilian: for   while   himself   contains
3   1   2   3   2

Auster,   Dum   sedet,   et   siccat   madidas
the South-Wind,   while   he rests,   and   dries   his wet
1

in   carcere   pennas,   Contemnunt   mediam
in (his)   prison   wings,   despise   the middle of
2   1   3   4

temeraria   lina   Charybdim.   Vos   anguilla
the rash   nets   Charybdis. .   You   an eel
1   2

manet,   longæ   cognata   colubræ,   Aut   glacie
awaits,   of the long   a relation   snake,   or   by the ice
2   1

aspersus   maculis   Tiberinus,   et   ipse   Vernula
sprinkled   with spots   a Tiberine,   and himself   an attendant

riparum   pinguis   torrente   cloacâ,   Et   solitus
of the banks   fat   with a rushing   sewer,   and accustomed

mediæ   cryptam   penetrare   Suburræ.   Ipsi
of mid   the dark-arched drain   to penetrate   Suburra. To(Virro)himself
3   2   1   4

pauca   velim,   facilem   si   præbeat   aurem;
a few (words)   I w'd (say),   an easy   if   he would lend   ear;
3   2   2

Nemo   petit,   modicis   quæ   mittebantur
Nobody   seeks,   to his humble   what   were sent
3   1   2

amicis   A Senecâ;   quæ   Piso   bonus,   quæ
friends   by Seneca;   what   Piso   the bounteous,   what

Cotta   solebat   Largiri   namque   et   titulis,
Cotta   used   to bestow;   for   than both   titles,

et   fascibus   olim,   major   habebatur   donandi
and   offices   formerly,·   greater   was regarded   of giving
                                                            2

gloria :   solum   Poscimus,   ut   coenes   civiliter:
the glory :   only   we ask,   that   you sh'd sup   civilly:
1

hoc   face,   et   esto,   Esto   (ut   nunc
this   do,   and   be,   be   (as are   now-a-days

multi)   dives   tibi,   pauper   amicis.   Anseris
many)   rich   to yourself,   poor   to your friends.   Of a goose
                                                            4   6

ante   ipsum   magni   jecur,   anseribus   par
before   himself (is placed) great   the liver,   to geese   equal
1   2   5   3   2   1

Altilis,   et   flavi   dignus   ferro   Meleagri
a crammed (fowl), and of yellow (haired) worthy   the spear   Meleager
              3   1   2

Fumat   aper :   post   hunc   raduntur   tubera,
smokes   a boar :   after   him   are scraped   truffles,
                                        2   1

si   ver   Tunc   erit,   et   facient
if   spring   then   be,   and   make
                                            3

optata   tonitrua   coenas   Majores:
wished-for   thunders   suppers   greater:
1   2

tibi   habe   frumentum,   Alledius
"to thyself   have   (thy) corn,"   Alledius

inquit,   O Libya,   disjunge   boves,   dum.
says,   "O Libya,   unyoke (your) oxen,   provided only

tubera   mittas.   Structorem   interea,   ne
truffles   you send."   The carver   meanwhile,   lest

qua   indignatio   desit,   Saltantem   spectes,
any   indignation   be wanting,   dancing   you behold,

et   chironomonta   volanti   Cultello,   donec
and   with nimble   flourishing   knife,   till
         2   1

peragat   dictata   magistri   Omnia;   nec
he can go through with   the lessons   of his master   all;   nor
                              2   1

minimo   sane   discrimine   refert,
with a very small   indeed   difference   does it bear (upon the matter)
3   1   4   2

Quo   gestu   lepores,   et   quo   gallina
with what   gesture,   hares,   and   with what   a hen

secetur.   Duceris   planta,   velut   ictus   ab
sh'd be cut.   You will be dragged   by the foot,   as   strucken   by
                                                            2

Hercule   Cacus,   Et   ponere foris,   si   quid
Hercules   Cacus,   and   put out of doors,   if   anything
    1

tentaveris   unquam   Hiscere,   tanquam   habeas
you attempt   ever   to mutter,   as it   you had

tria   nomina.   Quando   propinat   Virro
three   names.   When   does drink first   Virro
                        2   1

tibi,   sumitque   tuis   contacta   labellis
to you,   and take   by your   touched   lips
                       3   2

Pocula?   quis   vestrum   temerarius   usque adeò,
the cup?   who   of you   (is)   rash   enough,
 1

quis   Perditus,   ut   dicat   regi,   bibe?
who   (so)   lost,   as   to say   to the great man,   drink?

Plurima   sunt   quæ   Non   audent   homines
Very many (things)   there are   which   not   dare   men
                   5   4   1

pertusâ   dicere   læna.   Quadringenta   tibi   si
in a torn   say   coat.   Four hundred (sestertia)   to you   if
  2   6   3   3   2   1

quis   Deus,   aut   similis   Dis,   Et   melior
any   god,   or (one) like   the gods,   and   better than

fatis,   donaret;   homuncio,   quantus   Ex
the fates,   sh'd present;   poor sorry mortal,   how great   from

nihilo   fieres!   quantus   Virronis   amicus!
nothing   you w'd become!   how great   of Virro   a friend!
                         2   1

Da   Trebio,   pone   ad   Trebium :   vis,   frater,
"Give to Trebius,   set   before   Trebius: do you wish   brother,

ab   istis   Ilibus?   O Nummi,   vobis   hunc
some of   those   delicacies?   O Riches,   to you   this

præstat   honorem;   Vos   estis   fratres.
he vouchsafes   honor;   You   are   brothers.
  2   1

Dominus   tamen,   et   domini   rex   Si   vis
A lord   but,   and   of a lord   a sovereign   if   wish
  2   1   2   1   2

tu   fieri,   nullus   tibi   parvulus   aulâ
you   to become,   no   to you   little   in the hall
 1   3   2   4   1

Luserit   Æneas,   nec   filia   dulcior   illo.
shall play   Æneas,   nor   daughter   sweeter   than he.
     5

Jucundum   et   carum   sterilis   facit   uxor
A pleasant   and   dear   a barren   makes   wife
 4   1   3   2

amicum.   Sed   tua   nunc   Micale   pariat
friend.   But   thy   now   Micale   sh'd bring forth
       3   2   4

licet,   et   pueros   tres   In   gremium
through,   and   boys   three   into   the lap
1   2   1

patris   fundat   simul;   ipse   loquaci
of (th ir) father sh'd pour at the same time ; (Virro' himself in the prattling

gaudebit   nido ; ·   viridem   thoraca   jubebit
will rejoice   nest ;   a green   stomacher   he will command
2   1

Afferri,   minimasque   nuces,   assemque   rogatum,
to be brought, and tiny little   nuts,   and the penny   asked for,
                         2   1

Ad   mensam   quoties   parasitus   venerit
to (his)   table   as often as   parasite   shall come
       2   1   2   3

infans   Vilibus   ancipites   fungi   ponentur
the infant.   Before mean   doubtful   funguses   will be put
1   2

amicis,   Boletus   domino;   sed   qualem
friends,   a mushroom   before the lord;   but   such as
1

Claudius   edit,   Ante   illum   uxoris,   post
Claudius   ate,   before   that   of his wife,   after

quem   nihil   amplius   edit.   Virro   sibi,
which   nothing   more   he ate.   Virro   to himself,

et   reliquis   Virronibus   illa   jubebit   Poma
and   the other   Virros   those   will order   fruits
                               2   1

dari,   quorum   solo   pascaris   odore ;
to be given,   of which   alone   you may feed   on the odor ;
           3   2   1

Qualia ·   perpetuus   Phæacum   autumnus   habebat ;
such as   the perpetual   of the Phæacians   autumn   had ;
                        2   1

Credere   quæ   possis   surrepta   sororibus
to believe   which   you might be able   stolen   from sisters
3   1   2   2

Afris.   Tu   scabie   frueris   mali,   quod   in
the African. You   a scab   will enjoy   of an apple,   which   in
1

aggere   rodit   Qui   tegitur   parmâ   et   galeâ;
a trench   he gnaws.   who   is covered   with a shield   and   helmet;

metuensque   flagelli   Discit   ab   hirsuto   jaculum
and fearing   the whip   learns   from   the rough   a dart
                                               3

torquere   Capellâ.   Forsitan   impensæ   Virronem
to hurl   Capella.   Perhaps   expense   Virro
2   1   4   2

parcere   cred s :   Hoc   agit,   ut   doleas;
to spare   you may think :   this   he does,   that   you may grieve ;
3   1

nam   quæ   comœdia—mimus   Quis   melior
for   what   comedy—   mimic   what   (is) better
                               2   1

plorante gulâ? ergo omnia fiunt, Si
than a deploring gluttony? therefore all (things) are done, if

nescis, ut per lachrymas effundere
you know it not, that through tears to give vent to

bilem Cogaris, pressoque diu stridere molari.
vexation you may be forced, and with a pressed long to creak grinder.
2 3 1

Tu tibi liber homo, et regis conviva
You to yourself a free man, and a great man's guest

videris; Captum te nidore suœ putat
seem; (to be) taken you with the savor of his thinks
4 3 5 6 2

ille culinœ: Nec male conjectat: quis
he kitchen: nor badly does he guess: who
1 7 2

enim tam nudus, ut illum Bis ferat,
for so naked, that him twice w'd bear,
1

Hetruscum puero si contigit aurum, Vel
the Etruscan (him when) a boy if befell gold, or
2 5 1 4 3

nodus tantum, et signum de paupere
the knot only, and the mark from the poor

loro? Spes bene cœnandi vos decipit;
strap? The hope well of supping you deceives;
2 1

ecce dabit jam Semesum leporem, atque
"Lo he will give now a half-eaten hare, and
2 1

aliquid de clunibus apri: Ad nos jam
something from the buttocks of a boar: to us now

veniet minor altilis: inde parato, Intactoque
will come the lessened fat fowl":— then with prepared, and untouched

omnes, et stricto pane tacetis. Ille
you all, and cut bread are silent. He
4 1 2 3

sapit, qui te sic utitur: omnia ferre
is wise, who you thus uses: all things to bear

Si potes, et debes; pulsandum vertice
if you can, also you ought; to be beaten with a crown
2

raso Præbebis quandoque caput, nec
shaven you will offer sometime (your) head, nor
1

dura timebis Flagra pati, his epulis,
hard will you fear lashes to endure, these feasts,
2 1 2 3

et tali dignus amico.
and such worthy a friend.
1

SATIRE VI.

ARGUMENT.

Tho whole of this Satire, not only the longest, but the most complete of the Author's works, is directed against the female sex. It may be distributed under the following heads: Lust variously modified, imperiousness of disposition, fickleness, gallantry, attachment to improper pursuits, litigousness, drunkenness, unnatural passions, fondness for singers, dancers, &c.; gossipping, cruelty, ill-manners; outrageous pretensions to criticism, grammar and philosophy; superstitious and unbounded credulity in diviners and fortune-tellers; introducing supposititious children; poisoning their step-sons to possess their fortunes; and lastly, murdering their husbands.

Credo	pudicitiam,	Saturno	rege	moratum
I believe	chastity,	Saturn (being) King,		lingered

In	terris,	visamque	diu;	cùm	frigida
In	the lands,	and was seen	long;	when	a cold

parvas	Præberet	spelunca	domos	ignemque,
small	afforded	cavo	houses,	and the fire,
	3	2	1	

Laremque,	Et pecus,	et	dominos	communi
and household gold,	and the herd,	and (their) masters		in a common

clauderet	umbrâ:	silvestrem	montana	torum
enclosed	shade:	a rustic	a mountain	bed
2	1	5	2	6

cum	sterneret	uxor	Frondibus	et	culmo,
when	prepared	wife	with leaves	and	straw,
1	4	3			

vicinarumque	ferarum	Pellibus :	haud	similis
and of the neighboring	wild beasts	the skins :	not	like
2	3	1		

tibi,	Cynthia,	nec	tibi,	cujus	Turbavit
thee,	Cynthia,	nor	thee,	whose dimmed (with tears)	

5

nitides / bright / 1
extinctus / a dead / 3
passer / sparrow / 4
ocellos : / eyes : / 2
Sed / but

potanda / to be drunk / 3
ferens / bearing / 1
infantibus / by her children / 6
ubera / breasts / 2
magnis, / great, / 5

Et / and
sæpe / often
horridior / more rough
glandem / the acorn / 3
ructante / belching / 2

marito. / than the husband. / 1
Quippe / Since
aliter / differently
tunc / then
orbe / in the orb / 2
novo, / new, / 1

cœloque / and heaven / 2
recenti / recent / 1
Vivebant / lived
homines ; / men ; / 2
qui / who

rupto / from the bursted
robore / oak
nati, / born,
Compositique / and composed
luto / of clay

nullos / no / 2
habuere / had / 1
parentes. / parents.
Multa / Many
pudicitiæ / of chastity

veteris / old
vestigia / traces
forsan, / perhaps,
Aut / or
aliqua / some
Extiterant / existed

et / even
sub / under
Jove, / Jove,
sed / but
Jove / Jove
nondum / not yet
Barbato, / bearded,

nondum / not yet
Græcis / the Greeks
jurare / to swear
paratis / prepared
Per / by
caput / the head

alterius : / of another :
cùm / when
furem / a thief
nemo / no one
timeret / feared
Caulibus, / for his cabbages,

aut / or
pomis, / or apples,
sed / but
aperto / with an open
viveret / lived / 2
horto. / garden. / 1

Paulatim / Little by little
deinde / then
ad / to
superos / the gods
Astræa / Astræa
recessit / retired

Hâc / with this (her)
comite, / companion,
atque / and
duæ / the two
pariter / together / 3
fugêre / fled / 2

sorores. / sisters.
Antiquum / Ancient
et / and
vetus / old
est, / it is,
alienum, / another's,

Posthume, / Posthumus,
lectum / bed
Concutere, / to violate,
atque / and
sacri / of the sacred / 3

Genium / the genius / 2
contemnere / to despise / 1
fulcri. / couch.
Omne / Every
aliud / other

crimen / crime
mox / presently
ferrea / the iron
protulit / brought forth / 2
ætas. / age. / 1
Viderum / Sawing / 3

primos / the first / 4
argentea / the silver / 1
sæcula / ages / 2
mœchos. / adulterers.
Conventum / A meeting

tamen, et pactum, et sponsalia nostrâ
yet, and contract, and espousal in our

Tempestate paras; jamque a tonsore magistro
time you are preparing; and already by a barber master
2 1

Pecteris, et digito pignus fortasse dedisti.
you are combed, and to the finger the pledge perhaps have given.

Certe sanus eras ; uxorem, Posthume,
certainly sane you (once) were; a wife, Posthumus,

ducis ? Dic, . quâ Tisiphone ? quibus
do you lead? Say, by what Tisiphone? by what

exagitare colubris ? Ferre potes dominam
are you agitated snakes? To bear are you able mistress
3 1 2 1 4

salvis tot restibus ullam? Cum pateant
safe so many halters any? When are open
7 5 6 3

altæ, caligantesque fenestræ ? Cum tibi
high and dizzy windows? When to you

vicinum se præbeat Æmilius pons? Aut
near itself presents the Æmilian bridge? Or

si de multis nullus placet exitus ; illud
if from many no pleases exit; it

Nonne putas melius, quod tecum
do you not think better, that with you

pusio dormit? Pusio qui noctu non
a stripling sleeps? a stripling who by night not

litigat : exigit a te Nulla jacens illic
quarrels: exacts from you no lying there

munuscula, nec queritur quod Et lateri
little presents, nor complains that also (your) strength

parcas, nec, quantum jussit, anheles.
you spare, nor, as much as he commanded, that you pant

Sed placet Ursidio lex Iulia : tollere
But pleases Ursidius law the Iulian: to bring up
3 4 2 1 2

dulcem Cogitat hæredem, cariturus turture
a sweet he thinks heir, about to want turtle-fish
3 1 2

magno, mullorumque jubis, et captatore
a large, and of mullets the crests, and the inveigling
1

macello. Quid fieri non posse putes,
market place. What to happen not to be able do you think,
4 2 3 1

si jungitur ulla Ursidio ? si mœchorum
If is joined any (woman) to Ursidius? if of adulterers
2 1 3

notissimus olim Stulta maritali jam porrigit
the most notorious once (his) foolish to the nuptial now reach
1 2 6 8 4 5

ora capistro, Quem toties texit periturum
head halter, whom so often concealed about to perish
7 4 5 1

cista Latini ? Quid, quòd et antiquis
the chest of Latinus ? What, that even ancient
2 3

uxor de moribus illi Quæritur ? O medici
a wife of morals by him is sought ? O physicians

mediam pertundite venam : Delicias hominis !
the middle bore through vein : Delight of a man !
2 1

Tarpeium limen adora Pronus, et auratam
the Tarpeian threshold adore prone, and a gilded

Junoni cæde juvencam, Si tibi contigerit
for Juno slay heifer, if to you shall fall
5 4

capitis matrona pudici. Paucæ adeo Cereris
head a matron of chaste. Few so of Ceres
3 1 2 2 1 4

vittas contingere dignæ ; Quarum non
the fillets to touch (are) worthy ; whose not
3 2 1 4

timeat pater oscula. Necte coronam
w'd fear a father kisses. Weave a crown
3 5 2 1

Postibus, et densos per limina tende
for the doorposts, and thick over the threshold stretch

corymbos. Unus Iberinæ vir sufficit ? ocyus
ivy clusters. Does one for Iberina man suffice ? sooner
2 1

illud Extorquebis, ut hæc oculo contenta
that you will extort, that she with eye content
3 5 2

sit uno. Magna tamen fama est
be one. Great yet fame there is
1 4 3 1 4 2

cujusdam rure paterno Viventis ; vivat
of a certain (girl) at her father's country-house living ; let her live
2 1

Gabiis ut vixit in agro ; Vivat Fidenis,
at Gabii, as she lived in the country ; let her live at Fidenæ,

et agello cedo paterno. Quis tamen
and country-seat I yield the paternal. Who yet
3 1 2

affirmat nil actum in montibus, aut
affirms nothing done in mountains, or

iu   Speluncis?   adeò   senuerunt   Jupiter
in   caves?   so   have grown old   Jupiter
   5   1   4   6   2

et   Mars?   Porticibusne   tibi   monstratur
and   Mars?   In the portico   is there to you   shown
   3

fœmina   voto   Digna   tuo?   cuneis   an
a woman   wish   worthy   of your?   the benches
     3   1   2   4

habent   spectacula   totis   Quod   securus
have   the spectacles   in all   what   securely
1   2   3

ames,   quodque   inde   excerpere   possis?
you might love,   and what   thence   pick out   you might?

Chironomon   Ledam   molli   saltante   Batyllo,
The nimble   Leda   the soft   dancing   Bathyllus,
4   5   1   3   2

Tuccia   vesicæ   non   imperat :
Tuccia   herself   not   controls :

Appula   ganuit   Sicut   in   amplexu:
Appula   whines   as   in   an embrace:

subitum   et   miserabile   longum   Attendit   Thymele;
the quick   and   languishing   long   attends   Thymele ;
4   5   2   3   1

Thymele   tunc   rustica   discit.   Ast   aliæ,
Thymele   then   the rustic   learns.   But   others,
3   1   2

quoties   aulæa   recondita   cessant,   Et
as often as   stage ornaments   the packed away   cease,   and
     2   1

vacuo   clausoque   sonant   fora   sola   theatro,
empty   and shut up   sound   the courts   alone   the theatre (being),
5   6   3   1   2   4

Atque   á   plebeis   longè   Megalesia ;   tristes
and   from   the Plebeian   long   the Megalesian games;   sad

Personam,   thyrsumve   tenent,   et subligar   Acci.
the mask,   or thyrsus   they handle,   and   the sash   of Accius.

Urbicus   exodio   risum   movet   Atellanæ
Urbicus   with the interlude   laughter   moves   of Atellana
     3   2   1

Gestibus   Autonoës ;   hunc   diligit   Ælia
with the gestures of   Autonoe ;   him   loves   Ælia
                  3   2

pauper.   Solvitur   his   magno   comœdi   fibula.
poor.   Is loosened   for these   at a great (price)   of the comedian   the fibula.
1   3   4   5   2

Sunt,   quæ   Chrysogonum   cantare   vetent.
There are,   who   Chrysogonus   to sing   forbid.

Hispulla   tragœdo   Gaudet: an expectas,   ut
Hispulla   in a tragedian   rejoices :   do you expect,   that

Quintilianus   ametur ?   Accipis   uxorem,   de
Quintilian   can be loved?   you take   a wife,   by

quâ   citharœdus   Echion,   Aut   Glaphyrus
whom   the harper   Echion,   or   Glaphyrus

fiat   pater,   Ambrosiusve,   choraules.   Longa
may become a father,   or Ambrosius   the choral flute-player.   Long
                                                                     2

per   angustos   figamus   pulpita   vicos :
through   the narrow   let us fix   stages   streets:
  4   5   1   3

Ornentur   postes,   et   grandi   janua   lauro,
let be adorned the door posts, and with the grand the gate laurel,
                                      2   1

Ut   testudineo   tibi,   Lentule,   conopeo
that   in (his) vaulted to thee,   O Lentulus,   canopy
            3   1   2

Nobilis   Euryalum   mirmillonem   exprimat
the noble   Euryalus   the sword-player   may express
                3   4   2

   infans.   Nupta   senatori   comitata est
   infant.   married   to a senator accompanied
     1   2   3   4

Hippia   Ludium   Ad   Pharon   et   Nilum,
Hippia   a gladiator to   Pharos   and   the Nile,
  1   5

famosaque   mœnia   Lagi,   Prodigia,   et   mores
and the infamous walls   of Lagus, the Prodiges,   and   morals
                                          3   4

urbis   damnante   Canopo.   Immemor   illa
of the city condemning   Canopus.   Unmindful   she
                2   1

domûs,   et   conjugis,   atque   sororis,   Nil
of family,   and of husband,   and   of sister,   nothing

patriœ   indulsit ;   plorantisque   improba   gnatos,
for her country indulged ;   and (her) weeping wicked   children,
                                       2   1   3

Utque   magis   stupeas,   ludos,   Paridemque
and that   more   you may be astonished, the games,   and Paris

reliquit.   Sed   quanquam   in   magnis
left.   But   though   in   great

opibus,   plumâque   paternâ,   Et   segmentatis
riches,   and down   paternal,   and   in embroidered
                                                      3

dormisset   parvula   cunis,   Contempsit   pelagus ;
she had slept, a little one, cradle,   she despised   the sea;
    2   1

famam   contempserat   olim,   Cujus   apud
her reputation   she had contemned long ago, of which   among
                                                  2   5

molles   minima   est   jactura   Cathedras:
soft   the least   is   the loss   chairs:
  6   4   3   1   7

Tyrrhenos   igitur   fluctus,   latèque   sonantem
the Tyrrhene   therefore   waves,   and widely   sounding
                 2   1

Pertulit   Ionium,   constanti   pectore,   quamvis
sh⌣ bore   Ionian,   with undaunted   breast,   although
2   1

Mutandum   toties   esset   mare.   Justa
to be changed   so often   was   the sea.   Just
3

pericli   Si   ratio   est,   et   honesta,   timent;
of danger   if   cause   (there) is,   and   honest,   they fear;
7   1   6   2   4   5

pavidoque   gelantur   Pectore,   nec   tremulis
and with timorous   are frozen   breast,   nor   on (their) trembling
2   1   3   3

possunt   insistere   plantis :   Fortem   animum
can they   stand   feet: a brave   mind
1   2   4

præstant   rebus,   quas   turpiter   audent.
they show   in things,   which   basely   they dare.

Si   jubeat   conjux,   durum   est   conscendere
If   command   the husband,   hard   it is   to go aboard
2   1

navim ;   Tunc   sentina   gravis ; tunc   summus
a ship;   then   the bilge-water   (is) intolerable ;   then   the top

vertitur   aër.   Quæ   mœchum   sequitur,
is turned round   air.   Who   an adulterer   follows,
2   1

stomacho   valet :   illa   maritum   Convomit :
in stomach   is well :   she (her)   husband   bespews :

hæc   inte nautas   et   prandet,   et   errat
this (one)   among the sailors   both   dines,   and   wanders

Per   puppim,   et   duros   gaudet   tractare
through   the stern,   and   the hard   delights   to handle
3   1   2

rudentes.   Quâ   tamen   exarsit   formâ?   quâ
cables.   With what   yet   did she burn   a form? with what
2   1   4   3

capta   juventâ   Hippia ?   Quid   vidit,   propter
taken   youth   (was) Hippia ?   What did she see,   on account of
3   1   2

quod   ludia   dici   Sustinuit?   nam   Sergiolus
which   a gladiator's wife   to be called   she endured?   for   darling Sergius
3   2   1

jam   radere   guttur   Cœperat,   et   secto
now   to shave   his throat   had begun,   and   to his cut
3

requiem   sperare   lacerto.   Præterea   multa   in
rest   to hope for   arm.   Besides   many   in
2   1

facie   deformia;   sicut   Attritus   galea
(his) face   deformities;   as,   galled   with the helmet

mediisque   in   naribus   ingens   Gibbus,   et   acre
and in the midst of his   nostrils   a huge   wen,   and   the sharp

malum   semper   stillantis   ocelli.   Sed
evil   (of his)   ever   dropping   eye.   But

gladiator   erat;   facit   hoc   illos   Hyacinthos:
a gladiator   he was;   makes   this   them   Hyacinths:
                    2   1

Hoc   pueris,   patriæque,   hoc   prætulit   illa
This   to children,   and to country,   this   preferred   she

sorori,   Atque   viro :   ferrum   est,   quod
to sister,   and   husband :   the sword   it is,   which

amant :   hic   Sergius   idem   Acceptâ
they love :   this   Sergius   same   accepted
              2   1   2

rude   cœpisset   Veiento   videri.   Quid
the wand   had begun   Veiento   to seem.   What
  1   2   1   2

privata   domus,   quid   fecerit   Hippia   curas ?
a private   family,   what   may have done   Hippia   care you ?
   3   4   6   5   1

Respice   rivales   Divorum :   Claudius   audi
Consider   the rivals   of the Gods :   Claudius   hear
                                          3   1

Quæ   tulerit :   dormire   virum   cùm   senserat
what   endured :   to sleep (her)   husband   when   she had perceived
  2   5   4   2   3

uxor,   (Ausa   Palatino   tegetem   præferre
the wife,   (daring   to the Palatinian   a rug   to prefer
   1   3   6   5   4

cubile,   Sumere   nocturnos   meretrix   Augusta
bed,   to take   nocturnal   harlot   the August
  7   8   9   2   1

cucullos,)   Linquebat,   comite   ancillâ   non
hoods,)   left (him)   (her) companion   maidservant   not
   10   4   5

amplius   unâ;   Et   nigrum   flavo   crinem
more than   one;   and   (her) black   a yellow   hair
   2   3   4   1   5

abscondente   galero,   ·   Intravit   calidum   veteri
hiding   peruke,   she entered   warm   with an old
   3   2   2   3

centone   lupanar,   Et   cellam   vacuam,   atque
patched quilt   the brothel,   and   cell   the empty,   and
   4   1   2   1

suam :   tunc   nuda   papillis   Constitit   auratis,
her own :   then   naked   with nipples   she stood   gilded,
         2   4   1   3

titulum   mentita   Lyciscæ,   Ostenditque   tuum,
the name   having assumed   of Lycisca,   and shows   thy

g*nerose   Britannice,   ventrem.   Excepit blanda
O noble   Britannicus,   belly.   She received   bland
2   3   1

intrantes,   atque   ære   poposcit: Mox   lenone
the comers in,   and   money   asked: presently the bawd

suas   jam   dimittente   puellas,   Tristis   abit;
his   now   dismissing   girls,   sad   she goes away;
3   1   1

sed,   quod   potuit,   tamén   ultima   cellam
but,   what   she could,   yet   last   (her)   cell

Clausit,   adhuc   ardens   rigidæ   tentigine
shut,   still   burning

vulvæ,   Et   lassata   viris,   nondum   satiata
         and   wearied   with men,   but not   satiated

recessit: Obscurisque   genis   turpis,   fumoque
she with-drew: and with sullied   cheeks   defiled,   and with the smoke
                                              1   3

lucernæ   Fœda,   lupanaris   tulit   ad   pulvinar
of the lamp   foul,   of the brothel   she bore   to   the pillow
           2   3   1   4

odorem.   Hippomanes   carmenque   loquar
(of her husband)   the odor.   The love philters,   and charms shall I speak of
                      2   2   1

coctumque   venenum,   Privignoque   datum?
and boiled   poison,   and to a son-in-law   given?

faciunt   graviora   coactæ   Imperio   sexûs,
they do   worse (things) compelled   by the empire   of the sex;

minimumque   libidine   peccant.   Optima   sed
and least   from lust   they sin.   The best (of wives) but

quare   Cesennia   teste   marito?   Bis   quingenta
why (is)   Cesennia   the witness (her) husband?   Twice   five hundred
                       2   1

dedit,   tanti   vocat   ille   pudicam:
(sestertia) she gave,   for so much   calls   he   (her)   chaste:

Nec   Veneris   pharetris   macer   est,   aut
Nor   of Venus   from the quivers   lean   is he,   nor
       2   1

lampade   fervet: Inde   faces   ardent;   veniunt
with (her) lamp   he glows: thence   torches   burn;   come
                                                          2

á   dote   sagittæ.   Libertas   emitur;   coram
from (her) dowry   arrows.   Liberty   is bought;   before
    3   1

licet   innuat,   atque   Rescribat   vidua
tho' (her husband) she may nod,   and   answer   (her love-letter) a widow

est,   locuples   quæ   nupsit   avaro.   Cur
she is,   rich   who   has married   a miser.   Why
           2   1

desiderio   Bibulæ   Sertorius   ardet?   Si
with the desire   of Bibula   Sertonius   burns?   If
3   2   1

verum   excutias,   facies,   non   uxor   amatur.
the truth   you sift,   the face,   not   the wife   is loved.

Tres   rugæ   subeant,   et   se   cutis   arida
Three   wrinkles   let come,   and   itself   skin   (her) dry
2   3   1   4   2   1

laxet,   Fiant   obscuri   dentes,   oculique
relax,   let become   black   (her) teeth,   and (her) eyes
3

minores;   " Collige   sarcinulas,   dicet   libertus,
smaller ;   " Pack up   your bundles,"   will say   the freedman,
2   1

et   exi;   Jam   gravis   es   nobis,   et
and   be off;   now   offensive   you are   to us,   and

sæpe   emungeris;   exi   Ociús,   et   propera ;
often   blow your nose ;   be off   quickly,   and   hasten;

sicco   venit   altera   naso."   Interea   calet,
with a dry   is coming   another   nose."   Mean while   she is hot
3   2   1

et   regnat,   poscitque   maritum   Pastores,
and   reigns,   and demands of (her)   husband   shepherds

et   ovem   Canusinam,   ulmosqus   Falernas.
and   sheep   Canusian,   and elms   Falernan.
2   1   2   1

Quantulum   in   hoc?   pueros   omnes,
How very little   (is there) in   this ?   boys   all,
2   1

e gastula   tota,   Quodque   domi   non   est,
work-houses (of slaves)   whole   and what   at home   not   is,
2   1

et   habet   vicinus,   ematur.   Mense   quidem
and   has   (her) neighbor,   must be bought.   In the month   indeed
2   1

brumæ,   cùm   jam   mercator   Jason   Clausus,
of winter,   when   now   the merchant   Jason (is)   shut up,

et   armatis   obstat   casa   candida   nautis,
and   the armed   hinders   cottage   the white   sailors,
4   3   2   1   5

Grandia   tolluntur   crystallina,   maxima
great   are taken up   crystal vessels,   very large (vessels)
2   1   2

rursùs   Myrrhina,   deinde   adamas   notissimus,
and again   of myrrh,   then   an adamant   most famous,
1   3

et   Berenices   In   digito   factus   pretiosior :
and   of Berenice   on   the finger   made   more precious:
3   1   2

hunc   dedit   olim   Barbarus   incestæ,   dedit
this   gave   formerly   a Barbarian   to his incestuous;   gave
3   1   2   7   6

hunc   Agrippa   sorori,   Observant   ubi   festa
this   Agr'ppa   sister,   observe   where   festal
4   5   8   4   1   5

mero   pede   sabbata   reges,   Et   vetus
bare   foot   sabbaths   kings,   and   an ancient
              2   6   3

indulget   senibus   clementia   porcis.   Nullane
is indulgent   to old   clemency   swine.   Does none
      2   3   1

de   tantis   gregibus   tibi   digna   videtur?
from   so great   herds (of women)   to you   worthy   seem?

Sit   formosa,   decens,   dives,   fœcunda,
Let (her) be beautiful,   graceful,   rich,   fruitful,

      vetustos   Porticibus   disponat   avos,
(her)   old   in porticos   let (her) dispose   ancestors,
          3   1   2

      intactior   omni   Crinibus   effusis   bellum
(let her be) more chaste than every   with hair   dishevelled   the war
              1   3   4   6

dirimente   Sabinâ: (Rara   avis   in   terris,
ending   Sabine: (a rare   bird   in   the earth,
5   2

nigroque   simillima   cygno)   Quis   feret
and to a black   very like   swan)—   who   c'd bear
      2   1   3

uxorem,   cui   constant   omnia?   malo,   Malo
a wife,   in whom   are concentrated   (excellencies) all?   I'd rather rather

Venusinam,   quam   te,   Cornelia,   mater
a Venusian (girl),   than   you,   Cornelia,   mother

Gracchorum,   si   cum   magnis   virtutibus
of the Gracchi,   if   with   great   virtues

affers   grande   supercilium,   et   numeras   in
you bring   great   haughtiness,   and   number   in

      dote   triumphos.   Tolle   tuum,   precor,
(your) dowry   triumphs.   Take away   your,   I pray,
          2   1   2   1

Hannibalem,   victumque   Syphacem   In   castris,
Hannibal,   and conquered   Syphax   in (his)   camp,
                      2   1

et   cum   totâ   Carthagine   migra.   Parce,
and   with   all (your)   Carthage   depart.   "Spare

precor,   Pæan: et   tu,   Dea,   pone
I pray,   O Pæan: and   thou,   Goddess,   lay down

      sagittas;   Nil   pueri   faciunt,   ipsam
(thine) arrows;   nothing   the children   do,   herself
                                                                      3

configite   matrem;   Amphion   clamat :   sed
transfix   the mother;"   Amphion   cries :   but
1   2

Pæan   contrahit   arcum.   Extulit   ergo
Pæan   bends   (his)   bow.   He took off   therefore

gregem   natorum,   ipsumque   parentem,   Dum
the herd   of children,   and himself   the parent,   while
                    2   1

sibi   nobilior   Latonæ   gente   videtur,
to herself   more noble   of Latona   than the race   seems,
3   4   6   5   2

Atque   eadem   scrofâ   Niobe   fœcundior
and   the same   sow   Niobe   more fruitful
7   8   11   1   9

albâ.   Quæ   tanti   gravitas?   quæ
than the white.   What (is)   of so much   (value) gravity?   what
10   1   5   2   8

forma,   ut   se   tibi   semper   Imputet?
beauty,   that   herself   to you   always   she sh'd impute?
4

hujus   enim   rari,   summique   voluptas
of this   for   rare,   and highest   pleasure
2   1   3

Nulla   boni,   quoties   animo   corrupta
(there is) no   good,   as often as   mind   corrupted
2   1   3   1

superbo   Plus   aloes,   quam   mellis,   habet.
with a proud,   more   of aloes,   than   of honey,   she has.
2

Quis   deditus   autem   Usque   adeo   est,
Who   devoted (to his wife)   but   to such   a degree   is
2   4   1   5   3

ut   non   illam,   quam   laudibus   effert,
that   not   her,   whom   with praises   he extols,
        2

Horreat,   inque   diem   septenis   oderit horis?
he dreads,   and every   day   for seven   hates   hours?
1   2   1

Quædam   parva   quidem;   sed   non   toleranda
Some (things are)   trifling   indeed;   but   not   to be borne

maritis: Nam   quid   rancidius,   quàm
by husbands: for   what   more fulsome,   than

quòd   se   non   putat   ulla   Formosam,
that   herself   not   thinks   any one   beautiful,
    4   1   3   2

nisi   quæ   de   Tuscâ   Græcula   facta   est?
unless   who   from   a Tuscan   a little Greek   has   become?

De   Sulmonensi   mera   Cecropis?   omnia
from   a Sulmonian   a mere   Athenian?   every thing

Græcè;   Cùm   sit   turpe   minus   nostris
is) in Greek;   since   it is   disgraceful   less   to our   (ladies)
                                  2   1

nescire   Latine.   Hoc   sermone   pavent;
not to know   Latin.   In this   language   they fear ;

hoe   iram,   gaudia,   curas,   Hoc   cuncta
in this   anger,   joys,   cares,   in this   all
          2   3   4   5   6

effundunt   animi   secreta.   Quid   ultra?
they pour forth   of the mind   secrets.   What   more ?
    1   8   7

Concumbunt   Græce—   dones   tamen   ista
They copulate   in Greek—   you-may-grant   yet   those
                              2   1

puellis: Tune   etiam,   quam   sextus
(things) to girls: do you   also.   whom   the sixth

et   octagesimus   annus   Pulsat,   adhuc   Græce?
and   eightieth   year   beats.   still (speak)   in Greek ?

non   est   hic   sermo   pudicus   In   vetulâ:
not   is   this   language   a modest   in an old woman :
 3   2   1   5   4

quoties   lascivum   intervenit   illud,   Ζωή,
as often as   wanton   intervenes   that,   Ζωή
               3   1   2

καὶ   ψυχή,   modò   sub   lodice   relictis
καὶ   ψυχή, (words) just now   under   the coverlet   left
                                2   3   1

Uteris   in   turbâ: quod   enim   non   excitat
you use   in   public: what   for   not   does excite
                         2   1   5   4   2

inguen   Vox   blanda   et   nequam?   digitos
passion   word   an enticing   and   lewd ?   fingers
  3   8   6   7   2

habet.—   Ut   tamen   omnes   Subsidant
it has.—   That   yet   all   may subside
  1   2   1   3   5

pennæ   (dicas   haec   mollius   Æmo   Quanquam,
desires   (you-may-say   these (things)   softer than Æmus   although.
  4   2   3   4   5   1

et   Carpophoro)   facies   tua   computat
and   Carpophorus   face   your   computes
                      2   1

annos.   Si   tibi   legitimis   pactam,
(your) years.   If   to you   by lawful   (one) contracted,
               1   4   5   2

junctamque   tabellis   Non   es   amaturus,
and joined   tablets   not   you are   likely-to-love,
  3   6   2   1

ducendi   nulla   videtur   Causa;   nec   est
of marrying   no   there seems   cause ;   nor   is there
  2   1

quare   cœnam   et   mustacea   perdas,   Labente
(cause) why   a supper   and   bride-cakes   you sh'd lose,   ceasing
               2   1   4

officio,   crudis   donanda :   nec   illud,   Quod
(their) office to (your) crammed (guests) to be given : nor that, which
　　3　　　　　　　2　　　　　　　　　1

prima   pro   nocte   datur ;   cùm   lance
the first for night is-given ; when dish
　3　　　2　　　　　　　1　　　　　　　　　2

beatâ   Dacicus,   et   scripto   radiat   Germanicus,
In the happy Dacicus and with-the-inscribed is radiant Germanicus,
　1　　　　　　　　　　　3　　　　　2　　　　1

auro.   Si   tibi   simplicitas   uxoria,   deditus
gold.   If to you (is) simplicity uxorious, devoted
　　　　　　　　　2　　　　　　　1

uni   Est   animus :   submitte   caput   cervice
to one (your) mind : submit (your) head with a neck

paratâ   Ferre   jugum :   nullam   invenies
prepared to bear the yoke : no one you will find

quæ   parcat   amanti.   Ardeat   ipsa   licet,
who   can spare a lover. be enamored she herself though,
　　　　　　　　　　　　　　3　　　　2　　　　1

tormentis   gaudet   amantis,   Et   spoliis :
in the torments she rejoices of her lover, and spoils :
　　2　　　　　1　　　　　4

igitur   longe   minùs   utilis   illi
therefore far less useful to him
　　　　　　　　　　　　　　　　2

Uxor,   quisquis   erit   bonus,
(is) a wife, whoever will be a good,
　1

optandusque   maritus.   Nil   unquam   invitâ
and desirable husband. Nothing ever unwilling
　　　　　　　　　　　　　　　　　　　2

donabis   conjuge :   vendes   Hâc   obstante
will you give (your) wife: you will sell she opposing
　3　　　　　1　　　　　　　2　　　　3

nihil :   nihil,   haec   si   nolit,   emetur.   Hæc
nothing : nothing, she if is unwilling will be bought. She
　1　　　　　　　　　2　　　　1

dabit   affectus :   ille   excludetur   amicus
will dispose of (your) affections: that will be shut out friend
　　　　　　　　　　　　　　　2　　　　　1

Jam   senior,   cujus   barbam   tua   janua
now grown old, whose beard your gate

vidit.   Testandi   cùm   sit   lenonibus,   atque
has seen. Of making a will when there is to pimps, and

lanistis   Libertas,   et   juris   idem   contingat
fencers Liberty, and right the same happens
　　　　　　　　　　　　　　　　　　1

arenæ.   Non   unus   .tibi   rivalis   dictabitur
to the arena, not one to you rival (only) will be dictated
　　　　　　　1　　　　4　　　　2　　　　3

hæres.   "Pone   crucem   servo ."   "meruit
as heir. "Set up a cross for your slave :" "Has deserved
　　　　　　　　　　　　　　　　　　　　3　　5

quo   crimine   servus   Supplicium?   Quis
for what   crime   the slave   punishment?   What
1   2   4

testis   adest?   quis   detulit?   audi,   Nulla
witness   is there? who   gave information? hear,   No
                                                          1

unquam   de   morte   hominis   cunctatio   longa
ever   concerning   the death   of a man   delay   long
4   6   2   5

est."   "O demens,   ita   servus   homo   est?   nil
is."   "O madman,   so   a slave   a man   is?   nothing
3   2   1

fecerit,   esto: Hoc   volo,   sic   jubeo,   sit
he may have done, be it so: this   I wish, thus   I command, let be

pro   ratione   voluntas."   Imperat.   ergo   viro:
for   a reason   my will."   She governs   therefore (her) husband:

sed   mox   hæc   regna   relinquit,   Permutatque
but   presently   these   realms   leaves,   and changes

domos,   et   flammea   conterit: inde   Avolat,
houses,   and   (her) bridal veils   wears out: thence   she flies away,
                  1

et   spreti   repetit   vestigia   lecti.   Ornatas
and   of (her) despised seeks again   the footsteps   bed.   Adorned
       3   1   2   4

paulo   ante   fores,   pedentia   linquit   Vela
a little   before   the doors,   the pendent   she leaves   veils
2   3   1   3   1

domûs,   et   adhuc   virides   in   liminе
of the house,   and   yet   green   at   the threshold
2   2   3

ramos.   Sic   crescit   numerus;   sic   fiunt   octo
the boughs.   Thus   increases   the number;   thus   are made   eight
1

mariti   Quinque   per   autumnos: titulo   res
husbands.   Five   through   autumns: the title   a thing
              2   1   3   1

digna   sepulchri.   Desperanda   tibi   salvâ
worthy   of a sepulchre.   Must be despaired of   by you   alive
2   2   3   5

concordia   socru: Illa   docet   spoliis   nudi
concord   a stepmother: She   teaches   in the spoils   of a stripped
1   4   2   3

gaudere   mariti: Illa   docet,   missis   a
to rejoice   husband: She   teaches,   sent   by
1   2

corruptore   tabellis,   Nil   rude,   nil   simplex
a corrupter   to letters.   nothing   rude,   nothing   simple
                1

rescribere: decipit   illa   Custodes,   aut   ære
to write back: deceives   she   keepers,   or   with money
                        2   1

domat: tunc   corpore   sano   Advocat   Archigenem,
quiets (them:)   then   with body   sound   she calls in   Archigenes,
1

onerosaque   pallia   jactat.   Abditus   interea
and the heavy clothes   casts away.   Hidden   meanwhile

latet   arcessitus   adulter,   Impatiensque   moræ
lies   the sent-for   adulterer,   and impatient   of delay

silet,   et   præputia   ducit.   Scilicet expectas,
is silent,   and   the foreskin draws.   But   do you expect
                    2   1

ut   tradat   mater   honestos,   Aut   alios
that   sh'd infuse a mother honest,   or   other
         2   1

mores,   quàm   quos   habet?   utile   porrò
morals,   than   what   she has (herself)? profitable (it is) moreover

Filiolam   turpi   vetulæ   producere   turpem.
daughter   for a base   old woman to bring up   a base.
  5   1   2   3   4
Nulla   ferè   causa   est,   in   quâ   non
No   almost   cause   there is, in   which   not
  3   2   4   1
fœmina   litem   Moverit.   Accusat   Manilia,
a woman   the suit has stirred up. Accuses Manilia,
  1   5   2   4   2   1
si   rea   non   est.   Componunt   ipsæ   per
if   the accused not   she is. Compose   they   by
  3   2   1   4   1   2
se,   formantque   libellos,   Principium   atque
themselves and form   libels,   the exordium   and
  3   4
locos   Celso   dictare   paratæ.   Endromidas
the topics to Celsus to dictate prepared.   rugs
  5   3   2   1
Tyrias,   et   fœmineum   ceroma   Quis nescit?
the Tyrian, and   the female ceroma   who   knows not?
vel   quis   non   vidit   vulnera   pali,   Quem
or   who   not   has seen the wounds of the stake which
                 2   1
cavat   assiduis   sudibus,   scutoque   lacessit?
she hollows with continual wooden-swords. and with the shield provokes?
Atque   omnes   implet   numeros;   dignissima
and   all   fills up her parts;   most worthy
  2   1   3
prorsùs   Florali   matrona   tubâ;   nisi   si
altogether of the Floralian a matron trumpet; unless
  1   4   2
quid   in   illo   Pectore   plus   agitet,
something in   that   breast (of hers) more she may agitate,
          2   3   1
veræque   paratur   arenæ.   Quem   præstare
and for the real is prepared arena.   what   show
  2   1   5
potest   mulier   galeata   pudorem,   Quæ   fugit
can   woman   a helmeted modesty,   who   flees
  2   3   1

a   sexu,   et   vires   amat?   hæc   tamen
from   (her) sex, and feats-of-strength loves?   she   yet
              2   1   2   1

ipsa   Vir   nollet   fieri :   nam   quantula
herself a man would not   become: for   how little (is)

nostra   voluptas!   Quale   decus   rerum,   si
our   pleasure!   What   a fine-show of things,   if

conjugis   auctio   fiat,   Balteus,   et   maniceæ'
(your) wife's auction sh'd be,   (her) belt,   and   gauntlets,

et   cristæ   crurisque   sinistri   Dimidium
and   crests   and of her leg   left   the half
                        3   5   4   1

tegmen: vel   si   diversa   movebit   Prælia,
covering: or   if   different   she will stir up   battles,
   2   2   1

tu   felix,   ocreas   vendente   puellâ.   Hæ
you   happy,   her greaves   selling   (your) young wife. These
  2   1   3   2   1

sunt,   quæ   tenui   sudant   in   cyclade,
are   (the women) who a thin   sweat   in   gown.
                       3   1   2   4

quarum   Delicias   et   panniculus   bombycinus
whose   delica e [dobies] even a little piece   of silk

urit.   Aspice,   quo   fremitu   monstratos
burns.   Behold,   with what   a noise   the shown
                                                   2

perferat   ictus,   Et   quanto   galeæ   curvetur
she can convey hits,   and   with what   of helmet she can be bent
   1   2   3

pondere ;   quanta   Poplitibus   sedeat;   quàm   denso
a weight;   how great   on her hams   she can sit; with how   thick
   1

fascia   libro ;   Et   ride,   scaphium   positis
(her) swathe a fold;   and   laugh,   the scaphium   laid down
   2   1   4   3

cum   sumitur   armis.   Dicite   vos   neptes
when   is taken   [her] arms   say   ye   granddaughters
  1   5   2

Lepidi,   cæcive   Metelli,   Gurgitis   aut
of Lepidus,   or of blind   Metellus,   Gurges   or
                                            3   1

Fabii,   quæ   ludia   sumpserit   unquam   Hos
Fabius,   what   actress   took   ever   these
  2

habitus?   quando   ad   palum   gemat   uxor
habits?   when   at   a post   groans   the wife

Asylli?   Semper   habet   lites,   alternaque
of Asyllus?   Always   has   strifes,   and alternate
                 3   2

jurgia   lectus,   Inquo   nupta   jacet :   minimum
quarrels   the bed,   in which   a wife   lies :   very little
                1

dormitur   in illo.   Tunc   gravis   illa   viro,
is it slept   in that (bed).   Then   grievous   she   to her husband,

tunc   orbâ   tigride   pejor,   Cum   simulat
then   than a bereaved   tigress   worse,   when   she feigns
4

gemitus   occulti   conscia   facti,   Aut   odit
groans   of a hidden   conscious   deed,   or   hates
2   1   3

pueros,   aut   fictâ   pellice   plorat   Uberibus
the servants,   or   feigned   a mistress,   she wails   with fruitful
2   1   2

semper   lachrymis,   semperque   paratis   In
ever   tears,   and always   ready   in
1

statione   suâ,   atque   expectantibus   illam,
station   their   and   waiting for   her,
2   1

Quo   jubeat   manare   modo: .tu   credis
in what   she may command   to flow   manner: you   think (it)
2   3   1

amorem;   Tu tibi   tunc,   curruca,   places,
love;   you yourself   then,   O hedge-sparrow,   please,
4   1   2   3

fletumque   labellis   Exorbes;   quæ   scripta,
and the weeping   with (your) lips   suck up;   what   writings,

et quas   lecture   tabellas,   Si   tibi   zelotypæ
and what   w'd you read   letters,   if   to you   of the jealous
2   1   3

retigantur   scrinia   mœchæ!   Sed   jacet   in
were opened   the desks   strumpet!   But   she lies   in
1   2

servi   complexibus,   aut   equitis: dic,   Dic
a slave's   embraces,   or   a knight's: "Tell,   tell

aliquem,   sodes   hic,   Quintiliane,   colorem.
some,   I pray,   here   O Quintilian,   color (of excuse)."
4   1   2   3   5

Hæremus: dic   ipsa: olim   convenerat,
"We stick fast:" —"say   yourself"   "formerly   it was agreed,"

inquit,   Ut   faceres   tu   quod   velles;   necnon
says she,   "that   sh'd do   you   what   you w'd;   also
2   1   2

ego   possem   Indulgere   mihi: clames   licet,   et
I   might   indulge   myself: you sh'd clamor   though,   and
2   1

mare   cœlo   Confundas,   homo   sum.   Nihil
the sea   with heaven   confound,   human   I am.   Nothing
2   1

est   audacius   illis   Deprensis: iram   atque
is   more bold   than they   (when) detected: anger   and

animos   a crimine   sumunt.   Unde   hæc   monstra
courage   from (their) crime,   they take.   Whence   these   monstrous (things)
2

tamen,   vel quo   de   fonte   requiris?   Præstabat
yet,   or what   from source   do you ask?   rendered
1   2   3

castas   humilis   fortuna   Latinas   Quondam,
chaste   an humble   fortune   the Latin (women) formerly,
5   1   2   4

nec   vitiis   contingi   parva   sinebat   Tecta   labor,
nor   with vices to be touched (their) small did permit houses labor,
1   8   7   5   2 4   6   3

somnique   breves,   et   vellere   Thusco   Vexatæ,
and of sleep   short,   and   with the fleece   Tuscan   chafed,
2   1   2   1   2

duræque   manus,   ac   proximus   urbi   Hannibal,
and hard   (their) hands, and   very near   the city   Hannibal,
3   1   2   1

et   stantes   Collinâ   in   turre   mariti.   Nunc
and   standing   the Colline on   tower   (their) husbands.   Now
2   4   3   1

patimur   longæ   pacis   mala: sævior   armis,
we suffer   of a long   peace   the evils: more cruel than arms,
1   2   1

Luxuria   incubuit,   victumque   ulciscitur   orbem.
luxury   has invaded [us]   and the conquered   avenges   world.
                                2   1

Nullum   crimen   abest,   facinusque   libidinis,
no   crime   is absent,   and foul deed   of lust,

ex quo   Paupertas   Romana   perit: hinc   fluxit
since   poverty   Roman   perished: hence   flowed
          2   1

ad   istos   Et   Sybaris   colles,   hinc   et   Rhodos,
to   these   both   Sybaris   hills,   hence   and   Rhodes,
                        2   1   2   1

atque   Miletos,   Atque   coronatum,   et   petulans,
and   Miletus,   and   the crowned,   and   petulant,

madidumque   Tarentum.   Prima   perigrinos   obscœna
and drunken   Tarentum.   First   foreign   filthy
                           5   3   1

pecunia   mores   Intulit,   et   turpi   fregerunt
money   manners   brought in,   and   with base   weakened
2   4   5   3

secula   luxu   Divitiæ   molles.   quid   enim
the ages   luxury   riches   soft.   what   for
4   2   1   2   1

Venus   ebria   curat?   Inguinis   et   capitis
Venus   a drunken   cares?   of tail   and   head
3   2   1

quæ   sint   discrimina,   nescit;   Grandia   quæ
what   are   the differences,   she knows not;   huge   who
                                                   2

mediis   jam   noctibus   ostrea   mordet,   Cùm
at mid   even   nights   oysters   devours,   when
5   4   3   1

perfusa   mero   spumant   unguenta   Falerno,
mixed   with neat   foam   unguents   Falernian,
2   3   5   1   4

Cùm   bibitur   concha,   cùm   jam   vertigine
When   she drinks out of   the conch;   when   now   with a whirl

tectum   Ambulat,   et   geminis   exurgit   mensa
the roof   goes round,   and   with double   rises up   the table
              3   2   1

lucernis.   I   nunc,   et   dubita   quâ   sorbeat   aëra
candles.   Go   now, and   doubt   with what   snuffs up   the air
                                              3   4

sannâ   Tullia;   quid   dicat   notæ
a scoff   Tullia;   what   may say   to her acquaintance
1   2   2

Collacia   Mauræ;   Maura   Pudicitiæ
Collacia   Maura: Maura   of chastity
1   2   6

veterem   cum   præterit   aram.   Noctibus   hic
the old   when   passes by   altar.   o' nights   here
4   1   3   5   2   1

ponunt   lecticas,   micturiunt   hic;   Effigiemque
they put down   their sedans,   they urinate   here;   and the image

Deæ   longis   siphonibus   implent;   Inque
of the goddess   with long   siphons   they fill;   and in

vices   equitant,   ac   lunâ   teste   moventur:
turn   they ride,   and   the moon (being)   witness   are moved:

Inde   domos   abeunt.   Tu   calcas,   luce
Thence   to their homes   they go away.   you   tread,   the light

reversâ,   Conjugis   urinam,   magnos   visurus
having returned,   your wife's   urine,   (your) great   going to see
                         2   1

amicos.   Nota   Bonæ   secreta   Deæ,   cùm
friends.   Known (are)   of the good   the secrets   goddess,   when
         2   1

tibia   lumbos   Incitat,   et   cornu   pariter,
the pipe   the loins   incites,   and   with the horn   also,

vinoque   feruntur   Attonitæ,   crinemque   rotant,
and with wine   are driven   astonished,   and (their) hair   whirl,
              3   4

ululantque   Priapi   Mænades: O quantus   tunc
and howl   of Priapus   the Mænads: O how great   then
              2   1

illis   mentibus   ardor   Concubitûs!   quæ
to those   minds   the desire   of copulation!   what

vox   saltanto   libidine!   quantus   Ille   meri
a voice   dancing   their lust!   how great   that   wine
         2   1   3

veteris   per   crura   madentia   torrens!   Lenonum
of old   through   (their) legs   dripping   torrent!
2   4   6   5   1

ancillas positâ Laufella coronâ Provocat,
et tollit pendentis præmia coxæ: Ipsa
Medullinæ frictum crissantis adorat. Palmam
inter dominas virtus natalibus æquat.
Nil tibi per ludum simulabitur, omnia
fient Ad verum, quibus incendi jam
frigidus ævo Laomedontiades, et Nestoris
hernia possit. Tunc prurigo moræ impatiens:
tunc fœmina simplex; Et pariter toto
repetitus clamor ab antro: Jam fas
est; admitte viros: Jam dormit adulter?
Illa jubet sumpto juvenem properare cucullo:
Si nihil est, servis incurritur: abstuleris
spem Servorum, veniet conductus aquarius;
hic si Quæritur, et desunt homines:
mora nulla per ipsam, Quo minus
imposito clunem submittat asello. Atque

and

utinam	ritus	veteres,	et	publica	saltem
would that	rites	the ancient,	and	public	at least
	2	1			2

His	intacta	malis	agerentur	sacra:	sed
by those	untouched	evils	might be observed	worship:	but
5	4	6	3	1	

omnes	Noverunt	Mauri,	atque	Indi,	quæ
all	Know	the Moors,	and	Indians,	what
	3	1		2	

psaltria	penem	Majorem,	quam	sint	duo
singing-wench	a penis	greater,	than	are	two
	2	3	4	5	7

Cæsaris	Anticatones,	Illùc,	testiculi	sibi
Cæsar's	Anticatos,	in that place,	of a testicle	to himself
6	8	9	14	13

conscius	unde	fugit	mus,	Intulerit;	ubi
conscious	whence	flees	a mouse,	brought:	where
12	10	15	11	1	

velari	pictura	jubetur,	Quæcunque	alterius
to be veiled	picture	is ordered,	whatsoever	of the other
8	2	7	1	5

sexûs	imitata	figuram	est.	Et	quis
sex	imitates	the figure		And	who
6	3	4			

tunc	hominum	contemptor	numinis?	aut
then	of men	(was) a despiser	of the deity?	or

quis   Sympuvium   ridere   Numæ,   nigrumque
who   the earthern bowl   to deride   of Numa,   and the black
3   2   4   5

catinum,   Et   Vaticano   fragiles   de   monte
dish,   and   the Vatican   the brittle   from   mount
6   7   11   8   10   12

patellas   Ausus   erat?   Sed   nunc   ad
vessels   had   dared?   But   now   at
9   1

quas   non   Clodius   aras?   Audio,   quid
what (is there) not   a Clodius   altars?   I hear,   what
2   3   1   4

veteres   olim   moneatis   amici: Pone   seram,
ancient   of former days   you w'd advise   friends: "Put on   a lock,
1   3   5   2

cohibe;   Sed   quis   custodiet   ipsos   Custodes?
confine (her);"   But   who   will guard   themselves   the guards?
                2   1

Cauta   est,   et   ab   illis   incipit   uxor.
sly   is,   and   from   these   begins   (your) wife.
3   2   4   5   1

Jamque   eadem   summis   pariter,   minimisque
and now-a-days (there is) the same in the highest   equally,   and the lowest
        2

libido;   Nec   melior,   silicem   pedibus   quæ
lust;   nor   better, (is she)   flint   with her feet   who
1   4   1

conterit   atrum,   Quam   quæ   longorum
wears out   the black,   than   (she) who   of tall
2   3   3

vehitur   cervice   Syrorum.   Ut   spectet   ludos,
is carried   on the shoulder   Syrians.   That   she may see   plays,
1   2   4

conducit   Ogulnia   vestem,   Conducit   comites,
hires   Ogulnia   a dress,   hires   attendants,
2   1

sellam,   cervical,   amicas,   Nutricem,   et
a sedan,   a pillow,   female friend,   a nurse,   and

flavam,   cui   det   mandata,   puellam.   Hæc
a yellow-haired,   to whom she may give commands,   girl.   She
    2   3   4   1   2

tamen,   argenti   superest,   quodcunque   paterni,
yet,   silver   remains,   whatever of (her) paternal,
1   4   2   1   3

Lævibus   athletis,   ac   vasa   novissima
to well-oiled   athletes,   and   plate   very last
9   10   5   7   6

donat.   Multis   res   angusta   domi   est;
gives.   To many (women) circumstances narrow   at home   are;
8   3   2   4   1

sed   nulla   pudorem   Paupertatis   habet;
but   no one   the modesty   of poverty   has;
        2   1

nec   se   metitur   ad   illum,   Quem.
nor   herself   measures   at   that,   which
    2   1   2

dedit hæc, posuitque modum. Tamen utile
has given this, and laid down measure. Yet useful
4 3 5 1 3

quid sit, Prospiciunt aliquando viri ; frigusque,
what may be, foresee sometimes men; and cold,
1 2 3 2 1

famemque, Formicâ tandem quidam expavêre
and hunger, the ant at length some have feared
4 1 2 3

magistrâ. Prodiga non sentit pereuntem
(being) the teacher. A prodigal not perceives a perishing
5 3 2 4

fœmina censum : At velut exhaustâ redivivus
woman fortune : But as though in the exhausted reviving
1 5 4 2

pullulet arcâ Nummus, et è pleno semper
would bloom afresh chest money, and from a full always
3 5 1 3 4 2

tollatur acervo, Nonunquam reputat, quanti
w'd be taken heap, never she reflects how much
1 5

sibi gaudia constent. Sunt quas eunuchi
her (her) pleasures cost. There are whom eunuchs
2

imbelles, ac mollia semper Oscula delectent,
weak, and soft always Kisses delight,
1 2 1

et desperatio barbæ, Et quòd abortivo
and the despair of a beard, and because of an abortion
4

non est opus. Illa voluptas Summa tamen,
not is need. That pleasure (is) the highest yet,
3 2 1

quòd jam calidâ matura juventâ Inguina
that now in warm mature youth groins
2 1

traduntur medicis, jam pectine nigro. Ergo
are delivered to the surgeons,

expectatos, ac jussos crescere primum

Testiculos, postquam cœperunt esse bilibres,

Tonsoris damno tantùm rapit Heliodorus.

Conspicuus longè, cunctisque notabilis intrat

Balnea, nec dubie custodem vitis et horti

Provocat, a dominâ factus spado : dormiat

ille Cum dominâ : sed tu jam durum, Posthume,

jamque Tondendum eunucho Bromium committere

noli. Si gaudet cantu, nullius fibula durat
If she delights in singing, no one's fibula holds out

Vocem   vendentis   Prætoribus,   organa   semper
(his) voice   selling   to the Prætors,   the instruments (are) ever
   4   3   5

In   manibus :   densi   radiant   testudine   totâ
in (her) hands: thick   sparkle   lute   on the whole
                                3   2   1

Sardonyches: crispo   numerantur   pectine   chordæ,
Sardonyxes: with the trembling are-run-over-in-order quill the chords,
                     3   2   4   1

Quo   tener   Hedymeles   operam   dedit;   hunc
with which the tender Hedymeles   performed;   this

tenet,   hoc   se   solatur,   gratoque   iudulget
she holds, with this herself she solaces, and to-the-grateful indulges
                                                   3   1

basia   plectro.   Quædam.   de   numero
kisses   quill.   A certain [lady] from   the number
   2   4

Lamiarum,   ac   nominis   alti,   Cum   farre
of the Lamiæ,   and   name   of high,   with   meal
                         2   1

et   vino   Janum,   Vestamque   rogabat,   An
and   wine   Janus,   and Vesta   asked,   whether
               2   3   1

Capitolinam   deberet   Pollio   quercum   Sperare,
the Capitoline   ought   Pollio   oak   to-hope-for,
      4   2   1   5   3

et   fidibus   promittere.   Quid   faceret   plus,
and to-his-lyre promise [it].   What   c'd she do   more,
        2   1

Ægrotante   viro ?   medicis   quid   tristibus
being sick   [her] husband? the physicians what (being) sad,
   2   1   2   1

erga   Filiolum ?   stetit   ante   aram   nec   turpe
towards (her) little son? she stood before the altar, nor shameful

putavit   Pro   cithara   velare   caput;   dictataque
thought it)   for   a harp   to veil (her) head; and dictated

verba   Protulit,   (ut   mos   est)   et   apertâ
words   she uttered, [as the custom is] and being opened,
                                                       2

palluit   agnâ.   Dic   mihi   nunc,   quæso,
grew pale the lamb. "Tell   me   now   I pray,
   3   1

dic,   antiquissime   Divùm,   Respondes   his,   Jane
tell me, thou ancientest of gods, do you answer these, Janus
                                                              2

pater ?   magna   otia   cœli :   Non   est,
father ?   great   the leisure of heaven: not there is
   1   2   1

(ut   video)   non   est,   quid   agatur   apud
[as I see]   there is not, anything that is done among

vos.   Hæc   de   comœdis   te   consulit :   illa
you. This (woman) about comedians you consults: that
                                        2   1

tragœdum   Commendare   volet;   varicosus   fiet
a tragedian   recommend   would;   varicose   will become
                                      3   2

haruspex.   Sed   cantet   potius   quam   totam
the soothsayer.   But   let her sing   rather   than   the whole
1   3

pervolet   urbem   Audax,   et   cœtus   possit
sh'd fly through   city   (She) audacious,   and   the assemblies   she sh'd
2   1   4   2

quam   ferre   virorum;   Cumque   paludatis
than   endure   of men;   and with   robed
1   3

ducibus,   præsente   marito,   Ipsa   loqui
generals,   (being) present   (her) husband,   herself   converse
                        2   1

rectâ   facie,   strictisque   mamillis.   Hæc
with unembarassed   face,   and exposed   breasts.   This

eadem   novit,   quid   toto   fiat   in   orbe:
same   knows,   what   the whole   may be doing in   world:
                           3   1   2

Quid   Seres,   Quid   Thraces   agant: secreta
What   the Seres,   what   the Thracians   are engaged in: the secrets

novercæ,   Et   pueri: quis   amet: quis
of a step-mother,   and (her) boy: who   may love: what

decipiatur   adulter.   Dicet   quis   viduam
may be deceived   adulterer.   She will tell   who   a widow
2   1   2

prægnantem   fecerit,   et   quo   Mense,
pregnant   made,   and   in what   month,
            1

quibus   verbis   concumbat   quæque,   modis
with what   words   copulates   every (woman,)   ways
                     2   1   2

quot.   Instantem   regi   Armenio   Parthoque
in how many.   Menacing   King   the Armenian   and Parthian
1   2   5   3   4

Cometem   Prima   videt: famam,   rumoresque
the Comet   she first   sees: report,   and rumors
1   2

illa   recentes   Excipit   ad portas;   quosdam
she   recent   catches up   at the doors;   some
3   1

facit,   isse   Niphatem   In populos,   magnoque
she makes,   to have gone   the Niphates   over the peoples,   and by a great
          2   1   5

illic   cuncta   arva   teneri   Diluvio: nutare
there   all   the fields   to be held   Deluge: to totter
1   2   3   4   6   2

urbes,   subsidere   terras,   Quocunque   in
cities,   to sink down   lands,   whatsoever   in
1   2   1   1

trivio,   cuicunque   est   obvia,   narrat.   Nec
common-resort,   whomsoever   she   meets,   she tells: Nor

tamen   id   vitium   magis   intolerabile,   quam
yet   (is) that   vice   more   intolerable,   than

quod   Vicinos   humiles   rapere,   et   concidere
that   neighbors   [her] humble   to seize,   and   slash
        5   4   1   2

loris   Exorata   solet ;   nam   si   latratibus
with whips   entreated   she is wont ;   for   if   by barkings
    3

alti   Rumpuntur   somni :   fustes   huc   ocyùs
[her] deep   are broken   slumbers: "clubs   hither   quickly,"
        2   1

inquit,   Afferte,   atque   illis   dominum   jubet
she says,   "bring"   and   with them   the master   she orders

ante   feriri,   Deinde   canem ;   gravis   occursu,
first   to be beaten,   then   the dog;   terrible   to encounter,

teterrima   vultu,   Balnea   nocte   subit :
most frightful   in visage,   the baths   by night   she enters :

conchas,   et   castra   moveri   Nocte   jubet ;
bathing-vessels,   and   camp   to be moved   by night   she orders ;

magno   gaudet   sudare   tumultu :   Cum
with great   she rejoices   to sweat   tumult: When
    3   1   2

lassata   gravi   ceciderunt   brachia   massâ
tired   with the heavy   have fallen   [her] arms   mass
        3   2   1

Callidus   et   cristæ   digitos   impressit   aliptes,
the sly   and   upon the crest   [his] fingers   has pressed   anointer,
    2   1   6   5   4   3

Ac   summum   dominæ   femur   exclamare   coëgit,

Convivæ   miseri   interea   somnoque   fameque
guests   [her] wretched   meauwhile   with both sleep   and hunger
    2   1

Urgentur,   tandem   illa   venit   rubicundula,   totum
are urged,   at length   she   comes   flushed,   a whole
                2

Œnophorum   sitiens,   plenâ   quod   tenditur
flagon   thirsting after,   in full   which   is presented
    3   1   2   1   4

urnâ   Admotum   pedibus,   de   quo   sextarius
pitcher   placed   at her feet,   of   which   sextary
    3   2

alter   Ducitur   ante   cibum,   rabidam
another   is drained   before   food,   a rabid
    1   2

facturus   orexim,   Dum   redit,   et   loto
to promote   appetite,   till   it returns,   and with [her] washed
    1   3   3

terram   ferit   intestino.   Marmoribus   rivi   properant
the ground   strikes   inside.   on-the-marbles   rivers   hasten
    2   1   4   3   1   2

aut   lata   Falernum   Pelvis   olet :   nam
or   the wide Falernian   basin   smells of : for
          3   1   2

sic   tanquam   alta   in   dolia   longus   Deciderit
thus   as if   deep   into casks   a long   had fallen
                    2   1   2

serpens, bibit,   et   vomit.   Ergo   maritus
serpent, she drinks, and vomits.   Therefore (her) husband
1

Nauseat, atque   oculis   bilem   substringit
turns sick, and   with eyes (his) choler   restrains
                                  3   2

opertis. Illa   tamen   gravior,   quæ   cum
closed.   She   yet (is) more offensive, who   when
1

discumbere   cœpit,   Laudat   Virgilium,   perituræ
to-sit-at-table she begins, praises Virgil,   about-to-perish
2   1   3

ignoscit   Elisæ ;   Committit   vates   et   comparat ;
excuses • Elisa ;   she matches the poets and compares ;
1   2   3   1   2

inde   Maronem,   Atque   aliâ   parte   in
then   Maro,   and   on the other part   in

trutinâ   suspendit   Homerum.   Cedunt
the balance   she weighs   Homer.   yield
3   2   1   2

grammatici,   vincuntur   rhetores,   omnis   Turba
the grammarians, are overcome the rhetoricians, all   the crowd
1   2

tacet ;   nec   causidicus,   nec   præco   loquatur
is silent; neither lawyer,   nor   crier   can speak

Altera   nec   mulier :   verborum   tanta   cadit
another   nor   woman :   of words   so great (there) falls
2   1   4   2   1

vis ;   Tot   pariter   pelves,   tot   tintinnabula
a torrent;   so many   together   basons,   so many   bells
3   2   7   3   4   5

dicas   Palsari.   Jam   nemo   tubas,   nemo
you w'd say   to be struck. now   no one   trumpets,   no one
1   6   2   4   5

aera   fatiget,   Una   laboranti   poterit   succurrere
brazen (vessels) let weary, She alone the laboring could   succor
6   1   3   3   1   2

Lunæ.   Imponit   finem   sapiens   et   rebus
moon.   she imposes the end   wise   to things

honestis. Nam   quæ   docta   nimis   cupit
honest.   For (she)   who   learned   too   desires
                                4   3   1

et   facunda   videri,   Crure   tenus   medio
and   eloquent   to seem,   leg   up to   the middle of the
5   6   2   6   4   5

tunicas succingere debet, Cædere Sylvano
(her) coats to bind ought, to slay for Sylvanus
3   2   1   1   3

porcum, quadrante lavari. Non habeat
a hog, for a farthing to be washed. Not let have
2   2   1   2   8

matrona, tibi quæ juncta recumbit, Dicendi
the matron, to you who joined shares your bed, of speaking
3   6   4   5   7   10

genus, aut curtum sermone rotato Torqueat
a set-style, or the curt discourse with turned let her twist
9   4   3   2   1

enthymema, nec historias sciat omnes;
enthymeme, nor histories let her know all;
5   3   1   2

Sed quædam ex libris et non intelligat.
but some (things) from books and (some) not let her understand.

Odi Hanc ego, quæ repetit volvitque
Hate Her I, who repeats and turns over
2   1

Palæmonis artem, servatâ semper lege et
Palæmon's art, being observed always the law and
4   6   5   1

ratione loquendi, Ignotosque mihi tenet
manner of speaking, and, unknown to me quotes
2   3   4   3   2

antiquaria versus, Nec curanda viris
an antiquarian verses, not to be heeded by men
1   5   5

Opicæ castigat amicæ Verba. Solœcismum
of her unlettered corrects friend the words. A solecism
3   1   4   2   4

liceat fecisse marito. Nil non permittit
let it be permitted to have made [her] husband. Nothing not allows
1   3   2   3   2

mulier sibi, turpe putat nil, Quum
a woman herself, disgraceful she thinks nothing, when
1   4   3   2   1

virides gemmas collo circumdedit, et quum
green gems her neck she-has-placed around, and when
2   3   5   1   4

Auribus extensis magnos commisit elenchos.
ears to her extended large she-has-committed pearls.
5   4   2   1   3

Intolerabilius nihil est, quam fœmina dives.
more intolerable nothing is, than a woman rich.

Interea fœda aspectu ridendaque multo
meanwhile filthy to behold and to be laughed at with much

Pano tumet facies, aut pinguia Poppæana
pasto swells the face, or fat Poppæan
4   2   1   2   3

Spirat, et hinc miseri viscantur labra
breathes, and hence of the miserable are glued up the lips
1   2   4   1

mariti. Ad moechum veniet lotâ cute.
husband. To an adulterer she will come with washed skin.

Quando videri Vult formosa domi? moechis
When appear does she choose beautiful at home? for adulterers
2   1

foliata parantur; His emitur, quidquid
perfumes are prepared; for these is bought, whatever

graciles huc mittitis Indi. Tandem
ye slender hither send Indians. At length
3   2   1

aperit vultum et tectoria prima
she opens (her) countenance and coverings the first
3   2

reponit: Incipit agnosci, atque illo lacte
lays by; she begins to be known, and with that milk
1

fovetur, Propter quot secum comites
is cherished, on account of which with her her attendants
2   4

educit asellas, Exsul Hyperboreum si,
she leads forth she-asses, an exile, the Hyperborean if,
1   3   2   5   1

dimittatur ad axem. Sed quæ mutatis
she be sent to axis. But what changed
3   4   6   5

inducitur atque fovetur Tot medicaminibus
is covered over an l cherished with so many medicaments
1   2   3   4   6

coctæque siliginis offas Accipit et madidæ, facies
and of-boiled flour poultices receives and damp, a face
4   7   3   2   5   6

dicetur, an ulcus? Est pretium curæ,
shall it be called, or an ulcer? It is worth while,

penitus cognoscere, toto Quid faciant
exactly to know, through a whole what they do
4   1   2

agitentque die. Si nocte maritus Aversus
and agitate day. If at night the husband turned away
3

jacuit, periit libraria, ponunt Cosmetæ
hath lain, is half killed the housekeeper, put off the tire-women
2   1   2   1

tunicas, tarde venisse Liburnus
their clothes (to be whipped,) late to have come the Liburnian (slave)
4   3   1

Dicitur, et poenas alieni pendere somni
is said, and the penalties of another's to pay sleep
2   3   4   2   5

Cogitur: hic   frangit   ferulas,   rubet   ille
is forced: this one   breaks   rods,   reddens   that one
1   2   1

flagellio,   Ilic   scuticâ: sunt,   quæ
with the whip,   this one   with the thong: there are (women) who

tortoribus   annua   præstant.   Verberat,   atque
to their torturers   yearly salaries   pay.   He beats,   and

obiter   faciem   linit ;   audit   amicas,   Aut
at-the-same-time   her face   she enamels ;   listens to   her friends,   or

latum   pictæ   vestis   considerat   aurum,   Et
the broad   of an embroidered robe   examines   gold,   still
2   4   1   2

cædit ;   longi   relegit   transacta   diurni,
he lashes ;   of a long   she-pores-over   the items   diary,
3   1   2

Et   cædit ;   donec   lassis   cædentibus,   Exi
still   he lashes ;   until   being tired   the torturers,   "Begone"
                              2   1

Intonet   horrendum,   jam   cognitione   peractâ
she thunders   terribly,   now   the trial   gone through with
                              2   1

Præfectura   domus   Siculâ   non   mitior   aulâ.
the government   of (her) house   than a Sicilian (is) not   milder   court.
                              3   1   2

Nam   si   constituit   solitoque   decentius
For   if   she has made an   assignation and   than-usual more-becomingly
                                        4   3

optat   Ornari,   et   properat,   jamque   exspectatur
desires   to be dressed,   and   is in a hurry,   and already   is waited for
1   2

in   hortis,   Aut   apud   Isiacæ   potius
in   the gardens,   or   at   of the Isian   rather
                              2   4   1

sacraria   lenæ ;   Componit   crinem   laceratis
the chapels   bawd ;   arranges   ·(her)   hair   with torn
3   5   3   4   6

ipsa   capillis   Nuda   humeros   Psecas   infelix
herself   locks   naked (as to)   the shoulders   Psecas   unhappy
5   7   8   9   2   1

nudisque   mamillis.   Altior   hic   quare
and with naked   breasts.   too high   this   why
                              4   2   1

cincinnus ?   Taurea   punit   Continuo
curl ?   the cow-hide   punishes   immediately
3

flexi   crimen   facinusque   capilli.   Quid   Psecas
of a curled   the crime   and heinousness   lock.   What   has Psecas
3   1   2

admisit?   quænam   est   hic   culpa   puellæ,
committed?   what   is   here   the fault   of the girl,

si   tibi   displicuit   nasus   tuus ?   altera   lævum
if   you   has displeased   nose   your?   another   the left (side)
       4   3   2   1

Extendit, pectitque comas, et volvit, in orbem.
extends, and combs the locks, and rolls [them] into a circle.

Est in consilio matrona admotaque lanis
is in the council a matron and put to the wools
2 1u 2 1 2 3

Emeritâ quæ cessat acu : sententia prima
from the discharged who ceases needle : opinion first
5 1 4 2 4

Hujus erit; post hanc ætate atque
her shall be ; after her in age and
1 3

arte minores Censebunt, tanquam famæ discrimen
art the inferior shall judge, as if of her reputation the hazard
2 1

agatur aut animæ; tanta est quærendi
were in question or of (her) life ; so great , is of getting
2

cura decoris. Tot premit ordinibus, tot
the concern beauty, with so many she presses rows, with so many
1 2 1

adhuc compagibus altum Ædificat caput,
still joinings her high she builds head.

Andromachen a fronte videbis : Post minor
Andromache from the front you will see : behind less
2

est : credas aliam. Cedo, si breve
she is : you'd believe (her) another. allow (her,) if a short
1 2

parvi Sortita est lateris spatium, breviorque
of small she-is-allotted side space and shorter
4 1 5 3 2

videtur Virgine Pygmæa, nullis adjuta
she seems than a virgin pigmy, by no helped
1 2 1 2 1

cothurnis, Et levis erectâ consurgit ad
cothurni, and light with an erect rises to
2 3

oscula plantâ. Nulla viri cura interea,
kisses foot. (There is) no of her husband concern meanwhile,
4 1 2 1

nec mentio fiet Damnorum : vivit tanquam vicina
nor mention will be made of damages : she lives as a neighbor

marito. Hoc solo proprior :. quod amicos
to (her) husband : In this only nearer : that the friends

conjugis odit Et servos ; gravis est
of her husband she hates and his servants ; heavy she is

rationibus. Eccc furentis Bellonæ matrisque
in (her) expenses. Lo of mad Bellona and of the mother

deûm chorus intrat, et ingens Semivir,
of the gods a chorus enters. and a great half-man,

obscœno,   facies   reverenda   minori,   Mollia
by (his) obscene,   a face   to be revered   inferior,   his tender
.3   1   2   2

qui   ruptâ   secuit   genitalia   testâ;
who   with a broken   has cut   genitals   shell;
1   5   4   3

Jampridem   cui   rauca   cohors,   cui   tympana
now long   to whom   a hoarse   troop,   to whom   tabours
2   1   2

cedunt   Plebeia,   et   Phrygiâ   vestitur
yield   the plebeian,   and   with a Phrygian   is clothed
3   1   3   2

bucca   tiarâ.   Grande   sonat,   metuique
(whose) cheek   tiara.   Grandiloquently   he sounds,   and to be dreaded
1   5

jubet   Septembris   et   Austri   Adventum,
commands   of September   and   of the South Wind   the coming,
1   3   4   2

nisi   se   centum   lustraverit   ovis,   et
unless   herself   with a hundred   she purify   eggs,   and
2   3   1

xerampelinas   veteres   donaverit   ipsi   Ut
murrey-colored robes   (her) old   give   to him   that
4   3   1   2

quidquid   subiti   et   magni   discriminis   instat,
whatever   of sudden   and   great   peril   impends,

In   tunicas   eat,   et   totum   semel   expiet
into   the tunics   may pass,   and   the whole   at once   may expiate
2   4   1

annum.   Hibernum   fractâ   glacie   descendet
year.   the wintry   being broken   the ice   she will desend
3   5   3   2   1

in   amnem,   Ter   matutino   Tiberi   mergetur
into   river,   thrice   in the early   Tiber   be dipped
4

et   ipsis   Vorticibus   timidum   caput   abluet:
and   in the very   eddies   (her) timid   head   will bathe:

inde   Superbi   Totum   regis   agrum   nuda
thence   of the haughty   the whole   king   field   naked
8   6   9   7   4

ac   tremebunda   cruentis   Erepet   genibus.
and   trembling   on bloody   she-will-crawl-over   knees.
5   2   1   3

Si   candida   jusserit   Io,   Ibit   ad   Ægypti
If   white   sh'd command   Io,   she will go to   Egypt's
2   1

finem,   calidâque   petitas   A   Meroë   portabit
extremity,   and warm   fetched   from   Meroe   will bring
5   3   4   6   1

aquas,   ut   spargat   in   æde   Isidis,
waters,   that   she may sprinkle (them) on   the temple   of Isis.
2

antiquo quæ proxima surgit ovili. Credit
to the old which next rises sheepfold. She believes
4 1 3 2 2

enim ipsius dominæ se voce moneri.
for herself of the goddess herself by the voice to be admonished.
1 5 4 1 3 2

En animam et mentem, cum quâ di
Lo the soul and mind, with which the gods
Lo

nocte loquantur ! Ergò hic præcipuum
by night can speak ! Therefore he chief
2 1

summumque meretur. honorem Qui grege
and highest gains honor who by a flock
2 1 2

linigero circumdatus, et grege calvo
linen-bearing surrounded, and a tribe bald
1 2 1

Plangentis populi, currit derisor Anubis.
of lamenting people, runs the derider of Anubis.

Ille petit veniam, quoties non abstinet
He seeks pardon, as often as not abstains
2

uxor Concubitu sacris observandisque diebus ;
the wife from copulation on sacred and observable days ;
1

Magnaque debetur violato pœna cadurco.
and a great is due for a violated punishment coverlet.
2 3 1

Et movisse caput visa est argentea
and to nod (his) head was seen the silver
4 3 1

serpens : Illius lacrymæ meditataque murmura
serpent : His tears and meditated murmurs
2

præstant, Ut veniam culpæ non abnuat,
prevail, that pardon of her fault not may refuse,
4 5 3 2

ansere magno Scilicet et tenui popano
by a goose great that is to say and a thin cake
8 7

corruptus, Osiris. Quum dedit ille locum,
bribed Osiris. When has given he place,
6 1 2 1

cophino fœnoque relicto, Arcanam Judæa
(her) basket and hay being left, the Secret Jewess
5 2

tremens mendicat in aurem, Interpres legum
a trembling begs into ear, Interpretess of the laws
1 3 4 6

Solymarum, et magna sacerdos Arboris, ac
of Solyma, and great priestess of a tree, and

summi fida internuntia cœli. Implet et
of highest a faithful go-between heaven. fills and
3 1 3 3 1

illa   manum,   sed   parcins: ære   minuto,   Qualiacunque
she   her hand,   but   too sparingly: for a coin minute,   whatever
2   1   2   1   3

voles   Judæi   somnia   vendunt.   Spondet   amatorem
you wish   the Jews   dreams   sell.   promises   lover
5   1   4   2   4   6

tenerum,   vel   divitis   orbi   Testamentum
a tender,   or   of a rich   childless (man)   will
5   7   10   11   9

ingens,   calidæ   pulmone   columbæ   Tractato
a great,   of a warm   the lungs   dove   having been handled
8   13   12   14   15

Armenius   vel   Commagenus   haruspex;   Pectora
an Armenian   or   Commagenian   soothsayer;   the breasts
1   2   3

pullorum   rimatur   et   exta   catelli,   Interdum
of chickens   he searches   and   the entrails   of a whelp,   sometimes
2

et   pueri;   faciet,   quod   deferat   ipse.
and   of a child;   he will do,   what   would inform against he himself.
1   2   1

Chaldæis   sed   major   erit   fiducia: quidquid
in Chaldeans   but   greater   will be   (their) confidence: whatever
2   1

Dixerit,   Astrologus,   credent   a   fonte   relatum
shall say,   the Astrologer,   they will believe   from   the fount   brought
2   1

Hammonis;   quoniam   Delphis   oracula   cessant,
of Ammon;   since   at Delphi   the oracles   cease,

Et   genus   humanum   damnat   caligo   futuri.
and   race   the human   condemns   a darkness   of futurity.
5   4   3   1   2

Præcipuus   tamen   est   horum,   qui   sæpiùs,
the most eminent   yet   is   of these,   (he) who   oftener
2   1   4   3

exsul   Cujus   amicitiâ,   conducendâqe   tabellâ
an exile (has been),   by whose   friendship,   and venal   tablet

Magnus   civis   obit,   et   formidatus
a great   citizen   died,   and   (one) dreaded

Othoni.   Inde   fides   arti,   sonuit
by Otho.   Thence   confidence (is given) to (his) art,   has clanked
3

si   dextera   ferro   Lævaque,   si
if   (his) right hand   with iron   and (his) left,   if
1   2

longo   castrorum   in   carcere   mansit.   Nemo
the long   of camps   in   prison   he has remained.   No
3   5   2   4   1

mathematicus   genium   indemnatus   habebit.
astrologer   a genius   uncondemned   will have.
3   1   2

Sed | qui | pænè | perit, | cui | vix | in
But | (he) who | almost | has perished, | to whom | scarcely | to
 | | | | 5 | | 2

Cyclada | mitti | Contigit, | et | parvâ | ta ı dem
the Cyclades | to be sent | it has happened, | and | from little | at length
3 | 1 | 4 6 | | 3 | 1

caruisse | Seripho. | Cousulit | ictericæ | lento
to have been freed | Seriphos. | Consults | of her jaundiced | the slow
2 | 4 | 3 | 7 | 5

de | funere | matris, | Antè | tamen | de
about | death | mother, | before | but | about
4 | 6 | 8 | 10 | 9 | 11

te, | Tanaquil | tua : | quando | sororem
you, | Tanaquil | your : | when | (her) sister
12 | 2 | 1 | |

Efferat, | et | patruos ; | an | sit | victurus
she may carryout, and | | uncles ; | whether | may be | about-to-live
| | | | 2 | 3

adulter | Post | ipsam ? | quid | enim | majus
the adulterer | after | herself ? | what | for | greater (thing)
1 | | | 2 | 1

dare | numina | possunt ? | Hæc | tamen | ignorat
to give | the gods | are able ? | She | yet | is ignorant of
4 | 2 | 1 3 | 2 | 1

quid | sidus | triste | minetur | Saturni, | quo
what | star | the baleful | may threaten | of Saturn, | with what
| 2 | 1 | | 3 |

læta | Venus | se | proferat | astro, | Qui
propitious | Venus | herself | may shew | star, | what (is)
2 | 3 | | 4 | 1 |

mensis | damnis, | quæ | dentur | tempora
the mouth | for losses, | what | are given | times
| | | 2 | 1

lucro. | Illius | occursus | etiam | vitare | memento,
for gain | Of her | the meeting | also | to avoid | remember,
| 5 | 4 | 2 | 3 | 1

In | cujus | manibus, | ceu | pinguia | succina,
in | whose | hands, | like | unctuous | amber,

tritas | Cernis | ephemeridas ; | quæ | nullum
worn | you observe | diaries ; | who | no one
2 | 1 | | | 2

consulit, | et | jam | Consulitur : | quæ | castra
consults, | and | now | is consulted : | who | the camp
1 | | | | | 3

viro | patriamque | petente, | Non | ibit
(her) husband | and (his) country | going to, | not | will go
1 | 4 | 2 | 2 | 1

pariter, | numeris | revocata | Thrasylli. | Ad
along, | by the numbers | called back | of Thrasyllus. | to
| 2 | 1 | | 4

primum | lapidem | vectari | quum placet, | hora
the first | mile-stone | to be borne | when she pleases. | the hour
| | 8 | 1 2 |

sumitur   ex   libro :   si   prurit   frictus   ocelli
is taken   from   the book :   if   itches   the rubbed   of her eye
                                4   1   3

Angulus,   inspectâ   genesi   collyria   poscit.
angle,   being inspected   her nativity   ointment   she asks for.
2   4   3   2   1

Ægra   licèt   jaceat,   capiendo   nulla   videtur
Sick   though   she lie,   for taking   no   seems
                            5   1   3

Aptior   hora   cibo,   nisi   quam   dederit
more apt   hour   food,   than   that which   has allotted
4   2   2

Petosiris.   Si   mediocris   erit,
Petosiris.   If   of moderate means   she be,
1

spatium   lustrabit   utrinque   Metarum,
the space   she will travel   on both sides   of the goals,

et   sortes   ducet,   frontemque   manumque
and   lots   will draw,   and (her) forehead   and hand
     2   1

Præbebit   vati   crebrum   poppysma   roganti.
will show   to the fortune-teller   a frequent   stroking   asking
                          2   1

Divitibus   responsa   dabit   Phryx   augur,   et
To the rich   answers   will give   a Phrygian   augur,   and
              4   3   1   2

Indus   Conductus,   dabit   astrorum   mundique
Indian   a hired,   will give (them)   in the stars   and sphere
2   1   4   2   3

peritus   Atque   aliquis   senior,   qui   publica
skilled   and   some   elder,   who   the public
1

fulgura   condit.   Plebeium   in   circo   positum
lightnings   hides.   The plebeian   in   the circus   placed
                              4   3

est,   et   in   aggere   fatum.   Quæ   nullis
is   and   in   the mount   fate.   Who   to no
2   1   2

longum   ostendit   cervicibus   aurum,   Consulit   ante
long   shows   neck   gold,   Consults   before
4   1   3

Phalas,   delphinorumque   columnas,   An   saga
the Phalæ,   and of the dolphins   the columns,   whether   the blanket
                     2   1

vendenti   nubat,   caupone   relicto.   Hæ   tamen
seller   she-may-marry,   the victualler   being left.   These   yet
                                     2   1

et   partus   subeunt   discrimen,   et   omnes
both   of child-birth   undergo   the peril,   and   all
           3   1   2   2

Nutricis   tolerant   fortunâ   urgente,   labores ;
of a nurse   bear   (their) fortune   urging.   the toils ;
4   1   3

Sed   jacet   aurato   vix   ulla   puerpera   lec'o.
but   lies   in a gilded   hardly   any   lying-in-woman   bed.
4   5   1   2   3   6

Tantum   artes   hujus,   tantum   medicamina   possunt,
so much   the arts   of her,   so much   the drugs   prevail,
     4   1   2   3

Quæ   steriles   facit,   atque   homines   in   ventre
who   barren   makes   and   men   in   the womb
   2   1   2   4

necandos   Conducit.   Gaude,   infelix,   atque
to be killed,   conduces.   Rejoice,   thou wretch,   and
  3   1

ipse   bibendum   Porrige   quicquid   erit :   nam
thou thyself   to be drunk   reach forth   whatever   it shall be :   for
     2   1

si   distendere   vellet,   Et   vexare   uterum
if   to distend   she were willing, and   to distress   her womb
   2   1

pueris   salientibus,   esses   Æthiopis   fortasse
with children   leaping,   you sh'd be   of an Æthiop   perhaps
  2   1   3   1

pater :   mox   decolor   hæres   Impleret   tabulas
the father :   soon   a discolored   heir   might fill   (your) will
  1

nunquam   tibi   mane   videndus.   Transeo
never   by you   of a morning   to be seen.   I pass by
     2   3   1

suppositos,   et   gaudia,   votaque   sæpe
supposititious [children] and   the joys,   and vows   often

Ad   spurcos   decepta   lacus,   atque   inde
at   the dirty   baffled   lakes,   and   thence
2   3   1   4

petitos   Pontifices,   Salios,   Scaurorum   nomina
sought   Priests,   Salii,   of the Scauri   the names
  3   1   2   5   4

falso   Corpore   laturos.   Stat   Fortuna   improba
in a false   body   about to bear.   Stands   Fortune   mischievous
2   3   1   3   2   1

noctu   Arridens   nudis   infantibus.   Hos   fovet
by night   smiling at the   naked   infants.   These   she cherishes
  4

omnes,   Involvitque   sinu :   domibus   tunc
all,   and wraps in   (her) bosom :   houses   then
               4   1

porrigit   altis,   Secretumque   sibi   mimum
proffers (them)   to the high,   and a secret   for herself   sport
2   3   2   4   3

parat.   Hos   amat,   his   se   Ingerit,   atque
prepares: These   she loves,   with these herself   She charges,   and
  1

suos   ridens   producit   alumnos.   Hic   magicos
as her own smiling leads (them) forth   foster children.   This one   magical
  3   1   2   4   2

affert cantus, hic Thessala vendit Philtra,
offers incantations, this Thessalian sells philtres,
1   2   1

quibus valeat mentem vexare mariti, Et
by which she avails the mind to vex of her husband, and
   2   1

soleâ pulsare nates. Quo 1 desipis, inde
with a slipper beat (his) posteriors. That you are foolish, from thence
     2

est; Inde animi caligo, et magna
is; thence of mind darkness and great
1   2   1

oblivio rerum, Quas modo gessisti. Tamen
forgetfulness of things, which just now you did. Yet

hoc tolerabile, si non Et furere incipias,
this is tolerable, if not too to rave you begin,
     2   4   3   1

ut avunculus ille Neronis, Cui totam
as uncle that of Nero, for whom the whole
   2   1   3

tremuli frontem Cæsonia pulli Infudit.
of a trembling forehead Cæsonia colt infused.
5   4   1   2

Quæ non faciet, quod Principis uxor?
what [wife] not will do, what a prince's wife (did)?

Ardebant cuncta, et fractâ compage
were burning all [things] and broken the bond
2   1   2   1

ruebant, Non aliter, quam si fecisset
were falling to pieces, not otherwise than if had made
     2

Juno maritum Insanum. Minûs ergo
Juno (her) husband insane. Less therefore
1   2

nocens erat Agrippinæ Boletus: siquidem
hurtful was Agrippina's mushroom: since
1

unius præcordia pressit Ille senis,
of one the vitals oppressed that old man,
4   3   2   1

tremulumque caput descendere jussit In
and his trembling head to descend bade into
     2   1

cœlum et longam manantia labra salivam.
heaven, and a long dropping (his) lips slaver.
     3   2   1

Hæc poscit ferrum atque ignes, hæc
This demands sword and fires, this

potio torquet: Hæc lacerat mixtos Equitum
potion tortures: this lacerates mixed of Knights
     2   5

cum sanguine Patres. Tanti partus
with the blood Senators. Of so great (potency) the offspring
3   4   1

equæ!   quanti   una   venefica   constat !
of a mare!   of how great (woe)   one   sorceress   consists!

Oderunt   natos   de   pellice ;   nemo
They hate   those born   of   a mistress :   no one

repugnet,   nemo   vetet ;   jamjam   privignum
would object to   no one   w'd forbid (that) ;   now   a son-in-law
                                                      4

occidere   fas   est.   Vos   ego,   pupilli,
to kill   allowable   it is.   you   I,   orphans,
3   2   1   6   7

moneo   quibus   amplior   est   res,   Custodite
admonish   to whom   an ample   is   estate,   Guard (your)
8   2   4   3   5

animas,   et   nulli   credite   mensæ.   Livida
lives,   and   no   trust   table.   The livid
               2   1

materno   fervent   adipata   veneno.   Mordeat
with maternal   are warm   fat meats   poison.   Let bite
3   2   1   3   1

ante   aliquis,   quidquid   porrexerit   illa,   Quæ
first   some one   whatever   shall offer   she,   who
           2   2   1

peperit :   timidus   prægustet   pocula   pappas.
bore (you) :   the timid   let taste first   the cups   tutor.
              2   1   4   3

Fingimus   hæc,   altum   Satirâ   sumente
We feign   these (things),   the lofty   Satire   assuming
                              3   1   2

cothurnum   Scilicet,   et   finem   egressi   legemque
buskin   forsooth,   and the limit   having transgressed   and the law
                                    2   1

priorum,   Grande   Sophocleo   carmen   bacchamur
of former (writers),   grand   in Sophoclean   verse   we rant
                    2   4   3   1

hiatu,   Montibus   ignotum   Rutulis,   cœloque
strain,   to the Mountains   unknown   Rutulian,   and the sky
                2   1   3   2

Latino.   Nos   utinam   vani !   sed   clamat
Latin.   We   would that (were) false !   but   cries out
1   2   1   2

Pontia,   Feci,   Confiteor,   puerisque   meis
Pontia,   "I have done the deed !   I confess it,   and for boys   my
1   2   1

aconita   paravi,   Quæ   deprensa   patent :
the aconite   I prepared   which   detected   are patent :

facinus   tamen   ipsa   peregi.   Tunc   duos
the deed   still   I myself   perpetrated,"   "Didst thou,   two
2   1   3

unâ,   sævissima   vipera,   cœnâ?   Tunc   duos ?
at one   most cruel   viper   meal?"   "Didst thou,   two?
1   2

Septem,   si   septem   forte   fuissent.   Credamus
"Seven,   if   seven   haply   had been."   Let-us-believe

tragicis,   quidquid   de   Colchide   sævâ
in tragedies,   whatever   of   Colchis   stern
3   1

Dicitur   et   Procne :   nil   contrà   conor ;   et
is said   and   Progne :   nothing   against   I attempt,   and
2

illæ   Grandia   monstra   suis   audebant   temporibus;
those (women)   great   enormities   in their   dared   times ; .
2   3   1

sed   Non   propter   nummos.   Minor   admiratio
but   not   for the sake of   money.   Less   amazement

summis   Debetur   monstris,   quoties   facit
to the highest   is due   enormities,   as often as   makes
2   1   3   2

ira   nocentem   Hunc   sexum,   et   rabio
anger   injurious   this   sex,   and   fury
1   5   3   4

jecur   incendente   feruntur   Præcipites ;   ut
the liver   inflaming   they are carried   headlong ;   as
2   1

saxa   jugis   abrupta,   quibus   mons   Subtrahitur,
rocks   from cliffs   broken off,   from which   the mountain   is withdrawn

clivoque   latus   pendente   recedit.   Illam   ego
and from the   cliff the side   hanging   recedes.   Her   I
2   3   1

non   tulerim   quæ   computat,   et   scelus   ingens
not   c'd bear   who   makes calculations, and   crime   a great
2   1   2

Sana   facit.   Spectant   subeuntem   fata
in cold blood   commits.   They behold   undergoing   the fate
2

mariti,   Alcestim,   et,   similis   si   permutatio
of (her) husband,   Alcestis,   and,   a like   if   exchange
1   2   1

detur,   Morte   viri   cupient   animam
were allowed   by the death   of a husband   they will desire   the life
5   6   1   3

servare   catellæ.   Occurrent   multæ   tibi
to preserve   of a lap-dog.   Will meet   many   you
2   4   4   1   5

Belides   atque   Eriphylæ :   Mané   Clytæmnestram
Belides   and   Eriphylæ   in the morning :   a Clytemnestra
2   3

nullus   non   vicus   habebit.   Hoc   tantùm
no   not   street   will have.   This   only
2   1   3   4

refert,   quòd   Tyndaris   illa   bipennem   Insulsam
is the difference,   that   Tyndaris   that   axe   a bungling
2   1   4   3

et   fatuam   dextrâ   lævâque   tenebat   At
and   foolish   in (her) right   and left hand   held.   But

nunc   res   agitur   tenui   pulmone   rubetæ;
now   the thing   is done   with the thin   lungs   of a toad;

Sed   tamen   et   ferro,   si   prægustârit   Atrides
but   yet   too   with a sword,   if   has tasted beforehand   Atrides
               2   1   3   2

Pontica   ter   victi   cautus   medicamina   regis.
the Pontic   of the thrice conquered   cautious   antidotes   King.
   4   6   1   5   7

SATIRE VII.

ARGUMENT.

This Satire contains an animated account of the gen eral discouragement under which literature laboured at Rome. Beginning with poetry, it proceeds through the various departments of history, law, oratory, rhetoric, and grammar; interspersing many curious anecdotes, and enlivening each different head with such satirical, humorous, and sentimental remarks as naturally flow from the subject.

Et	spes,	et	ratio	studiorum	in	Cæsare
Both	the hope,	and	reason	of studies	(is) in	Cæsar

tantùm :	Solus	enim	tristes	hâc	tempestate
only :	he alone	for	the sad	at this	time
	2	1		3	4

Camœnas	Respexit,	quum	jam	celebres
muses	has regarded	when	now	famous

notique	poetæ	Balneolum	Gabiis,	Romæ
and noted	poets	a small bath	at Gabii,	at Rome
		3	4	6

conducere	furnos	Tentarent :	nec	fœdum
to hire	ovens	would try ;	nor	foul
2	5	1		4

alii,	nec	turpe	putarent	Præcones	fieri,
others,	nor	base	would think (it)	criers	to become,
2			1 3	2	1

quum,	desertis	Aganippes	Vallibus,	esuriens
when,	being deserted	of Aganippe	the vales,	hungry
	3	2	1	

migraret	in	atria	Clio.	Nam,	si	Pieriâ
w'd migrate	to	courts	Clio.	For,	if	the Pierian
2			1			6

quadrans	tibi	nullus	in	umbrâ	Ostendatur,
farthing	to you	no	in	shade	is shown,
2	4	1	5	7	3

ames	nomen	victumque	Machæræ,	Et	vendas
you may love	the name	and living	of Maschera,	and	sell

potiùs,   commissa   quod   auctio   vendit
rather   the intrusted what   auction   sells
              2   1

Stantibus,   œnophorum,   tripodas,   armaria,   cistas,
to the standers-by, a wine-pot, tripod, book-cases, chests,

Alcyonem   Pacci,   Thebas   et   Terea Fausti.
the Alcyone   of Paccius,   the Thebes and   Tereus of Faustus.

Hoc   satius,   quàm   si   dicas   sub   judice,
This (is) better,   than   if   you sh'd say before a judge,

Vidi,   Quod   non   vidisti.   Faciant   equites
"I have seen," what not   you have seen. may do (this) knights
                    3   1   2   4   3

Asiani   Quanquam,   et   Cappadoces   faciant,
As at c   although,   and   Cappadocian   may do (this),
  2   1

equitesque   Bithyni,   Altera   quos   nudo   traducit
and knights   Bithynian,   the other whom   with bare brings over
                             2   1   5   4

Gallia   talo.   Nemo   tamen   studiis   indignum
Gaul   foot.   no one   yet,   (his) studies unworthy
3   2   1   5

ferre   laborem   Cogetur   posthac,   nectit
to bear   a toil   shall be compelled hereafter, joins
3   4   2

qu'cunque   canoris _   Eloquium   vocale   modis,
whoever   to tuneful eloquence   lofty   measures,
1   3   6   5   4

laurumque   momordit.   Hoc   agite,   O juvenes:
and the laurel has bitten. this   do,   O young men:
2   1

circumspicit,   et   stimulat   vos,   Materiamque
is looking around, and encourages you,   and matter
 3

sibi   Ducis   indulgentia   quærit.   Si   qua
for itself of the Emperor the indulgence seeks.   If   any
          2   1

aliunde   putas   rerum   exspectanda   tuarum
elsewhere   you think   affairs   to be expected of your
7   1   5   6   4

Præsidia,   atque   ideo   croceæ   membrana
protection,   and   therefore of (your) yellow the parchments
                                  2   1

tabellæ   Impletur: lignorum   aliquid   posce
tablet   is filled: of faggots   some   call for
                        3   2   1

ociùs,   et,   quæ   Componis,   dona   Veneris,
quickly,   and,   what   you compose,   give   of Venus,
                                          2

Thelesine,   marito: Aut   claude,   et   positos
Telesinus,   to the husband; or   shut up,   and laid by
  1   3   4

tineâ   pertunde   libellos.   Frange   miser
with the moth   bore through (your) books.   Break,   wretch,
    2   1   3

   calamos,   vigilataque   prœlia   dele,   Qui
(your) pens,   and (your) watched   battles   blot out,   who

facis   in   parva   sublimia   carmina   cella,
makest   in   a small   sublime   verses   cell,
   3   4   1   2

Ut   dignus   venias   hederis,   et · imagine
that   worthy   you-may-come-forth   of ivy,   and   image
    2   1   2

macrâ.   Spes   nulla   ulterior :   didicit   jam
a meagre.   Hope (there is) none   beyond :   has learned   now
   1   3   5   4

dives   avarus   Tantûm   admirari,   tantûm
the rich   miser   only   to admire,   only
   1   2

laudare   disertos,   Ut   pueri   Junonis   avem.
to praise   the eloquent,   as   boys   Juno's   bird.

Sed   defluit   ætas   Et   pelagi   patiens,
But   is ebbing away (your) age,   both   of the sea   enduring,
            2   1   2   3   1

et   cassidis,   atque   ligonis.   Tædia   tunc
and   of the helmet,   and   of the spade.   weariness   then

subeunt   animos,   tunc   seque   suamque
creeps-upon   the spirits,   then   both itself   and its
                         5

Terpsichoren   odit   facunda   et   nuda   senectus.
Terpsichore   hates   eloquent   and   naked   old age
           4   1   2   3

Accipe   nunc   artes,   ne   quid   tibi   conferat
Hear   now   (his) arts,   lest   anything   to you   sh'd give
                           6   5   4

iste   Quem   colis,   et   Musarum   et
that (one)   whom   you court,   both   of the Muses   and
   1   2   3   2   3

Apollinis   œde   relictâ.   Ipse   facit   versus,
of Apollo   the temple   being forsaken. himself   makes   verses·
               1

atque   uni   cedit   Homero   Propter   mille
and   alone   yields   to Homer   because of   a thousand
           3   1   2

annos;   et,   si   du'cedine   famæ   Succensus
years (before him); and,   if   with the sweetness of fame   inflamed
                       2   3

recites,   Maculonus   commodat   ædes.   Hæc
you recite (your verses), Maculonus   lends (you   a house.   This
   4

longè   ferrata   domus   servire   jubetur.   In
long   barred   house   to serve (you) is commanded.   in
  2   3   1   ·   1

quâ   sollicitas   imit.tur   auua   portas.   Scit
wh.eu   anxious   imitat s   the door   gates. He knows
         3   2   1

dare   libertes   extremâ   in   parte   sedentes
(how) to place (his) freedmen the extreme   in   part   sitting
                  3   2   4   1

Ordinis,   et   magnas   comitum   disponere   voces.
of the rows,   and   the loud   of his a tendants to dispose voices.
                 2   4   1

Nemo   dabit   regum,   quanti   subsellia   con-tent
No one   will give of the great lords, as much as the benches cost,
         2   1

Et   quæ   conducto   pendent   anabathra   tigillo,
and   which   from the hired   hang   the stairs   beam,
         2   5   1

Quæque   reportandis   posita est   orchestra   cathedris.
and which   to-be-carried-back   is set   the orchestra with chairs.
        2   5   3   1   4

Nos   tamen   hoc   agimus,   tenuique   in
We   yet   this   do,   and the light   in
   2   1   3   4   3

pulvere   sulcos   Ducimus,   et   litius   sterili
dust   furrows   draw,   and   the shore with a barren
              2   1   2

versamus   aratro.   Nam   si   discedas.   laqueo
turn   plough.   For   if   you w d desist, in a snare
 1   5

tenet   ambitiosi   Consuetudo   mali :   tenet
holds (you) of ambitious   the habit   evil :   holds
   4   2   1   3   4

insanabile   multos   Scribendi   cacoethes,   et
incurabl   many   of writing   itch,   and
                          3   2

ægro   in   corde   senescit.   Sed   vatem egregium,
the sick in   heart   grows old.   But   the poet,   excellent,
  3   2   4

cui   non   sit   publica   vena,   Qui   nihil
to whom not   is   a common   vein,   who   nothing
       2   1

expositum   soleat   deducere,   nec   qui   Communi
stale   is wont   to spin out,   nor   who with a common

feriat   carmen   triviale   monetâ;   Hunc,   qualem
stamps   verse   trivial   die,   him, such (a one) as
         4   3   1

nequeo   monstrare,   et   sentio   tantum,
I cannot   show,   and   feel   only,

Anxietate   carens   animus   facit,   omnis
anxiety   free from   a mind   makes,   of very
  5   2   4   2

acerbi   Impatiens,   cupidus   silvarum,   aptusque
(thing) bitter impatient,   desirous   of the woods, and disposed
  3   1

bibendis   Fontibus   Aonidum.   Neque   enim
for drinking   the fountains   of the Aonides.   Neither   for
                                       2   1

cantare   sub   antro   Pierio,,   thyrsumve   potest
to sing   in   cave   the Pierian,   or the thyrsus   is able
           2   1   2   3 6

coutingere   sana   Paupertas   atque   æris   inops,
to handle   sober   Poverty   and   of money   void,
1   4   5

quo   nocte   dieque   Corpus   eget :   satur
which   night   and day   the body   needs :   satisfied

est,   quum   dicit   Horatius,   Evoe !   Quis
is   when   he says   Horace,   "Evoe!"   What
  2   3   1

locus   ingenio,   nisi   quum se   carmine   solo
place (is there) for genius,   unless   when themselves   with verse   alone
6   1   2

Vexant,   et   dominis   Cirrhæ   Nysæque   feruntur
trouble   and   by the lords of Cirrha   and Nysa   are borne along
5

Pectora   nostra,   duas   non   admitteutia
breasts   our,   two   not   admitting
4   3   3   1   2

curas ?   Magnæ   mentis   opus   nec   de   lodice
cares ?   of a great   mind   (it is) the work   nor about   a blanket
                              1   3   5

parandâ   Attonitæ,   currus,   et   equos
getting   of (one) bewildered,   chariots   and   horses
4   2   2

faciesque   deorum   Adspicere,   et   qualis
and the faces   of the gods   to behold,   and   what
1

Rutulum   confundat   Erinnys.   Nam si   Virgilio
the Rutulian   appals   an Erinnys.   For if   to a Virgil
3   2   1

puer   et   tolerabile   deesset   Hospitium,
a boy   and   tolerable   were wanting   lodging,
2   1

caderent   omnes   a   crinibus   hydri: Surda
would fall   all   from   her hair   the serpents: the silent
3   1   2

nihil   gemeret   grave   buccina.   Poscimus, ut
nothing   w'd groan   disastrous   trumpet.   Do we demand that
3   2   1

sit   Non   minor   antiquo   Rubrenus Lappa
sh'd be   not   less   than the ancient   Rubrenus Lappa
2   3   4   1

cothurno,   Cujus   et   alveolos   et   lænam   pignerat
buskin,   whose   both   platters   and   cloak   had pawned
2   1   2

Atreus?   Non   habet   infelix   Numitor,   quod
Atreus,?   Not   has   unhappy   Numitor,   what
1   4   3   1   2

mittat   amico;   Quintillæ,   quod   donet,
he may send   to (his) friend;   to Quintilla,   what   he can give,
4   2   5

habet;   nec   defuit   illi,   Unde   emeret
he has: nor   was there wanting   to him,   with which   he might buy
1

multâ   pascendum   carne   leonem   Jam
with much   to be fed   flesh   a lion   already
3   2   4   1

domitum :   constat   leviori   bellua   sumptu
tamed: stands (him)   in less   the beast   expense
2   3   1

Nimirum,   et   capiunt   plus   intestina   poetæ.
doubtless   and   hold   more   the intestines   of a poet.
3   4   1

Contentus   famâ   jaceat   Lucanus   in   hortis
content   with fame   may lie   Lucan   in   gardens
2   1

Marmoreis :   at   Serrauo   tenuique   Salcio   Gloria
adorned with marble: but   to Serranus   and to thin   Saleius   glory
3

quantalibet   quid   erit,   si   gloria   tantum   est?
however great,   what   will be,   if   glory   only   it is?
1   2   3   2   1

Curritur   ad   vocem   jucundam,   et   carmen
It is run   to   voice   the pleasing,   and   poem
2   1

amicæ   Thebaïdos,   lætam   fecit   quum   Statius
of the favorite   Thebais,   glad   has made   when   Statius
5   3   1   2

urbem,   Promisitque   diem :   tantâ   dulcedine
the city   and has promised   a day :   with so great   sweetness
4

captos   Afficit   ille   animos,   tantâque   libidine
the captivated   affects   he   minds,   and with so great   desire
3   1   2

vulgi   Auditur :   sed,   quum   fregit   subsellia
of the multitude   is heard :   but,   when   he has broken   the benches

versu,   Esurit,   intactam   Paridi   nisi   vendat
with his verse, he hungers,   his untouched   to Paris   unless   he sells
4   3   1   2

Agaven.   Ille   et   militiæ   multis   largitur
Agave.   He   also   of military service   on many   bestows
4   2   1

honorem,   Semestri   vatum   digitos   circumligat
the honor,   with Semestrian   of poets   the fingers   he binds around
3   4   3   2   1

auro.   Quod   non   dant   proceres,   dabit
gold.   What   not   give   nobles,   will give
3   2   1   2

histrio.   Tu   Camerinos,   Et   Barcas,   tu
an actor.   thou   the Camerini,   and   Barcæ,   thou
1   2   4   5   6

nobilium   magna   atria   curas ?   Præfectos   Pelopea
of nobles   the great   courts   dost care for ?   prefects   Pelopea
9   7   8   1   3   3   1

facit,   Philomela   tribunos.   Haud   tamen
makes,   Philomela   tribunes.   not   yet
2   3   1

invideas   vati,   quem   pulpita   pascunt.
envy   the poet,   whom   the stage   maintains.
2

Quis   tibi   Mæcenas ?   quis   nunc   erit
who   to you   (is) a Mæcenas ?   who   now   will be

aut   Proculeius,   Aut   Fabius?   quis   Cotta
either   a Proculeius,   or   a Fabius ?   who   a Cotta

iterum ?   quis   Lentulus   alter?   Tunc   par
again?   who   Lentulus   another ?   Then   equal
2   1

ingenio   pretium :   tunc   utile   multis   Pallere,
to genius (was) the reward: then   (it was) useful   to many   to be pale,

et   vinum   toto   nescire   Decembri.   Vester
and   wine   for a whole   not to know   December.   Your
2   3   1   2

porro   labor   fœcundior,   historiarum   Scriptores:
moreover   labor   (is) more abundant,   of histories   ye writers:
1   2   1

petit   hic   plus   temporis   atque   olei   plus ;
asks   this   more   of time   and   of oil   more ;
2   1

Namque   oblita   modi   milesima   pagina   surgit
For   forgetful   of measure   the thousandth   page   arises

Omnibus,   et   multâ   crescit   damnosa   papyro.
to (you) all,   and   from much   grows   ruinous   pape▪▪
3   1   2

Sic   ingens   rerum   numerus   jubet,   atque
thus   the great   of things   number   requires,   and
2   1

operum   lex.   Quæ   tamen   inde ·   seges ?
of (such) works   the law.   What   yet   thence   harvest ?
2   1   2   1   4   3

terræ   quis   fructus   apertæ ?   Quis   dabit
earth   what   the fruit   of the opened ?   Who   will give
4   1   2   3   3

historico,   quantum   daret   acta   legenti ?
an historian   as much as   he would give   registers   to-one-collecting?
2   1

Sed   genus   ignavum,   quod   lecto   gaudet
"But (they are)   race   an idle,   which   in a couch   rejoices
2   1

et   umbrâ.   Dic   igitur,   quid   causidicis
and   the shade."   Tell me   then,   what   to the lawyers
4

civilia   præstant   Officia,   et   magno   comites
civil   afford   offices,   and   a great (their) attendants
1   3   2   4   2

in   fasce   libelli ?   Ipsi   magna   sonant,   sed
in   bundle   the briefs ?   They themselves   aloud   bawl   but
3   5   1   2   1

tunc,   quum   creditor   audit   Præcipuè,   vel
then   when   the creditor   hears   especially,   or
2   1

si   tetigit   latus   acrior   illo,   Qui   venit
it'   has touched (his) side (one) more keen   than he,   who   comes
3   4   1   2

ad   dubium   grandi   cum   codice   nomen.
to   a doubtful   a big   with   account-book   debt.
4   5   2   1

Tunc   immensa   cavi   spirant   mendacia   folles
then   immense   their hollow   breathe   lies   bellows
4   1   3   2

Conspuiturque   sinus.   Verum   deprendere   messem
and is slavered   the bosom.   But   to calculate   the harvest
2   1   3

Si   libet ;   hinc   centum   patrimonia   causidicorum,
if   it pleases: on this side   of a hundred   the patrimonies   lawyers,
1   2   2   1

Parte   alia   solum   russati   pone   Lacernæ.
on the side   other   only   (that) of the red clad   put   Lacerna.
2   1   2   3   1   4

Consedêre   duces :   surgis   tu   pallidus   Ajax
have taken seats   the chiefs :   risest   thou   a pale   Ajax
2   1   2   1

Dicturus   dubia   pro   libertate,   bubulco   Judice.
about to plead   doubtful   for   liberty,   a herdsman   being judge.
2   1

Rumpe   miser   tensum   jecur,   ut   tibi   lasso
Break,   wretch,   your stretched   liver,   that   to you fatigued

Figantur   virides,   scalarum   gloria,   palmæ.
may be affixed   green,   of (your) stairs   the glory,   palms.
3   1   5   4   2

Quod   vocis   pretium ?   siccus   petasunculus,
what   of (your) voice (is) the reward ?   a dry   bit-of-bacon,
2   1

et   vas   Pelamidum ; aut   veteres,   Afrorum
and   a dish   of sprats ;   or   old,   of the Africans
3

epimenia,   bulbi ;   Aut   vinum   Tiberi   devectum,
the-monthly-provender onions ;   or   wine   the Tiber   brought down,
2   2   1

quinque   lagenæ.   Si   quater   egisti,   si
five   bottles;   if   four times   you-have-pleaded,   if

contigit   aureus   unus,   Inde   cadunt   partes
befals   gold piece   one,   thence   fall   shares
2   1   2   1

ex   fœdere   pragmaticorum.   Æmilio   dabitur,
from   the agreement   of the pragmatics.   To Æmilius   will be given,

quantùm   licet,   et   meliùs   nos   Egimus :
as much as   the law allows, although   better   we   have pleaded :
3   1   2

hujus enim stat currus aëneus, alti
his for stands chariot a brazen, stately
8 1 4 3 2 6

Quadrijuges in vestibulis, atque ipse
four horses in vestibules, and himself
5 6 7 9

feroci Bellatore sedens curvatum hastile
on a fierce war-horse sitting a bent spear
2

minatur Eminus, et statuâ meditatur
brandishes aloft, and statue meditates
1 4 1

prœlia luscâ Sic Pedo conturbat, Matho
battles with a blinking. Thus Pedo gets involved, Matho
2 3

deficit: exitus hic est Tongilli, magno
fails: the end this is of Tongillus, a large
3 1 2 5

cum rhinocerote lavari Qui solet, et
with rhinoceros to bathe who is wont, and
4 3 1 2

vexat lutulentâ balnea turbâ, Perque
vexes with a dirty the baths crowd, and through
2 1

forum juvenes longo premit assere Medos,
the forum the young with a long presses pole Medes,
2 4 1 5 3

Emturus pueros, argentum, murrhina, villas.
going to bid for boys, silver, myrrhine-vases, villas.

Spondet enim Tyrio stlataria purpura
gains-him-credit for with Tyrian foreign purple
6 1 4 2 3

filo. Et tamen est illis hoc utile:
thread. and yet is to them this useful:
5 2 1 3

purpura vendit Causidicum, vendunt amethystina:
purple sells the lawyer, sell (him) violet-robes:
2 1

convenit illis Et strepitu, et facie majoris
it suits them both with the bustle, and show of a greater
2

vivere census. Sed finem impensæ non
to live income (than they really have). But a limit to expense not
1 5 4

servat prodiga Roma. Fidimus eloquio?
observes prodigal Rome. Do we trust in (our) eloquence?
3 1 2

Ciceroni nemo ducentos Nunc dederit
to Cicero no one two hundred now w'd give
4 1 3 2

nummos, nisi fulserit annulus ingens.
sesterces, unless shone ring a great.
3 2 1

Respicit hæc primúm, qui litigat, an
regards these (things) first, (he) who litigates, whether
3 1 2

tibi	servi	Octo,	decem	comites,	an
to you	slaves (are)	eight,	ten	attendants,	whether
	2	1			

post	te	sella,	togati	Ante	pedes.
after	you (is)	a sedan,	gownsmen	before (your)	feet.

Ideo	conductâ	Paulus	agebat		Sardonyche,
Therefore	with a hired	Paulus	used-to-plead		Sardonyx,
	3	1	2		

atque	ideo	pluris,	quàm	Cossus	agebat,
and	therefore at a higher fee,		than	Cossus	pleaded,
		2		3	1

Quàm	Basilus.	Rara	in	tenui	facundia
than	Basilus.	rare (is)	in	a thread bare	eloquence
			2	3	1

panno.	Quando	licet	Basilo	flentem
coat.	when	is it allowed	Basilus	a weeping
4				2

producere	matrem?	Quis	bene	dicentem
to produce (in court) mother?		who	well	(tho') pleading
1			4	3

Basilum	ferat?	Accipiat	te	Gallia,	vel
Basilus	c'd endure?	let receive	you	Gaul,	or
2	1	1 3		2	

potiùs	nutricula	causidicorum	Africa,	si
rather	the foster-nurse	of pleaders,	Africa,	if

placuit	mercedem	imponere	linguæ.	Declamare
it has pleased (you) a reward		to set upon (your) tongue.		to declaim
				2

doces?	O ferrea	pectora	Vecti!	Quum
do you teach?	O the iron	heart	of Vectius!	when
1				

perimit	sævos	classis	numerosa	tyrannos
destroys	cruel	class	(his) numerous	tyrants.
3	4	2	1	

Nam	quæcunque	sedens	modò	legerat,	hæc
For,	whatever	sitting	just	it had read,	these
			2	1 3	

eadem	stans	Proferet,	atque	eadem	cantabit
same (things)	standing	it will utter,	and	the same	will sing

versibus	isdem.	Occidit	miseros	crambe
in verses	the same.	Kills	the miserable	the cabbage
		3	4	1

repetita	magistros.	Quis	color,	et	quod
repeated	masters.	What	the color,	and	what
2					

sit	causæ	genus,	atque	ubi	summa
may be	of the cause	the character,	and	where	the chief
	2	1			

Quæstio,	quæ	veniant	diversæ	forté	sagittæ,
question,	what	may come	diverse	perhaps	arrows,
		4	1	3	2

Nôsse	velint	omnes	mercedem	solvere	nemo,
Know	would	all,	the reward	pay	nobody.
3	2	1	3	2	1

Mercedem   apellas?   quid   enim   scio?   Culpa
"Pay   do you call for?   what   forsooth   do I know?"   The fault

docentis   Scilicet   arguitur,   quòd   lævâ
of the teacher   you-may-be-sure   is blamed,   because   the left
                                                              2

in   parte   mamillæ   Nil   salit   Arcadico   juveni,
in   part   of the breast   nothing   leaps   to the Arcadian   youth,
   1

cujus   mihi   sextâ   Quâque   die   miserum
whose   to me   sixth   every   day   the miserable
   9   4   3   5   7

dirus   caput   Hannibal   implet;   Quidquid   id   est,
dire   head   Hannibal   fills: Whatever   it   is,
   1   8   2   6

de   quo   deliberat,   an   petat   Urbem   A
about   which   he deliberates,   whether   he seek   the city   fror

Cannis,   an   post   nimbos   et   fulmina,   cautus,
Cannæ,   or   after   storms   and   thunderbolts,   cautious,

Cicumagat   madidas   a   tempestate   cohortes.
he sh'd lead about   wet   from   the tempest   (his) cohorts.
              2   3   4   1

Quantùm   vis   stipulare,   et   protinus   accipe,
for as much as   you will   bargain,   and   immediately   take,
   2   1

quod   do,   Ut   toties   illum   pater   audiat.
what   I give,   that   as often   him   (his) father   sh'd hear
               4   3   1   2

Ast   alii   sex   Vel   plures   uno   conclamant
But   other   six   or   more   with one   cry together
                     3   2

ore   sophistæ   Et   veras   agitant   lites,
mouth   sophists   and   real   agitate   causes,
   4   1   2   1

raptore   relicto: Fusa   venena   silent,   malus
the ravisher   being left;   the mixed   poisons   are silent,   the bad

ingratusque   maritus,   Et   quæ   jam   veteres   sanant
and ungrateful   husband,   and   what   now   old   heal
                              2   4   3

mortaria   cæcos.   Ergo   sibi   dabit   ipse
medicines   blindmen.   Therefore   to himself   will give   he himself
   1   3   2   1

rudem,   si   nostra   movebunt   Consilia,   et   vitæ
the wand   if   our   will move   Counsels,   and   of life
   4   2   1   4

diversum   iter   ingredietur,   Ad   pugnam   qui
a different   way   will enter upon,   to   real-engagement   who
   2   3   1   6   7   1

rhetoricâ   descendit   ab   umbra,   Summula   ne
the rhetorical   has descended   from   shadow,   the small sum   lest
   4   2   3   5   2   1

pereat,   quâ   vilis   tessera   venit   Frumenti:
sh'd perish from   which   the vile   ticket   comes   for corn:
   3

quippe hæc merces lautissima. Tenta,
since this (is) a reward most splendid. Try,

Chrysogonus quanti doceat, vel Pollio quanti
Chrysogonus for how much teaches, or Pollio how much
2   1   2   1

Lautorum pueros, artem scindens Theodori.
of quality the children, the art dividing of Theodorus.
2   1   2   1

Balnea sexcentis, et pluris porticus, in quâ
Baths (are) at six hundred, and at more a portico, in which
  2   1

Gestetur dominus, quoties pluit. Anne serenum
may be carried the lord, as often as it rains. can he fair (weather)

Exspectet, spargatve luto jumenta recenti ?
wait for, or dash mud (his) cattle with fresh ?
  2   4   1   3

Hic potiùs : namque hic mundæ nitet
here (in the portico) rather: for here of the clean shines
      2   4

ungula mulæ. Parte aliâ longis Numidarum
the hoof mule. In part another, with tall of Numidia
1   3   2   1   2   4

fulta columnis Surgat, et algentem rapiat
supported columns, let arise. and the cool catch
1   3   1   3   5   4

cœnatio solem. Quanticunque domus,
a supper-room sun. However much the house (may have cost)
2

veniet, qui fercula docte Componat ; veniet,
he shall come who the dishes scientifically can arrange; he shall come

qui pulmentaria condat. Hos inter
who made-dishes can season. These amidst
2   1

sumptus sestertia Quintiliano, Ut multum,
expenses sestertia Quintilian, as a great deal,
  2   6   3   4

duo sufficient. Res nulla minoris
two will suffice. Thing no less
1   5   2   1   5

Constabit patri, quàm filius. Unde igitur
will cost a father, than (his) son. Whence therefore
3   4

tot Quintilianus habet saltus ? Exempla
so many Quintilian has forests ? examples
3   2   1

novorum Fatorum transi : felix et pulcher
of new fates pass over : the fortunate both handsome

et acer, Felix, . et sapiens, et nobilis,
and witty, the fortunate both wise, and noble,

et generosus, Appositam nigræ lunam
and generous, set upon (his) black the crescent
  3   4   2

subtexit   alutæ: Felix,   orator   quoque   maximus
subjoins   shoe: the fortunate,   an orator   also   very great
 1   5

et   jaculator;   Et,   si   perfrixit,   cantat
and   a disputant;   and,   if   he is hoarse,   sings

bene.   Distat   enim,   quæ   Sidera   te
well.   There is a difference   for,   what   stars   you
       2   1   2

excipiant   modò   primos   incipientem   Edere
receive   just   the first   beginning   to utter
 1   1   4   2   3

vagitus,   et   adhuc   a   matre   rubentem.
cries,   and   as yet   from (your) mother   red
           2   3   1

Si   Fortuna   volet,   fies   de   rhetore
If   Fortune   wills it,   you will become from   a rhetorician

consul: Si   volet   hæc   eadem,   fies   de
a consul: If   wills   this   same,   you will become from
           3   1   2

consule   rhetor   Ventidius   quid   enim?   quid
a consul   a rhetorician.   Ventidius   what   for?   what
              3   2   1

Tullius?   anne   aliud,   quàm   Sidus,   et
Tullius?   was it   other,   than   a star,   and

occulti   miranda   potentia   fati?   Servis   regna
of hidden   the wonderful   power   fate?   to slaves   kingdoms
 3   1   2   4   5

dabunt,   captivis   Fata   triumphos.   Felix
will give,   to captives   the Fates   triumphs.   Fortunate
 2   6   1   5   3

ille   tamen   corvo   quoque   rarior   albo.
that   yet   than a crow   (is)   also   rarer   white.
 2   1   6   8   4   5   7

Pœnituit   multos   vanæ   sterilisque   cathedræ,
It has repented   many   of the vain   and barren   chair,

Sicut   Thrasymachi   probat   exitus,   atque
as   of Thrasymachus   proves   the exit,   and
       2   3   1

Secundi   Carrinatis: et   hunc   inopem   vidistis,
of Secundus   Carrinas: and   him   poor   you saw,

Athenæ,   Nil   præter   gelidas   ausæ   conferre
O Athens,   nothing   but   cold   having dared to bestow
          3   4   5   1   2

cicutas.   Di,   majorum   umbris   tenuem
hemlock.   (grant) ye Gods,   of our ancestors   to the shades   thin
          2   1   3

et   sine   pondere   terram,   Spirantesque
and   without   weight   earth,   and breathing
 5   6   7   4

crocos,   et   in   urnâ   perpetuum   ver,
crocuses,   and   upon (their) urn   perpetual   spring,

Qui   præceptorem   sancti   voluêre   parentis
who   a preceptor   of a revered   wished   parent
    2   5   1

Esse   loco.   Metuens   virgæ   jam   grandis
to be   in the place.   fearing   the rod   now   grown up
3   4   4   5   2   3

Achilles   Cantabat   patriis   in   montibus :
Achilles   sang   (his) paternal   on   mountains :
1   6   8   7

et   cui   non   tunc   Eliceret   risum   citharœdi
and   from whom   not   then   would elicit   laughter   of the harper
     3   1   2   8   5

cauda   magistri ?   Sed   Rufum   atque   alios
the tail   (his) master ?   But   Rufus   and   others
4   6

cædit   sua   quæque   juventus :   Rufum,   qui
wounds   their own   each   youth :   Rufus,   who
4   2   1   3

toties   Ciceronem   Allobroga   dixit.   Quis
so often   Cicero   an Allobrogian   called.   who

gremio   Enceladi   doctique   Palæmonis   affert
to the lap   of Enceladus   and of the learned   Palæmon   brings
  2   1

Quantum   grammaticus   meruit   labor?   et tamen ex   hoc,
as much as   grammatical   has deserved   labor ?   and yet from   this,
        2   1

Quodcunque   est, (minus   est   autem,   quàm   rhetoris
whatever   it is,   (less   it is   but,   than   the rhetorician's
               3   2   1

æra)   Discipuli   custos   præmordet   Acœnonoëtus,
pay)   of the scholar   the keeper   bites first   Acœnonoetus,
       3   2   1

Et,   qui   dispensat,   franget   sibi.   Cede,
and, (he) who   manages,   will break   for himself.   Yield,

Palæmon,   Et   patere   inde   aliquid   decrescere,
Palæmon,   and   suffer   thence   something   to decrease,

non   aliter,   quàm   Institor   hibernæ   tegetis
not   otherwise,   than   a dealer   in winter   rug

niveique   cadurci.   Dummodo   non   pereat,
and snow-white   sheeting.   Only   not   let it be lost,

mediæ   quòd   noctis   ab   horâ   Sedisti,
of mid   that   night   from   the hour   you have sat,
4   1   5   2   3

quâ   nemo   faber,   quâ   nemo   sederet,
in which   no   smith,   in which   nobody   would sit,

Qui   docet   obliquo   lanam   deducere   ferro ;
who   teaches   with the crooked   wool   to draw out   iron;
                3   2   1   4

Dummodo   non   pereat   totidem   olfecisse
only   not   let it be lost   as many   to have smelt
                  2   1

lucernas,   Quot   stabant   pueri,   quum   totus
lamps,   as   were standing   boys,   when   all
                       2   1

decolor   esset   Flaccus,   et   hæreret nigro   fuligo
discolored   was   Flaccus,   and   adhered to black soot
                                        2   3   1

Maroni.   Rara   tamen   merces,   quæ   cognitione ,
Maro.   Rare   yet   the pay,   which the cognizance
  4   2   1   4

tribuni   Non   egeat.   Sed   vos   sævas   imponite
of the tribune not may need. But   ye   cruel   impose
   5   2   1 3   3   1

leges,   Ut   præceptori   verborum   regula   constet,
laws,   that to the preceptor of words   the rule be clear,
                    4   2   1   3

Ut   legat   historias,   auctores   noverit,   omnes,
that he read   histories,   authors   sh'd know,   all,
                    3   1   2

Tanquam   ungues   digitosque   suos :   ut   forte
as   nails   and fingers   his own: that by chance
             2   1

rogatus,   Dum   petit   aut   thermas   aut   Phœbi
being asked, while he seeks either the hot baths or of Phœbus
                                                          2

balnea, dicat Nutricem Anchisæ,   nomen patriamque
the baths, he may tell the nurse of Anchises, the name and country
  1

novercæ   Anchemoli,   dicat,   quot   Acestes   vixerit
of the step-mother of Anchemolus, may tell how many Acestes lived
                                                                 2

annos,   Quot   Siculus   Phrygibus   vini   donaverit
years, how many the Sicilian to the Phrygians of wine presented
  1   3   2

urnas.   Exigite,   ut   mores   teneros   ceu
urns.   Exact   that   morals the tender   as
  1   Exact   3   2

pollice   ducat,   Ut   si   quis   cerâ   vultum
with (his) thumb he mould, as   one   in wax   a face
                     1

facit :   exigite,   ut   sit   Et   pater   ipsius
models :   exact,   that   he be even a father of his

cœtus,   ne   turpia   ludant,   Ne   faciant   vicibus.
flock,   lest base tricks, they play, lest they do   by turns.

Non   est   leve   tot   puerorum   observare   manus,
not it is a light (matter) of so many   boys   to watch the hands,
 2   1   3   1   2

oculosque   in   fine   trementes.   Hæc   inquit,
and eyes   in   the corner twinkling. these (things) he says,
              2   3   1

cures ;   et,   quum   se   verterit   annus,   Accipe,
take care of; and, when itself shall have turned the year, Accept,
                              3   2   1

victori   populus   quod   postulat   aurum
for a (stage) victor the people which   demand a piece of gold.
    5   3   2   4   1

SATIRE VIII.

ARGUMENT.

Juvenal demonstrates in this Satire, that distinction is merely personal; that though we may derive rank and titles from our ancestors, yet if we degenerate from the virtues by which they obtained them, we cannot be considered truly noble. This is the main object of the Satire; which, however, branches out into many collateral topics— the profligacy of the young nobility; the miserable state of the provinces, which they plundered and harassed without mercy; the contrast between the state of debasement to which the descendants of the best families had sunk, and the opposite virtues to be found in persons of the lowest station and humblest descent.

STEMMATA   quid   faciunt?   quid   prodest,   Pontico,
pedigrees   what   do?   what   profits it,   Ponticus,
3   1   2

longo   Sanguine   conseri,   pictosque   ostendere
by a long   descent   to be valued: and the painted   to show
                                        2   1

vultus   Majorum,   et   stantes   in   curribus
countenances   of Ancestors,   and   standing   in   chariots
                                     2

Æmilianos,   Et   Curios   jam   dimidios,   humerosque
Æmiliani,   and   the Curii   now   half,   and (as to) the shoulders
1   1

minorem   Corvinum,   et   Galbam,   auriculis
less   Corvinus,   and   Galba,   ears
3   2   and   2

nasoque   carentem?   Quis   fructus   generis
and nose   wanting?   What   fruit   of kindred
            1   5

tabulâ   jactare   capaci   Corvinum,   posthac
tablet   to boast of   in the capacious   Corvinus,   afterwards
4   1   3   2

multâ   contingere   virgâ   Fumosos   equitum
by many a   to trace   branch   smoky   of the Knights
2   1   2

cum   dictatore   magistros,   Si   coram   Lepidis
with   a dictator   masters,   if   in the presence of   the Lepidi
             1

malé   vivitur?   Effigies   quò   Tot   bellatorum,
ill   it is lived?   The effigies   whither (tend)   of so many   warriors,
              2   1

si   luditur   alea   pernox   Ante   Numantinos?
if   be played   die   the nightly   before   the Numantini?
    3   2   1

si   dormire   incipis   ortu   Luciferi,   quo
if   to sleep   you begin   at the rising   of Lucifer,   at which
    2   1

• signa   duces   et   castra   movebant?   Cur
(their) standards   the generals   and   camps   were moving?   Why
    3   1   2

Allobrogicis   et   magnâ   gaudeat   arâ   Natus
in the Allobrogici   and   the great   should rejoice   altar   (tho') born
    8   9   10   1 3   11   7

in   Herculeo   Fabius   lare,   si   cupidus,   si
in   a Herculean   Fabius   family,   if   covetous,   if
4   5   2   6

Vanus,   et   Euganeâ   quantumvis   mollior
vain,   and   than an Euganean   ever so much   softer
              3   1   2

agnâ;   si   tenerum   attritus   Catinensi   pumice
lamb;   if (his) tender   having rubbed   with a Catinensian   pumice
        2   1   4

lumbum   Squalentes   traducit   avos,   emptorque
loins,   (his) rugged   he shames   sires,   and a buyer
    3   2   1

veneni   Frangendâ   miseram   funestat   imagine
of poison   should   be broken   the miserable   he saddens   with an image
             5   2   1   4

gentem?   Tota   licet   veteres   exornent
family?   the entire   though   the old   sh'd adorn
3   5   1   2   4

undique   ceræ   Atria,   nobilitas   sola   est
on every side   waxen figures   halls,   nobility,   the sole   is
7   3   6   5   3   2

atque   unica   virtus.   Paulus,   vel   Cossus,
and   only   virtue.   Paulus,   or   Cossus,
    4   1

vel   Drusus,   moribus   esto: Hos   ante
or   Drusus,   in morals   be you   These   before
                           2   1

effigies   majorum   pone   tuorum: Præcedant
the effigies   ancestors   put   of your: let precede
4   6   1   5   1   3

ipsas   illi,   te Consule   virgas.   Prima   mihi
themselves   them,   you (being) Consul,   the fasces.   (as) first   me
7   2   4   6   3   2

debes   animi   bona.   Sanctus   haberi,
you owe of the mind the virtues. (a man) of-spotless-integrity to be regarded
1   5   4   3   2

Justitiæque   tenax   factis   dictisque   mereris?
and of justice   tenacious   in deeds   and words   do you deserve?
                                                                                      1

Agnosco   procerem.   Salve,   Gætulice,   seu
I acknowledge   the nobleman.   Hail,   Gætulicus,   or

tu   Silanus,   quocunque   alio   de   sanguine,
thou   Silanus,   whatever   other   from   blood,
                              2   3   1

rarus   Civis   et   egregius   patriæ   contingis
a rare   citizen   and   choice,   country   thou-fallest-to-the-lot-of
                                                    3   1

ovanti.   Exclamare   libet,   populus   quod
(thy) rejoicing.   to exclaim   it is permitted,   the people   what
     2   2   1

clamat,   Osiri   Invento.   Quis   enim   generosum
call out   to Osiris   when found.   Who   for   noble
                                                    2   1   3

dixerit   hunc,   qui   Indignus   genere,   et
w'd call   him,   who (is)   unworthy   of (his) race,   and
1   2

præclaro   nomine   tantùm   Insignis?   Nanum
for an illustrious   name   only   remarkable?   the dwarf

cujusdam   Atlanta   vocamus;   Æthiopem   cygnum;
of some one   Atlas   we call;   an Ethiopian,   a swan;

parvam   extortamque   puellam   Europen :   canibus
a little   and deformed   wench,   a Europa: dogs
                                                                                      2

pigris,   scabieque   vetustâ   Levibus,   et
to lazy,   and with mange   an inveterate   smooth,   and
I   2   4   3   1

siccæ   lambentibus   ora   lucernæ,   Nomen   erit
of a dry   licking   the edges   lamp,   the name   will be
3   1   2

pardus,   tigris,   leo,   si   quid   adhuc   est,
leopard,   tiger,   lion, [or]   if   anything   yet   there is,
                                                    2   3   1

Quod   fremat   in   terris   violentiùs.   Ergo
which   rages   on   earth   more violently.   Therefore
6   4   5

cavebis,   Et   metues,   ne   tu   sis
you will beware,   and   fear,   lest   you   be

Creticus   aut   Camerinus.   His   ego quem
(on this principle) a Creticus.   or   a Camerinus,   in these (words)   I   whom
                                                                        5   3   1

monui ?   tecum   est   mihi   sermo,   Rubelli
have admonished?   with you is   my   discourse,   Rubellius
2   4

Plaute. Tumes alto Drusorum stemmate, tanquam
Plautus. You-are-puffed-up with-the-high of the Drusi pedigree, as if
                2   1

Feceris ipse aliquid, propter quod nobilis
had done you yourself something, for which noble
2   1   2

esses, Et te conciperet, quæ sanguine
you sh'd be, and you she conceived, who with the blood
1   2   1

fulget Iuli; Non quæ ventoso conducta
shines of Iulus; not (she) who the windy being hired
1   4   1

sub aggere texit. Vos humiles, inquis,
under rampart has woven. "Ye (are) low," say you,
3   2

vulgi pars ultima nostri, Quorum nemo
populace part the last of our, of whom no one
4   2   1   3

queat patriam monstrare parentis ; Ast
can the country show of his parent; but
     2   1

ego Cecropides. Vivas, et originis hujus
I (am) a Cecropi." may you live, and origin of this
                            2   1

Gaudia longa feras; tamen imâ plebe
the joys long bear; yet from the lowest of the people
3   1   2

Quiritem Facundum invenies : solet hic
Roman an eloquent you will find: is accustomed this one
2   1   2   1

defendere causas Nobilis indocti. Veniet
to defend the causes noble of the ignorant. (There) will come
                    2   1

de plebe togatâ, Qui juris · nodos et
from the people gowned, (one) who of law the knots and
                     1   3   2

legum ænigmata solvat. Hic petit Euphraten
of statutes the enigmas can untie. This seeks the Euphrates
5   4   2   3

juvenis, domitique Batavi Custodes aquilas,
youth, and of conquered Batavus the guardian eagles,
1   3   4   1   2

armis industrius ; at tu Nil, nisi Cecropides,
in arms industrious ; but thou (art) nothing, but a Cecropid,
6   5

truncoque simillimus Hermæ. Nullo quippe
and to a mutilated most like Herma. in no since
2   1   2   1

alio vincis discrimine, quàm quòd Illi
other you excel point-of-difference, than that to him
       2   1   1

marmoreum caput est, tua vivit imago.
a marble head is, thy lives image.
                           2   1

Dic	mihi,	Teucrorum	proles,	animalia
Tell	me,	of Trojans	offspring,	animals
		2	1	4

muta	Quis	generosa	putct,	nisi	fortia?
dumb	who	highly bred	thinks,	unless	spirited?
3	1	5	2		

nempe	volucrem	Sic	laudamus	equum,
for	a swift	thus	we praise	horse,
	3	1	2	

facili	cui	plurima	palma	Fervet,	et
an easy (conqueror)	for whom	many a	palm	glows,	and
2	1				

exsultat	rauco	victoria	Circo.	Nobilis	hic
exults	in the hoarse	victory	Circus.	Noble	that
2		1			

quocunque	venit	de	gramine,	cujus
(horse) whatever	he comes	from	pasture,	whose
2	4	1	3	

Clara	fuga	ante	alios.	et	primus	in
famous	speed (is)	before	others,	and	(is) first	on
2	1				2	

æquore	pulvis:	Sed	venale	pecus	Corythæ
the plain (whose) dust:	But (is) offered for sale	the brood of Corytha
1		3	1	2

posteritas	et	Hirpini,	si	rara	jugo
the posterity	and	of Hirpinus,	if	seldom	on (their) yoke
2	1			3	

victoria	sedit.	Nil	ibi	majorum	respectus,
victory	has perched.	No	in-their-case	of ancestors	regard,
1	2	2	1	4	3

gratia	nulla	Umbrarum:	dominos	pretiis
(is had) favor	no	of shades:	(their) masters	prices
2	1		3	5

mutare	jubentur	Exiguis,	tritoque	trahunt
to change	they are obliged	for paltry,	and with a galled	they draw
2	1	4	3	1

epiredia	collo	Segnipedes,	dignique	molam
wagons	neck	slow of foot,	and worthy	the mill
2				2

versare	Nepotis.	Ergò,	ut	miremur	te,
to turn	of Nepos.	Therefore.	that	we may admire	you,
1					

non	tua,	primum	aliquid	da,	Quod
not	yours,	first	something	exhibit,	which
			2	1	

possim	titulis	incidere	præter	honores,
I may	among (your) titles	inscribe	besides	the honors,
	2	1		

Quos	illis	damus	et	dedimus,	quibus
which	to them	we give	and	have given,	to whom

omnia	debes.	Hæc	satìs	ad	juvenem,
all (things)	you owe.	these (things are) enough	to	the youth,

quem   nobis   fama   superbum   Tradit,   et
whom   to us   fame   proud   delivers,   and
            3   1   2

inflatum,   plenumque   Nerone   propinquo.   Rarus
puffed up,   and full of   Nero (his) kinsman.   Rare
                                                              2

enim   fermè   sensus   communis   in   illâ
for   in general (is) sense   common   in   that
1

Fortunâ.   Sed   te   censeri   laude   tuorum,
rank of life. But   you   to be valued   for the renown of your (ancestors,)

Pontice,   noluerim,   · sic   ut   nihil   ipse
Ponticus,   I sh'd be unwilling,   so   that   nothing   you yourself
                                                          3   1

futuræ   Laudis   agas.   Miserum   est   aliorum
of future   praise   sh'd do.   Miserable   it is   of others
4   2   2   1   5

incumbere   famæ,   Ne   collapsa
to rest on   the fame,   lost   ,   having fallen
3   4   2

ruant   subductis   tecta   columnis.
tumble into ruins taken from under   the house   the columns.
5   4   1   3

Stratus   humi   palmes   viduas   desiderat
strewed   on the ground   the vine   the widowed longs for
2   3   1   5   4

ulmos.   Esto   bonus   miles,   tutor   bonus,
elms.   Be you   a good   soldier,   guardian   a good,
                                               2   1

arbiter   idem   Integer.   Ambiguæ   si   quando
an umpire   likewise   of integrity. of a doubtful if   ever
                                         5   1   2

citabere   testis   Incertæque   rei ;   Phalaris
you shall be summoned as a witness and uncertain   cause;   Phalaris
3   4   2

licet   imperet   ut   sis   Falsus,   et   admoto
tho'   sh'd command   that   you be   False,   and   brought near
1   4

dictet   perjuria,   tauro,   Summum   credo
sh'd dictate   perjuries   with (his) bull, the highest   believe it
1   2   3   2   1

nefas   animam   præferre   pudori,   Et
impiety   life   to prefer   to honor,   and

propter   vitam   vivendi   perdere   causas.
for the sake of life   of living   to lose   the ends.
                            3   1   2

Dignus   morte   perit,   cœnet   licet   ostrea
worthy of   death   he perishes, he sh'd sup on though   oysters
2   3   1   2   1   5

centum   Gaurana,   et   Cosmi   toto   mergatur
a hundred   Gauran,   and   of Cosmus   in the whole sh'd immerse
3   4   2   4

aëno.   Exspectata   diu   tandem   provincia
cauldron.   Expected   long   at length   the province
3   5   4   2   3

quum	te	Rectorem	accipiet,	pone	iræ
when	you	[as its] ruler	shall receive,	put	to anger
1	7	8	6		

fræna	modumque,	pone	et	avaritiæ;	miserere
checks	and a measure,	put	also	to avarice;	pity

inopum	sociorum.	Ossa	vides	regum
the poor	allies.	the bones	you see	of Kings
		2	1	

vacuis	exsucta	medullis.	Respice,	quid
empty	sucked out	the marrow.	Regard,	what
	2	1		

moneant	leges,	quid	curia	mandet,	Præmia
may admonish	the laws,	what	the Senate	enjoines,	Rewards
2	1				

quanta	bonos	maneant,	quàm	fulmine
how great	the good	await,	how	with a stroke
	2	1	2	1 4

justo	Et	Capito	et	Numitor	ruerint,
just	both	Capito	and	Numitor	came to ruin,
3					

damnante	senatu,	Piratæ	Cilicum.	Sed	quid
condemning	the Senate,	Pirates	of the Cilicians.	But	what
2	1				

damnatio	confert,	Quum	Pausa	eripiat,
(their) condemnation	avails,	When	Pansa	seizes,
2	1			

quidquid	tibi	Natta	reliquit?	Præconem,
whatever	you	Natta	left?	a crier,
	3	1	2	

Chærippe,	tuis	circumspice	pannis.	Jamque
Chærippus,	for your	look about for	tattered-clothes.	And now
3	4	1		

tace.	Furor	est	post	omnia	perdere
be silent.	Madness	it is	after	all	to lose

naulum.	Non	idem	gemitus	olim,
(your) passage-money.	(There was) not	the same	lamentation,	formerly

neque	vulnus	erat	par	Damnorum,	sociis
nor	the wound	was	equal	of losses,	our allies
	2	1	4	3	

florentibus	et	modò	victis.	Plena	domus
flourishing	and	just now	conquered.	full	house
				4	3

tunc	omnis,	et	ingens	stabat	acervus
then (was) every		and	a great	(there) was standing	heap
1	2		2	1	

Nummorum,	Spartana	chlamys,	conchylia
of money,	a Spartan	cloak,	purples

Coa,	Et	cum	Parrhasii	tabulis	signisque
of Cos,	and	with	of Parrhasius	pictures	and statues
			2	1	

Myronis,   Phidiacum   vivebat   ebur,   nec non
of Myron   Phidian   breathed   ivory.   also
                  2   1

Polycleti   Multus   ubique   labor :   raræ   sine
of Polycletus   much   everywhere   labor: few   without
4   1   3   2   2

Mentore   mensæ.   Inde   Dolabella   est atque
Mentor   tables.   Thence   Dolabella   is   and
         1   2   1

hinc   Antonius,   inde   Sacrilegus   Verres:
hence   Antony,   then   the sacrilegious   Verres :

referebant   navibus   altis   Occulta   spolia,
they brought back   ships   in deep-laden   hidden   spoils,
                  2   1

et   plures   de   pace   triumphos.   Nunc
and   more   from   peace   triumphs.   Now
             2   3   1

sociis   juga   pauca   boum,   grex   parvus
to our allies   (are) yokes   a few   of oxen,   stock   a small
         2   1   2   1

equarum,   Et   pater   armenti   capto
of mares,   and   the father   of the herd   from-the-captured
                                           2

eripietur   agello ;   Ipsi   deinde   Lares,
will-be-snatched-away   field;   the very   then   Lares,
1   2   1

si   quod   spectabile   signum,   Si   quis   in
if   any   observable   image,   if   any   in
                                        3

ædiculâ   deus   unicus.   Hæc   etenim   sunt
the small shrine   god is   one single   these   for   are
4   2   1   2   1

Pro   summis :   nam   sunt   hæc   maxima. Despicias
for   the highest: since   are   these   the greatest.   may despise
                    2   1   2

tu   Forsitan   imbelles Rhodios,   unctamque Corinthum:
you   perhaps   unwarlike Rhodians,   and anointed   Corinth:
1

Despicias   meritò.   Quid   resinata   juventus,
You may despise (them) deservedly.   What   a resin-smeared   youth,
                                       2   3

Cruraque   totius   facient   tibi   levia   gentis?
and legs   of a whole   will do   to you   the smooth   nation?
4 6   7   1 9   10   5   8

Horrida   vitanda   est   Hispania,   Gallicus
Rugged   must be avoided   Spain,   the Gallic
            2   1

axis,   Illyricumque   latus;   parce   et   messoribus
axle,   and the Illyrian   coast ;   spare   too   reapers
                                       2

illis,   Qui   saturant   urbem,   Circo   scenæque
those   who   overstock   the city,   for the circus   and the theatre
1   2   3

vacantem.	Quanta	autem	inde	feres
having leisure.	How great	but	thence	will you bring
1	2	1	7	6

tam	diræ	præmia	culpæ,	Quum	tenues
of so	dire	rewards	a fault,	since	the slender
4		3	5 .	1	6

nuper	· Marius	discinxerit	Afros?	Curandum
lately	Marius	has disgirdled	Africaus?	care-must-be-taken
4	2	3	5	

in primis,	ne	magna	injuria	fiat	Fortibus
especially,	lest	great	injury	be done	to the brave

et	miseris.	Tollas	licèt	omne	quod
as well as	wretched.	You may take away	though	every, thing)	which
		2	1		

usquam	est	Auri	atque	argenti ;	scutum
anywhere	is	of gold	and	silver;	the shield

gladiumque	relinques,	Et	jacula	et	galeam :
and sword	you will leave,	and	darts	and	helmet ;

spoliatis	arma	supersunt.	Quod	modò
to (them) plundered	arms	remain.	What	just now

proposui	non	est	sententia :	verùm	Credite,
I have set forth	not	is	an opinion :	but	believe,
	2	1			

me	vobis	folium	recitare	Sibyllæ.	Si
me	to you	a leaf	to recite	of the Sibyl.	if
	2	3	1		

tibi	sancta	cohors	comitum,	si	nemo
to you [be]	a virtuous	cohort	of attendants,	if	no

tribunal	Vendit,	Accersecomes,	si	nullum
(your) tribunal	sells,	minion,	if	no
3	2	1		

in	conjuge	crimen,	Nec	per	conventus
in	(your) wife	crime,	Nor	through	the district-courts
2		3	1		

et	cuncta	per	oppida	curvis	Unguibus
and	all	through	the towns	with crooked	talons
	2		1		

ire	parat	nummos	raptura	Celæno :	Tunc
to go she	contrives	money	to seize	a Celæno :	then
4	1	3		5	2

licet	a	Pico	numeres	genus ;	altaque
may	from	Picus	you reckon	descent ;	and high
	3	4		2	1 3

si	te	Nomina	delectant,	omnem	Titanida
if	you	names	delight,	the whole	Titan
2	6	1	5		

pugnam	Inter	majores	ipsumque	Promethea
conflict	among (your)	ancestors	and himself	Prometheus
			2	1

ponas ;	De	quocuuque	voles	proavum
you may place ;	from	whatever	you please	a great grandfather
	4	5	7	3

tibi	sumito	libro.	Quòd	si	præcipitem
to yourself	take	book.	But	if	headlong
2	1	6			4

rapit	ambitio	atque	libido,	Si	frangis
hurry (you)	ambition	and	lust,	if	you break
3	1		2		

virgas	sociorum	in	sanguine,	si	te	Delectant
rods	of allies	in	the blood,	if	you	delight
	3	1	2			3

hebetes	lasso	lictore	secures :	Incipit
blunt	being wearied	the lictor	axes :	begins
1	5	4	2	4

ipsorum	contra	te	stare	parentum	Nobilitas,
themselves	against	you	to stand	of (your) sires	the nobility,
3	6		5	2	1

claramque	facem	præferre	pudendis.	Omne
and a clear	torch	to carry before	(your) shameful deeds.	every

animi	vitium	tanto	conspectius	in	se
of the mind	vice	by so much	more conspicuous	in	itself
2	1	2	3		5

Crimen	habet,	quanto	major,	qui	peccat,
crime	has,	by how much	greater,	(he) who	offends,
4	1	6	10	7	8

habetur.	Quò	mihi	te	solitum	falsas
is accounted.	Why	to me (do you vaunt)	yourself	accustomed	false
0					2

signare	tabellas	In	templis.	quæ	fecit
to sign	wills	in	the temples,	which	built
1					2

avus,	statuamque	parentis	Ante	triumphalem?
[your] grandsire,	and statue	of (your)father	before	the triumphal?
1	3	4	1	2

quò	si	nocturnus	adulter	Tempora	Santonico
why,	if	a nightly	adulterer	(your) brows	by a Santonic
				2	4

velas	adoperta	cucullo?	Præter	majorum
you veil	covered	cowl?	Past	(his)	ancestors:
1	3			

cineres	atque	ossa	volucri	Carpento	rapitur
ashes	and	bones	in rapid	car	is whirled

pinguis	Damasippus,	et	ipse	Ipse	rotam
the fat	Damisrppus,	and	himself,	himself	the wheel
					3

adstringit	multo	sufflamine	Consul :	Nocte
binds	with many	a drag-chain	a Consul:	by night
2			1	

quidem;	sed	luna	videt,	sed	sidera	testes
indeed:	but	the moon	sees,	but	the stars	[being] witnesses

Intenduut	oculos.	Finitum	tempus	honoris
strain	(on him their) eyes.	Finished	the time	of office
		5	2	3

Quum   fuerit,   clarâ   Damasippus   luce
when   shall have been, in-the-clear Damasippus   light
1   4   2   1

flagellum   Sumet,   et   occursum   nunquam
the whip   will take,   and   the meeting   never
                                         3   1

trepidabit   amici   Jam   senis,   ac   virgâ
tremble at   of a friend now   old,   and   with the switch
2

prior   annuet,   atque   maniplos   Solvet,
the first   will nod,   and   the trusses (of hay) will untie,

et   infundet   jumentis   hordea   lassis.   Interea,
and   pour in   beasts   barley   to the tired. meantime,
                          3   1   2

dum   lanatas   torvumque   juvencum   More
while   sheep   and the stalwart   bullock   after the manner

Numæ   cædit   Jovis   ante   altaria,   jurat
of Numa   he slays   Jove's   before   altars,   he swears by
                         2   1

Solam   Eponam   et   facies olida   ad   præsepia
alone   Epona   and   faces the stinking at   stalls
2   1   3   2   4

pictas.   Sed   quum   pervigiles   placet   instaurare
painted.   But   when   open-all-night he pleases   to renew
1   4   1   2

      popinas;   Obvius   assiduo   Syrophœnix
[his visits to] the taverns ; meeting [him] with [his] assiduous a Syrophœnician
              3   6   3   1

udus   amomo   Currit,   Idumææ   Syrophœnix
reeking   perfume   runs,   of the Idumæan a Syrophœnician
2   4   5   3   1

incola   portæ,   Hospitis   affectu   dominum
inhabitant   gate,   of-a-host   with-the-studied-courtesy   "lord"
2   2   1   2

regemque   salutat,   Et   cum   venali   Cyane
and "king"   he salutes (him), and   with   for-sale   Cyane
3   1   3   2

succincta   lagenâ.   Defensor   culpæ   dicet
tucked-up   a bottle.   A defender   of (his) fault will say
1   4

mihi,   fecimus   et   nos   Hæc   juvenes.
to me,   "have done   also   we   these (things when) young men."
             3   2   1

Esto.   Desisti   nempe,   nec   ultra   Fovisti
Be it so.   You left off   surely,   nor   further   cherished

      errorem.   Breve   sit,   quod   turpiter
(your) error.   Brief   let be,   what   basely

audes.   Quædam   cum   primâ   resecentur
you dare.   Some   with   the first   sh'd be cut off
                            3   4   2

crimina   barbâ.   Indulge   veniam   pueris.
crimes   beard.   Indulge   favor   to boys.
1

Damasippus ad illos Thermarum calices
Damasippus to those of the warmbaths cups
                                            3 2

inscriptaque lintea vadit, Maturus bello,
and inscribed linen signs goes, ripe for war,

Armeniæ Syriæque tuendis Amnibus, et
Armenia's and Syria's for guarding rivers, and
2 3 1 4

Rheno atque Istro. Præstare Neronem
the Rhine and Ister. To insure Nero

Securum valet hæc ætas. Mitte Ostia,
safe is able this age. Send to Ostia,
3 1 2

Cæsar, Mitte; sed in magnâ legatum
Cæsar, send; but in a great (your) legate
in legate
3 4 2

quære popinâ. Invenies aliquo cum præcussore
seek tavern. you will find (him) some with cut-throat
1 2 1

jacentem, Permixtum nautis, et furibus,
lying, mixed up with sailors, and thieves,

ac fugitivis, Inter carnifices, et fabros
and run-aways, among executioners, and makers

sandapilarum, Et resupinati cessantia tympana
of coffins, and lying-on-his-back the ceasing drums
4 1 2

Galli. Æqua ibi libertas, communia
Of-a-priest-of-Cybele. [is] equal there liberty, in common
3 2 3 1 2

pocula, lectus Non alius cuiquam, nec
cups, couch not another to any one, nor
1 3 1 2

mensa remotior ulli. Quid facias, talem
a table more remote to any. What w'd you do, such
3

sortitus, Pontice, servum? Nempe in
having-obtained-by-lot, Ponticus, a slave? Surely into
2 1 4 2

Lucanos, aut Tusca ergastula mittas.
the Lucanians, or the Tuscan workhouses you w'd send [him]
3 1

At vos, Trojugenæ, vobis ignoscitis, et
But you, Trojugenæ, yourselves excuse, and

quæ Turpia cerdoni, Volesos Brutumque
what [things] (are) base to a cobler, the Volesi and a Brutus
2

decebunt. Quid, si nunquam adeo fœdis
will become. What, if never so foul
1

adeòque pudendis Utimur exemplis, ut
and so shameful we use examples, that
2 1

non   pejora   supersint?   Consumptis
not   worse   remains behind?   Squandered
                                                  2

opibus   vocem,   Damasippe,   locâsti   Sipario,
[your] riches [your] voice, Damasippus,   you hired   to the stage,
1

clamosum   ageres   ut   Phasma   Catulli.
the noisy   you-might-act that   Phasma   of Catullus.
3   2   1

Laureolum   Velox   etiam   bene   Lentulus
Laureolus   Velox   also   well   Lentulus
6   1   4   5   2

egit,   Judice me,   dignus   verâ   cruce.   Nec
acted,   I being judge,   worthy   a real   cross.   Nor
3

tamen   ipsi   Ignoscas   populo ;   populi
yet   the very   can you excuse people ;   people
              2   1   3

frons   durior   hujus,   Qui   sedet,   et   spectat
the front [is] harder   of this,   Who   sits,   and   beholds
1   4   2

triscurria   patriciorum,   Planipedes   audit   Fabios,
the buffooneries of the patricians, the barefooted hears   Fabii,
                                    2   1

ridere   potest   qui   Mamercorum   alapas.
laugh at   can   who   of the Mamerci   the slaps.
3   2   1   2   1

Quanti   sua   funera   vendant,   Quid   refert ?
At what price their   deaths   they may sell, What   matters it ?

vendunt   nullo   cogente   Nerone,   nec   dubitant
they sell   no   compelling   Nero,   nor   hesitate
                            2   1

celsi   prætoris   vendere   ludis.   Finge tamen
of the lofty prætor   to sell   to the games. imagine yet
3   4   1   2

gladios   inde,   atque   hinc   pulpita
the swords (of a tyrant) on-the-one-hand and   on-the-other   the stage

pone :   Quid   satius?   Mortem   sic   quisquam
place: Which   (is) better ? Death   so   anyone
                                   5   3   2

exhorruit,   ut   sit   Zelotypus   Thymeles,   stupidi
has dreaded, that he sh'd be jealous of Thymele,   of stupid
1   4   2

collega   Corinthi ?   Res   haud   mira   tamen,
the colleague Corinthus?   The thing (is) not   wonderful however,
1

citharædo   Principe,   mimus   Nobilis.
a harper   the Prince (being) a buffoon   (that) the noble (should be)
2   1   2   1

Hæc   ultra,   quid   erit   nisi   ludus?
These (things) beyond,   what   will there be but   the amphitheatre?
2   1

Et   illud   Dedecus   Urbis   habes: nec
and   that   disgrace   of the city   you have: neither
    3

mirmillonis   in   armis,   Nec   clypeo   Gracchum
of a mirmillo   in   the arms,   nor   with the shield   Gracchus
    5   4   6   7   1

pugnantem,   aut   falce   supinâ;   (Damnat   enim
fighting,   or   faulchion   flat.   (he condemns   for
    2   8   10   9   2   1

tales   habitus;   sed   damnat,   et   odit)   Nec
such   equipments;   yea   condemns,   and   hates)   Nor

galeâ   frontem   abscondit;   movet   ecce
with a helmet   his face   does he conceal;   he wields   see!
    3   2   1   2   1

tridentem,   Postquam   libratâ   pendentia   retia
a trident,   after   from (his) poised   hanging   the nets
                3   2   1

dextrâ   Nequidquam   effudit,   nudum   ad spectacula
right hand   without effect   he has cast,   exposed   to the spectators
         2   1   3

vultum   Erigit,   et   tota   fugit   agnoscendus
(his) face   he erects,   and by-the-whole   flees   to be recognised
    2   1   3   1   2

arenâ.   Credamus   tunicæ,   de   faucibus
arena   let us trust   to the tunic,   from   (his) jaws
                                          5

aurea   quum   Porrigat,   et   longo   jactetur
a golden   since   reaches,   and   from the long   is tossed
    2   1   4   6   8   7

spira   galero,   Ergò   ignominiam   graviorem
band   cap,   Therefore   ignominy   a heavier
    3   9   1   5   4

pertulit   omni   Vulnere,   cum   Graccho
bore   than any   wound,   with   Gracchus
    3   6   7   10   11

jussus   pugnare   secutor.   Libera   si   dentur
commanded   to fight   the Secutor.   Free   if   were given
    8   9   2   2   1   4

populo   suffragia,   quis   tam   Perditus,   ut
to the people   suffrages,   who   so   lost,   that
    5   3

dubitet   Senecam   præferre   Neroni?   Cujus
he w'd hesitate   Seneca   to prefer   to Nero?   for whose
         2   1

supplicio   non   debuit   una   parari   Simia,
punishment   not   ought   one   to be prepared   ape,
                   3   1   4   2

nec   serpens   unus,   nec   culeus   unus?
nor   serpent   one,   nor   sack   one?
         2   1   2   1

Par   Agamemnonidæ   crimen;   sed   causa   facit
(was) equal   of the son of Agamemnon, the crime: but the motive makes
    3   2   1

rem	Dissimilem.	Quippe	ille,	deis	au ctoribus
a thing	unlike.	Since	he,	the gods [being] instigators	

ultor	Patris	erat	cæsi	media inter
the avenger	of a father	was	slain	amidst (his)
	2	1		

pocula;	sed	nec	Electræ	jugulo	se	polluit
cups;	but	neither	with Electra's	throat	himself	he polluted

aut	Spartani	Sanguine	conjugii,	nullis	aconita
nor	of Spartan	with the blood	wedlock,	for no	poison
	2	1	3	2	1

propinquis	Miscuit;	in	scenâ	nunquam
relations	did he mix;	on	the stage	never
				2

cantavit	Orestes:	Troïca	non	scripsit.
sang	Orestes	Troies	not	wrote.
	1		2	1

Quid	enim	Virginius	armis	Debuit
What	for	Virginius	with (his) arms	ought
2	1	4	5	3

ulcisci	magis,	aut	cum	Vindice
to avenge	rather,	or	with	Vindex
7	6		2	

Galba?	Quid	Nero	tam	sævâ	crudâque
Galba?	What	Nero	so	cruel	and bloody
1		2			

tyrannide	fecit?	Hæc	opera,	atque	hæ
in a tyranny	did?	These	the works,	and	these
3	1				

sunt	generosi	Principis	artes	Gaudentis
are	of a noble	Prince	the arts	rejoicing
	2	3	1	

fœdo	peregrina	ad	pulpita	cantu	Prostitui,
with foul	foreign	on	stages	singing	to be prostituted,
	3		2	1	

Graiæque	apium	meruisse	coronæ.
and of a Grecian	the parsley	to have deserved	crown.
3	2		1

Majorum	effigies	habeant	insignia	vocis:
of (your) ancestors	the statues	let have	the insignia of (your)	voice:
3	2	1	4	

Ante	pedes	Domiti	longum	tu	pone
before	the feet	of Domitius	the long	you	place
			3	2	1

Thyestæ	Syrma	vel	Antigones,	seu
of Thyestes	train	or	of Antigone,	or
5	4			

personam	Menalippes,	Et	de	marmoreo
the mask	of Menalippe,	and	from	a marble
			3	4

citharam	suspende	colosso.	Quid,	Catilina,
a harp	suspend	colossus.	What,	O Catiline,
2	1			

tuis	natalibus,	atque	Cethegi,	Inveniet
than thy	lineage,	and (that)	of Cethegus,	shall find
5				1 3

quisquam	sublimius?	Arma	tamen	vos
any one	more lofty?	arms	yet	you
2	4	3	1	2

Nocturna	et	flammas	domibus	templisque
nocturnal	and	flames	for houses	and temples

parûstis,	Ut	Braccatorum	pueri,	Senonumque
prepared,	as (though you were)	of the Gauls	sons,	and of-the-Senones
		2	1	2

minores,	Ausi,	quod	liceat	tunicâ	punire
the posterity,	having dared,	what	it w'd be right	coat	to punish
1				3	1

molestâ.	Sed	vigilat	Consul,	vexillaque
with-a-pitched.	But	is vigilant	the Consul,	and banners
2		2	1	3

vestra	coërcet.	Hic	novus	Arpinas,	ignobilis,
your	restrains.	This	new	man of Arpinum,	ignoble,
2	1				

et	modò	Romæ	Municipalis	Eques,	galeatum
and	lately	at Rome	a municipal	Knight,	a helmeted
					3

ponit	ubique	Præsidium	attonitis,
puts	everywhere	safeguard	for the terrified (people,)
1	2		

et	in omni gente	laborat.	Tantum	igitur
and	everywhere	labours.	So much	therefore
			7	1

muros	intra	toga	contulit	illi	Nominis
the walls	within	the toga	conferred	on him	of name
6	5	2	3	4	8

et	tituli,	quantum	non	Leucade,	quantum
and	title,	as	not	from Leucas,	as [not]
	9				

Thessaliæ	campis	Octavius	abstulit	udo
of Thessaly	from the plains	Octavius	brought away	wet
2	1			2

Cædibus	assiduis	gladio. Sed	Roma	parentem,
slaughters	with continual	by the sword. But	Rome	the parent,
4	3	1		

Roma	patrem	patriæ	Ciceronem	libera
Rome	the father	of his country	Cicero	set free
	4		3	1

dixit.	Arpinas	alius	Volscorum	in monte
called.	Arpinian	another	of the Volsci	in the mountain
2	2	1	5	3 4

solebat	Poscere	mercedes	alieno	lassus
used	to demand	wages	with another's	tired
			2	1

aratro;	Nodosam	post	hæc	frangebat
plough;	a knotty	after	this	he broke
	4	1	2	3

vertice   vitem,   Si   lentus   pigrâ   muniret
with [his] head vine,   if   idle   with a lazy he fortified
6   5   3   1

castra   dolabrâ.   Hic   tamen   et   Cimbros
the camp   axe.   he   yet   both   the Cimbri
2   2   1

et   summa   pericula   rerum   Excipit,   et
and   the greatest   dangers   of affairs   sustains,   and

solus   trepidantem   protegit   Urbem.   Atque
alone   the trembling   protects   City.   and
            2   1

ideo,   postquam   ad   Cimbros   stragemque
so,   after   to   the Cimbri   and the slaughter

volabant,   Qui   nunquam   attigerant   majora
flew,   that   never   had touched   greater
        2   3   4

cadavera,   corvi,   Nobilis   ornatur   lauro
carcasses,   the crows,   [his] noble   is adorned   laurel
            1   2   4

collega   secundâ.   Plebeiæ   Deciorum
colleague   with-the-second.   plebeian   of the Decii
1   3   2

animæ,   plebeia   fuerunt   Nomina :
the souls,   plebeian   were   [their] names :
1

pro   totis   legionibus   hi   tamen
for   whole   legions   these   yet
3   2   1

et pro   Omnibus   auxiliis,   atque   omni   pube
and for   all   auxiliaries,   and   all   the flower

Latinâ,   Sufficiunt   dis   infernis   Terræque
of Latium   Suffice   for the gods   infernal   and the earth
                                                    2

parenti :   Pluris   enim   Decii,   quam   quæ
parent :   of more (value)   for   (were) the Decii, [to them] than   than   what
                2   1

servantur   ab   illis.   Ancillâ   natus   trabeam,
were preserved   by   them.   of-a-servant-maid   born   the robe,

et   diadema   Quirini,   Et   fasces   meruit
and   diadem   of Romulus,   and   the fasces   deserved
                                                5

regum   ultimus   ille   bonorum.   Prodita
Kings   last   that   of good.   Betrayed
4   2   1   3   7

laxabant   portarum   claustra   tyrannis   Exsulibus
were loosening   of the gates   the fastenings   tyrants   to exiled
4   6   5   9   8

juvenes   ipsius   Consulis,   et   quos   Magnum
the youths   himself   of the Consul,   and   whom   great (thing)
1   3   2   2

aliquid   dubia   pro   libertate   deceret,   Quod
some   doubtful   for   liberty   might become,   Which
1   4   3

(13)

miraretur   cum   Coclite   Mucius   Et   quæ
might admire   with   Cocles   Mucius,   and   who
    4   2   3   1   2

Imperii   fines   Tiberinum   virgo   natavit.
of the empire (then) the limit the Tiber   the virgin   swam.
    6   5   4   1   3

Occulta   ad   patres   produxit   crimina   servus
[their] hidden   to   the fathers   produced   crimes   a slave
    5   7   8   4   6   1

Matronis   lugendus :   at   illos   verbera   justis
by matrons   to be bewailed :   but   them   stripes   with just
    3   2   3   1   4

Afficiunt   pœnis,   et   legum   prima   securis.   Malo
affect   punishments, and   of the laws   the first   axe.   I had rather
    2

pater   tibi   sit   Thersites,   dummodo   tu   sis
father   to you   were   Thersites,   provided   you   were
    3   4   2   1

Æacidæ   similis,   Vulcaniaque   arma   capessas,
Achilles   like,   and the Vulcanian   arms   c'd wield,
    2   1

Quàm   te   Thersitæ   similem   producat   Achilles.
than   you   Thersites   like   sh'd produce   Achilles.
          3   5   4   2   1

Et   tamen,   ut   longè   repetas,   longèque
and   yet,   however   far   you go back,   and (however) far

revolvas   Nomen,   ab   infami   gentem
you trace   your name   from   an infamous   (your) race
                                 3   4   2

deducis   asylo.   Majorum   primus   quisquis
you deduce   asylum.   ancestors   the first   whoever
    1   5   3   1   4

fuit   ille   tuorum,   Aut   pastor   fuit,
was   that   of your,   either   a shepherd   was
    6   5   2

aut   illud,   quod   dicere   nolo.
or   that,   which   to say   I am unwilling.

SATIRE IX.

ARGUMENT.

The Satire consists of a dialogue between the poet and one Nævolus, a dependant of some wealthy debauchee, who, after making him subservient to his unnatural passions, in return, starved, insulted, hated, and discarded him. The whole object seems to be, to inculcate the grand moral lesson, that, under any circumstances, a life of sin is a life of slavery.

SCIRE	velim,	quare	toties	mihi,	Nævole,
Know	I would,	why	so often	me,	Nævolus,

tristis	Occurras	fronte	obductâ,	ceu	Marsya
sad	you meet,	with brow	clouded,	like	Marsya

victus.	Quid	tibi	cum	vultu,	qualem
conquered.	What	to you	with	a countenance,	such as

deprénsus	habebat	Ravola,	dum	Rhodopes
the detected	had	Ravola,	when	Rhodope
	2	1		

udâ	terit	inguina	barbâ ?	Nos	colaphum
with a wet	rubs	his groins	beard ?	We	a box on the ear
3	1	2			2

incutimus	lambenti	crustula	servo.	Non
give	licking	the sweet-meats	to a slave.	Not
1	4		3	

erat	hûc	facie	miserabilior	Crepereius
was	than this	face	more woe-begone	Crepereius
4	2	3	1	

Pollio,	qui	triplicem	usuram	præstare
Pollio,	who	triple	interest	to pay
		3	4	2

paratus	Circuit	et	fatuos	non	invenit.
ready	went around	and	fools	not	found.
1			3	2	1

Unde	repentè	Tot	rugæ ?	certè	modico
Whence of-a-sudden	so many	wrinkles ?	certainly	with a moderate (sum)	

contentus   agebas   Vernam   equitem,   conviva
content   you-acted   slave   the knight,   guest
                     2   1   2

joco   mordente   facetus,   Et salibus   vehemens
jest   with biting   a facetious,   and with witticisms   quick
4   3   1   2   1

intra   pomœria   natis.   Omnia   nunc   contrà :
within   the-city-bounds,   born.   All   now   the reverse :
4   3

vultus   gravis,   horrida   siccæ   Silva comæ,
countenance   a heavy,   a rough   of dry   wood   hair,
2   1   1   3   2

nullus   totâ   nitor   in   cute,   qualem
no   all   sleekness   in   your skin,   such as
1   4   2   3

Bruttia   præstabat   calidi   tibi   fascia   visci :
the Bruttian   afforded   of warm   you   plaster   pitch ;
1   5   3   6   2   4

Sed   fruticante   pilo   neglecta   et   squaladi
But   with growing   hair   neglected   and   foul
4   2   3

crura.   Quid   macies   ægri   veteris,   quem
(your) legs (are).   What (means) the leanness of a sick   old (man),   whom
1

tempore   longo   Torret   quarta   dies,   olimque
time   for a long   parches   a fourth   day,   and long since
2   1   3   1   2

domestica   febris ?   Deprèndas   animi   tormenta
familiar   fever ?   you may detect   of a mind   the torments
                                2   1

latentis   in   ægro   Corpore,   deprèndas   et
lurking   in   a sick   body,   you may detect   also

gaudia :   sumit   utrumque   Iudè   habitum
the joys :   takes   each   from thence   habit
4   1   5   2

facies.   Igitur   flexisse   videris   Propositum
the face.   Therefore   to have turned   you seem   (your) purpose
3   2   1

et   vitæ   contrarius   ire   priori.   Nuper
and   life   contrary   to go   to (your) former.   Lately
4   2   1   3   2

enim,   ut   repeto,   fanum   Isidis,   et
for,   as   I recollect,   the temple   of Isis,   and
1

Ganymeden   Pacis   et   advectæ   secreta
the Ganymede   of [the temple of] Peace and   of the imported   the secret
3   1

palatia   Matris,   Et   Cererem   (nam   quo
palaces   mother [of the gods], and   Ceres   [for   in what
2

non   prostat   fœmina   templo ?)   Notior
not   stands-for-hire   a woman   temple ?]   more known
3   2   5   6   4   1   2

Aufidio   mœchus   celebrare   solebas,
than Aufidius   an adulterer   to frequent   you used
3   1   5   4

(Quod   taceo)   atque   ipsos   etiam   inclinare
(waich not to mention) and   themselves   even   to incline to
      2   1   6   4   3

maritos.   Utile   et   hoc   multis   vitæ   genus :
the husbands. useful   even this to many   of life   kind
      5   3   2   1

at   mihi   nullum   Inde   operæ   pretium.   Pingues
but   to me   no   thence of (my) pains reward.   greasy
                          3   2   1

aliquando   lacernas,   Munimenta   togæ,   duri
sometimes   cloaks,   defences   of the gown,   of a hard
      2   1

crassique   coloris,   et   malè   percussas   textoris
and homely   color,   and   badly   stricken   weaver
                                                            3

pectine   Galli   Accipimus,   tenue   argentum
with-the-slay of a Gallic We receive,   thin   money
      1   2

venæque   secundæ.   Fata   regunt   homines.   Fatum
and of the vein second.   The fates   rule   men.   Fate
      2   1

est   in   partibus   illis   Quas   sinus   abscondit :
is   in   parts   those   which   the lappet (of the toga) hides:
                 2   1

nam   si   tibi   sidera   cessant,   nil   faciet   longi
for   if   you   (your) stars   fail,   nothing will do   of the long
             3   1   2   6   5   2

mensura   incognita   nervi :   Quamvis   te   nudum
the measure unknown   nerve :   though   you   naked
      1   4   3   5   6

spumanti   Virro   labello   Viderit,   et   blandæ,
with foaming Virro   lip   sh'd see,   and   kind,
      2   1   3   4

assiduæ,   densæque,   tabellæ   sollicitent :
assiduous,   and numerous,   letters   sh'd solicit:

Ἀὸτὸς   γάρ   ἐφέλχεται   ἀνδρα   χίναιδος.
a very   for   seduces   a man   catamite.
      2   1   4   3

Quod   tamen   ulterius   monstrum,   quàm   ·mollis
What   yet   worse   monster   than   an effeminate
      2   1   4   3

avarus?   Hæc   tribui,   deinde   illa   dedi
miser?   "These (things) I bestowed,   then   those   I gave

mox   plura   tulisti.   Computat   ac   covet.
soon   more   you had.   He-reckons-up   and   sins on.

Ponatur   calculus,   adsint   Cum   tabulâ
Let-be settled the account, let be present with   the account-book

pueri :   numera   sestertia   quinque   Omnibus
the slaves: number   sestertia   five   all
                                                    2

in   rebus :   numerentur   deinde   labores.   An
in   things :   let be reckoned   then   (my) labors.
1

facile   et   pronum   est,   agere   intra   viscera

penem Legitimum, atque illic histernæ occurrere
cœnæ? Servus erit minus ille miser, qui
       slave   will be   less   that   miserable,   who
                 2

foderit agrum, Quam dominum. Sed tu
shall dig the field, than (his) master. But you

sanè tener et puerum te, Et pulchrum,
truly [are] delicate and a boy, yourself, and beautiful,

et dignum cyatho cœloque putabas. Vos
and worthy of the cup and heaven thought. [will] you

humili asseculæ, vos indulgebitis unquam
an humble dependant, will you indulge ever

    Cultori, jam nec morbo donare
one-who-pays-court, (who are) now not to [your] disease to give
                                                    2

parati? En cui tu viridem umbellam, cui
ready?" Behold to whom you a green parasol, to whom
  1

succina mittas Grandia, natalis quoties
ambers you must send large, his birth-day as often as

redit, aut madinum ver Incipit; et stratâ
returns, or wet spring begins; and on a pillowed
                                                      2

positus longâque cathedrâ munera fœmineis
placed and long couch gifts for the female
  1   2   4

tractat secreta calendis. Dic, passer, cui
he handles set apart calends. Say, sparrow, for whom
  1   3   5

tot montes, tot prædia servas Appula, tot
so many mountains, so many farms you keep Appulian, so many
                               2   3   1

milvos intra tua pascua lassos? Te Trifolinus
kites within your pastures tired? You a Trifoline
             2   1

ager fœcundis vitibus implet, Suspectumque
estate with fruitful vines fills. and looking up
                                              2

jugum Cumis, et Gaurus inanis. Nam quis
the hill at Cumæ, and Gaurus caverned. For who
  1   2   1

plura linit victuro dolia musto?
more seals up destined-to-live casks with wine?
  2   1   5   3   4

Quantum erat exhausti lumbos donare
How great (a matter) had it been of an exhausted the loins to present
                          3   2   1

clientis Jugeribus paucis? meliusne hic
client acres with a few? is it better this
  4   2   1

rusticus infans, Cum matre, et casulis, et
rustic infant, with mother, and hovel, and

collusore catello, Cymbala pulsantis legatum
playmate cur, the Cymbals beating the legacy
                      5   4   2

fiet amici? Improbus es, quum poscis,
sh'd become of a friend? "Impudent you are, when you ask"
  1   3

ait : sed pensio clamat, Posce ; sed
he says; "but rent cries out, 'Beg' but

appellat puer unicus, ut Polyphemi Lata
calls slave my only, as Polyphemes' broad
  3   2   1

acies, per quam solers evasit Ulixes.
eye, by which crafty escaped Ulysses
                  2   1

Alter emendus erit : namque hic non
another will-have-to-be-bought : for this does not

sufficit : ambo Pascendi: Quid agam brumâ?
suffice: both (are) to be fed What shall I do in winter?

spirante, quid oro, Quid dicam scapulis
whistl.ng, what, I pray, What shall I say to the shoulders
  3   4   5

puerorum Aquilone Decembri Et pedibus ?
of [my] slaves north wind the December and to [their] feet?
            2   1

durate atque exspectate cicadas? Verum,
bear up and wait for the grasshoppers?" But,

ut dissimules, ut mittas cætera,
however you may dissemble, however you may pass by other (matters ,

quanto Metiris pretio, quod ni tibi
at how great do you reckon it a price, that unless to you
         2   1

deditus essem, Devotusque cliens, uxor tua
a resigned I had been and devoted client, wife your
  2   1   2   1

virgo maneret? scis certe quibus ista
a virgin would remain? you know certainly by what those (things)
  4   3   5

modis, quám sæpe rogaris, Et quæ
methods, how often you asked, and what
  1   2   3   4

pollicitus ; fugientem sæpe puellam Amplexu
promised; the flying how often girl in (my) embrace

rapui : tabulas quoque ruperat, et jam
I caught : the marriage contract also she had broken, and now

Signabat; totâ vix hoc ego nocte redimi,
was signing (another); in a whole hardly this I night redeemed,
               5   2   4   1   6   3

Te plorante foris. testis mihi lectulus, et tu,
you whimpering outside-the-door. a witness to me (is)the bed, and you,

Ad   quem   pervenit   lecti   sonus,   et   dominæ
to   whom   came through   of the bed   the sound,   and   the lady's
                                        2   1

vox.   Instabile,   ac   dirimi   coeptum,   et   jam
groan.   unstable,   and   to-be-broken-off   begun,   and   now
                2   4   3   5   6

pæue   solutum   conjugium   in   multis   domibus
nearly   dissolved   wedlock   in   many   houses
7   8   1   10

servavit   adulter!   Quo   te   circumagas?   quæ
has preserved   an adulterer!   Whither   yourself   can you turn?   what
            9

prima   aut   ultima   ponas?   Nullum   ergo   meritum
first   or   last   can you place?   No   therefore   merit

est,   ingrate   ac   perfide,   nullum,   Quòd
is there,   ungrateful   and   perfidious (man),   none,   that

tibi   filiolus,   quod   filia   nascitur   ex   me?
to you   a little son,   that   a daughter   is born   from   me?

Tollis   enim,   et   libris   actorum   spargere
you-bring [them] up for,   and   in the books   of the acts   to publish
2   1   2

gaudes   Argumenta   viri.   Foribus   suspende
you delight   the evidence   of virility.   at the doors   suspend
1

coronas,   Jam   pater   es: dedimus   quod
garlands,   now   a father   you are: we have given   what
            2   1

famæ   opponere   possis: Jura   parentis
to scandal   oppose   you can: the rights   of a parent
3   2   1

habes,   propter   me   scriberis   hæres,   Legatum
you have,   by-means-of   me   you-are-written   heir,   the legacy

omne   capis,   nec   non   et   dulce   caducum.
all   you take,   nor   not   also   a pleasant   windfall.

Commoda   præterea   jungentur   multa   caducis·
advantages   moreover   will be joined   many to the windfalls.
2   3   1

Si   numerum,   si   tres   implevero,   Justa
if   the number,   if   three   I fill up.   Just
                                            4

doloris,   Nævole,   causa   tui.   Contra   tamen
grief [is]   Nævolus,   the cause   of thy.   in reply   yet
3   5   1   2   5   1

ille   quid   affert: Negligit   atque   alium
he   what   brings: "He neglects [me],   and   another
4   2   3   2

bipedem   sibi   quærit   asellum.   Hæc   soli
two-legged   for himself   seeks   ass.   These [things] alone
3   5   1   4   3   6

commissa   tibi   celare   memento,   Et   tacitus
committed   to yourself to conceal remember,   and   silent.
4   5   2   1

nostras   intra   te   fige   querelas.   Nam
our   within   you   fix   complaints.   For
4   2   3   1

res   mortifera   est   inimicus   pumice   levis.
thing   a deadly   is   an enemy with pumice-stone smooth.
7   6   5   1   3   2

Qui   modò   secretum,   commiserat   ardet,
(he) who   lately   the secret,   committed   burns,

et   odit,   Tanquam   prodiderim,   quidquid
and   hates,   as if   I betrayed,   whatever

scio.   Sumere   ferrum,   Fuste   aperire   caput,
I know.   to take   the sword, with a club to open (my) head,

candelam   apponere   valvis,   Non   dubitat.
a candle   to put   to my doors,   not   he hesitates.

Nec   contemnas   aut   despicias,   quòd   His
neither   contemn   nor   despise,   that   to these

opibus   nunquam   cara   est   annona   veneni.
riches   never   dear   is   the provision of poison.

Ergò   occulta   teges,   ut   curia   Martis
Therefore   secrets   you conceal, as   the court   of Mars

Athenis.   O Corydon,   Corydon,   secretum
at Athens. [JUV.] O Corydon,   Corydon,   secret
                                                    2

divitis   ullum   Esse   putas?   Servi   ut
of a rich man any   to be   do you think? (his) servants though
3   1   2   1

taceant;   jumenta   loquentur,   Et   canis
sh'd be silent; the cattle   will speak,   and   the dog

et   postes,   et   marmora.   Claude   fenestras,
and   the posts, and   the marbles.   Shut   the windows,

Vela   tegant   rimas,   junge   ostia,   tollite
let curtains cover   the chinks, close   the doors, take

lumen   E medio;   taceant   omnes,   propè
the light   out of the midst; let be silent all,   near
                                                    4

nemo   recumbat: Quod   tamen   ad   cantum
no one   let-lie: What   yet   at   the crowing
2   1   3   2   1   6

galli   facit   ille   secundi,   Proximus   ante
cock   does   he   of the second, the next   before
8   4   3   7   3

diem   caupo   sciet;   audiet   et   quæ
day   vintner   will know; will hear   and   what
4   1   2   2   1

Finxerunt · pariter · librarius, · archimagiri,
have fabricated · together · the steward, · the master-cooks,
4 · 5 · 1 · 2

Carptores. · Quod · enim · dubitant · componere
the carvers. · What · for · do they scruple · to frame
3 · 2 · 1

crimen · In · dominos, · quoties · rumoribus
crime · against (their) masters, · as often as · by rumors
3 · 3

ulciscuntur · Baltea? · Nec · deerit, · qui
are revenged · straps ? · nor · will-there-be-wanting (one), who
2 · 1

te · per · compita · quærat · Nolentem, · et
you · along · the public-thoroughfares · seeks · unwilling, · and
2 · 1

miseram · vinosus · inebriet · aurem. · Illos
(your) wretched · smelling-of-wine · inebriates · ear. · them
3 · 1 · 2 · 4 · 3

ergò · roges, · quidquid · paulò · antè · petebas
therefore · ask, · what · a little · before · you begged
1 · 2

A · nobis: · Taceant · illi: · sed · prodere
from · us: · be silent · (that) they: · why · betray
2 · 1

malunt · Arcanum, · quàm · subrepti · potare
they would rather · a secret, · than · of stolen · to drink
2

Falerni, · Pro · populo · faciens · quantum
Falernian, · for · the people (when) · sacrificing · as-much-as
1 · 6 · 5 · 3

Saufeia · bibebat. · Vivendum · rectè est, · cùm
Saufeia · used to drink. · one sh'd live · rightly, · as well
4 · 5

propter · plurima, · tum · his · Præcipuè · causis,
on-account-of · many things. · as · for these · especially · causes,
2 · 1

ut · linguas · mancipiorum · Contemnas: · nam
that · the tongue · of servants · you may despise: · for

lingua · mali · pars · pessima · servi. · Deterior
the tongue (is) · of a bad · part · the worst · servant. · worse
3 · 2 · 1

tamen · hic, · qui · liber · non · erit · illis,
yet · (is) he, · who · free · not · will be · (than) those

Quorum · animas · et · farre suo · custodit · et
whose · lives · both · with his corn · he preserves · and

ære. · Idcirco · ut · possim · linguam · contemnere
money (N.Ev.) · therefore · that · I may be able · the tongue · to despise

servi, · Utile · consilium · modò, · sed · commune,
of a servant, · useful · counsel · just-now, · but · common,

dedisti: · Nunc · mihi · quid · suades · post
you have given: · now · me · what · do you advise · after

damnum	temporis,	et	spes	Deceptas ?
loss	of time,	and	hopes	deceived ?

Festinat	enim	decurrere	velox	Flosculus,
hastens	for	to flee away	the short-lived	little-flower,
9	1	10	2	3

angustæ	miseræque	brevissima	vitæ	Portio :
of a contracted	and miserable	the very brief	life	portion :
6	7	4	8	5

dum	bibimus,	dum	serta,	unguenta,	puellas
while	we drink,	while	garlands,	ointments,	girls

Poscimus,	obrepit	non	intellecta	senectus·
we call for,	creeps upon (us)	not	perceived	old age.
4		2	3	1

Ne	trepida :	nunquam	pathicus	tibi
(Juv) not	fear :	never	a pathic	to you
2	1	3	1	5

deerit	amicus,	Stantibus	et	salvis	his
will-be-wanting	friend,	standing	and	safe	these
4	2	3			1

collibus ;	undique	ad	illos	Convenient,
hills ;	from everywhere	to	them	will flock,
2				

et	carpentis	et	navibus,	omnes,	Qui
both	in carriages	and	ships,	all.	who

digito	scalpunt	uno	caput.	Altera	major
finger	scratch	with one	the head.	Another	greater
4	1	3	2		

Spes	superest :	tu	tantùm	crucis	imprime
hope	remains :	thou	only	on cringe	impress
		3	1	5	2

dentem.	Hæc	exempla	para	felicibus :
(thy) tooth (Næv.)	These	examples	prepare	for the fortunate :
4				

at	mea	Clotho	Et	Lachesis	gaudent,
but	my	Clotho	and	Lachesis	rejoice,

si	pascitur	inguine	venter.	O parvi,
if	is fed	by the groin	(my) belly.	O little,
	2	3	1	

nostrique	Lares,	quos	thure	minuto,	Aut
and our	Lares,	whom with frankincense	minute,	or	

farre,	et	tenui	soleo	exorare	coronâ,
meal,	and	with a slender	I am wont	to supplicate	garland,
			2	3	1

Quando	ego	figam	aliquid,
when	I	shall fix	anything,
	2	1	

quo	sit	mihi	tuta	senectus
by which	may be	to me	secure	an old-age
			2	1

A	tegete	et	baculo?	viginti	millia
from	the rug	and	staff?	twenty	thousand (sesterces)

fœnus　Pignoribus　positis,　argenti　vascula
(as) interest　with pledges　put down,　silver　the little vessels
　　　　　　　　　　　　　　　　　　　3　　　1

puri,　sed　quæ　Fabricius　censor　notet,
of pure,　but　which　Fabricius,　the censor　w'd note,
2

et　duo　fortes　De　grege　Mœsorum,　qui
and　two　strong (ones)　from　the herd　of the Mœsi,　who

me　cervice　locatâ　Securum　jubeant
me　(their) neck　being placed (under me)　secure　may command
4　　1　　　2　　　6　　3

clamoso　insistere　Circo.　Sit　mihi　præterea
in the noisy　to stand　Circus.　Let there be　to me　besides
7　　　5

.　curvus　cœlator,　et　alter,　Qui　multas
stooping (over his work)　an engraver, and　another,　who　many
2　　1

facies　fingat　cito.　Sufficient　hæc,　Quando
faces　can paint　quickly.　Will suffice　these (things,)　Since
　　　　　　　　2　　1

ego　pauper　ero.　Votum　miserabile,　nec
I　poor　shall (ever) be.　Wish　a wretched　nor
I　　　　　　　　　　　　　1

spes　His　saltem :　nam,　quum　pro　me
(is there) hope　for these　even :　for　when　for　me

Fortuna　rogatur,　Affigit　ceras　illâ　de　nave
Fortune　is invoked,　she puts　wax (in her ears)　that　from　ship
　　　　　　　　　　　　　　3　　2　　4

petitas,　Quæ　Siculos　cantus　effugit　remige
fetched,　which　the Sicilian　songs .　escaped　rower
1　　　　　　　　　　　　　　　　　3

surdo
with a deaf.
1　2

SATIRE X.

ARGUMENT. ·

The subject of this inimitable Satire is the vanity of human wishes. From the principal events of the lives of the most illustrious characters of all ages, the poet shows how little happiness is promoted by the attainment of what our indistinct and limited views represent as the greatest of earthly blessings. Of these he instances wealth, power, eloquence, military glory, longevity, and personal accomplishments; all of which, he shows have proved dangerous or destructive to their respective possessors. Hence, he argues the wisdom of acquiescing in the dispensations of Heaven; and concludes with a form of prayer, in which he points out with great force and beauty the objects for which a rational being may presume to approach the Almighty.

Omnibus	in	terris,	quæ	sunt	a	Gadibus
all	in	lands,	which	are	from	Gades
2	1					

usque	Auroram	et	Gangen,	pauci	dignoscere
even to	the east	and	Ganges,	few	to know apart

possunt	Vera	bona	atque	illis	multùm
are able	real	blessings	and [those]	from them	much
				3	1

diversa,	remotâ	Erroris	nebulâ.	Quid	enim
different,	being removed	of error	the mist.	What	for
2	3	2	1	2	1

ratione	timemus	Aut	cupimus?	quid	tam
with reason	do we fear	or	desire?	what	with so

dextro	pede	concipis,	ut	te	Conatus	non
right	a foot	do you conceive,	that	you	of the attempt	not

pœniteat	votique	peracti?	Evertère	domos
it repents	and of [your] wish	accomplished?	Have overthrown	families
			3	5

(14)

totas,   optantibus   ipsis,   Di   faciles.
whole,   desiring (it)   themselves,   gods   the easy.
4   7   6   2   1

Nocitura   togâ,   nocitura   petuntur
things-that-will-injure   in-peace,   that-will-injure   are-asked-for
                2

Militiâ.   Torrens   dicendi   copia   multis,   Et
in war.   The torrent   of speaking   copiousness   to many,   and
1   2   1   5   6

sua   mortifera   est   facundia.   Viribus   ille
their   fatal   is   eloquence.   in strength   that [man]
7   4   3   8   3   1

Confisus   periit   admirandisque   lacertis.   Sed
having trusted   perished   and wondrous   muscle.   But
2   6   4   5

plures   nimiâ   congesta   pecunia   curâ
many   with too much   heaped up   money   care
16   3   2   1   4

Strangulat,   et   cuncta   exsuperans   patrimonia   census,
strangles,   and   all   surpassing   patrimonies   a revenue
15   5   8   7   9   6

Quantò   delphinis·   balæna   Britannica   major.
as much as   [than] dolphins   whale   the British   (is) greater.
10   14   12   11   13

Temporibus   diris   igitur   jussuque   Neronis,
in times   dire   therefore   and by the command   of Nero,

Longinum   et   magnos   Senecæ   prædivitis
Longinus   and   the great   Seneca   of the too-wealthy
4   5   6   9   8

hortos   Clausic   et   egregias,   Lateranorum
gardens   blockaded   and   the splendid,   of the Laterani
7   3   10   12   14

obsidet   ædes   Tota   cohors :   rarus   venit
besieged   mansion   a whole   cohort :   rarely   comes
11   13   1   2

in   cœnacula   miles.   Pauca   licèt   portes
into   garrets   the soldier.   (but) few   though   you are carrying
                3   1   2

argenti   vascula   puri,   Nocte   iter   ingressus
silver   vessels   of pure,   by night (your)   journey   having entered on
6   4   5   3   2   1

gladium   contumque   timebis,   Et   motæ
the sword   and bludgeon   you will dread,   and   moved
                4

ad   lunam   trepidabis   arundinis   umbram :
at   moonlight   will tremble at   of a reed   the shadow :
5   1   3   2

Cantabit   vacuus   coram   latrone   viator.
will sing   the empty   before   the robber   traveller.
3   1   2

Prima   fere   vota   et   cunctis   notissima
the first   generally   prayers   and   in all   the best known
2   1   2   1

templis	Divitiæ,	crescant	ut	opes,	ut
the temples	(are that) riches,	may increase	that	influence,	that
3		3	1	2	

maxima	toto	Nostra	sit	area	foro.
the largest	in the whole	our	may be	chest	forum.
4	5	1	3	2	6

Sed	nulla	aconita	bibuntur	Fictilibus,	Tunc
But	no	aconite	is drunk	from earthen ware,	Then

illa	time,	quum	pocula	sumes	Gemmata,	et
it	fear,	when	cups	you take	jewelled,	and

lato	Setinum	ardebit	in	auro.	Jamne
the broad	Setine	glows	in	gold.	now
4	1	2	3		

igitur	laudas,	quod	de	sapientibus	alter
then	do you not praise (the fact,)	that	of	the sages	one

Ridebat,	quoties	de	limine	moverat	unum
used to laugh	as often as	from	(his) threshold	he had moved	one
					2

Protuleratque	pedem;	flebat	contrarius	alter?
and had advanced	step;	used to weep	contrary	the other?
1		3	2	1

Sed	facilis	cuivis	rigida	censura	cachinni:
But	easy	to any one.(is)	the harsh	censure	of a sneering laugh;

Mirandum est	unde	ille	oculis	suffecerit
It is to be wondered,	whence	that	to the eyes	supplied enough
			3	2

humor	Perpetuo	risu	pulmonem	agitare
moisture.	With perpetual	laughter	his lungs	to shake
1				

solebat	Democritus,	quanquam	non	essent	urbibus
used	Democritus,	although	not (there) were		cities
			2	1	4

illis	Prætexta,	et	trabeæ,	fasces,	lectica,
in those	the prætexta,	and	trabeæ	fasces,	litter,
3					

tribunal.	Quid,	si	vidisset	prætorem	curribus
tribunal.	What,	if	he had seen	the prætor	car
					3

altis	Exstantem,	et	medio	sublimem	in
in-the-lofty	standing-preeminent,	and	the mid	raised-on-high	in
2	1		3	1	2

pulvere	Circi	In	tunicâ	Jovis,	et	pictæ
dust	of the Circus	In	the tunic	of Jove,	and of the embroidered	
4					6	

Sarrana	ferentem	Ex	humeris	aulæa	togæ,
the Tyrian	wearing	from	(his) shoulders	hangings	toga,
4	1	2	3	5	7

magnæque	coronæ	Tantum	orbem,	quantò
and of a great	crown	so great	a circle,	as

cervix	non	sufficit	ulla?	Quippe	tenet	sudans
neck	not	suffices	any?	Since	holds	sweating
3	1	4	2		3	2

hanc	publicus,	et,	sibi,	consul
it	the official,	and,	himself, (too much)	the consul
	1		4	2

Ne	placeat,	curru	servus	portatur	eodem.
lest	may please,	car	the slave	is borne	in the same.
1	3	4	1	2	3

Da	nunc	et	volucrem	sceptro	quæ	surgit
add	now	also	· the bird	sceptre	which	rises
			4		1	2

eburno,	Illinc	cornicines,	hinc	præcedentia
from (his) ivory,	on that side	the trumpeters,	on this	marching before
3				4

longi	Agminis	officia,	et	niveos	ad
of a long	train	the offices,	and	snow-white-toged	at
2	3	1			2

fræna	Quirites,	Defossa	in	loculis	quos
the bits	Quirites,	buried deep	in	(his) chest	whom
3	1	4	5	6	2

sportula	fecit	amicos.	Tunc	quoque	materiam
the sportula	has made	friends.	Then	also	matter
3	7	1			

risûs	invenit	ad	omnes	Occursus	hominum,
for laughter	he found	at	all	meetings	of men,

cujus	prudentia	monstrat,	Summos	posse
whose	sagacity	shows,	(that) the highest	may
				6

viros,	et	magna	exempla	daturos,
men,	and	great	examples,	destined-to-give,
1	2	4	5	3

Vervecum	in	patriâ	crassoque	sub
of mutton-heads	in	a country	and a foggy	beneath
10	8	9	12	11

aere	nasci.	Ridebat	curas,	nec non	et
atmosphere	be born.	He used to laugh at	the cares,	also	and
	7			2	1

gaudia	vulgi,	Interdum	et	lacrymas,
the joys	of the common herd,	Sometimes	even	(their) tears,

quum	Fortunæ	ipse	minaci	Mandaret
while	Fortune	he himself	to threatening	would consign
	5	1	4	2

laqueum	mediumque	ostenderet	unguem.	Ergò
a halter	and the middle	would show (her)	nail.	Therefore
3	5 7	6	8	

supervacua	hæc	aut	perniciosa	petuntur
superfluous	these	or	destructive (things)	are asked for
2	1			3 4

Propter	quæ	fas	est	genua	incerare
for	which	right	it is (in our eyes)	the knees	to waxen
				2	1

deorum.	Quosdam	præcipitat	subjecta	potentia
of the gods.	Some	hurls headlong	exposed	power
	6	5 7	2	1

magnæ Invidiæ ; mergit longa atque insignis
to great / envy ; / sinks (others) the long / and / splendid
3 4 5 1 2

honorum Pagina; descendunt statuæ, restemque
of honors / list; / down come (their) statues, / and the rope
4 3 2

sequuntur. Ipsas deinde rotas bigarum impacta
follow. / Themselves / then / the wheels / of the chariot / the vigorous
1 3 1 2

securis Cædit, et immeritis fraguntur crura
axe / hacks, / and / of the innocent / are broken / the legs
2 4 1

caballis. Jam stridunt ignes, jam follibus
horses. / now / roar / the fires, / now / with the bellows
3 5

atque caminis Ardet adoratum popu'o
and / the furnace / glows / (once) worshipped / by the people
6 4 2 3

caput, et crepat ingens Sejanus: deinde ex
the head, / and / crackles / great / Sejanus: / then / from
1 3 1 2

facie toto orbe secundâ Fiunt urceoli,
the head / in the whole / world / second / are made / pitchers,
2 3 1

pelves, sartago, patellæ. Pone domi
basins, / a frying-pan, / platters. / "Put / at home
2

lauros, duc in Capitolia magnum
bays, / lead / into / the Capitol / a huge
1

Cretatumque bovem: Sejanus ducitur unco
and chalk-whitened / ox: / Sejanus is being dragged along by the hook

Spectandus: gaudent omnes. Quæ labra!
a glorious sight: / rejoice / all. / "what / lips!
2 1

quis illi Vultus erat! nunquam, si
what / to him / a face / was! / never, / if
3 1 2

quid mihi credis, amavi Hunc hominem.
any thing / me / you believed, / liked I / this / man."

Sed quo cecidit sub crimine? quisnam
"But / what / did he fall / under / charge? / who
2 4 1 3

Delator? quibus indiciis? quo teste
the accuser? / on what / information? / by what / witness

probavit? Nil horum: verbosa et grandis
did he prove (it)?" "Nothing of these: / a wordy / and / lengthy

epistola venit A Capreis. Bene habet;
epistle / came / from / Capreæ." / "well / it holds;
2 1

nil plus interrogo. Sed quid Turba
nothing / more / I ask. / But / what / the mob

(14*)

Remi ?   Sequitur   Fortunam,   ut   semper
of Remus ?" "It follows   Fortune,   as (mobs) always (do)

et   odit   Damnatos.   Idem   populus,   si
and hates the comdemned." the same people,   if

Nursia   Tusco   Favisset,   si   oppressa
Nursia the Tuscan had favored, if   oppressed
                                        5

foret   secura   senectus   Principis,   hâc ipsâ
had been the secure old-age   of the prince, in that very
   4   1   2   3

Sejanum   diceret   horâ Augustum. Jampridem,
Sejanus w'd have saluted hour (as) Augustus. Long ago,
  3   2   1

ex   quo   suffragia . nulli   Vendimus,
from which (time) suffrage   to no one we sell,

effudit   curas :   nam   qui dabat olim
it has thrown off cares : for (the people) who gave away formerly

Imperium, fasces,   legiones,   omnia,   nunc
military-command, fasces, legions,   all (things), now

se Continet,   atque   duas tantùm res
itself restrains, and   two   only   things
                       3   5   4

anxius   optat, .   Panem   et   Circenses.
anxious desires,   bread and the games-of-the-Circus.
  1   2

Perituros audio   multos.   Nil   dubium ;
"doomed to perish I hear many (are)." "No   doubt ;
   3   1   2

magna est   fornacula : pallidulus mi Brutidius
great is the little furnace : a little pale me Brutidius
                        3   5   2

meus   ad   Martis   fuit obvius aram. Quàm
my [friend] at of Mars met   the altar." "How
  1   6   8   4   7

timeo,   victus   ne   poenas   exigat   Ajax,
I fear, conquered lest punishments may wreak Ajax,
          2   1   5   4   3

Ut   male   defensus ! curramus   præcipites,
as badly defended ! let us rush   headlong,

et   Dum   jacet   in   ripâ, calcemus Cæsaris
and while he lies on the bank, let us trample Cæsar's

hostem. Sed   videant   servi,   ne   quis
foe.   But let see (the act) the slaves, lest any one
                1   3   2

neget,   et   pavidum   in   jus   Cervice
deny (it), and (his) terrified to   trial (his) neck
                   2   4

obstrictâ dominum   trahat.   Hi   sermones
bound   master   drag." These (were) the speeches
             3   1

Tunc de Sejano, secreta hæc murmura vulgi.
then about Sejanus, the secret these murmurs of the populace.
                          2   1

Visne salutari, sicut Sejanus? habere
do-you-wish to be saluted, as Sejanus (was)? to have

Tantundem, atque illi summas donare curules?
as much, and on one the highest to bestow curule honors?
                      2   1

Illum exercitibus præponere? tutor haberi
another armies to place over? the guardian to-be-esteemed
                                    2   1

Principis angustâ Caprearum in rupe sedentis
of the prince the narrow of Capreæ on rock sitting
      3   5   2   4   1

Cum grege Chaldæo? Vis certè pila,
with (his) herd Chaldæan? Do you wish at least javelins,
        2   1

cohortes, Egregios equites, et castra domestica?
cohorts, picked cavalry, and camp a domestic?
                              2   1

Quidni Hæc cupias? et qui nolunt occidere
Why not these sh'd you covet? and (they) who are unwilling to kill

quenquam, Posse volunt. Sed quæ præclara
any one to-have-the-power wish. But what brilliant

et prospera tanti, Ut rebus
and prosperous (things are) of so great (worth) that to the

lætis par sit mensura malorum? Hujus,
good-luck equal is the measure of ills? of him,
  5   4   3   1   2

qui trahitur, prætextam sumere mavis,
who is dragged along, the prætexta put on w'd you rather

An Fidenarum Gabiorumque esse potestas, Et
or of Fidenæ and Gabii be the magistrate, and

de mensurâ jus dicere, vasa minora
about measure the law speak, measures scanty

Frangere pannosus vacuis ædilis Ulubris?
break up, the ragged to deserted ædile Ulubræ?
                        2   1

Ergo quid optandum foret, ignorâsse
Therefore what ought to-be-desired, to have been ignorant
                                          3

fateris Sejanum: nam qui nimios optabat
you confess Sejanus; for (he) who excessive coveted
  1   2   2   1

honores, Et nimias poscebat opes, numerosa
honors, and excessive prayed for influence, numerous
              2   1   2

parabat Excelsæ turris tabulata, unde altior
was preparing of a lofty tower stories, whence deeper
  1   4   5   3

esset   Casus,   et   impulsæ   præceps   immane
might be   the fall,   and   of his impelled   the headlong-descent   enormous
3   2   1

ruinæ.   Quid   Crassos,   quid   Pompeios   evertit?
ruin.   What   the Crassi,   what   the Pompeys   overthrew?
4

et   illum,   Ad   sua   qui   domitos   deduxit
and   him,   to   his   who   the subdued   brought down
3   4   1   6   2

flagra   Quirites ?   Summus   nempe   locus
lashes   Quirites?   the highest   why   place
5   2   1

nullâ non arte   petitus,   Magnaque   numinibus   vota
by-every-device   sought,   and ambitious   divinities   prayers
4   1

exaudita   malignis.   Ad   generum   Cereris
heard   by malign.   to   the son-in-law   of Ceres
2   3

sine   cæde   et   vulnere   pauci   Descendunt
without   slaughter   and   wound   few   descend
2

reges,   et   siccâ   morte   tyranni.
Kings,   and   a bloodless   death   (few)   tyrants [die.]
1

Eloquium   ac   famam   Demosthenis   aut   Ciceronis
The eloquence   and   renown   of Demosthenes   or   Cicero
16

Incipit   optare,   et   totis   Quinqua'ribus   optat,
begins   to long for,   and   through all (his)   Quinquatrian holidays   longs,
14   15

Quisquis   adhuc   uno   partam   eolit   asse
Whoever   as yet   by a single   purchased   pays-court-to   as
1   5   6   4   2   7

Minervam,   Quem   sequitur   custos   angustæ
Minerva,   whom   follows   the guard   of his narrow
3   8   13   10   11

vernula   capsæ.   Eloquio   sed   uterque   perit
a little slave   satchel.   From eloquence   but   each   perished
9   12   2   1   3   5

orator :   utrumque   Largus   et   exundans   leto
orator: each   The copious   and   overflowing   to destruction
4   6   1   2   7

dedit   ingenii   fons.   Ingenio   manus   est
gave   of genius   fountain.   by genius   his hand   was
5   4   3

et   cervix   cæsa;   nec   unquam   Sanguine
and   head   cut off;   nor   ever   with the blood
3

causidici   maduerunt   rostra   pusilli.   O fortunatum
pleader   reeked   the rostra   of a contemptible   "O fortunate
5   1   2   4

natam   me   consule   Romam !"   Antoni   gladios
born   I (being)   consul   Rome ! '   Antony's   swords
2   3   4   1

potuit   contemnere,   si   sic   Omnia   dixisset.
he were able   to despise,   if   thus   all (things)   he had said.

Ridenda   poëmata   malo,   Quàm   te   conspicuæ,
Laughable   poems   I choose rather,   than   thee   of distinguished
                                          3

divina   Phillippica,   famæ,   Volveris   a   primâ
divine   Philippic,   fame,   art rolled up   from   the first
 1   2   2   4   5

quæ   proxima.   Sævus   et   illum   Exitus
which   next.   A cruel   also   him   exit
 1   3   1   2   4   1

eripuit,   quem   mirabantur   Athenæ   Torrentem,
snatched away,   whom   used to admire   Athens,   a torrent (of eloquence),
    3   2   1

et   pleni   moderantem   fræna   theatri.   Dis
and   of the crowded   controlling   the reins.   theatre.   With gods
       3   1   2

ille   adversis   genitus,   fatoque   sinistro,   Quem
he   adverse   (was) born,   and fate   inauspicious,   whom
 2   1

pater   ardentis   massæ   fuligine   lippus   A
(his) father   of the glowing   mass   with the grime   blear-eyed   from
                  3   4   2   1

carbone,   et   forcipibus   gladiosque   parante Incude,
the coal,   and   pincers,   and sword   preparing   anvil,

et   luteo   Vulcano   ad   rhetora   misit.   Bellorum
and   sooty   Vulcan   to the rhetorician   sent.   Of wars
                                               2

exuviæ   truncis   affixa   tropæis   Lorica,
the spoils   to the truncated   fastened   trophies   the cuirass,
 1   5   4   6   3

et   fractâ   de   casside   buccula   pendens
and   the battered   from   helm   the cheek-piece   hanging
       10   9   11   7   8

Et   curtum   temone   jugum,   victæque
and   shorn   of its pole   the car,   and of the captured
      13   14   12   16

triremis   Aplustre,   et   summo   tristis   captivus in arcu,
galley   the streamer,   and the top (of the)   the sad   captive   in arch
 17   15   21   18   19   20 22

Humanis   majora   bonis   creduntur: ad   hæc   se
(than all) human   greater   blessings   are believed: for   these   himself
            25   24   26   23

Romanus,   Graiusque,   ac   barbarus   endoperator
Roman,   and Greek,   and   barbarian   general

Erexit;   causas   discriminis   atque   laboris
exerted;   causes   of peril   and   of hardship

Inde   habuit.   Tantò   major   famæ   sitis
thence   he had.   so much   greater   for fame   the thirst

est,   quàm   Virtutis.   Quis   enim   virtutem
is,   than   for virtue.   Who   for   virtue
                         2   1   4

amplectitur ipsam, Præmia si tollas?
embraces herself, the reward if you take away?
3   3   1   2

Patriam tamen obruit olim Gloria
(their) country yet has ruined ere now the glory
6   1   5   2   3

paucorum, et laudis ti:ulique cupido
of a few, and of praise and of title the desire
4   2   3   1

Hæsuri saxis cinerum custodibus; ad
(that is) to adhere on the stones of [their] ashes the defenders; for
                          2   1

quæ Discutienda valent sterilis mala
which to be burst asunder avails of the barren the mischievious
                          5   3   1

robora ficûs; Quandoquidem data sunt
strength fig-tree; since are assigned
2   4   5

ipsis quoque fata sepulcris. Expende
themselves even fates to sepulcres. weigh
3   1   4   2

Hannibalem: quot libras in duce summo
Hannibal: how many pounds in general the highest
                                    2   1

Invenies? hic est, quem non capit
will you find? this is [he], whom not contains
                                      3   2

Africa Mauro Percussa Oceano, Niloque
Africa by the mauritanian lashed Ocean, and Nilo
1   5   4   6   3

admota tepenti, Rursus ad Æthiopum
stretched to steaming, again [in another direction] to of the Æthiopes
1   2   2

populos altosque elephantos. Additur imperiis
the peoples and lofty elephants. is added to the domains
1   2   3

Hispania: Pyrenæum Transsilit. Opposuit
[of Carthage] Spain: the Pyrenees he bounds across. opposed
      1   2

natura Alpemque nivemque: Diducit scopulos,
nature both the Alps and [their] snow: he cleaves the rocks,
1

et montem rumpit aceto. Jam tenet
and the mountain rends with vinegar. Now he holds
     2   1

Italiam: tamen ultrà pergere tendit:
Italy: yet beyond to proceed he strives:

Actum, inquit, nihil est, nisi Pœno
"Achieved," he says, "naught is, unless with Carthaginian

milite portas Frangimus, et mediâ
soldiery the gates [of Rome] we break, and in-the-midst [of]
                                                      3

vexillum — pono — Suburâ. — O qualis — facies,
my standard — I plant — the Subura. — O what a — face
2 — 1 — 4

et — quali — digna — tabellâ, — Quum — Gætula
and — of what — worthy — a picture, — when — the Gætulian
2 — 1

ducem — portaret — bellua — luscum! — Exitus
general — bore — beast — the one-eyed! — the issue
4 — 2 — 1 — 3 — 4

ergo — quis — est? — o gloria! — vincitur — idem
then — what — is? — o glory! — is conquered — the same
3 — 1 — 2 — 5 — 2

Nempe, — et — in — exsilium — præceps — fugit,
why, — and — into — exile — headlong — flees,
1

atque — ibi — magnus — Mirandusque — cliens
and — there — a great — and to-be-admired — client

sedet — ad — prætoria — regis — Donec
sits — at — the palace — of the king — until

Bithyno — libeat — vigilare — tyranno·
the Bithynian — it pleases — to wake — monarch.
2 — 1 — 4 — 3

Finem — animæ, — quæ — res — humanas — miscuit
an end — to the soul, — which — things — human — confounded

olim, — Non — gladii, — non — saxa — dabunt, — nec — tela;
once, — not — swords, — not — stones — will give, — nor — darts;

sed — ille — Cannarum — vindex — et — tanti — sanguinis
but — that — for Cannæ — atoner — and — of so much — blood
2 — 1

ultor — Annulus. — I, — demens, — et — sævas — curre
the avenger, — a ring. — Go, — madman, — and — the rugged — hurry
3 — 1

per — Alpes, — ut — pueris — placeas — et declamatio
through — Alps, — that — boys — you may please — and a declamation
2

fias! — Unus — Pellæo — juveni — non — sufficit
become! — One — the Pellæan — youth — not — suffices
4 — 3 — 2

orbis; — Æstuat — infelix — angusto — limite — mundi,
world: — he chafes — unhappy — in the narrow — limit of the universe
1

ut — Gyari — clausus — scopulis — parvaque
as — Gyarus, — [one] confined — in the rocks — and little
3 — 1 — 2 — 4

Seripho: — Quum — tamen — a — figulis — munitam
Seriphos: — When — yet — by — the brick-makers — fortified
2 — 1 — 6 — 7 — 5

intraverit — urbem, — Sarcophago — contentus — erit.
he shall have entered the city, — with a sarcophagus — content — he will be.
3 — 1

Mors — sola — fatetur, — Quantula — sint hominum
Death — alone — confesses, — How little great — are — of men
2

corpuscula.   Creditur   olim   Velificatus
the puny bodies.   Is believed   of yore   (to have been) sailed through
1   2   4   3

Athos,   et   quidquid   Græcia   mendax   Audet
Athos,   and   whatever   Greece   lying   dares
1   2   1

in   historia :   constratum   classibus   isdem
in   history: (to have been) bridged over   fleets   by the same
2   4   8

suppositumque   rotis   solidum   mare :   credimus
and placed-under   wheels   solid   the sea :   we believe
5   7   8   6   1

altos   Defecisse   amnes,   epotaque   flumina
deep   to have failed   rivers,   and (to have been) drunk up   streams
2   1   2   1

Medo   Prandente,   et   madidis   cantat
by the Mede,   lunching,   and   moist (with wine)   sings
5   3

quæ   Sostratus   alis,   Ille   tamen   qualis
what   Sostratus   with pinions,   he   yet   what
1   2   4   4   1   2

rediit   Salamine   relictâ,   In   Corum   atque
returned   Salamis   left behind,   upon   Corus   and
3   5   6

Eurum   solitus   sævire   flagellis   Barbarus,
Eurus   accustomed   to rage   with scourges   a barbarian,
7   2   3   4   1

Æolio   nunquam   hoc   in   carcere   passos,
the Æolian   never   in this (sort)   in   prison   having suffered,
12   8   10   11   13   9

Ipsum   compedibus   qui   vinxerat   Ennosigæum.
himself   in gyves   who   had bound   Ennosigæus.
5   3   1   2   4

Mitius   id   sané,   quòd   non   et   stigmate
too mild   that   in faith,   that   not   also   of branding
3

dignum   Credidit   Huic   quisquam   vellet
(him) worthy   he thought.   This (man)   any   would
2   1   5   2   1

servire   deorum?   Sed   qualis   rediit?
serve   of the gods?   But   how   did he return ?
4   3

nempe   unâ   nave,   cruentis   Fluctibus,   ac
why   in one   ship,   through bloody   . waves,   and

tardâ   per   densa   cadavera   prorâ.   Has
with slow   through   the dense   corpses   prow.   These
2   1

toties   optata   exegit   gloria   pœnas.   Da
so often   prayed for   exacted   glory   the penalties.   "Grant
3   4   5   2   1

spatium   vitæ,   multos   da,   Jupiter,   annos!
length   of life,   many   grant,   O Jupiter,   ' years!"
3   1   2

Hoc	recto	vultu	solum,	hoc	et
this	with-the-erect	look (of health)	only,	this	also,
1	3	4	2		

	pallidus	optas.	Sed		quam
	pallid (with sickness)	you pray for.	But		with how

continuis	et	quantis	longa		senectus
unremitting	and	how great	(is) a long		old age
			2		3

Plena	malis?	Deformem	et	tetrum	ante
full	its?	misshapen	and	loathsome	before
4	1				

omnia	vultum,	Dissimilemque	sui,		deformem
all	(its) face,	and unlike	its [former] self,		an ugly

pro	cute	pellem,	Pendentesque		genas,
instead of	a skin	hide,	and flaccid		cheeks,
2		1			

et	tales	adspice	rugas,	Quales	umbriferos
and	such	behold	wrinkles,	as	(her) shady
		2	1		4

ubi	pandit	Tabraca	saltus,	In	vetulâ
where	extends	Tabraca	woods,	in	[her] old
1	3	2		5	6

scalpit	jam	mater	simia	buccâ.	Plurima
scratches	long since a	mother	the ape	jowl.	very many
4	2	3	1	7	

sunt	juvenum	discrimina:		pulchrior	ille
are	of youth	the differences:		handsomer	that
	2	1			

Hoc,	atque	ille	alio;	multùm	hic
than this,	and	that	than another;	much	this
				2	1

rubustior	illo.	Una	senum	facies,	cum
more robust	than that.	one (and the same) of old men [are]	the faces,	with
			2	1	3

voce	trementia	membra,	Et	jam	leve
the voice	trembling	the limbs,	and	now	a smooth
4	2	1			

caput,	madidique	infantia	nasi.	Frangendus
pate,	of a running	the second-childhood	nose.	must be mumbled
	2	1		2

misero	gingivâ	panis	inermi:	Usque
by-the-poor-wretch gum	bread	with-a-toothless:	even
3	5	1	4	

adeò	gravis	uxori,	natisque,	sibique,	Ut
so	grievous	to his wife,	and children,	and himself,	that

captatori	moveat	fastidia	Cosso.	Non
to the legacy hunter	he w'd move	disgusts	Cossus.	not
3	1	2		

eadem	vini	atque	cibi,	torpente	palato,
the same	of wine	and	food, [being] torpid	the palate,
	2		3	5	4

Gaudia:	nam	coitûs	jam	longa	oblivio:
[are] the joys:	for	of coition	already long [is] the forgetfulness:
1					

vel   si   Coneris,   jacet   exiguus   cum   ramice
or   if   you attempt (it,)

nervus;   Et   quamvis   totâ   palpetur   nocte
jacebit.   Anne   aliquid   sperare   potest   hæc
inguinis   ægri   Canities?   quid,   quod   meritò
suspecta   libido   est,   Quæ   Venerem   affectat
sine   viribus?   Aspice   partis   Nunc   damnum

alterius :   nam   quæ   cantante   voluptas,
    for   what   in-a-singer   pleasure,
       2   1

Sit   licèt   eximius   citharœdus,   sitve
he-may-be   though   an eminent   harper,   or he may be
   2   1

Seleucus,   Et   quibus   auratâ   mos   est
Seleucus,   and [those] to whom   in a gold-bedecked   the custom   is
                                4   1   2

fulgere   lacernâ?   Quid   refert,   magni   sedeat
to glitter   robe?   what   matters it,   of the great   he may sit
   3   2   4

quâ   parte   theatri,   Qui   vix   cornicines
in-what   part   theatre,   who   scarcely   the born-blowers
  1   3

exaudiat   atque   tubarum   Concentus?   clamore
can hear   and   of trumpets   the general-clang?   of clamor
                    2   1

opus   est,   ut   sentiat   auris,
need   is,   that   may distinguish   [his] ear,
                       2   1

Quem   dicat   venisse   puer,   quot   nuntiet
Whom   says   to have come   the slave,   how many   he reports
          2   1   2

horas.   Præterea   minimus   gelido   jam   in   corpore
hours.   Besides   the very little   (his) cold   now   in   body
  1   4   2   3   5

sanguis   Febre   calet   solâ ;   circumsilit   agmine
blood   by fever   is warm   only;   leaps around   a troop
  1   2   1   4

facto   Morborum   omne   genus :   quorum   si   nomina
being formed of diseases   every   kind :   of which   if   the names
          3   1   2

quæras,   Promptiùs   expediam,   quot   amaverit
you sh'd ask,   sooner   I c'd tell,   how many   loved
                                               3

Hippia   mœchos,   Quot   Themison   ægros
Hippia   adulterers,   how-many   Themison   patients
  2   1   2   1

autumno   occiderit   uno,   Quot   Basilus
autumn   killed   in one,   how many   Basilus
  5   3   4   2

socios,   quot   circumscripserit   Hirrus   Pupillos,
partners-in-business   how many   defrauded   Hirrus   wards:
      1   3   6   5   4

quot   longa   viros   exsorbeat   uno   Maura
how may   long   men   exhausts   in one   Maura
  2   1   4   5   3

die,   quot   discupulos   inclinet   Hamillus.
day,   how many   pupils   corrupts   Hamillus.
6   2   1

Percurram · citius,   quot   villas   possideat   nunc,
I c'd run through   more   quickly   how many villas   he possesses   now,

Quo   tondente,   gravis   juveni   mihi   barba
who   clipping,   the heavy   a youth   to me   beard
      3   2   1

sonabat.   Ille   humero,   hic   lumbis,
sounded.   That (old man)   in the shoulder,   this one   in the loins

hic   coxâ   debilis,   ambos   Perdidit   ille
this (one) in the hip (is) disabled,   both   has lost   that (one)
      3   2   1

oculos,   et   luscis   invidet :   hujus   Pallida
eyes,   and   the one-eyed   envies :   this one's   bloodless

labra   cibum   accipiunt   digitis   alienis.
lips   food   receive   fingers   from others'.
  2   1   4   3

Ipse   ad   conspectum   cœnæ   diducere
He himself   at   the sight   of (his) dinner   to distend
  4   5   2

rictum   Suetus   hiat   tantùm,   ceu   · pullus
(his) jaws   accustomed,   gapes   only,   like   the young one
3   1

hirundinis,   ad   quem   Ore   volat   pleno
of the swallow,   to   whom   beak   flies   with full
      5   3   4

mater,   jejuna.   Sed   omni   Membrorum
the mother-bird,   fasting.   But   than all   of limbs
1   2   2

damno   major   dementia,   quæ   nec   Nomina
loss   greater   (is) the idiocy,   which   neither   the names
1

servorum,   nec   vultum   agnoscit   amici,   Cum
of the slaves,   nor   the face   recognises   of the friend   with

quo   præteritâ   cœnavit   nocte ;   nec   illos,
whom   on-the-previous   he supped   night :   nor   those,
  2   1

Quos   genuit,   quos   eduxit.   Nam   codice
whom   he begot,   whom   he brought up.   For   will
          2

sævo   Hæredes   vetat   esse   suos ;   bona
by a cruel,   heirs   he prohibits   to be   his own ;   (his) goods
1   4   1   3   2   2

tota   feruntur   Ad   Phialen :   tantùm   artificis
all   are-made-over   to   Phiale :   so much   of an artful
1   3

valet   halitus   oris,   Quod   steterat   multis
avails   the breath mouth,   which   had stood (for hire) for many
1   2

in   carcere   fornicis   annis.   Ut   vigeant
in   the dungeon of a brothel years.   Though   are-in-vigor
2   3   1   3

sensus   animi,   ducenda   tamen   sunt
the faculties   of the mind,   to be led forth yet   are
1   2   5   1   4

Funera   natorum,   rogus   adspiciendus   amatæ
the funerals   of (his) children, the pyre   to-be-gazed-at   of a loved
2   3

Conjugis   et   fratris,   plenæque   sororibus   urnæ.
wife   and   brother,   and full   of sisters   urns.
                               2   3   1

Hæc   data   poena   diù   viventibus,   ut,
This (is) imposed   the penalty   on the   long-lived,   that
             2   1

renovatâ   Semper   clade   domus,   multis   in
renewed   ever   with-the-death-blow in the house, many   in
4   3   1   2   2   in

luctibus,   inque   Perpetuo   mœrore,   et   nigrâ
griefs,   and in   perpetual   mourning,   and   black

veste   senescant.   Rex   Pylius,   magno   si
vesture   they-must-grow-old. King   the Pylian,   to great   if
            2   1   4   1   1

quidquam   credis   Homero,   Exemplum   vitæ
anything   you trust   Homer,   an instance   of life
3   2   1

fuit   a   cornice   secundæ.   Felix   nimirum,   qui
was   from   the crow   second.   Happy   no doubt (was he) who
                 2   3   1

tot   per   sæcula   mortem   Distulit,   atque
so many   for   generations   death   put off,   and
2   1

suos   jam   dextrâ   computat   annos,   Quique
his   now   on the right hand   reckons   years,   and who
3   1   5   2   4

novum   toties   mustum   bibit.   Oro,
the new-made   so often   wine   has drunk.   I pray,
2   1

parumper   Attendas,   quantum   de   legibus
for a little space attend,   how much   of   the decrees
                                                     3

ipse   queratur   Fatorum,   et   nimio   de
he himself complains   of the fates,   and   a too prolonged   of
1   2   2   1

stamine,   quum   videt   acris   Antilochi   barbam
thread-of-life   when   he sees   of the spirited Antilochus   beard
                                     8   2

ardentem,   quum   quærit   ab   omni,   Quisquis
the blazing.   when   he asks   from   every,   whatever
1

adest   socius,   cur   hæc   in   tempora
is pres nt companion.   why   these   into   times
  2   1   3   2   4

duret,   Quod   facinus   dignum   tam   longo
he lasts, what   crime   worthy of   so   long
  1

admiserit   ævo?   Hæc   eadem   Peleus,   raptum
he-has-committed an age? These same (things) Peleus,   snatch'd away,
    2   1   4

quum   luget   Achillem,   Atque   alius,   cui
when   he mourns Achilles,   and (that) other,   to whom
 1   2

fas   Ithacum   lugere   natantem.   Incolumi
(was) the fate Ithacensian to grieve the floating. (remaining) safe
              3   1   2   2

Trojâ   Priamus   venisset   ad   umbras
Troy   Priam   w'd have gone to   the shades
  1

Assaraci   magnis   solennibus,   Hectore   funus
of Assaracus with great solemnities,   Hector   (his) corpse

Portante,   ac   reliquis   fratrum   cervicibus,
bearing,   and   on the other of his brothers necks,
                                        2   1

inter   Iliadum   lacrymas,   ut   primos   edere
amid   of the Trojans the tears,   that so the first   to utter
             2   1   4   3

planctus   Cassandra   inciperet,   scissâque   Polyxena
wailings   Cassandra   w'd begin,   and with rent Polyxena
   5   1   2   1

pallâ,   Si   foret   exstinctus   diverso   tempore,   quo
in tatters, if he had   died   at a different time (from that) in which

non   Cœperat   au laces   Paris   ædificare   carinas.
not   had begun   (his) audacious Paris to build   keels.
 3   2   4   1   5
            6

Longa   dies   igitur   quid   contulit?   omnia
a long   life   therefore   what   d. l confer?   all (things)
 4   5   2   1   3   6

vidit   Eversa,   et   flammis   Asiam   ferroque
he saw   overthrown, and   by flames   Asia   and the sword
                                   3

cadentem   Tunc   miles   tremulus   positâ
falling.   Then   soldier   the tottering put aside
  2   2   1   6

tulit   arma   tiarâ,   Et   ruit   ante   aram
down d (his) arms [his] crown, and   fell   before   the altar
  3   4   5

summi   Jovis,   ut   vetulus   bos,   Qui
of supreme Jove,   as   an old   ox,   who

domini   cultris   tenue   et   miserabile   collum
to [his] master's knife [his] thin and   miserable   neck

Præbet,   ab   ingrato   jam   fastiditus   aratro.
yields.   by   the ungrateful long since scorn'd   plough.
              3   4   1   2

Exitus   ille   utcumque   hominis: sed   torva
the death   that   however   of a man :   but [his] fierce

canino   Latravit   rictu,   quæ   post   hunc
with canine   barked   jaws,   who   after   him
7   6   8   2   4   5

vixerat,   uxor.   Festino   ad   nostros,
lived,   wife.   I hasten   to   our own [countrymen,]
3   1

et   regem   transeo   Ponti,   Et   Crœsum,
and   the king   pass by   of Pontus,   and   Crœsus,
2   1

quem   vox   justi   facunda   Solonis   Respicere
whom   voice   of the just   the eloquent   Solon   to have respect
2   1   2

ad   longæ   jussit   spatia   ultima   vitæ.
to   of a long   commanded   scenes   the last   life.
3   6   1   5   4

Exsilium,   et   carcer,   Minturnarumque
Exile,   and   prison,   and of-Minturnæ
2

paludes,   Et   mendicatus   victâ   Carthagine
the marshes   and   begged   in conquered   Carthage
1   2   3

pauis,   Hinc   causas   habuêre.   Quid   illo
bread,   hence [their] causes   had.   What   than that
1   1   10

cive   tulisset   Natura   in   terris,   quid
citizen   c'd have-produced   Nature   in   the world,   what [could]
11   2   6   3   9   4

Roma   beatius   unquam,   Si   circumducto
Rome   more happy   ever,   If   surrounded
5   8   7

captivorum   agmine,   et   omni   Bellorum
of captives   by a train,   and   all   of wars
2   1   2

pompâ,   animam   exhalâsset   opimam,   Quum
the pomp,   soul   he-had-breathed-forth his glutted,   when
1   3   1   2

de   Teutonico   vellet   descendere   curru?
from (his)   Teutonic   he w'd   alight   car?
2   1

Provida   Pompeio   dederat   Campania   febres
in (her) foresight   to Pompey   had given   Campania   fevers
4   3   1   2

Optandas: sed   multæ   urbes   et   publica
to be prayed for: but   many   cities   and   public

vota   Vicerunt.   Igitur   Fortuna   ipsius   et
prayers   prevailed.   therefore   the fortune   of himself   and

Urbis   Servatum   victo   caput   abstulit.
of the City   the preserved   (to him) conquered   head   took off
2   4   3   1

Hoc   cruciatu   Lentulus,   hâc   poenâ   caruit
this   torture   Lentulus,   this   penalty   wanted
2

cociditque	Cethegus	Integer,	et	jacuit
and fell	Cethegus	unmutilated,	and	lay
	1			2

Catilina	cadavere	toto.	Formam	optat
Catiline	with corpse	entire.	beauty	prays for
1			8	7

modico	pueris,	majore	puellis	Murmure,
with a subdued	for (her) boys,	with a greater	for (her) girls	murmur,
10	9	12	13	11

quum	Veneris	fanum	videt	anxia	mater,
when	Venus'	temple	she visits	the anxious	mother,
3	5	6	4	1	2

Usque	ad	delicias	votorum.	Cur	tamen,
even	to	the delight	of vows.	"Why	yet,"
				2	1

inquit,	Corripias?	Pulchrâ	gaudet	Latona
she says,	"sh'd you chide?	in the beautiful	delights	Latona
		3		1

Dianâ.	Sed	vetet	optari	faciem	Lucretia,
Diana."	But	forbids	to be prayed for	a face	Lucretia,
		2	7	3	1

qualem	Ipsa	habuit:	cuperet	Rutilæ
such as	she herself	had:	w'd desire	of Rutila
4	5	6	2	5

Virginia	gibbum	Accipere,	atque	suam
Virginia	the wen	to receive,	and	her (face)
1	4	3		

Rutilæ	dare.	Filius	autem	Corporis	egregii
to Rutila	to give.	a son	but	of person	exquisite
		2	1		

miseros	trepidosque	parentes	Semper	habet.
wretched	and fearful (his)	parents	always	keeps.
4	5	3	1	2

Rara	est	adeò	concordia	formæ	Atque
Rare	is	so	the union	of beauty	and
2		1			

pudicitiæ.	Sanctos	licèt	horrida	mores
chastity.	Unsullied	though	austere (in virtue)	morals
	5	1		6

Tradiderit	domus,	ac	veteres	imitata
may-have-handed-down the house,		and	the ancient having-imitated	
4	2		2	1

Sabinos;	Præterea	castum	ingenium	vultumque
Sabines,	besides	a chaste	mind	and a face
	6	7	8	9

modesto	Sanguine	ferventem	tribuat	natura
with modest	blood	glowing	may bestow	nature
11	12	10	5	2

benignâ	Larga	manu;	(quid	enim	puero
with benignant	bountuous	hand;	(want	for	on a youth
3	1	4	2	1	3

conferre	potest	plus	Custode	et	curâ
to confer	is able	more	than a guardian	and	care
12	4 11	3	7	8	10

natura   potentior   omni ?)   Non   licet   esse
nature   more powerful   all ?)   it is not   permitted (them) to be
5   6   9

viris :   nam   prodiga   corruptoris   Improbitas
men :   for   the prodigal   of the corrupter   villainy
2   1

ipsos   audet   tentare   parentes.   Tanta   in
themselves   dares   to assail   the parents.   so great   in
6   3   4   5

muneribus   fiducia.   Nullus   ephebum   Deformem
bribes   (is) the confidence.   No   a youth   deformed
6   7

sæva   castravit   in   arce   tyrannus :   Nec
(his) cruel   castrated   in   palace   tyrant: nor
3   5   2   4   1

prætextatum   rapuit   Nero   loripedem,   vel
stripling   seized   Nero   a bow-legged,   or
4   2   1   3

Strumosum,   atque   utero   pariter,   gibboque
neck-swelled,   and   in (his) belly   equally,   and hump

tumentem.   I,   nunc,   et   juvenis   specie
swelling.   Go,   now,   and   youth   in the appearance
4   2

lætare   tui,   quem   Majora   expectant   discrimina.
exult   of your,   whom   greater   await   perils.
1   3   2   1

Fet   adulter   Publicus,   et   pœnas   metuet,
he will become adulterer   a public,   and   punishments   will dread.
2   1   3   1

quascunque   maritus   Exigit   iratus ;
whatsoever   husband   inflicts   an enraged ;
2   5   6   4

nec   erit   felicior   astro
nor   will be be   more lucky   than the star

Martis,   ut   in   laqueos   nunquam   incidat:
of Mars,   though   into   the nets   never   he may fall :

exigit   autem   Interdum   ille   dolor   plus,
exacts   but   sometimes   that   grief   more

quam   lex   ulla   dolori   Concessit.   Necat   hic
than   law   any   to grief   concedes.   slays   this one
2   1

ferro,   secat   ille   cruentis   Verberibus,
with the sword   cuts   that one   with bloody   stripes,
2   1

quosdam   mœchos   et   mugilis   intrat.   Sed
some   adulterers   also   the mullet   enters.   But

tuus   Endymion   dilectæ   fiet   adulter   Matronæ:
your   Endymion   of a beloved   will become   the adulterer   matron:
3   1   2

mox   cum   dederit   Servilia   nummos,
soon   when   shall-have-given   Servilia   money,
2   1

Fiet   et   illius   quam   non   amat;
he will become also hers whom not he loves;

exuet   omnem   Corporis   ornatum.   Quid
and will despoil (her) of every of the body adornment.
                           2   1

enim   ulla   negaverit   udis   Inguinibus,   sive   est
                                                  whether is
                                                              2

hæc   Hippia,   sive   Catulla?   Deterior   totos
sho a Hippia, or a Catulla? a depraved all
1   3

habet   illic   fœmina   mores.   Sed   casto
has there woman (her) morals. "But (one) chaste
2   5   1   4

quid   forma   nocet?   quid   profuit   immo
what does beauty harm? what . profited nay
                            2   1

Hippolyto   grave   propositum?   quid   Bellerophonti?
Hippolytus his virtuous resolve? what Bellerophon?

Erubuit   nempe   hæc,   ceu   fastidita,   repulsa.
reddened why she as if scorned, repulsed.
3   1   2

Nec   Sthenobœa   minus   quam   Cressa,   excanduit
Nor Sthenobœa less than Cressa, burned

et   se   Concussêre   ambæ.   Mulier   sævissima
and themselves roused both. a woman most cruel
            3   2   1

tunc   est,   Quum   stimulos   odio   pudor
then is, when spurs to (her) hate shame
                         3   1

admovet.   Elige   quidnam   Suadendum   esse   putes,
puts. Choose what ought-to-be-advised you think
2   2   1

cui   nubere   Cæsaris   uxor   Destinat?
[him] whom to marry Cæsar's wife purposes?
               4   1   2   3

Optimus   hic et   formosissimus   idem   Gentis
the best this and most beautiful same of the race
3   1   4   2

patriciæ   rapitur   miser   exstinguendus
patrician is seized, wretched [man], to be extinguished

Messalinæ   oculis: dudum   sedet   illa
by Messalina's eyes: long since sits she

parato   Flammeolo,   Tyriusque   palam   genialis
with prepared bridal-veil and-the-Tyrian openly marriage-bed
                                                      3   1

in   hortis   Sternitur,   et   ritu   decies
in the gardens is spread, and rite a million(sesterces)
                            2   2

centena dabuntur   Antiquo;   veniet   cum   signatoribus
will be given according to the antique; will come with the signers
                           1   2   3   4

auspex.   Hæc   tu   secreta   et   paucis
the soothsayer.   these (acts)   you   secret   and   to a few
1   4   2   5   6   8

commissa   putabas?   Non,   nisi   legitime,
entrusted   did think?   Not,   unless   in-due-form,
7   1   3   3   5

vult   nubere.   Quid   placeat,   dic: Ni
she will,   marry.   What   may please [you,]   say: unless
1   2   4

parere   velis,   pereundum   erit   ante   lucernas.
to obey   you are willing   you   must die   before   night fall.

Si   scelus   admittas,   dabitur   mora
if   the crime   you do commit,   will-be-afforded   delay
                           3   2

parvula,   dum   res   Nota   Urbi   et
a very brief,   until   the thing   known   to the city   and
1

populo   contingat   Principis   aures.   Dedecus
the people   reaches   the Prince's   ears.   The dishonor

ille   domûs   sciet   ultimus: interea   tu
he   of [his] house   will know   last: meanwhile   do you

Obsequere   imperio   si   tanti   vita   dierum
obey   [her] behest   if   so much [worth]   the life   days
                                                        2

Paucorum.   Quidquid   melius   leviusque
of a few.   whichever   the better   and the smoother (course)
1

putaris,   Præbenda est   gladio   pulchra
you shall consider,   must be presented   to the sword   beauteous
                        5   6   2

hæc   et   candida   cervix.   Nil   ergò
this   and   white   neck.   Nothing   then
1   3   4

optabunt   homines?   Si   consilium   vis,
shall pray for   men?   if   counsel   you wish,
1   3   2

Permittes   ipsis   expendere   numinibus,
you will permit   themselves,   to determine   the deities,
                2   3   1

quid   Conveniat   nobis.   rebusque   sit   utile
what   may be expedient   for us,   and circumstances (what) may be useful
                                 4   1   2

nostris.   Nam   pro   jucundis   aptissima
to our.   For   instead   of merely   pleasant (things) most fit
3

quæque   dabunt   Di.   Carior   est   illis
everything   will give   the gods.   dearer   is   to them
3   2   1

homo,   quam   sibi.   Nos   animorum   Impulsu,
man,   than   to himself.   We   of our minds   by the impulse,
                                     2   1

et   cæcâ   magnâque   cupidine   ducti,   Conjugium
and   by blind   and great   desire   led on,   wedlock

petimus,   partumque   uxoris: at illis   Notum,
seek,   and the issue   of a wife: but to them   it is known,

qui   pueri,   qualisque   futura sit   uxor.
what   our children,   and of what character   shall be   (our) wife.

Ut   tamen   et   poscas   aliquid,   voveasque
that   yet   also   you may ask   something,   and may vow
2   1   4   3

sacellis   Exta,   et   candiduli   divina
to (their) shrines   the entrails,   and   of the white   the consecrated
3   1

tomacula   porci;   Orandum est,   ut   sit
mince-meat   porker;   You must pray   that,   there be
2   4

mens   sana   in   corpore   sano.   Fortem
a mind   sound   in   a body   sound.   a brave
2

posce   animum,   mortis   terrore   carentem,
ask for   spirit,   of death   the dread   wanting,
1   3   2   1

Qui   spatium   vitæ   extremum   inter   munera
which   scene   of life   the last   among   the boons
3   4   2

ponat   Naturæ,   qui   ferre   queat   quoscunque
places   of Nature,   which   endure   can   whatsoever
1

labores,   Nesciat   irasci,   cupiat   nihil,   et
labors,   Knows not   to be angry,   covets   nothing,   and

potiores   Herculis   ærumnas   credat   sævosque
more desirable   of Hercules   the cares   believes   and cruel
6   5   2   1   3

labores   Et   Venere,   et   cœnis,   et   plumâ
labors   (than) both   Venus,   and   banquets, and   the downy couch
4

Sardanapali.   Monstro,   quod   ipse   tibi
of Sardanapalus.   I show,   what   thou thyself   to thyself

possis   dare: semita   certe   Tranquillæ
mayst be able   to give: path   surely   of a tranquil
2   3

per   virtutem   patet   unica   vitæ.   Nullum
through   virtue   is open   the only   life.   No
6   7   5   1   4

numen   habes,   si   sit   prudentia: nos   te,
divinity   thou hast,   if (there) is   foresight: we   thee,
3

Nos   facimus,   Fortuna,   Deam,   cœloque   locamus.
We   make,   O Fortune,   a Goddess,   and in heaven   place (thee)
1   2   2   1

SATIRE XI.

ARGUMENT.

Under the form of an invitation to his friend Persicus, Juvenal takes occasion to enunciate many admirable maxims for the due regulation of life. After ridiculing the miserable state to which a profligate patrician had reduced himself by his extravagance, he introduces the picture of his own domestic economy, which he follows by a pleasing view of the simplicity of ancient manners, artfully contrasted with the extravagance and luxury of the current times. After describing with great beauty the entertainment he proposes to give his friend, he concludes with an earnest recommendation to him to enjoy the present with content, and await the future with calmness and moderation.

ATTICUS   eximiè   si   cœnat,   lautus
ATTICUS   sumptuously   if   dines, a splendid (fellow)
2   4   1   3

habetur;   Si   Rutilus,   demens.   Quid
he is considered;   if   Rutilus (does so, he is thought) mad.   what
                                                       2

enim   majore   cach'nno   Excipitur   vulgi,
for   with greater   laughter   is received   of the people,
1   4   5   3   6

quàm   pauper   Apicius?   Omnis   Convictus,
than   impoverished   Apicius?   every   dinner-party,

thermæ,   stationes,   omne   theatrum   De
the baths,   knots-of-loungers,   every   theatre (talk)   about

Rutilo.   Nam   dum   valida   ac   juvenilia
Rutilus.   For   while (his) sturdy   and   youthful

membra   Sufficiunt   galeæ,   dumque   ardens
limbs   Suffice   for the helmet,   and while (he is) hot

sanguine,   fertur,   Non   cogente   quidem,
in blood,   he is driven,   (not   forcing   indeed,
                    2

sed   nec   prohibente   tribuno,   Scripturus
but   neither   prohibiting   the tribune.)   to write out
                     1

leges,   et   regia   verba   lanistæ.   Multos
the rules,   and   imperial   commands   of-the-trainer-of-gladiators.   many

porrò   vides,   quos   sæpè elusus   ad   ipsum
moreover   you see,   whom   the often eluded   at   the very
                         4   5

Creditor   introitum   solet   exspectare   macelli,
creditor   entrance   is wont   to-look-out-for of the market,
  1   6   2   3

Et   quibus   in   solo   vivendi   causa   palato
and   to whom   in   alone   of living   the cause the palato
                 4   6   2   1   5

est.   Egregiùs   cœnat,   meliùsque   miserrimus
is.   the more-sumptuously   sups,   and the better   the great st wretch
  3   10   9   1

horum,   Et   citò   casurus   jam   perlucente
of these,   and   soon   about to fall alr ady letting the light through
  2   3   4   5   7   8

ruinâ.   Interea   gustus   elementa   per   omnia
the ruin.   meanwhile   delicacies   the elements   through   all
  6   2   5   3   4

quærunt,   Nunquam   animo   pretiis   obstantibus.
they seek,   never   (their) desire   prices standing-in-the-way-of.
  1   2   4   1   3

Interiùs   si   Attendas,   magis   illa   juvant,
more closely   if   you attend,   more   those [things] please

quæ   pluris   emuntur.   Ergò   haud
which   for more   are bought.   Therefore   not
                         2

difficile   est,   perituram   arcessere
a difficult [matter of conscience]   it is,   to be squandered   to procure
  3   1   6   4

summam,   Lancibus   oppositis,   vel   matris   imagine
a sum   plates   being pawned,   or   of a mother   image
  5   3   2

fractâ,   Et   quadringentis   nummis   condire
a broken,   and   with the four-hundred   sesterces   to season
  1

gulosum   Fictile :   sic   veniunt   ad   miscellanea
a gluttonous   earthen-dish :   thus   they come   to   the hotchpotch

ludi.   Refert   ergò,   quis   hæc
of the (gladiatorial) school.   It matters   therefore,   who   these

eadem   paret :   in   Rutilo   nam   Luxuria
same (things) procures :   in   Rutilus   for   luxuriousness
               2   1

est ;   in   Ventidio   laudabile   nomen   Sumit,
it is ;   in   Ventidius   a praise-worthy   name   it takes,

et   a   censu   famam   trahit.   Illum   ego
and   from (his) estate   credit   derives.   him   I
                        2   1

jure   Despiciam,   qui   scit,   quanto   sublimior
rightly   sh'd despise,   who   knows,   how much   more lofty

Atlas   Omnibus   in   Libyâ   sit   montibus;
Atlas   than all   in   Libya   is   the mountains;
            2   4   1   3

hic   tamen   idem   Ignoret,   quantùm   ferratâ
this   yet   same (man) knows not,   how much   an iron-bound
 2   1   4

distet   ab   arcâ   Sacculus.   E   cœlo   descendit
differs   from   chest   a little-purse.   From heaven   descended
  2   3   1

γνῶθι σεαυτὸν,   Figendum   et   memori   tractandum
"KNOW THYSELF," (a maxim) to be fixed and in-the-mindful to be cherished
                        2   1

pectore,   sive   Conjugium   quæras,   vel   sacri
breast,   whether   matrimony   you seek,   or   of the sacred
                                                        3

in   parte   senatûs   Esse   velis: nec   enim
in   a part   senate   to be   you wish: not   for
1   2   2   1   4   1

loricam   poscit   Achillis   Thersites,   in   quâ
the armour   asks for   of Achilles   Thersites,   in   which
  6   3   5   2

se   transducebat   Ulixes   Ancipitem,   seu
himself   exposed   Ulysses   a doubtful,   or whether
3   2   1   4

tu   magno   discrimine   causam   Protegere
you   of great   risk   cause   to defend
 1   6   5   3

affectas;   te   consule,   dic   tibi,   qui sis,
aim;   yourself   consult,   tell   yourself,   who you are,
  2   2   1

Orator   vehemens,   an   Curtius   et   Matho
an orator   vehement,   or   a Curtius   and   a Matho

buccæ.   Noscenda est   mensura   sui
(mere) cheeks. must be known   the measure of one's-ownself
            3   1   2

spectandaque   rebus   In   summis   minimisque;
and kept-in-view   matters   in   the highest   and least;
                4   1   2   3

etiam   quum   piscis   emetur,   Ne   mullum
even   when   a fish   shall be bought,   lest   a mullet

cupias,   quum   sit   tibi   gobio   tantùm
you desire,   when   there is   to you   a gudgeon   only
                                        1   2

In   loculis.   Quis   enim   te,   deficiente
in   the purse   What   for   you,   failing
        3   2   1   5   7

crumenâ,   Et   crescente   gulâ,   manet exitus,
[your] purse,   and   increasing   gluttony,   awaits   end,
    6   8   10   9   4   3

ære paterno   Ac   rebus   mersis   in ventrem,
(your) patrimony   and   estate   sunk   into [your] belly,

fœnoris   atque   Argenti   gravis,   et   pecorum
of interest   and   silver   heavy,   and   flocks
2   3   4

agrorumque   capacem?   Talibus   a   dominis
and lands   capacious?   such   from   masters
   1   2   1

post   cuncta   novissimus   exit
after   all   last   goes forth

Annulus,   et   digito   mendicat   Pollio   nudo.
the ring,   and   with finger   begs   Pollio   bare.
    3   2   1   4

Non   præmaturi   cineres,   nec   funus
Not   prematur (are)   the ashes (of the funeral pile)   nor   death

acerbum   Luxuriæ;   sed   morte   magis
bitter   to luxury;   but (than)   death   more
   4   2

metuenda   senectus.   Hi   plerùmque   gradus:
to-be-dreaded   ol l-age.   These (are) commonly   the steps :
3

conducta   pecunia   Romæ   Et   coram   dominis
(is) borrowed   money   at Rome   and   before-the faces-of   the owners
2   1

consumitur :   inde   ubi   paulùm,   Nescio   quid,
is spent :   then   when   a little,   I know not   what,

superest,   et   pallet   fœnoris auctor,   Qui
remains,   and   grows pale   the money-lender,   (they) who
   2   1

vertère   solum,   Baias   et   ad   ostrea
have changed (their) soil,   to Baiæ   and   to   shell-fish

currunt.   Cedere   namque   foro   jam   non   est
run away.   to quit   for   the forum   now-a-days   not   is
    2   1   2   1

deterius,   quàm   Esquilias   a   ferventi   migrare
more discreditable,   than   to Esquiline   from   hot   to remove
   2   3   1

Suburâ.   Ille   dolor   solus   patriam   fugientibus,
Subura.   This   grief   the only   (their) country   to those fleeing,
   2   1   4   3

illa   Mœstitia   est,   caruisse   anno   Circensibus
this   the (only) sorrow   is,   to have lost   year   the Circensian (games)
    2

uno.   Sanguinis   in facie   non   hæret   gutta :
for one.   of blood   in their face   not   remains   a drop:
1   3   5   1   4   2

morantur   Pauci   ridiculum   effugientem   ex   Urbe
delay   few   ridiculous -   fleeing   from   the city
2   1   5   4

pudorem.   Experiere   hodie,   nunquid   pulcherrima
modesty.   You-shall-prove   to-day,   whether (these things)   very fine
3

dictu,   Persice,   non   præstem   vitâ   vel
to-be-talked-about,   Persicus,   I do not   exhibit   in my life   or

moribus   et   re;   Sed   laudem   siliquas   occultus
morals   and   in deed;   but   praise   pulse [while] in secret

ganeo;   pultes   coram   aliis   dictem
[I am] a glutton: pottage   in-the-presence   of others   I order   of my

puero,   sed   in   aure   placentas   Nam,
slave,   but   in   his ear   cheese-cakes.   For,

quum   sis   conviva   mihi   promissus,
since   you are   guest   my   promised,
           3   1   2

habebis   Evandrum,   venies   Tirynthius,
you shall have   an Evander,   you shall come   a Tirynthian,

aut   minor   illo   Hospes,   et   ipse   tamen
or   less   than he   a guest,   and   himself   yet
     2   1   2   1

contingens   sanguine   cœlum,   Alter   aquis:
akin to   by blood   heaven,   the one   by water:
           2   1

alter   flammis   ad   sidera   missus.   Fercula
the other   by flames   to   the skies   sent.   the courses of dishes

nunc   audi   nullis   ornata   macellis.   De
now   hear   by no   furnished   markets.   From [my]
           2   1

Tiburtino   veniet   pinguissimus   agro   Hædulus,
Tiburtian   shall come   the fattest   farm   little kid,
           2   3   1

et   toto   grege   mollior,   inscius   herbæ,
and   than the whole   flock   more tender,   ignorant   of grass,

Necdum   ausus   virgas   humilis   mordere
not yet   having ventured   the twigs   of the low   to browse on
           2   3   1

salicti,   Qui   plus   lactis   habet,   quam
willow-bed,   Which   more   of milk   has, [in his veins]   than

sanguinis;   et   montani   Asparagi,
blood;   and   mountain   Asparagus,

posito   quos   legit   villica
having-been-laid-down which   gathered   (my) farm-steward's wife
     5   1   3   2

fuso.   Grandia   præterea   tortoque   calentia
(her) spindle.   huge   besides   and in twisted   warm
     4   2   3   5   4

fœno   Ova   adsunt   ipsis   cum   matribus
hay   eggs   are-on-hand   themselves   with   the mothers,
6   1   3   1   2

et   servatæ   Parte   anni,   quales   fuerant
and   kept   a portion   of the year,   as   they had been
     2

Latin	in	vitibus,	uvæ:	Signinum	Syriumque
Gloss	on	the vines,	grapes:	the Signian	and Syrian
No.			1		

pyrum,	de	corbibus	isdem	Æmula
pear,	from	baskets	the same,	rivalling (those)
		2	1	3

Picenis	et	odoris	mala	recentis,	Nec
of Picenum	and	odor	apples	of a fresh,	nor
3	4	6	1	5	

metuenda	tibi,	siccatum	frigore	postquam
to be feared	by you,	dried	by the cold	since
		4	5	1

Autumnum	et	crudi	posuere	pericula
(their) Autumnal moisture	and	of crude	they have lost	the dangers
3	6	8	2	7

succi.	Hæc	olim	nostri	jam	luxuriosa
juice.	This	in-past-times	for our	already	a luxurious
9		2	6	3	4

senatus	Cœna	fuit.	Curius,	parvo	quæ
senate	supper	was.	Curius,	in (his) little	which
7	5	1		8	6

legerat	horto,	Ipse	focis	brevibus	ponebat
he had gathered	garden,	himself	over [his] little fires		used-to-place
7	9	1	3		2

oluscula,	quæ	nunc	Squalidus	in	magnâ
pot-herbs,	which	now	the squalid	in [his]	heavy
4			2		3

fastidit	compede	fossor,	Qui	meminit,
scorns	fetter	digger,	who	remembers,
5	4	1		

calidæ	sapiat	quid	vulva	popinæ.	Sicci
of the reeking	tastes	how	the vulva	cook-shop.	of the smoked
3	5	1	2	4	2

terga	suis,	rarâ	pendentia	crate,
flitches	swine,	from the wide-barred	hanging	rack,
1	3	5	4	6

Moris	erat	quondam	festis	servare
the custom	it was	formerly	for festal	to keep
2	1	3	5	4

diebus,	Et	natalitium	cognatis	ponere
days,	and [as] a birth-day-treat before [one's] relations			to set
		3		1

lardum,	Accedente	novâ,	si	quam	dabat
bacon,	being added	fresh,	if	any	afforded
2	3	1	4	7	6

hostia,	carne.	Cognatorum	aliquis,	titulo
a-sacrificial-victim	meat.	of the kin	someone,	with the title
5	2	2	1	

ter	consulis,	atque	Castrorum	imperiis	et
of "thrice	consul,"	and	of camps	the command and	
			3	2	4

dictatoris	honore	Functus,	ad	has	epulas
of dictator	the honor	having discharged,	to	these	feasts
6	5	1			

(16*)

solito   maturius   ibat,   Erectum   domito
[than] usual   earlier   used to go, thrown-over-his-shoulder the subdued
3   2   1   6   3

referens   a   monte   ligonem.   Quum   tremerent
bearing back   from   mountain (his)   spade.   When (men)   trembled at
1   2   4   5   2

autem   Fabios,   durumque   Catonem,   Et
but   the Fabii,   and the stern   Cato,   and
1

Scauros,   et   Fabricios,   postremò   severos
the Scauri,   and   the Fabricii, (when) in fine   the severe
                                                 4

Censoris   mores   etiam   collega   timeret;
of the Censor   character   even (his)   colleague   feared;
6   5   1   2   3

Nemo   inter   curas   et   seria   duxit
No one   among   cares   and   serious (things)   considered (it was)
1   4   2

habendum   Qualis   in   oceani   fluctu   testudo   nataret,
to be ranked   What-kind-of in   Ocean's   wave   tortoise   swam,
3   3   1   2

Clarum   Trojugenis   factura   ac   nobile
a splendid   for the Trojugenæ   destined-to-make and   noble
2   5   1   3

fulcrum   Sed   nudo   latere   et   parvis
couch-foot   but   bare (of ornament) with side   and   small
4   2   1

frons   ærea   lectis   Vile   coronati   caput
front   the brazen   sofas,   the rude   of a vine crowned   head
3   2   1   2   4   3

ostendebat   aselli,   Ad   quod   lascivi   ludebant
displayed   ass,   near   which   the frolicksome   used to play
1   3

ruris   alumni.   Tales   ergò   cibi,   qualis
of the country   lads.   such   then   the food,   as
2   1

domus   atque   supellex.   Tunc   rudis   et
the house   and   the furniture.   Then   rude   and
                                    1   3   4

Graias   mirari   nescius   artes,   Urbibus   eversis,
Grecian   to admire   unknowing   arts,   cities having been overthrown
7   6   5   8   16   17

prædarum   in   parte   reperta   Magnorum
of the booty   in   (his) part   found   of great
15   14   13   11

artificum   frangebat   pocula   miles,   Ut
artists   used to break   the drinking-cups   the soldier,   that
12   9   10   2

phaleris   gauderet   equus   cælataque   cassis
in his trappings   might rejoice (his) horse   and (his)embossed   helmet
3   2   1

Romuleæ   simulacra   feræ   mansuescere
of the Romulean   likenesses   wild beast   to grow tame
5   4   6   8

jussæ   Imperii   fato,   geminos   sub   rupe
bidden   of the empire   by the fate,   the twin   beneath   the rock
7   10   9   11   13   14

Quirinos,   Ac   nudam   effigiem   clypeo
Quirini,   and   the naked   image   with buckler
12   15   16   17   20

venientis   et   hastâ   Pendentisque   dei,
coming down   and   spear   and hanging (over him)   of the god
19   21   22   18

perituro   ostenderet   hosti.   Argenti   quod
about-to-perish   might display   to (his) enemy.   of silver   what
3   1   2

erat,   solis   fulgebat   in   armis.   Ponebant
there was,   alone   shone   in   arms,   They put,
4   1   2   3

igitur   Tusco   farrata   catino   Omnia
therefore,   in a Tuscan   (their) meal-foods   dish   all
4   3   2

tunc,   quibus   invideas,   si   lividulus
in those days   which   you w'd envy,   if   in-any-degree-envious
1

sis.   Templorum   quoque   majestas   præsentior
you were.   of temples   also   the majesty   (was) more present
2   3   1

et   vox   Nocte   ferè   mediâ   mediamque
and   a voice   about   midnight   and the midst of
2   3   4   6

audita   per   Urbem,   Littore   ab   Oceani
heard   through   the city,   the shore   from   of ocean
1   5   7   4   3   5

Gallis.   venientibus,   et   dis   Officium   vatis
the Gauls.   coming,   and   the gods   the office   of a prophet
1   2

peragentibus,   his   monuit   nos.   Hanc   rebus
discharging,   of-these-things   warned   us.   This   affairs
3   1   2   1   7

Latiis   curam   præstare   solebat   Fictilis
for the Latian   care   to show   used (while still) of earthenware,
6   2   5   4   8

et   nullo   violatus   Jupiter   auro.   Illa
and   by no   profaned   Jupiter   gold.   Those
9   11   10   3   1

domi   natas   nostrâque   ex   arbore   mensas
at home   grown   and our own   from   tree   tables
6   5   7   9   8   10   4

Tempora   viderunt;   hos   lignum   stabat   in
times   saw: these   the wood   was applied   to
2   3   2   4   5   1

usus,   Annosam   si   forte   nucem   dejecerat
uses,   full-of-years   if   perchance   a walnut-tree had prostrated
3   6   1   2   5   4

Eurus.   At   nunc   divitibus   coenandi   nulla
Eurus.   But   now   to the rich   in dining   (there is) no
3   3   1

voluptas,   Nil   rhombus,   nil   dama   sapit:
pleasure,   nothing   the turbot,   nothing   the venison   tastes:
2

putere   videntur   Unguenta   atque   rosæ,
to stink   seem   perfumes   and   roses,
4   3   1   2

latos   nisi   sustinet   orbes   Grande
the broad   unless   sustains   circumferences (of the tables)   a huge
5   1   4   2

ebur,   et   magno   sublimis   pardus   hiatu,
ivory,   and   with wide   a rampant   leopard   gaping (jaws)
3   3   1   2   4

Dentibus   ex   illis,   quos   mittit   porta
tusks   (made) from   those,   which   sends   the gate
3   1   2   3   1

Syenes,   Et   Mauri   celeres,   et   Mauro
of Syene,   and   Moors   the swift,   and (than) the Moor
2   3   1

obscurior   Indus,   Et   quos   deposuit
duskier (in hue)   the Indian,   and   which   has deposited
2   1   2

Nabatæo   bellua   saltu,   Jam   nimios,
in a Nabathæan   the huge-beast   glen,   now   too great,
3   1   4

capitique   graves.   Hinc   surgit   orexis,
and to the head   burdensome.   Hence   arises   appetite,
2   1

Hinc   stomacho   bilis: nam   pes   argenteus
Hence   in the stomach   gastric-juice: for   a (table) foot   of silver

illis,   Annulus   in   digito   quod   ferreus.
(is) to them,   ring (would be)   on the finger   what   an iron.
3   1   2

Ergò   superbum   Convivam   caveo,   qui   me
Therefore   a proud   guest   I shun,   who   me

sibi   comparat,   et   res   Despicit   exiguas.
with himself   compares,   and   means   despises (my)   scanty.
     3   1   2

Adeò   nulla   uncia   nobis   Est   eboris
insomuch   that not   an ounce   to us   is   of ivory,

nec   tessellæ,   nec   calculus   ex   hâc
neither   (my) dice   nor   counter   of   this

Materiâ :   quin   ipsa   manubria   cultellorum
material: nay   the very   handles   of (my) knives

Ossea.   Non   tamen   his   ulla   unquam
(are) of bone.   Not   yet   from these   any   ever
     2   1   8   3   5

opsonia   fiunt   Raucidula,   aut   ideo   pejor
viands   become   rank,   or on-that-account   the worse
4   6   7

gallina   secatur.   Sed   nec   structor   erit
does my hen   cut up.   But   neither   a carver   will there be

cui   cedere   debeat   omnis   Pergula,   discipulus
to whom   to yield   ought   every   carving-school, a pupil
           4   3   1   2

Trypheri   doctoris,   apud   quem   Sumine
of Trypherus   the professor   at whose   house   sow's udder
                                                                 4

cum   magno   lepus,   atque   aper,   et
with   a great   the hare,   and   the wild-boar, and
2   3   1

pygargus,   Et   Scythicæ   volucres,   et
the white antelope, and   Scythian   birds,   and

phœnicopterus   ingens,   Et   Gætulus   oryx,
flamingo   huge,   and   Gætulian   wild-goat

hebeti   lautissima   ferro   Cæditur,   et
with a blunted   a most sumptuous knife   is carved,   and
5   1   6   4   7

totâ   sonat   ulmea   cœna   Suburâ.
though the whole resounds   (though of elm supper   Suburra.
9   8   3   2   10

Nec   frustrum   capreæ   subducere,   nec
Neither   a slice   of roe   to-take-dexterously-off, nor

latus   Afræ   Novit   avis
the side   of an African   knows   bird
                           2   1

noster   tirunculus,   ac   rudis   omni
our   little novice,   and   untutored   all (his)

Tempore,   et   exiguæ   frustis   imbutus   ofellæ.
life,   and   of a small in pieces   initiated (only) cutlet.
                     3   2   1

Plebeios   calices,   et   paucis   assibus   emptos
Plebeian   cups,   and   for a few   pence   bought
8

Porriget   incultus   puer   atque   a   frigore
will hand (you) unadorned   a slave   and only   from   the cold
7   2   1   3   5   6

tutus: Non   Phryx.   aut   Lycius,   non
protected: not   a Phrygian, or   a Lycian,   not
4

a   mangone   petitus   Quisquam   erit,   et
from   a slave-dealer got   any one   will he be, and
3   2   1

magno.   Quum   posces,   posce   Latinè.
at a great (price). When   you-ask-for-anything, ask   in Latin.

Idem   habitus   cunctis,   tonsi,   rectique
(There is) the same dress   to all,   close-cropt,   and straight

capilli,   Atque   hodie   tantùm   propter
hair,   and   to-day   only   on account of

convivia   pexi   Pastoris   duri   hic   est
company   combed.   shepherd   of a hardy   this one   is
                          2   1

fllius, ille bubulci. Suspirat longo non
the son, that one of a neat-herd. he sighs after for a long not
                                                 4   2

visam tempore matrem, Et casulam et
seen time (his) mother, and (his) little hut and
3   5   1   3

notos tristis desiderat hædos, Ingenui
the familiar sad pines for kids, of ingenuous
      1   2   2

vultûs puer, ingenuique pudoris, (Qua'es
face a boy, and of ingenuous modesty, (such as (those)
     1

esse decet, quos ardens purpura vestit,)
to be it becomes, whom brilliant purple clothes,)
2   1

Nec pugillares defert in balnea raucus
Testiculos, nec vellendas jam præbuit alas
Crassa nec opposito pavidus tegit iuguina;
gutto. Hic tibi vina dabit, diffusa in
He you wines will give, racked in

montibus illis, A quibus ipse venit,
mountains those, from which he himself comes,
2   1

quorum sub vertice lusit: Namque una
whose under summit he has played: for one
2   1

atque eadem est vini patria atque
and the same is of the wine the country and
                       2   1

ministri. Forsitan expectes, ut Gaditana
of the attendant.

canoro Incipiat prurire choro, plausuque
probatæ Ad terram tremulo descendant
clune puellæ. Irritamentum Veneris languentis,
et acres Divitis urticæ. Major tamen
ista voluptas Alterius sexûs : magis ille
incenditur, et mox Auribus atque oculis
concepta urina movetur. Non capit has
nugas humilis domus. Audiat ille Testarum
crepitus cum verbis, nudum olido stans
Fornice mancipium quibus abstinet: ille
fruatur Vocibus obscœnis; omnique libidinis
arte, Qui Lacedæmonium pytismate lubricat
orbem : Namque ibi Fortunæ veniam damus.
     Alea turpis, Turpe et adulterium
gambling (is) disgraceful, disgraceful too (is) adultery

mediocribus.　　Hæc　　eadem　　　illi　　　Omnia
in (those) of moderate means.　These same (things) those (who are rich)　all
　　　　　　　　　　　　2　　　　　3　　　　5　　　　　1

quum ′　faciant,　　hilares　　nitidique　　　vocantur.
when　　　do,　　　jovial　　and splendid (fellows) they are called.
4　　　　　6

Nostra　　dabunt　　alios　　　hodie　　　convivia
Our　　　will give　　other　　to-day.　　banquet
　　　　　3　　　　　4　　　　　2　　　　　1

ludos :　　Conditor　　Iliados　　cantabitur,　atque
entertainments:　the author　of the Iliad　shall be chant. d,　an l
　　　　　　　　　　　　　　　　　　　　　　1

Maronis　Altisoni　　dubiam　　facientia　carmina
Maro　of high-sounding　doubtful　rendering　the verses
4　　　　3　　　　　　7　　　　　　5　　　　　2

palmam.　　Quid　　refert,　　tales　　versus　　quâ
the palm.　　What　　matters it,　such　　verses　with what
6　　　　　　　　　　　　　　3　　　　　4　　　　　1

voce　　legantur?　　Sed　　nunc　　dilatis　　averte
voice　may be read?　But　　now　　being put off　lay aside
2

negotia　　curis,　　Et　　gratam　　requiem　　dona
business　　cares,　　and　　a pleasing　respite　　grant
　　　　　1

tibi,　　quando　　licebit,　　Per　　totam　　cessare
yourself　since　　it-will-be-permitted,　through　the whole　to be idle
　　　　　　　　　　　　　　　　　2　　　　　　　　　　1

diem :　　non　　fœnoris　　ulla　　Mentio,　　nec,
day :　　not　　of interest in money　any　　mention,　　nor,

primâ　　si　　luce　　egressa　　reverti　　Nocte
　　　　if　　at daybreak having gone out　to return　at night

solet,　　tacito　　bilem　　tibi　　contrahat　uxor,
she is accustomed,　silent　the bile　to you　let stir up (your) wife
　　　　　6　　　　　4　　　　5　　　　1　　　3　　　2

Humida　　suspecti ;　　referens　　multitia　　rugis,

Vexatasque　comas,　et　vultum,　auremque　calentem.

Protinus　　ante　　meum　　quidquid　　dolet,
forthwith,　　before　　my　　whatever　grieves (you)
　　　　　　　　　　　　　　3　　　　　4

exue　　limen :　　Pone　　domum　et　servos,
divest yourself of　threshold:　Put aside　house　and　servants,
2　　　　　1

et　quidquid　frangitur　illis,　　Aut　perit:
and　whatever　is broken　by them,　or　is wasted:

ingratos　　ante　　omnia　　pone　　sodales.　Interea
ungrateful　before　　all　　put aside　friends.　Meanwhile
4　　　　　1　　　　2　　　　3

Megalesiacæ　　spectacula　mappæ　Idæum　solenne
of the Megalesian　the spectacles　napkin　the Idæan　solemnity
2　　　　　　　　1

colunt,　　similisque　　triumpho　Præda　caballorum
grace,　　and like one　in a triumph　the prey　of horses

Prætor sedet ; ac, mihi pace Immensæ
the Prætor sits; and, me without offence of the immense
                   1   4   5   6

nimiæque licet si dicere, plebis,
and over-grown it be permitted if to say it, crowd
   7   3   2   9   8

Totam hodie Romam circus capit, et
entire to-day Rome the circus takes in, and
 4   2   5   1   3

fragor aurem Percutit, eventum
the applause (my) ear strikes, the success
    2   1   3

viridis quo colligo panni. Nam, si
of the green from which I infer cloth. For, if
         1   2

deficeret, mœstam attonitamque videres Hanc
it sh'd fail, sad and astonished you w'd see this

urbem, veluti Cannarum in pulvere victis
city, as if of Cannæ in the dust conquered
                 5   3   4   2

Consulibus. Spectent juvenes, quos clamor
for Consuls. Let behold [the games] young men, whom shouting
  1   1   3   2

et audax Sponsio, quos cultæ decet
and bold betting, whom a spruce it becomes
                           3   1

assedisse puellæ ; Spectent hoc nuptæ,
to sit by damsel; Let behold that married women,
   2   1   3   4   2

juxta recubante marito, Quod pudeat
near reclining the husband, which it w'd shame
 3   2   1

narrâsse aliquem præsentibus ipsis. Nostra
to have narrated any one, being present themselves Our
  2   1   1   2

bibat vernum contracta cuticula solem,
let imbibe the vernal wrinkled skin sun,
 1 5   3   4

Effugiatque togam. Jam nunc in balnea
and shun the toga. Already now into the bath

salvâ Fronte licet vadas, quanquam solida
with unblushing brow you may go, although a solid

hora supersit Ad sextam. Facere hoc
hour remains to the sixth. To do this

non possis quinque diebus Continuis,
you may not be able for five days continuous
                       2   1

quia sunt talis quoque tædia vitæ
because there are of such also tædia a life
          2   1   5   3

Magna. Voluptates commendat rarior usus.
great. Pleasures enhances a rarer indulgence
 4   4   3   1   2

SATIRE XII.

ARGUMENT.

Catullus, a valued friend of the poet, had narrowly escaped shipwreck. In a letter of rejoicing to their common friend, Corvinus, Juvenal describes the danger that his friend had incurred, and his own hearty and disinterested delight at his preservation, contrasting his own sacrifices of thanksgiving at the event, with those offered by the designing legacy-hunters, by which the rich and childless were attempted to be ensnared.

NATALI, Corvine, die mihi dulcior hæc
(than my) NATAL, Corvinus, day to me sweeter (is) this
    1   2

lux, Quâ festus promissa deis animalia
day, in which the festal promised to the gods the animals
               1   5   6   4

cespes Exspectat. Niveam Reginæ ducimus
turf awaits. a snow-white to the queen (of the gods) we lead
  2   3   2   4   1

agnam : Par vellus dabitur pugnanti
lamb: a similar fleece shall be given to (her) fighting
  3

Gorgone Maura. Sed procul extensum
Gorgon with the Mauritanian. But (his) far stretched
  2   1   7   8

petulaus quatit hostia funem, Tarpeio
the petulant shakes victim rope, for Tarpeian
  1   6   2   9   4

servata Jovi, frontemque coruscat : Quippe
reserved Jove, and [his] forehead brandishes: Since he is
  3   5   2   1

ferox vitulus, templis maturus et aræ,
a spirited calf, for temples ripe, and for the altar,
                  2   1

Spargendusque mero quem jam pudet
and ready to be-sprinkled with wine which now it shames

ubera	matris	Ducere,	qui	vexat
the teats	of [his] mother	to drain,	who	butts

nascenti	robora	cornu.	Si	res	ampla
with his sprouting	the oaks	horn.	If	fortune	an ample
2	1			2	1

domi,	similisque	affectibus	esset,	Pinguior
at home,	and equal	to [my] wishes	were,	fatter [than]
4			3	2

Hispullâ	traheretur	taurus,	et	ipsâ
Hispulla	sh'd be drawn [to sacrifice]	a bull,	and from [his] very
3	8	1	4	5

Mole	piger,	nec	finitimâ	nutritus	in
bulk	slow-paced,	nor	a neighboring	fed	in
6	7		3	1	2

herbâ,	Læta	sed	ostendens	Clitumni
pasture,	the joyous	but	giving-evidence-of	of Clitumnus
	5		4	7

pascua	sanguis	iret,	et a	grandi	cervix
pastures	(his) blood	sh'd flow,	and by	a strong	a neck
6	2	3	5	4	1

ferienda	ministro,	Ob	reditum
requiring-to-be-struck	assistant,	on account of	the return
2	5		

trepidantis	adhuc,	horrendaque	passi
trembling	still,	and horrible [things]	having suffered
2	3	4 8	5 7

Nuper,	et	incolumem	sese	mirantis
lately,	and	safe	himself	wondering at
6	9	12	11	10

amici.	Nam	præter	pelagi	casus,	et
of (my) friend.	For	besides	of the sea	the dangers,	also
1			2	1	2

fulguris	ictum	Evasit	densæ	cœlum	abscondére
the lightning's	stroke	he escaped	thick	the sky	hid
		1		3	2

tenebræ	Nube	unâ,	subitusque	antennas
darkness	cloud	with one,	and a sudden	the yard-arms
1	2	1		3

impulit	ignis	Quum	se	quisque	illo
struck	thunderbolt	when	himself	everyone	by it
2	1		3	1	5

percussum	crederet,	et	mox	Attonitus
struck	believed,	and	at once	amazed
4	2			

nullum	conferri	posse	putaret	Naufragium
no	to be compared	to be able	thought	shipwreck
2	5	4	1	3

velis	ardentibus.	Omnia	fiunt	Talia,	tam
to sails	burning.	All (things) are made	such,	so
6					

graviter,	siquando	poetica	surgit	Tempestas.
strongly,	whenever	a poetical	arises	tempest.
		2		1

Genus   ecce   aliud   discriminis: audi   Et
K nd   behold   another   of peril: hear   a..l
8   1   2

miserere   iterum,   quanquam   sint   cætera
pity   a second-time,   although   are   the rest
                                              2   1

sortis   Ejusdem: pars   dira   quidem,   sed
sort   of the same: part   a dreadful   indeed,   but
4   3   2   1

cognita   multis,   Et   quam   votivâ   testantur
known to   many,   and   which   with a votive   attest
                                  4   8

fana   tabellâ   Plurima.   Pictores   quis   nescit
temples   tablet   full many.   (Painters   who   knows not
2.   1   3   1   2

ab   Iside   pasci?   Accidit   et   nostro
by   Isis   to be maintained?)   happens   a so   to our
        6   4   3

similis   fortuna   Catullo.   Quum   plenus
a similar   fortune   Catullus.   When   full
1   2   4

fluctu   medius   foret   alveus,   et   jam,
with the wave   the middle   was   hold,   and   now,
1   4   3   2

Alternum   puppis   latus   evertentibus   undis,
the alternate   of (his) ship   side   heaving up   the waves,
3   5   4   2   1

Arbori   incertæ   nullam   prudentia   cani
m ist   to the uncertain,   no   the foresight   of the hoary
8   7   5   1   2

Rectoris   conferret   opem;   decivere   jactu
pilot   could render   aid;   to compound by casting overboard
3   4   6   2   4

Cœpit   cum   ventis,   imitatus   castora,   qui
he began   with   the winds,   having imitated   the beaver,   who
1   3

se   Eunuchum   ipse   facit,   cupiens   evadere
himself   a eunuch   himself   makes,   desiring   to escape

damno   Testiculi: adeo   medicatum   intelligit
with the loss   of a testicle: so   medicinal   he understands

inguen.   Fundite.   quæ   mea   sunt,   dicebat,
the privy-member [to be]   "cast out,   which   mine   are,"   said,
                                           2   4   3

cuncta,   Catullus,   Præcipitare,   volens   etiam
"all [things,]   Catullus,   to pitch over,   willing   even
1   3   1   2

pulcherrima,   vestem   purpuream,   teneris
[his] most beautiful [things],   a robe   of purple,   for luxurious
                                                              3

quoque   Mæcenatibus   aptam,   Atque   alias,   quarum
even   Mæcenases,   fit,   and   others,   whose
2

generosi graminis ipsum Infecit natura
of the generous pasture very has tinged the quality
4 5 1 6 3

pecus, sed et egregius fons Viribus
fleece, moreover also the excellent spring-water, powers
2 2

occultis, et Bæticus adjuvat aër. Ille
with [its] hidden, and the Bætic assists atmosphere. He
1 2 1

nec argentum dubitabat mittere, lances
neither [his] silver hesitated to cast away, salver

Parthenio factas, urnæ cratera capacem,
by Parthenius made, of-three-gallons a bowl capable,
3 1 2

Et dignum sitiente Pholo, vel conjuge
and worthy the thirsting Pholus, or the wife

Fusci. Adde et bascaudas, et mille
of Fuscus. Add also bascaudæ, and a thousand

escaria, multum Cælati, biberat quo
chargers, much of chased [work,] had drunk from which
2 1

callidus emptor Olynthi. Sed quis nunc
the cunning purchaser of Olynthus. But what now
2

alius, qua mundi parte, quis audet
other [man] in what of the world part, who dares
1 2 1

Argento præferre caput, rebusque salutem?
to his silver to prefer [his] head, and to [his] property (his) safety?
3 1 2 4

Non propter vitam faciunt patrimonia quidam,
Not for-the-sake-of living make fortunes some,
2 1

Sed vitio cæci propter patrimonia vivunt.
but from vice blind for the sake of fortunes they live.

Jactatur rerum utilium pars maxima:
is-thrown-overboard (even) of things useful part the greatest:
5 3 4 2 1

sed nec Damna levant. Tunc, adversis
but neither do (these) losses relieve the ship. Then, the perils

urgentibus, illuc Recidit, ut malum fero
being urgent, to that pass it came, that the mast to the axe

submitteret, ac se Explicat angustum:
he submitted, and himself extricates reduced-to-straits:

Discriminis ultima quando Præsidia
of danger [it is] the last resource when helps

afferimus, navem factura minorem. I nunc,
we apply, the ship designed to make less. Go now,

et   ventis   animam   committe,   dolato,   Confisus
and   to the winds [your] life   commit,   to a hewn,   trusting
                                                      2   1

ligno,   digitis   a   morte   remotus   Quatuor,
plank,   fingers   from   death   removed   four,
              3   1   2

aut   septem,   si   sit   latissima   tædal   Mox
or   seven,   if   be   the thickest   the pine!   and then
                            2   1

cum   reticulis,   et   pane   et   ventre   lagenæ,
with   net-bags,   and   bread   and   a belly   of a flagon,

Adspice   sumendas   in   tempestate   secures.
look after   to-be-taken-in-hand   in   the tempest   the hatchets.
                  2   3   4   1

Sed   postquam   jacuit   planum   mare,   tempora
But   after   lay   level   the sea,   the times
                        2   3   1   2

postquam   Prospera   vectoris,   fatumque   valentius
after   propitious [were]   of the pilot,   and destiny   more prevailing over
  1

Euro,   Et   pelago,   postquam   Parcæ   meliora
Eurus,   and   the deep,   after   Parcæ   better
                                                  2   6

benignâ   Pensa   manu   ducunt   hilares,   et
with a benign   tasks   hand   draw   the cheerful,   and
  4   7   5   3   1

staminis   albi   Lanificæ;   modicâ   nec
thread   of a white   (are) spinsters,   than a moderate   nor
  3   2   1   4   1

multum   fortior   aurâ   Ventus   adest: inopi
much   stronger   breeze   the wind   is: with a poor
  2   3   5   3

miserabilis   arte   cucurrit   Vestibus   extentis,
the wretched   contrivance   ran along   (the sailor's) clothes   spread out,
  1   4   5   6   7

et,   quod   superaverat   unum,   Velo   prora
and   which   had remained   alone;   sail   prow
  8   11   13   12   10   2

suo.   Jam   deficientibus   Austris,   Spes
with its.   Now   subsiding   the south-winds,   the hope
  9   2   3   1

vitæ   cum   sole   redit: tum   gratus   Iulo,
of life   with   the sun   returns: then   pleasing   to Iulus,
                                                  1   4   5

Atque   novercali   sedes   prælata   Lavino,
and   to (his) step-mother   (as) an abode   preferred   Lavinium,
  6   9   7   8   10

Conspicitur   sublimis   apex,   cui   candida
is beheld   the lofty   peak,   to which   the white
  11   2   3   1

nomen   Scrofa   dedit.   (lætis   Phrygibus   mirabile
name   Sow   gave,   to the glad land   Phrygian   wonderful
  4   2   5   3   2

(17*)

sumen,)   Et   nunquam   visis   triginta   clara
an udder,   and   never before   seen   for thirty   famous
1   4   5   2   1

mamillis.   Tandem   intrat   positas   inclusa
teats.   At length   (the ship) enters   built   the enclosed
3   2   4

per   æquora   moles,   Tyrrhenamque   Pharon
through   waters   the moles,   and the Tuscan   Pharos
3   5   1

porrectaque   brachia   rursum,   Quæ   pelago
and extended   the arms   back,   which   sea
1   3   2   3

occurrunt   medio,   longèque   relinquunt   Italiam.
jut-out   into the middle,   and far   leave behind   Italy.
1   2

Non   sic   igitur   mirabere   portus,
Not   thus   therefore   will you wonder at   the harbors,

Quos   natura   dedit.   Sed   truncâ   puppe
Which   nature   has made.   But   with mutilated   bark

magister   Interiora   petit   Baianæ   pervia
the master   the inner   steers for   to a Baian   pervious
2   1   7   6

cymbæ   Tuti   stagna   sinûs.   Gaudent   ibi
wherry   of the safe   still-waters   harbor.   rejoice   there
8   4   3   5   6   1

vertice   raso   Garrula   securi   narrare
with crowns   shaven [their] garrulous   the secure   to narrate
4   5   8   2   7

pericula   nautæ.   Ite   igitur,   pueri,   linguis
dangers   sailors.   Go,   then,   boys,   with tongues
9   3

animisque   faventes,   Sertaque   delubris   et
and minds   favoring,   and garlands   in the temple   and
1   3

farra   imponite   cultris,   Ac   molles
meal   place   on the sacrificial-knives,   and   the soft
2   2

ornate   focos   glebamque   virentem: Jam
adorn   hearths   and turf-altar   green: soon
1   2   1

sequar,   et   sacro,   quod   præstat,   ritè
I shall follow,   and   the sacred rite,   which is most important,   duly having

peracto,   Indè   domum   repetam,   graciles
been performed,   then   home   I shall return,   slender
8

ubi   parva   coronas   Accipiunt   fragili   simulacra
where [my] little   chaplets   receive   with brittle   images
1   2   9   7   5   3

nitentia   cerâ.   Hic   nostrum   placabo   Jovem,
shining   wax.   Here   my own   I shall propitiate   Jove.
4   6   2   1

laribusque   paternis   thura   dabo   atque
and to (my) lares   paternal   incense   I shall give   and

omnes   violae   jactabo   colores.   Cuncta
all   of the violet shall scatter colors.   all (things)
2   4   1   3

nitent: longos   erexit   janua   ramos,   Et
look bright: long   has set up   the gateway   branches,   and
3   2   1

matutinis   operatur   festa   lucernis.   Nec
with morning-lighted celebrates the festivities lamps.   nor
3   1   2   1

suspecta   tibi   sint   hæc,   Corvine.   Catullus,
suspected   by you   let be   these (things), Corvinus.   Catullus,
5   6   2 4   3

Pro   cujus   reditu   tot   pono   altaria,   parvos
for   whose   return   so many   I erect   altars,   little
                              2   1   3

Tres   habet   hæredes.   Libet   exspectare,   quis
three   has   heirs.   You-may   look-out-for (one), who
2   1

ægram   Et   claudentem   oculos   gallinam
a sick   and   closing [her]   eyes   hen
2   4   5   6   3

' impendat   amico   Tam   sterili.   Verùm
w'd expend   on a friend so   unproductive. But
1

hæc   nimia   est   impensa: coturnix   Nulla
this (even) too-great   is   an outlay: quail   no
          2   1   2   1

unquam   pro   patre   cadet.   Sentire   calorem
ever   for   a father   will fall. to feel   a fever
4   6   7   3 5   7   8

Si   cœpit   locuples   Gallita,   et   Paccius,
if   begins   rich   Gallita,   and   Paccius,
1   6   2   3   4

orbi,   Legitimè   fixis   vestitur tota   tabellis
childless, in-due-form   affixed   is clothed the whole with-votive-tablets
5   6   5   3   1   4

Porticus: exsistunt,   qui   promittant   hecatomben,
temple-porch: there are,   who   w'd promise   a hecatomb,
2

Quaenus   hic   non   sunt   nec   venales
Since   here   not   are   neither   for-sale
             2   5   4   1   6

elephanti,   Nec   Latio,   aut
elephants,   nor   in Latium,   or
3

usquam   nostro   sub   sidere   talis
anywhere   our   In   climate   such
              2   1

Belua   concipitur;   sed   furvà   gente   petita,
a beast   is generated;   but   from the dusky nation   fetched,
                                      2   3   1

Arboribus   Rutulis   et   Turni   pascitur
in the forests Rutulian   and   of Turnus   he is fed
2   3   4   6   1

agro,   Cæsaris   armentum,   nulli   servire   paratum
field,   Cæsar's   herd,   no   to serve   prepared
5   3   2   1

Privato: siquidem   Tyrio   parere   solebant
private (individual:)   since   Tyrian   to obey   used
          1   6   5   4

Hannibali,   et   nostris   ducibus,   regique   Molosso,
Hannibal,   and   our   generals,   and King   Molossus,
7

Horum   majores,   ac   dorso   ferre   cohortes,
their   ancestors,   and   on (their) back   to bear   cohorts,
2   3

Partem   aliquam   belli,   et,   euntem   in
portion   no mean   of the war,   and   going   into
2   1   2   3

prœlia   turrim.   Nulla   igitur   mora   per
battles   a tower.   No   therefore   delay   through
       1   2   1

Novium,   mora   nulla   per   Histrum   Pacuvium,
Novius,   delay   none   through   Hister   Pacuvius,

quin   illud   ebur   ducatur   ad   aras,   Et   cadat
that not   that   ivory   is led   to the   altars.   and   falls

ante   lares   Gallitæ,   victima   sola   Tantis
before   the lares   of Gallita,   a victim   alone   such great
                                         2

digna   deis,   et   captatoribus   horum.
worthy of   gods,   and   the favor-courters of these (i.e. the rich and childless).
1

Alter   enim,   si   concedas   mactare,   vovebit
one-or-other   for   if   you allow (him)   to sacrifice,   will vow
2   1

De   grege   servorum   magna   aut   pulcherrima
from (his) flock   of slaves   the grown-up   or   the most beautiful
                                         2

quæque   Corpora;   vel   pueris   et   frontibus
all   bodies;   or   on (his) boys   and   the brows
1

ancillarum   Imponet   vittas: et,   si   qua
of (his) female slaves   will place   fillets: and,   if   any

est   nubilis   illi   Iphigenia   domi,   dabit
is   marriageable   to him   Iphigenia   at home,   he will give
3   4   2   5

hanc   altaribus;   etsi   Non   sperat   tragicæ
her   to the altars;   though   he does not   hope for   of the tragic
                                         3

furtiva   piacula   cervæ.   Laudo   meum
the furtive   substitution   stag.   I commend   my
1   2

civem,   nec   comparo   testamento   Mille
fellow-citizen,   and   do not compare   to a will   a thousand

rates: nam,   si   Libitinam   evaserit   æger,
ships: for,   if   Libitina   shall have escaped   the sick man
                           3   2   1

Delebit   tabulas,   inclusus   carcere   nassæ
he will destroy   [his]   will,   inclosed   in the prison   of the weel

Post   meritum   sane   mirandum,   atque
after   a service   so truly   wonderful,   and

omnia   soli   Forsan   Pacuvio
all   alone   perhaps   to Pacuvius
4   6   1   5

breviter   dabit.   Ille   superbus
in a few words   will give.   He   proud
2   3

Incedet   victis   rivalibus.   Ergò   vides,
will strut over (his)   defeated   rivals.   Therefore   you see,

quàm   Grande   operæ pretium   faciat   jugulata
how   great   a recompense   may gain (for him)   the slain
                                          3   1

Mycenis.   Vivat Pacuvius,   quæso,   vel
Mycenian maid.   may Pacuvius live,   I pray,   even
2

Nestora   totum: Possideat,   quantum   rapuit
Nestor: a whole   may he possess,   as much as   plundered
                                                        2

Nero: montibus   aurum   Exæquet;   nec
Nero: to mountains   [his] gold   may-he-make equal;   nor
1   4   2   3

amet   quenquam,   nec   ametur   ab   ullo!,
may-he-love   anybody,   nor   be loved   by   any one!

SATIRE XIII.

ARGUMENT.

Calvinus had left a sum of money in the hands of a confidential person, who, when he came to redemand it, forswore the deposit. The indignation and fury expressed by Calvinus at this breach of trust, reached the ear of his friend Juvenal, who endeavors to sooth and comfort him under his loss. The different topics of consolation follow one another naturally and forcibly, and the horrors of a troubled conscience were perhaps never depicted with such impressive solemnity as in this Satire.

EXEMPLO	quodcunque	malo	committitur,
EXAMPLE	whatever	with bad	is committed,
4	1	3	2

ipsi	Displicet	auctori.	Prima	est	hæc
himself	displeases	the author.	the first	is	this
3	1	2	3	2	1

ultio,	quòd	se	Judice	nemo	nocens
revenge,	that	himself [being] judge	no one	guilty

absolvitur,	improba	quamvis	Gratia	fallaci
is absolved,	the corrupt	although	influence	by the false
	2	1	3	6

Prætoris	vicerit	urnâ.	Quid	sentire
of the Prætor	may-have-gained-his-cause	urn.	what	feel
4	5	7		3

putas !	omnes,	Calvine,	recenti	De	scelere
do you think	all,	Calvinus,	the recent	about	villany
1	2		2	1

et	fidei	violatæ	crimine?	Sed	nec	Tam
and	of faith	violated	the charge?	But	neither	so
	2	3	1

tenuis	census	tibi	contigit,	nt	mediocris
slender	our income	to you	has fallen,	that	of a moderate

Jacturæ	te	mergat	onus;	nec	rara	videmus,
loss	you	s'd sink	the weight;	nor	rarely	do we see,
3	5	4	1

Quæ pateris. Casus multis hic
(the things) which you are suffering. a misfortune to many this (is)
2 4 1

cognitus, ac jam Tritus, et e medio
known, and now trite, and from the midst
3 2

Fortunæ ductus acervo. Ponamus nimios
of Fortune's drawn heap. Let us lay aside excessive
1

gemitus: flagrantior æquo Non debet
complaints: more violent than (what is) just not ought
6 4 3

dolor esse viri, nec vulnere major.
grief to be a man's, nor (than) the wound greater.
2 5 1 2 1

Tu quamvis levium minimam exiguamque
you whereas of light the least and trifling
2 1 9 6 7

malorum Particulam vix ferre potes,
ills particle scarcely to bear are able,
10 8 4 5 3

spumantibus ardens Visceribus, sacrum tibi
with foaming burning bowels, a sacred to you
2 1 6 5

quòd non reddat amicus Depositum.
because not returns (your) friend deposit.
1 4 3 2

Stupet hæc, qui jam post terga
Can he be amazed at these (things), who already behind (his) back

reliquit Sexaginta annos, Fonteio Consule
has left sixty years, Fonteius [being] Consul
2

natus? An nihil in melius tot rerum
born? nothing for the better of so many things
1 2 3 5 6

proficis usu? Magna quidem, sacris
do you profit by the experience? great indeed, in the sacred
1 4 7

quæ dat præcepta libellis, Victrix Fortunæ
which gives the precepts books, the conqueror of Fortune
2 6 8 4 5

Sapientia. Ducimus autem Hos quoque
Wisdom. We deem yet those also
3 2 1

felices, qui ferre incommoda vitæ, Nec
happy, who to bear the inconveniences of life, nor
2

jactare jugum, vitâ didicêre magistrâ.
to cast off the yoke, life have learned (being their) mistress.
1

Quæ tam festa dies, ut cesset prodere
What so solemn day, that it fails to disclose
2 3 1

furem,   Perfidiam,   fraudes,   atque   omni
a thief,   perfidy,   frauds,   and   every
                                                        4

ex   crimine   lucrum   Quæsitum,   et   partos
from   crime   gain   sought,   and   gotten
3   5   1   2   2

gladio   vel   pyxide   nummos?   Rari   quippe
by the sword or   poison   money?   rare   forsooth (are)
                                  1

boni: numerus   vix   est   totidem,   quot
the good: the number   scarcely   is   so many,   as

Thebarum   portæ,   vel   divitis   ostia   Nili.
of Thebes   the gates, or   of fertilizing   the mouths Nile.
2   1   2   1

Nona   ætas   agitur,   pejoraque   sæcula   ferri
the ninth age   is now passing, and worse   periods   of iron
                                                                2

Temopribus,   quorum   sceleri   non   invenit
(than) the times, of which   for the villany not   has found
1   2   1   6   5   7

ipsa   Nomen   et   a   nullo   posuit   natura
herself   a name   and   from no   has imposed (one) nature
4   8   9   11   12   10   3

metallo.   Nos   hominum   divûmque   fidem
metal.   We   of men   and gods   the faith
                       3   2

clamore   ciemus,   Quanto   Fæsidium   laudat
with clamor   invoke,   with-as-much-as   Fæsidius   praises
                1   4   3

vocalis   agentem   Sportula.   Dic,   senior,
the vocal   pleading   Sportula.   Say,   old man,
1   2

bullâ   dignissime,   nescis,   Quas   habeat
the bulla   most worthy of, know you not,   what   has
2   1   4

Veneres   aliena   pecunia?   nescis,   Quem   tua
charms   another's   money?   know-you-not,   what   your
1   2   3   2

simplicitas   risum   vulgo   moveat,   quum
simplicity   a laugh   in-the-crowd   may excite,   when
3   1   5   4

Exigis   a   quoquam,   ne   pejeret,   et   putet   ullis
you exact from anyone, (that) he sh'd not forswear, and   sh'd think to any
                                                                       4

Esse   aliquod   numen   templis,   aræque
to be   any   divinity   temples,   and to the altar
3   1   2

rubenti?   Quondam   hoc   indigenæ   vivebant
red [with blood]?   Formerly   in this   the aborigines lived
                                 3   1   2

more,   priùs quàm   Sumeret   agrestem   posito
manner,   before   took   the rustic   laid down
           3   4   7

diademate | falcem | Saturnus | fugiens; | tunc,
[his] diadem | sickle | Saturn, | fleeing; | then,
6 | 5 | 1 | 2 |

quum | virguncula | Juno, | Et | privatus | adhuc
when | a little maid | Juno [was], | and | private | as yet
| 2 | 1 | | 3 | 2

Idæis | Jupiter | antris. | Nulla | super
in the Idæan | Jupiter | caves. | no | above
1 | | | | 3

nubes | convivia | cœlicolarum, | Nec | puer
the clouds | feasts | of the heavenly habitants, | nor | boy
| 1 | 2 | | 2

Iliacus, | formosa | nec | Herculis | uxor | Ad
Trojan, | beauteous | nor | of Hercules | wife | at
1 | 2 | 1 | 4 | 3 |

cyathos, | et | jam | siccato | nectare | tergens
the cups, | and | now | drained | the nectar | wiping
1 | | | 2 | 1 | 4

Brachia | Vulcanus | Liparæâ | nigra | tabernâ.
[his] arms | Vulcan | with the Liparæan | black | forge.
5 | 3 | 7 | 6 | 8

Prandebat | sibi | quisque | deus, | nec | turba
dined | by himself | every | god, | nor | (was) the crowd
3 | | 1 | 2 | |

deorum | Talis, | ut | est | hodie, | contentaque
of gods | such, | as | it is | now-a-days, | and content
| | | | | 2

sidera | paucis | Numinibus | miserum | urgebant
the stars | with a few | divinities | the wretched | pressed on
1 | | | 2 | 1

Atlanta | minori | Pondere. | Nondum | aliquis
Atlas | with a less | weight. | Not yet | any one

sortitus | triste | profundi | Imperium, | aut
shared | the gloomy | of the deep | Empire. | or
| | 2 | 1 |

Siculâ | torvus | cum | conjuge | Pluton.
(his) Sicilian | (was there) the grim | with | wife | Pluto.
5 | 1 | 4 | 6 | 3

Nec | rota, | nec | Furiæ, | nec | saxum,
nor [Ixion's] wheel, | | nor | the Furies, | nor [Sisyphus'] stone,
| 2 | | | |

aut | vulturis | atri | Pœna; | sed | infernis
or | vulture | of the black | punishment; | but | infernal
| 3 | 2 | 1 | | 4

hilares | sine | regibus | umbræ. | Improbitas
jocund | without | Kings | the shades [were]. | Villany
2 | 3 | | 1 |

illo | fuit | admirabilis | ævo. | Credebant
in that | was | [a thing] to be wondered at | age. | They believed
| 2 | | 1 |

hoc | grande | nefas, | et | morte | piandum,
this | a great | crime, | and | by death | to be expiated,

Si | juvenis | vetulo | non | adsurrexerat, | et | si
if | a youth | to an elderly [man] | not | had risen | and | if
| | 4 | 2 | 1 | 3 |

(18)

Latin	Latin	Latin	Latin	Latin	Latin
Barbato	cuicunque	puer,	licet	ipse	videret
bearded	to any one	a boy,	though	he himself	might see
3	2	1			
Plura	domi	fraga,	et	majores	glandis
more	at home	strawberries,	and	greater	of acorn
2	1				2
acervos.	Tam	venerabile		erat	præcedere
heaps.	so	venerable		was it	to precede
1					
quatuor	annis,	Primaque	par	adeò	sacræ
by four	years.	and the first (was)	equal	so	to sacred
		2	4	3	
lanugo	senectæ!	Nunc,	si		depositum
down	old age!	now,	if		a deposit
1					5
non	infitietur	amicus,		Si	reddat
not	sh'd deny	a friend,		if	he sh'd give back
3	2 4	1			
veterem	cum	totâ	æruginc		follem,
an old	with	all the	rust		purse,
	2				1
Prodigiosa	fides,	et	Tuscis	digna	libellis,
[it is] prodigious	honesty,	and	the Tuscan	worthy	books,
			2	1	
Quæque	coronatâ	lustrari	debeat		agnâ.
and which	by a crowned	to be expiated	ought		she-lamb.
	3	2	1		
Egregium	sanctumque		virum	si	cerno,
an excellent	and upright		man	if	I behold,
bimembri	Hoc	monstrum		puero,	aut
to a double-limbed	this	monster		boy,	or
3	1	2			
miranti	sub	aratro	Piscibus	inventis,	et
the wondering	under	plough	to fishes.	found,	and
4	3		1	2	
fœtæ	comparo	mulæ,	Sollicitus,		tanquam
with foal	I compare	a mule,	solicitous,		as though
2	3	1			
lapides	effuderit	imber,	Examenve		apium
stones	had poured forth	a shower	or a swarm		of bees
3	2	1			
longâ	consederit	uvâ	Culmine		delubri,
in a long	had settled	cluster	on the top		of a temple,
2	1				
tanquam	in	mare	fluxerit	amnis	Gurgitibus
as though	into	the sea	had flowed	a river	with gulfs
	3		2	1	
miris,	et	lactis	vortice	torrens.	Intercepta
wondrous,	and	of milk	with a whirlpool	rushing.	intercepted
		3	2	1	4
decem	quereris	sestertia	fraude		Sacrilegâ?
ten	do-you-complain-of	sestertia	fraud		by impious?
2	1	3	6		5

Quid   si   bis centum   perdidit   alter   Hoc
What   if   two hundred   has lost   another   in this
                  3   2   1   5

arcana   modo?   majorem   tertius   illâ
secret   [sestertia]   manner?   a greater   a third   than that
4   2   1   4

Summam,   quam   patulæ   vix   ceperat   angulus
sum,   which   of his wide scarce   had contained, the corner,
3   2   5   4   1

arcæ?   Tam   facile   et   pronum   est
chest?   so   easy   and   natural   is it
3

superos   contemnere   testes,   Si   mortalis   idem
the gods above   to contemn   (who are) witnesses if mortal   the same
2   1   2   4

nemo   sciat!   Adspice,   quantâ   voce   neget;
no   know!   see,   with how great a voice he denies (it;)
1   3   3

quæ   sit   ficti   constantia   vultûs.   Per
what   there is of feigned steadiness   countenance.   by
                   2   3   1

solis   radios,   Tarpeiaque   fulmina   jurat,
the sun's   rays,   and the Tarpeian   thunderbolts   he swears,

Et   Martis   frameam,   et   Cirrhæi   spicula
and   of Mars   the glaive,   and   of the Cirrhæan   the darts
        2   1   2   1

vatis,   Per   calamos   venatricis .   pharetramque
prophet,   by   the shafts   huntress   and quiver
                                   4   1   2

Puellæ,   Perque   tuum,   pater   Ægæi,
of the Virgin,   and by   thy,   father   of Ægeus
3   3   4

Neptune,   tridentem;   Addit, et   Herculeos   arcus,
O Neptune,   trident;   He adds also   the Herculean   bows,
2   1

hastamque   Minervæ,   Quidquid   habent   telorum
and the spear   of Minerva,   Whatever   have   of weapons
                                            3

armamentaria   cœli.   Si   verò   et   pater
the armories   of heaven. If   indeed   also   a father
1   2

est: Comedam,   inquit,   flebile   nati
he is: "I w'd eat,"   he says,   the to-be-lamented   of my son
                                                            2

Sinciput   elixi,   Pharioque   madentis   aceto.   Sunt,
head   boiled,   and with Pharian dripping   vinegar.   There are,
1   3   4   6   5

in   Fortunæ   qui   casibus   omnia   ponant,
in   of Fortune   who   the accidents all (things) place,
4   6   1   5   3   2

Et   nullo   credant   mundum   rectore   moveri,
and   no one   believe   the world (being) ruler   to move,
        4   1   2   5   3

Naturâ   volvente   vices   et   lucis   et   anni; -
nature   bringing round the vicissitudes both of light and   the year,

Atque · ideo   intrepidi   quæcunque   altaria
and   therefore   fearless   whatsoever [any] altars
                                    3   2

tangunt.   Est   alius,   metuens   ne   crimen
they touch.   there is   another,   fearing   lest   crime
   1   3

pœna   sequatur: Hic   putat   esse   deos,
punishment   may follow: he   thinks (there) are   gods,
   1   2

et   pejerat,   atque   ita   secum: Decernat
and   forswears,   and   thus (thinks) with himself: "let decree
                                                               1   3

quodcunque   volet,   de   corpore   nostro   Isis,
whatever   she will,   concerning   body   our   Isis,
                                                                2

et   irato   feriat   mea   lumina   sistro,
and with (her) angry   strike   my   eyes   sistrum,
                              2   3   1

Dummodo   vel   cœcus   teneam,   quos   abnego,
so that   even   blind   I may keep,   which   I deny,
                                                2

nummos.   Et   phthisis,   et   vomicæ   putres,
the money.   Both   consumption,   and   sores   putrid,
   1

et   dimidium   crus   Sunt   tanti?   Pauper
and   a half   leg   are they   of so much (consequence)?   (if) poor
                                                                        4

locupletem   optare   podagram   Ne   dubitet
the rich   to wish for   gout   Let not   hesitate
   7   6   8   1 2   5

Ladas,   si   non   eget   Anticyrâ, ·   nec
Ladas,   if   not   he needs   Anticyra,   nor
   3   2   1

Archigene.   Quid   enim   velocis   gloria   plantæ
Archigenes.   What   for   of a swift   the glory   foot
                    2   1   5   4

Præstat,   et   esuriens   Pisææ   ramus   olivæ?
avails,   and   the hungry   of the Pisæan   branch   olive?
   3   2   1

Ut   sit   magna,   tamen   certè   lenta   ira
Though may be   great,   yet   surely   slow   the anger
           3   4   5   6   8   1

deorum   est.   Si   curant   igitur   cunctos
of the gods   it is.   If   they care   therefore   all
   2   7   2

punire   nocentes,   Quando   ad   me   venient?
to punish   the guilty,   When   to   me   will-they-come?
   1   2   1

sed   et   exorabile   numen   Fortasse   experiar;
but   also   exorable   the deity   perhaps   I may find;
 1   3   6   5   2   4

solet   his   ignoscere.   Multi   Committunt
he is wont   these (things) to forgive.   Many   commit

eadem   diverso   crimina   fato: Ille   crucem
the same   with a different   crimes   fate: one   the cross
                 2   1   2

sceleris   pretium   tulit,   hic,   diadema.
of wickedness (as) a reward   has borne,   another,   a diadem.
     4   3   1

Sic   animum   diræ   trepidum   formidine   culpæ
Thus (their) mind   of dire   agitated   by the fear   guilt
                        3   1   2

Confirmant.   Tunc   te   sacra   ad   delubra
they fortify.   Then   you   the sacred   to   shines
                                     3   2

vocantem   Præcedit,   trahere   immo   ultro
calling (him)   he precedes,   to draw (you)   or rather   of-his-own-accord
    1   3   1   4

ac   vexare   paratus.   Nam,   quum   magna
an I   to worry [you]   [he is] ready.   For,   when   great
 5   6   2

make   superest   audacia   causæ,   Creditur   a
to a bad   remains   impudence   cause,   it is believed   by
  3   2   1

multis   fiducia.   Mimum   agit   ille,
many [to be]   the confidence [of innocence.]   a farce   acts   he

Urbani   qualem   fugitivus   scurra   Catulli:
of the witty   such as   the runaway   buffoon   Catullus:
   4   1   2   3

Tu   miser   exclamas,   ut   Stentora   vincere   possis,
You poor-wretch   cry out,   that   Stentor   overcome   you might,
                                           3   2   1

Vel   potius,   quantum   Gradivus   Homericus:
or   rather,   as much as   Gradivus   the Homeric:
                                       2

Audis,   Jupiter,   hæc,   nec   labra   moves,
Hearest thou, O Jupiter, these (things) and not (thy) lips   movest,
                                      1   3   2

quum   mittere   vocem   Debueras,   vel
when   to send forth   (thy) voice   thou oughtest,   whether

marmoreus,   vel   aëneus?   aut   cur   In   carbone
(thou art) of marble,   or   of brass?   or   why,   on   coal

tuo,   chartâ   pia   thura   solutâ   Ponimus,
thy.   wrapper   the pious   frankincense   from the loosened   place we,
 1   5   2   3   4   1

et   sectum   vituli   jecur,   albaque   porci
and   the cut   of a calf   liver,   and the white   of a hog
         2   1   2

Omenta?   Ut   video,   nullum   discrimen   habendumest
entrails?   As   I see,   no   difference   is to be reckoned
    1

Effigies   inter   vestras,   statuamque   Vagelli.
images   between   your,   and the statue   of Vagellius.
   3   1   2

(18*)

Accipe, quæ contrá valeat solatia
Hear (now,) what on-the-other-hand he can consolations
              2   3   1

ferre, Et qui nec Cynicos nec
bring, and who neither the Cynics, nor

Stoica dogmata legit A Cynicis tunicâ
the Stoic doctrines has read from the Cynics (only) by a tunic

distantia; non Epicurum Suspicit exigui
differing, not Epicurus admires of a small
         2   3   1   3

lætum plantaribus horti. Curentur
happy in the plants garden. may-be-taken-care-of
1   2   3

dubii medicis majoribus ægri; Tu venam
the dubious physicians by greater sick; do you (your) vein
1   5   4   2   2

vel discipulo committe Philippi. Si nullum
even to the apprentice commit of Philip. If no
                1

in terris tam detestabile factum Ostendis,
in the world so detestable deed you show,
4 5   2   3   1

taceo ; nec pugnis cædere pectus Te
I am silent; nor with (your) fists to beat (your) breast You
            5   3   4   2

veto, nec plana faciem contundere
do I forbid, nor with open (your) face to bruise
1   3   2   1

palmâ, Quandoquidem accepto claudenda est
palm, since having-been-received must-be-shut
                    2   4

janua damno, Et majore domûs gemitu,
the gate loss and with greater of the house lamentation,
3   1   2   1

majore tumultu Planguntur, nummi, quàm
with greater tumult is bewailed money, than
               2   1

funera. Nemo dolorem Fingit in hoc casu,
deaths. Nobody grief feigns in this case,

vestem deducere summam Contentus, vexare
the garment to sever the-upper-part-of content, to vex
4   2   3   1

oculos humore coacto: Ploratur lacrymis
the eyes with moisture constrained: is deplored with tears
         2   1   3   4   6

amissa pecunia veris. Sed si cuncta
lost money true. But if all
1   2   5   2

vides simili fora plena querelâ;
you see with the like the courts filled complaint:
1   5   3   4

Si,   decies   lectis   diversâ   parte   tabellis,
if,   ten-times   being-read   by the opposite   party   the tables,
       3   2   4   1

Vana   supervacui   dicunt   chirographa   ligni,
(are) vain   of the useless   they say   the hand-writings   wood,
5   3   1   2   4

Arguit   ipsorum   quos   litera   gemmaque
convicts   of themselves   whom   the letter   and gem
4   3   1   2   2

princeps   Sardonychum,   loculis   quæ   custoditur
a principal   of a Sardonyx,   in cases   which   is guarded
1   2   3   1   2

eburnis: Te v',   O delicias!   extra   communia
of ivory: you,   my dear fellow!   beyond   the common
4   2

censes   Ponendum?   Qui   tu   gallinæ   filius
do you think (are) to be put?   How (are) you   of a hen   the chick
1   2   4   1

albæ,   Nos   viles   pulli   nati   infelicibus
white, (while) we (are) a vile   brood   hatched   from unlucky
3

ovis?   Rem   pateris   modicam,   et   mediocri
eggs?   matter   you suffer   a moderate,   and   with moderate
3   1   2

bile   ferendam,   Si   flectas   oculos   majora
choler   to be borne,   if   you bend (your) eyes   greater
                                                              2

ad   crimina.   Confer   Conductum   latronem,
to   crimes.   Compare   the hired   robber,
1

incendia   sulphure   cœpta   Atque   dolo,   primos
burnings   with sulphur   begun   and   by guile,   the first
              2   1   4

quum   janua   colligit   ignes;   Confer   et   hos,
when   the gate   collects   fires;   compare   also   those,
1   2   3

veteris   qui   tollunt   grandia '   templi   Pocula
of an old   who   carry off   the massive   temple   cups
5   1   2   3   6   4

adorandæ   robiginis,   et   populorum   Dona,   vel
of venerable   rust,   and   of nations   the gifts,   or
                                        2   1

antiquo   positas   a   rege   coronas.   Hæc   ibi
an ancient   deposited   by   king   crowns.   these   there
4   2   3   5   1   2   5

si   non   sunt,   minor   exstat   sacrilegus,   qui
if   not   are, (one)   less   there-stands-forth   sacrilegious,   who
1   4   3   2   1

Radat   inaurati   femur   Herculis,   et   faciem
may scrape   of a gilded   the thigh   Hercules,   and   the face
                        1

ipsam   Neptuni;   qui   bracteolam   de   Castore ducat.
itself   of Neptune;   who   the leaf-gold   from   Castor may-draw-off.
                              2   1

An   dubitet,   solitus   totum   conflare   Tonantem?
Sh'd he   hesitate,   accustomed   a whole   to melt   Thunderer?
                         2   1

Confer   et   artifices,   mercatoremque   veneni,
compare   also   the compounders,   and the vender   of poison.

Et   deducendum   corio   bovis   in   mare,   cum
and (him) deserving-to-be-launched in-the-hide of an ox into the sea,   with

quo   Clauditur   adversis   innoxia   simia   fatis.
whom   is shut up   by adverse   the harmless   ape   fates.
                              2   3   1

Hæc   quota   pars   scelerum,   quæ   custos
this   how small   a part   of the crimes,   which   the guardian
3   1   2   2

Gallicus   Urbis   Usque   a   lucifero,   donec   lux
Gallicus   of the City   even   from   dawn,   until   the sun
1

occidat,   audit?   Humani   generis   mores   tibi   nôsse
sets,   hears?   of the human   race   the morals   you   to know
                     5   6   4   1   3

volenti   Sufficit   una   domus.   Paucos   consume   dies,   et
wishing   suffices   one   house.   a few   spend   days,   and
2   9   7   8   2   1

Dicere   te   miserum,   postquam   illinc   veneris,
to call   yourself   miserable,   after   thence   you have come,
2

aude.   Quis   tumidum   guttur   miratur   in
dare.   Who   a goitred   throat   wonders at   in
1   2   1

Alpibus?   aut   quis   In   Meroe   crasso
the Alps?   or   who (wonders at)   in   Meroe   (than) a chubby
                                      3

majorem   infante   mamillam?   Cærula   quis
bigger   infant   a breast?   the blue   who
2   4   1   3   1

stupuit   Germani   lumina,   flavam   Cæsariem,
has-been-amazed-at   of a German   eyes,   (at his) yellow   hair,
2   5   4

et   madido   torquentem   cornua   cirro?   Nempe
and (at him) with moistened   twisting   horns   curl?   Forsooth
1   3   1   2   2

quòd   hæc   illis   natura   est   omnibus   una.
because   this   to them   nature   is   all   one.
1   3   7   5   6   8   4

Ad   subitas   Thracum   volucres   nubemque
to   the sudden   of the Thracians   birds   and the cloud
            2   1   2

sonoram   Pygmæus   parvis   currit   bellator
clangorous   the Pygmean   (his) little   runs   warrior
1   4   2   1

in   armis: Mox   impar   hosti   raptusque   per
in   arms: soon   unequal   to the enemy   and snatched   through
3

aera   curvis   Unguibus   a   sævâ   fertur   grue.
the air   with crooked   talons   by   a cruel   he is borne   crane.
                   2   3   1   4

Si videas hoc Gentibus in nostris, risu
If you sh'd see this nations in our, with laughter
                        3   1   2

quatiare; sed illic, Quanquam eadem assidué
you w'd be shook; but there, though the same constantly
                                              3

spectentur prœlia, ridet Nemo, ubi tota
may be seen battles, laughs nobody, when the whole
           1   2   1
2

cohors pede non est altior uno. Nullane
cohort foot not is higher (than) one. "No
       5   2   1   3   4   2

perjuri capitis fraudisque nefandæ Pœna
of a perjured head and of fr'ud atrocious punishment
                                          3

erit? Abreptum crede hunc graviore
shall there be?" dragge'l-away suppose this (man) with a heavier
1   3   1   2

catenâ Protenus, et nostro (quid plus velit ira?)
chain immediately, and at our (what more would anger?)
                      2

necari Arbitrio: manet illa tamen jactura,
to-be-kill'd will: remains that yet loss.
1   3   4   2   1   3

nec unquam Depositum tibi sospes erit.
nor ever the deposit to you safe will be."
    2   3   6   5   1 4

Sed corpore trunco Invidiosa dabit minimus
"But, from (his) body maimed, enviable will give the least
     2   1   4   3   1

solatia sanguis: At vindicta bonum vitâ
consolations blood: but revenge (is) a good [than] life
5   2   3   4   2

jucundius ipsâ. Nempe hoc indocti, quorum
more pleasant itself." Truly this the ignorant [think], whose
1

præcordia nullis Interdum aut levibus
breasts from none sometimes or from slight
          4   3

videas flagrantia causis. Quantulacunque adeò
you-may-see burning causes. How small so ever
1   2

est occasio, sufficit iræ. Chrysippus non
is the occasion, it is sufficient for anger. Chrysippus not
                                             2

dicet idem, nec mite Thaletis
will say the same, nor the mild of Thales
1   2

Ingenium, dulcique senex vicinus Hymetto,
disposition, and to-sweet the-old-man neighbor Hymettus,
1   3   1   2

Qui partem acceptæ sæva inter vincla
who a part of the received cruel amid chains
6   7   2   1   3

cicutæ / hemlock [8] — Accusatori / to the accuser [9] — nollet / w'd not [4] — dare. / give. [5] — Plurima / very many [5]

felix / happy [1] — Paulatim / by degrees [4] — vitia / vices [6] — atque / and [7] — errores / errors [9] — exuit / puts off [3]

omnes / all [8] — Prima / first — docet / teaches — rectum / the right — Sapientia: / Wisdom: [2]

quippe / since [1] — minuti / of a minute [6] — Semper / always [4] — et / and — infirmi / weak [8] — est / est [3] — animi / mind [11]

exiguique / and little [9 10] — voluptas / the pleasure [5] — Ultio. / revenge. [2] — Continuò / at once — sic / •thus

collige, / conclude, — quòd / because — vindictâ / in revenge — Nemo / no one — magis / more — gaudet, / rejoices,

quàm / than — fœmina. / a woman. — Cur / Why — tamen / yet [2] — hos / these [1] — tu / you [6] — Evasisse / to-have-escaped [4] [7]

putes, / sh'd think, [3 5] — quos / whom — diri / of a dire [3] — conscia / conscious [2] — facti / deed — Mens / the mind [1]

habet / keeps — attonitos, / in terror, — et / and — surdo / with-an-unheard [2] — verbere / thong [3] — cædit, / lashes,

Occultum / a secret [4] — quatiente / shaking [3] — animo / conscience (their) [1] — tortore / tormentor [2] — flagellum? / scourge?

Pœna / (is their) punishment [3] [4] — autem / nay [1] — vehemens / vehement [2] — ac / and — multo / much — sævior / more cruel

illis, / than those, — Quas / which — et / both — Cædicius / Cædicius [2] — gravis / severe [1] — invenit, / invented,

et / and — Rhadamanthus / Rhadamanthus — Nocte / night — dieque / and day — suum / their [2] — gestare / to carry [1]

in / in (their) [4] — pectore / breast [5] — testem. / witness. [3] — Spartano / Spartan [2] — cuidam / to a certain [:] — respondit / gave-answer

Pythia / the Pythian — vates: / prophetess: — Haud / not — impunitum / unpunished — quondam / in-time-to-come

fore, / he sh'd be, — quòd / because — dubitaret / he hesitated — Depositum / a deposit [2] — retinere, / to retain, [1]

et / and — fraudem / the fraud — jure tueri / to defend — Jurando. / by an oath. — Quærebat / he asked [2]

enim / for [1] — quæ / what [3] — numinis / of the divinity [6] — esset / was [4] — Mens, / the mind, [5] — et / and — an / whether — hoc / this [3]

illi / to him [5] — facinus / deed [4] — suaderet / advised [2] — Apollo? / Apollo? [1] — Reddidit / he restored (it)

ergò metu, non moribus; et tamen omnem
therefore from fear, not from principle; and yet every

Vocem adyti dignam templo veramque
word of the shrine worthy the temple and true
2

probavit Exstinctus totâ pariter cum
he proved having been extinguished all together with
1 3 1 2

prole domoque, Et, quamvis longâ deductis
(his) progeny and house, and, although from a long derived
2 4 3

gente, propinquis. Has patitur
clan, kin. These suffers
5 1 5

pœnas peccandi sola voluntas.
punishments of sinning alone the wish.
1 4 3 2

Nam scelus intra se tacitum qui cogitat
For wickedness within himself secret who meditates
5 6 7 4 1 2

ullum, Facti crimen habet. Cedo, si
any, of the act the guilt he has. "Tell me, (what) if
3 10 9 8

conata peregit? Perpetua anxietas nec
[his] attempts he has accomplished? a perpetual anxiety [is his], nor

mensæ tempore cessat, Faucibus ut morbo
of-the-table at the time does it cease, with jaws as by disease
3 2 1 2 3

siccis interque molares Difficili crescente cibo:
dry, and between [his] grinders the difficult increasing food:
1 2 1

Setina misellus Exspuit; Albani veteris
(his) Setine (wines) the wretch spits out; Abanian of old
4 3

pretiosa senectus Displicet. Ostendas melius,
the precious old age Displeases. Show (him) better,
1 2

densissima ruga Cogitur in frontem, velut
the thickest wrinkle is gathered on his forehead, as

acri ducta Falerno. Nocte brevem si fortè
by sour drawn Falernian. In the night a brief if haply
2 1 5 1 2

indulsit cura soporem, Et toto versata toro
has indulged care sleep, and over-the-whole tossed bed
4 3 3 2 4

jam membra quiescunt: Continuò templum
now (his) limbs are at rest: immediately the temple
6 1 5 7

et violati numinis aras, Et, quod
and of the violated divinity the altars, and, (what
2 3 1

præcipuis mentem sudoribus urget, Te videt
with especial (his) mind pains urges,) thee he sees
3 2 4 1

in   somnis: tua   sacra   et   major   imago
in   his dreams: thy   sacred   and   greater   image
                                   2   3   1

Humanâ   turbat   pavidum,   cogitque   fateri.
(than) human disturbs the trembling (wretch), and compels (him) to confess.

Hi   sunt   qui,   trepidant,   et   ad   omnia
These   are (they)   who   tremble,   and   at   all

fulgura   pallent,   Quum   tonat,   exanimes
lightning-flashes,   pale,   when   it thunders,   dead (with terror)

primo   quoque   murmure   cœli;   Non   quasi
at-the-first   even   rumbling   of the sky;   not   as if
    2   1

fortuitus,   nec   ventorum   rabie,   sed   Iratus
by chance,   nor   of winds   by the rage,   but   in wrath
                            2   1

cadat   in   terras   et   judicet   ignis.   Illa
falls   upon   the earth   and   is-fraught-with-justice   fire.   That
   2   1

nihil   nocuit,   curâ   graviore   timetur   Proxima
nothing   harmed,   concern   with heavier   is feared   the next
                      2   1   5   3

tempestas,   velut   hoc   dilata   sereno.   Præterea,
tempest,   as if   by this   deferred   calm.   moreover,
    4   2   1

lateris   vagili   cum   febre   dolorem   Si   cœpere
of the side   a watchful   with   fever   a pain   if   they have begun
    2   4   3   5   1

pati,   missum   ad   sua   corpora   morbum   Infesto
to suffer,   sent   to   their   bodies   the disease   a hostile
          3   4   2   6

credunt   a   numine: saxa   deorum   Hæc   et
they believe   by   divinity: the stones   of the gods   These (things) and
    1   5   3   6   2   4

tela   putant.   Pecudem   spondere   sacello
darts   they think.   sheep   to vow   to the shrine
    5   1   3   1

Balantem,   et   Laribus   cristam   promittere   galli
a bleating,   and   to the Lares   the comb   to promise   of a cock
    2   2   3   1

Non   audent: quid   enim   sperare   nocentibus
They do not   dare: what   for   to hope for   to the guilty
                     2   1   5   4

ægris   Concessum?   vel   quæ   non   dignior
sick   (is)   vouchsafed?   or   what   not more worthy of
  5   3   2   3

hostia   vitâ?   Mobilis   et   varia   est   ferme
victim   life?   fickle   and   variable   is for-the-most-part
  1

natura   malorum.   Quum   scelus   admittunt,
the character   of the bad.   When   crime   they admit,
                                    2   1

superest   constantia.   Quid   fas   Atque
is super abundant (their) resolution.   What (is)   right   and   (what is)
    4   3

nefas, tandem incipiunt sentire peractis
wrong, at length they begin to feel, being-perpetuated
                          2

Criminibus. Tamen ad mores natura recurrit
(their) crimes. yet to morals nature recurs
1   5 7   1   4

Damnatos, fixa et ˙ mutari nescia: Nam quis
(its) depraved, fixed and immutable: For who
6   2   3

Peccandi finem posuit sibi? quando recepit
of sinning an end has proposed to himself? when recovered he
4   3   1   2

Ejectum semel attrita de fronte ruborem?
banished once (his) hardened from brow the blush (of shame)?
3   2   5 4   6   1

Quisnam hominum est, quem tu contentum
who of men is there, whom you content
                         2

videris uno Flagitio? Dabit in laqueum
shall see with one base action? will get into a snare
1   3   5   6

vestigia noster Perfidus, et nigri patietur carceris
(his) feet our Perfidious (friend). and of a gloomy will suffer dungeon
4   1   2   3   1   4

uncum, Aut maris Ægæi rupem, scopulosque
the hook, or sea of the Ægean a crag. and the cliffs
2   3   2   1

frequentes Exsulibus magnis. Pœnâ gaudebis
swarming with exiles of rank. Punishment you-will-rejoice
                    3   1

amarâ Nominis invisi, tandemque fatebere
in the bitter of (his) name hated, and at length you-will-confess
2   2   1

lætus, Nec surdum nec Tiresiam quenquam
with joy, neither deaf nor a Tiresias any one

esse deorum.
to be of the gods.

19   .

SATIRE XIV.

ARGUMENT.

The whole of this Satire is directed to the one great end of self-improvement. By showing the dreadful facility with which children copy the vices of their parents, the poet points out the necessity as well as the sacred duty of giving them examples of domestic purity and virtue. After briefly enumerating the several vices, gluttony, cruelty, debauchery, etc., which youth imperceptibly imbibe from their seniors, he enters more at large into that of avarice; of which he shows the fatal and inevitable consequences. Nothing can surpass the exquisiteness of this division of the Satire, in which he traces the progress of that passion in the youthful mind from the paltry tricks of saving a broken meal to the daring violation of every principle, human and divine. Having placed the absurdity as well as the danger of immoderate desires in every point of view, he concludes with a solemn admonition to rest satisfied with those comforts and conveniences which nature and wisdom require, and which a decent competence is easily calculated to supply.

PLURIMA   sunt,   Fuscine,   et   famâ   digna
very many (things)   there are,   Fuscinus,   both   reputation   worthy of
                                        3   1

sinistrâ,   Et   nitidis   maculam   hæsuram   figentia
a sinister,   and   on splendid   a spot   that-will-stick   fixing
2   4   3   1

rebus,   Quæ   monstrant   ipsi   pueris   traduntque
things,   which   point out   themselves   to (their) children   and deliver
              3   2   5   4

parentes.   Si   damnosa   senem   juvat   alea,
parents.   If   the destructive   the old man   delights   die,
1   3   2   1

ludit   et   hæres   Bullatus,   parvoque   eadem
plays   also the heir   wearing-the-bulla,   and in (his) little   the same
3   4   1   2   4   2

movet   arma   fritillo.   Nec   melius   de   se
shakes   weapons   dice-box.   Nor   better   of   himself
1   3   5   7   8

cuiquam   sperare   propinquo   Concedet   juvenis,   qui
any   to hope   relation   will allow   the youth,   who
4   6   5   1   3   2

radere   tubera terræ,   Boletum   condire,   et eodem
to peel   truffles,   a mushroom   to season,   and in the same
2   3   5   4   6   10

jure   natantes   Mergere   ficedulas   didicit,   nebulone
sauce   swimming,   to immerse   beccaficos has learned, (h's)   gourmand
11   9   7   8   1

parente,   Et   canâ   monstrante   gulâ.   Quum   septimus
parent,   and hoary   showing (him)   gluttony.   When   the seventh
2   1

annus   Transierit   puero,   nondum   omni
year   has passed over   the boy,   not as yet   every
3   1

dente   renato,   Barbatos   licet   admoveas
tooth   renewed,   bearded   though   you sh'd range
2   4   1   2

mille   inde   magistros,   Hinc   totidem,   cupiet
a thousand   there   masters,   here   as many,   he will d. sire
3   6   5

lauto   cœnare   paratu   Semper,   et   a   magnâ
in sumptuous   to sup   style   always,   and   from   a great
2   1   3   4

non   degenerare   culinâ.   Mitem   animum   et   mores
not   to degenerate   kitchen.   a mild   disposition   and a character
1   2   5

modicis   erroribus   æquos   Præcipit,   atque
to moderate   errors   indulgent   inculcates,   and
2   1

animas   servorum   et   corpora   nostrâ   Materiâ
the souls   of slaves   and   bodies   of our own   matter
3   1   2   5   6

constare   putat   paribusque   elementis;   An
to consist   thinks   and of similar   elements;   or
4

sævire   docet   Rutilus,   qui   gaudet   acerbo
to be cruel   does teach   Rutilus,   who   delights   in the bitter
2   1

Plagarum   strepitu,   et   nullam   Sirena   flagellis
of stripes   sound,   and   no   Siren   to whips
2

Comparat,   Antiphates   trepidi   laris,   ac
compares,   the antiphates   of (his) trembling household,   and

Polyphemus,   Tum   felix,   quoties   aliquis
Polyphemus,   then   happy,   as often as   any one

tortore	vocato	Uritur	ardenti		duo	propter
the tormentor	being called	is burned	with a hot		two	on-account-of
					3	2

lintea	ferro?	Quid	suadet	juveni	lætus
towels	iron?	What	advises he	a youth	joyous
4	1				

stridore	catenæ,	Quem	mirè afficiunt	inscripta
at the clank	of a chain,	whom	wonderfully delight	branded
			5 6	1

ergastula	carcer	Rusticus?	Exspectas,	ut non
slaves,	jail	a country?	Do you expect,	that not
2	4	3		4

sit	adultera	Largæ	Filia,	quæ	nunquam
sh'd be	an adulteress	of Larga	the daughter,	who	never
3 5	6	2	1		

maternos	dicere	mœchos	Tam	citò	nec
(her) mother's	say over	gallants	so	quickly	nor
3	2	4		5	6

tanto	poterit	contexere	cursu,	Ut	non
with so much	c'd	join together	rapidity,	that	not
8	1	7	9		

ter decies respiret?	Conscia	matri	Virgo
thirty times she must take breath?	a confidante	to the mother	the virgin .
			2

fuit:	ceras	nunc	hûc	dictante	pusillas
was:	tablets	now	this (mother)	dictating	(her own) little
1	4	1	5	6	3

Implet,	et	ad	mœchos	dat	eisdem	ferre	cinædis.
She fills,	and	to	the gallants	gives	to the same	to carry	agents
2		5	6	1	2	4	3

Sic	natura	jubet:	velociùs	et	citiùs	nos
Thus	nature	commands:	more swiftly	and	speedily	us
						5

Corrumpunt	vitiorum	exempla	domestica,	magnis
corrupt	of vices	examples	domestic (proceeding)	from great
4	3	2	1	2

Quum	subeunt	animos	auctoribus.	Unus	et
when	they impress	(our) minds	influencers.	One	or
1	4	5	3		

alter	Forsitan	hæc	spernant	juvenes,	quibus
two	perhaps	these (things)	may spurn	young men,	whose
	2	4	3	1	

arte	benignâ	Et	meliore	luto	finxit	præcordia
with art	benign	and	with better	clay	has formed	hearts
2	3		4	5	7	1

Titan :	Sed	reliquos	fugienda	patrum	vestigia
Titan:	But	the rest	to be shunned	of (their) fathers	the footsteps
6	5	3		2	1

ducunt,	Et	monstrata	diù	veteris	trahit
lead	and	shown them	long	of old	draws them on
4		5	4	2	

orbita	culpæ.	Abstineas	igitur	damnandis:
the routine	depravity.	abstain	therefore	from [things] to be condemned:
1	3			

hujus enim vel Una potens ratio est, ne
oi this for at least one powerful reason there is, lest
2 1

crimina nostra sequan'ur Ex nobis geniti;
crim s our sh'd follow from us [those] begotten;
6 5 4 2 3 1

quoniam dociles imitand's Turpibus ac pravis
since docile in imitating base and wicked (things)
3

omnes sumus, et Catilinam Quocunque iu
all we are: and a Catiline whatsoever in
2 1 2 1

populo videas, quocunque sub axe: Sed nec
people you may see, whatsoever under clime: but neither
2 1

Brutus eri:, Bruti nec avunculus usquam.
a Brutus will be, of Brutus nor an uncle anywhere.
4 3 1 2

Nil dictu fœdum visuque hæc limina
nothing to be said foul and to be seen those thresholds
2 1

tangat, Intra quæ puer est. Procul hinc,
sh d touch with n which a child is. Far hence,

procul inde puellæ Lenonum, et cantus
far thence the girls of bawds, and the songs

pernoctantis parasiti. Maxima debetur puero
rioting-through-the-night of the parasite. The greatest is due to a child
2 1 2

reverentia. Si qu'd Turpe paras, ne tu
reverence. If any base (thing) you-are-preparing, not thou
1 2 3

pueri contempseris annos: Sed peccaturo
of [thy] child despise the yea s: But about to sin
5 1 4 7

obstet tibi fi'ius infans. Nam si quid
let hinder you (your son infant. For if anything
1 5 6 2 4 3 2

dignum Censor's fecerit irâ Quandoque, et
worthy of the Censor he sh l do the anger (since, also
3 5 1

similem tibi se non corpore tantùm Nec
like to you himself not in body only nor
3 4 2

vultu dederit, morum quoque fi'ius,
in countenance he wil show, of [your] morals also the son.)
1 5

et qui Omn'a dete.'ùs tua per ves igia
and who all the worse your by foot steps
4 2 5 3 6

peccet, Corripies n'mirum et cas'igabis acerbo
may sin, you will reprove forsoo i and chastise with bitter
1

(19*)

Clamore, ac post hæc tabulas mutare
clamor, and after these [things] [your] will to change
                                  3   2

parabis. Unde tibi frontem
you-will-set-about. Whence (do you take) to yourself the front
1

libertatemque parentis, Quum facias pejora
and liberty of a parent, when you do worse [things]
                                            1 3

senex, vacuumque cerebro Jam pridem caput
an-old-man, and void of brain long since head
2   3   4   5   2

hoc ventosa cucurbita quærat? Hospite
this the exhausted cupping-glass is-looking-out-for? a guest
1

venturo, cessabit nemo tuorum. Verre
about to come, will be idle no one of yours. "Sweep
                  3   1   2

pavimentum, nitidas ostende columnas,
the pavement, shining display the columns,
                  3   1   2

Arida cum totâ descendat aranea telâ;
the shrivelled with the whole let come down spider web;
2   5   6   1   4   3   7

Hic leve argentum, vasa aspera tergeat
this (one) the smooth silver, vessels the embossed let clean
2   4   5   8   7   1 3

alter; Vox domini furit instantis, virgamque
another;" the voice of the master blusters forth urging, and a rod
6   2

tenentis. Ergò miser trepidas, ne stercore
holding. Therefore wretch dost thou tremble. lest dung
1   3

fœda canino Atria displiceant oculis venientis
foul with canine (your) halls sh'd displease the eyes of (your) coming"
1   2

amici, Ne perfusa luto sit porticus; et
friend, lest overspread with mud sh'd be the porch; and

tamen uno Semodio scobis hæc emundat servulûs
yet with one half-bushel of saw-dust these c'd clean little-slave
                                  4   3   2

unus. Illud non agitas, ut sanctam filius
one. it do you not manage, that pure (your) son
1   4   1

omni Adspiciat sine labe domum, vitioque
any may see without stain (your) house, and vice
6   2   5   7   3   8 10

carentem? Gratum est, quòd patriæ
wanting? deserving-of-acknowledgment it is, that to (your) country
9   3

civem populoque dedisti, Si facis,
a citizen and people you-have-given, if you-bring-it-to-pass,
2   1

ut patriæ sit idoneus; utilis agris,
that for (his) country he may be fit; useful to (her) lands,
   3   1   2

Utilis et bellorum et pacis rebus
useful both of wars and of peace in managing
   3   1

agendis. Plurimùm enim intererit, quibus
the affairs. very much for it will import, in what
   2   2   1

artibus, et quibus hunc tu Moribus
arts, and in what him you moral habits
                        4   2   1

instituas. Serpente ciconia - pullos Nutrit,
train. With a serpent a stork [her] young ones nourishes,
   3

et inventâ per devia rura lacertâ:
and found through out-of-the-way fields with a lizard:
          2   1

Illi eadem sumptis quærunt animalia pinnis.
They the same being taken seek animals [their] feathers.
   4   2   3   5   1

Vultur, jumento et canibus crucibusque relictis,
the vulture, cattle and dogs and gibbets being left behind,

Ad fœtus properat, partemque cadaveris
to (her) young hastens, and part of a carcass

affert. Hic est ergò cibus magni quoque
brings. This is therefore the food of a great also
                                                        3

vulturis, et se Pascentis, propriâ quum
vulture, and of one herself feeding, in her own when
   1   2   1   5   1

jam facit arbore nidos. Sed leporem aut
now she makes tree nests. But the hare or
   2   3   6   4   8

capream famulæ Jovis et generosæ In
the kid the ministers of Jove and noble in
   9   1   2   3   6

saltu venantur aves: hinc præda cubili
the forest hunt birds: hence prey in (their) nest
   7   5   4

Ponitur: inde autem, quum se matura levârit
is put: thence too, when itself the mature has raised (on wing)
                             4   1   3   5

Progenies, stimulante fame, festinat ad illam,
progeny, stimulating hunger, it hastens to that,
   2   2   1

Quam primam prædam rupto gustaverat ovo.
which first prey being broken it-had-tasted the egg.
   2   3   1   6   4   5

Ædificator erat Cetronius, et modo curvo
a builder was Cetronius, and now on-the-crooked

Littore   Cajetæ,   summâ   nunc   Tiburis   arce,
shore   of Caieta,   on the highest   now   of Tibur   peak,
                2   1   4   3

Nunc   Prænestinis   in   montibus,   alta   parabat
now   the Prænestine   in   mountains,   the high   was preparing
        2   1   3   5   4

Culmina   villarum,   Græcis   longèque   petitis
tops   of villas,   with Grecian   and far   sought

Marmoribus, vincens   Fortunæ   atque   Herculis   ædem,
marbles,   surpassing   of Fortune   and   of Hercules   the temple,
                      2   3   1

Ut   spado   vincebat   Capitolia   nostra   Posides.
as   the eunuch   out-did   Capitols   our   Posides.
                2   4   3   1

Dum   sic   ergo   habitat   Cetronius,   imminuit
while   thus   therefore   dwells   Cetronius,   he diminished

rem,   Fregit   opes ;   nec   parva   tamen   mensura
(his) estate,   he impaired   [his] wealth; nor   small   yet   the measure
                             6   1   3

relictæ   Partis   erat: totam   hanc   turbavit   filius
left   of the portion   was: all   this   squandered   [his] son
  5   4   2   4   1 3

amens,   Dum   meliore   novas   attolit   marmore
senseless,   while   with better   new   he reared   marble
  2   3   2   1

villas.   Qu'dam   sortiti   metuentem   sabbata
villas.   some   having-for-their-lot   fearing   sabbaths
                                2   3

patrem,   Nil   præter   nubes   et   cœli   numen
a father,   nothing   beside   the clouds   and   of the sky   the divinity
  1   2   1

adorant;   Nec   distare   putant   humanâ   carne
adore;   nor   to differ   do they think   from human   flesh
                    6   1   7   8

suillam,   Quâ   pater   abstinuit;   mox   et
pork,   from which   the father   abstained: soon   also (their)
  2   3   4   5

præputia   ponunt: Romanas   autem   soliti
foreskins   they put away: the Roman   but   accustomed
                     4   1   2

contemnere   leges,   Judaïcum   ediscunt,   et   servant,
to despise   laws,   the Jewish   they study,   and   observe,
  3   4   1   2

ac   metuunt   jus,   Tradidit   arcano   quodcunque
and   fear   law,   delivered   in the secret   whatsoever
      3   3   1

volumine   Moses.   Non   monstrare   vias,   eadem
volume   Moses.   not   to show   the ways,   the same
         2   3

nisi   sacra   colenti;   Quæsitum   ad   fontem
unless   sacred rites   to [one] observing;   the-sought-for   to   fountain
 1   4   2   5   4   6

solos	deducere	verpos.	Sed	pater	in
alone	to conduct	the circumcised.	But	the father (is)	in
3	1	2			

causâ,	cui	septima	quæque	fuit	lux
fault,	to whom	seventh	every	was	day
		2	1	4	3

Ignava,	et	partem	vitæ	non	attigit	ullam·
Idle,	and	part	of life	not	he touched	any.
		4	5	2	1	

Sponte	tamen	juvenes	imitantur	cætera:
of-their-own-accord	however	young men	imitate	other [vices]:

solam	Inviti	quoque	avaritiam	exercere
alone	against-their-will	even	avarice	to exercise
2	4	3	1	6

jubentur.	Fallit	enim	vitium	specie
they are commanded.	deceives	for	the vice	under the appearance
5	3	1	2	

virtutis	et	umbrâ,	Quum	sit	triste
of virtue	and	shadow,	since	it is	grave
3	1	2			

habitu	vultuque	et	veste	severum.
in bearing	and countenance	and	in dress	severe.

Nec	dubiè	tanquam	frugi,	laudatur	avarus,
nor	doubtfully,	as	frugal,	is praised	the miser,

Tanquam	parcus	homo,	et	rerum	tutela	suarum
as	a sparing	man,	and	things	a safeguard of his own	
				3	1	2

Certa	magis,	quàm	si	fortunas	servet	easdem
certain	more,	than	if	fortunes	sh'd keep	the same
2	1			7	5	6

Hesperidum	serpens,	aut	Ponticus.	Adde	quòd
of the Hesperides	the serpent,	or	of Pontus.	add	that
2	1	3	4		

hunc,	do	Quo	loquor,	egregium	populus
this [man]	of	whom	I speak,	an excellent	the people
				3	1

putat	acquirendi	Artificem:	quippe	his
think	of [his own] fortune	Artificer:	since	to these
2	5	4		

crescunt	patrimonia	fabris.	Sed	crescunt
increase	patrimories	workmen.	But	they increase
3	2	1		

quocunque	modo,	majoraque	fiunt	Incude
by whatsoever	mode,	and greater	become	by the anvil
				2

assiduâ,	semperque	ardente	camino.	Et	pater
assiduous,	and ever	glowing	forge.	and	the father
1					

ergò	animi	felices	credit	avaros,	Qui
therefore	of mind	happy	believes	the covetous,	who
	4	3	1	2	

miratur	opes,	qui	nulla	exempla	beati
admires	wealth,	who	no	examples	of a happy

Pauperis   esse   putat.   juvenes   hortatur,
poor-man   to be   thinks: [his] young men   he exorts,

ut illam Ire viam pergant. et eidem incumbere
that that to go way they continue, and to the same apply themselves
        3   1   2   2   1

sectæ.   Sunt   quædam   vitiorum   elementa:
sect.   There are   certain   of vices   elements:
                                  2   1

his protenus illos Imbuit, et cogit minimas
with these in regular order them he imbues, and compels the most petty
                                                    2

ediscere   sordes.   Mox   acquirendi   docet
to learn   stinginess.   By-and-by   of acquiring   he teaches
 1

insatiabile   votum.   Servorum ventres modio
an insatiable   wish.   the servants, bellies with a measure
                                                     2

castigat   iniquo,   Ipse   quoque   esuriens:
he chastises   unjust,   himself   also   hungering:
 1

neque enim omnia sustinet unquam Mucida
neither for all does he bear ever the musty
  2   1   7   3   5   4   8

cærulei panis consumere frusta, Hesternum
of blue bread to consume pieces, yes e day's
 11   21   6   9   3

solitus medio servare minutal Septembri:
accustomed in mid to keep hash September:
 1   5   2   4

nec non differre in tempora cœnæ
nor not to defer to the times supper

Alterius conchem æstivam cum parte lacerti
of another bean the summer with a piece of stock-fish
 1   2   1   2

Signatum, vel dimidio putrique siluro, Filaque
sealed up, or a half rotten siurus, and the threads
 1   3

sectivi numerata includere porri. Invitatus
of chopped numbered to shut up leek. invited
 4   2   1   5   2

ad hæc aliquis de ponte negabit. Sed quò
to these anyone from a bridge will refuse. But why
    3   1

divitias hæc per tormenta coactas. Quum
riches these by torments scraped-together, since
        3   2   4   1

furor haud dubius, quum sit manifesta phrenesis,
madness undoubted, since it is manifest phrensy,

Ut locuples moriaris, egentis vivere fato?
that rich you may die, of (one) in want to live with the fate?
                        3   1   2

Interea pleno quam turget sacculus ore,
meanwhile, with full though swells the sack mouth,
          4   1   3   2

Crescit amor nummi, quantùm ipsa pecunia
grows the love of money, as much as itself money
3 1 2 4 6 5

crevit; Et minus hanc optat, qui non
has grown; and less it he covets, who not
2 1 2

habet. Ergò paratur Altera villa tibi,
has (it). Therefore is being prepared another villa for you,
1

quum rus non sufficit unum, Et proferre
since country-seat is not sufficient one, and to extend
2 1 2

libet fines; majorque videtur Et melior
it pleases (your) borders; and greater seems and better
1

vicina seges: mercaris et hanc, et
the neighbouring corn-land: you buy also this, and

Arbusta, et densâ montem qui canet
the groves, and with dense the hill which whitens
4 1 2 3

olivâ. Quorum si pretio dominus non vincitur
olive. of which if price the owner not is prevailed on
6 1 3 2 4

ullo, Nocte boves macri, lassoque famelica
with any, by night the oxen lean, and with tired the fam shed
5 2 1 3 1

collo Jumenta ad virides hujus mittentur aristas;
neck cattle to the green of this (man) will be sent corn:
4 2 to 6 8 5 7

Nec priùs inde domum, quàm tota novalia
nor thence home, before the whole crop

sævos In ventres abeant. ut credas falcibus
(their) ravenous into bellies goes, so that you w'd believe (it) by sickles
3 2 4 1 2

actum. Dicere vix possis, quàm multi talia
done. Tell hardly you c'd, how many such things
1 3 2 1

plorent, Et quot venales injuria fecerit agros.
lament, and how many for sale injury (like this) has made fields.
4 2 3 1

Sed qui sermones? quàm fœdæ buccina
"But what speeches? how of foul the trumpet
2

famæ? Quid nocet hoc? inquit. Tunicam
fame?"— "What does this hurt?" says he. The pod

mihi malo lupini, Quam si me toto
to me I had rather of a lupin, than, if me in-the-whole
5 2

laudet vicinia pago, Exigui ruris paucissima
sh'd praise the neighborhood district, of a little farm the very scanty
4 1 3 4 5 2

farra secantem. Scilicet et morbis et debilitate
crops cutting." Forsooth both diseases and weakness
3 1

carebis, Et luctum et curam effugies, et
you will want, and grief and care you will escape, and

tempora vitæ Longa tibi post hæc fato
times of life long to you after these (things) fate
2 3 1 2

meliore dabuntur, Si tantum culti solus
with a better will be given, if so much of cultivated you only
1 3 4 1

possederis agri, Quantum sub Tatio populus
possess ground, as under Tatius people
2 2

Romanus arabat. Mox etiam fractis ætate
the Roman used to plough. Afterward even to (those) broken with age
1

ac Punica passis Prœlia, vel Pyrrhum
and the Punic having suffered wars, or Pyrrhus
2 1

immanem, gladiosque Molossos, Tandem pro multis
the cruel, and swords Molossian, at length for many

vix jugera bina dabantur Vulneribus. Merces
scarce acres two a piece were given wounds. Reward
2 4 3 5 6 1 2

ea sanguinis atque laboris Nullis visa unquam
that of blood and of toil to none seemed ever
1

meritis minor, aut ingratæ Curta fides patriæ.
(than) deserts less, or of an ungrateful the scant faith country.
2 1 3 1 2 4

Saturabat globula talis Patrem ipsum,
used to satisfy a little glebe such the father himself,
3 2 1

turbamque casæ, quâ fœ'a jacebat Uxor, et
and the troop of (his) cottage, in which the pregnant was lying wife, and
2 1

infantes ludebant quatuor, unus Vernula, tres
children were playing four, one a little-slave, three
2 1

domini: sed magnis fratribus horum, A
freeborn: but for-the-grown-up brothers of these, from

scrobe vel sulco redeuntibus, altera cœna
the trench or furrow returning, another supper

Amplior et grandes fumabant pultibus ollæ. Nunc
more ample and the great smoked with pottage pots. Now
2 3 1

modus hic agri nostro non sufficit horto.
measure this of ground for our is not sufficient garden.
2 1 2 3 1

Inde fere scelerum causæ, nec plura venena
Thence commonly of villanies the causes, nor more poisons
2 1

Miscuit, aut ferro grassatur sæpius ullum
has mixed, or with the sword assaults oftener any
1 6 7 10 9 8 2

Humanæ mentis vitium, quàm sæva cupi'o
of the human mind vice, than the fierce lust
4 5 3

Indomiti censûs: nam dives qui fieri vult,
of unbounded income: for rich who would be,

Et cito vult fieri. Sed quæ reverentia
also quickly would be. But what reverence

legum, Quis metus aut pudor est unquam
of the laws, what fear or shame is there ever

properantis avari? Vivite contenti casulis
of a hastening miser? "Live contented little-cottages
2

et collibus istis, O pueri, Marsus dicebat
and hills with those, O youths," the Marsian used-to-say
1

et Hernicus olim Vestinusque senex; panem
and Hernician formerly and Vestine sire; bread

quæramus aratro, Qui satis est mensis:
let us seek by the plough, which enough is for (our) tables:

laudant hoc numina ruris, Quorum ope
approve this the deities of the country, by whose aid
3 4 1 2

et auxilio, gratæ post munus aristæ,
and intervention, of-the-grateful after the gift corn,
3 1 2 4

Contingunt homini veteris fastidia quercûs.
there happen to man of the old loathings oak.
2 1

Nil vetitum fecisse volet, quem non
Nothing forbidden to do does-he-desire, whom not
2 1 2

pudet alto Per glaciem perone tegi;
it shames with a high through ice country-boot to be covered;
1 4 2 3 5 1

qui submovet Euros Pellibus inversis.
who keeps off the East winds by skins inverted.
2 1

Peregrina ignotaque nobis Ad scelus atque
foreign and unknown to us to crime and
3 4

nefas, quæcunque est, purpura ducit.
impiety, whatsoever it is, purple leads."
5 1 2

Hæc illi veteres præcepta minoribus:
these those olden-times (fathers) precepts (gave) to (their) children:
2 3 1 4 5

at nunc Post finem autumni mediâ de nocte
but now after the end of autumn at midnight

(20)

supinum   Clamosus   juvenem   pater   excitat:
the supine   th · clamorous   youth   father   rouses:
4   1   5   2   3

Accipe   ceras,   Scribe,   puer,   vigila,   causas
take   the tablets,   write,   boy,   wake up,   indictments

age,   perlege   rubras   Majorum   leges,   aut
draw,   read over   tne red   of (our) forefathers   laws,   or
                       2   1

vitem   posce   libello.   Sed   caput   intactum
a centurion's-post ask for   by a petition.   But (your) head   untouched

buxo   naresque   pilosas   Annotet,   et   grandes
with box   and nostrils   hairy   must observe,   and   (your) brawny
      2   1   2   3   5

miretur   Laelius   alas.   Dirue   Maurorum
must admire   Laelius   shoulders.   destroy   of the Moors
4   1   6   2

attegias,   castella   Brigantum,   Ut   locupletem
tae huts,   the forts   of the Brigantes,   that   the enriching
1   5

aquilam   tibi   sexagesimus   annus   Afferat;
eagle   to you   the sixteenth   year   may bring;
6   4   1   2   3

aut,   longos   castrorum   ferre   labores   Si   piget,   et
or,   the long   of the camp   to bear   labors   if   it irks   and
     4   6   3   5   1   2

trepidum   solvunt   tibi   cornua   ventrem
(your) trembling   relax   your   the horns   belly
7   5   6   1   8

Cum   lituis   audita,   pares,   quod   vendere
with   the clarions   heard,   you-may-procure,   what   to sell
3   4   2

possis   Pluris   dimidio,   nec   te   fastidia
you may be able   at more   by a half,   nor   you   the dislike
                               6   2

mercis   Ullius   subeant   ablegandæ   Tiberim
trade   of any   let steal upon   (that is) to be banished   the Tiber
4   3   1   5   2

ultra: Neu   credas   ponendum   aliquid   discriminis
beyond   nor   believe   to be put   any   difference
1   3   1   2

inter   Unguenta,   et   corium.   Lucri   bonus   est
between   perfumes,   and   leather.   Of gain   good   is

odor   ex   re   Quâlibet.   Illa   tuo   sententia
the smell   from   thing   whatever.   That   your   sentiment
                2   1   2   8   3

semper   in   ore   Versetur,   dis   atque   ipso
always   in   mouth   let be turned,   the gods   and   himself
5   7   9   1   6   11   12   14

Jove   digna,   poëtæ: Unde   habeas,   quærit
Jove   worthy,   of the poet: whence   you have,   asks
13   10   4   3   4   2

nemo :   sed   oportet   habere.   Hoc   monstrant
nobody: but   it behooves   to have.   This   (maxim) point out
1   3

vetulæ pueris repentibus assæ: Hoc discunt
old women to boys creeping dry: This learn
2   1   3

omnes ante alpha et beta puellæ. Talibus
all before Alpha and Beta girls. with such
1   2   4

instantem monitis quemcunque parentem Sic possem
instant admonitions whatsoever parent thus I w d
3   5   1   2

affari: Dic. o vanissime, quis te Festinare
address: "Say, O most empty-headed, who you to hasten
                                    2   3

jubet? meliorem præsto magistro Discipulum.
bids? better I warrant (than) the master the pupil.
1   3   1   2

Securus abi: vinceris, ut Ajax
without care go-about-your-business: you-will-be-outdone, as Ajax
2   1

Præteriit Telamonem, ut Pelea vicit Achilles.
outstripped Telamon, as Peleus excelled Achilles.
4   3   2

Parcendum teneris: nondum implevere
you must spare the tender (ones): not as yet have filled
                                    4

medullas Maturæ mala nequitiæ. Quum pectere
(their) marrows of mature the evils wickedness. When to comb
5   2   1   3

barbam Cœperit et longi mucronem admittere
(his) beard he has begun and of the long the edge to apply
                           3   2   1

cultri, Falsus erit testis, vendet perjuria
razor, a false he will be witness, he will sell perjuries
4   2   1

summâ Exiguâ et Cereris tangens aramque
sum for a small and of Ceres touching both the altar
2   1

pedemque. Elatam jam crede nurum,
and foot. Borne forth (to burial) already believe [your] daughter-in-law
                4   3   1   2

si limina vestra Mortiferâ cum dote subit.
if thresholds your a death-bringing with dowry she enters.
if   2   1   5   4   6   3

Quibus illa premetur Per somnum
By what will she be pressed Per in sleep
         2   3   4

digitis! nam quæ terrâque marique
fingers! for (what) things both by land and sea
1

Acquirenda putas, brevior via conferet
(are) to be acquired you suppose, a shorter way will confer
        2   1

illi. Nullus enim magni sceleris labor.
upon him. (there is) no for of great · wickness labor.
        4   1   2   3

Hæc ego nunquam Mandavi, dices olim,
"These [things] I never recommended," you will say hereafter,

nec   talia   suasi.   Mentis   causa   malæ   tamen
"nor   such   counselled."   mind   the cause   of a bad   yet
                                      4   2   3   1

est   et   origo   penes   te.   Nam   quisquis   magni
is   and (its) origin   with   you.   For   whoever   of a great
7   5   6   3

census   præcepit   amorem,   Et   lævo   monitu
income   has inculcated   the love,   and   by sinister   lessons
4   1   2

pueros   producit   avaros,   Dat   libertatem,   et
boys   produces   avaricious,   grants   license,   and
3   1   2

totas   effundit   habenas   Curriculo: quem
all   loosens   the reins   to the chariot's course: whom
2   1

si   revoces,   subsistere   nescit,   Et   te   contempto
if   you-w'd-recall,   to stop   he knows not,   and   you   contemned

rapitur   metisque   relictis.   Nemo   satis
is-hurried-on   the goal even   being left behind.   no one   enough
                                                     2

credit   tantùm   delinquere,   quantum   Permittas:
thinks [it]   so much   to offend,   as   you may permit:
1   4   3

adeò   indulgent   sibi   latiùs   ipsi.   Quum
so much   indulge   themselves the more widely they themselves.   when
                3   4   1   2

dicis   juveni,   stultum,   qui   donet   amico,
you say   to a youth, (that man is) a fool,   who   gives   to a friend,

Qui   paupertatem   levet   attolatque   propinqui;
who   the poverty   lightens   and raises up   of a relative;

Et   spoliare   doces,   et   circumscribere,   et   omni
both   to rob   you teach (him), and   to cheat,   and   by every
2   3   1

Crimine   divitias   acquirere,   quarum   amor   in
crime   riches   to acquire,   of which (as great) a love (is) in
                2   1

te,   Quantus   erat   patriæ   Deciorum   in   pectore
you,   as (there) was of (their)   country   of the Decii   in   the breast
                                               2   1

quantùm   Dilexit   Thebas,   si   Græcia   vera,
as much as   loved   Thebes,   if   Greece [is]   true,
                    2   3

Menœceus: In   quorum   sulcis   legiones   dentibus
Menœceus: in   whose   furrows   legions from the teeth
1

anguis   Cum   clypeis   nascuntur,   et   horrida
of a serpent   with   bucklers   are born   and   horrid

bella   capessunt   Continuo,   tanquam   et
wars   undertake   at once,   as though   also

tubicen   surrexerit   una.   Ergò   ignem,   cujus
a trumpeter   had arisen   with-them.   Therefore   the fire   whoso

scintillas ipse dedisti, Flagrantem latè
sparks yourself have given, raging far-and-wide

et rapientem cuncta videbis. Nec tibi
and seizing all [things] you will see, nor to your

parcetur misero, trepidumque magistrum
will it be spared miserable self, and the trembling master
1 3

In caveâ magno fremitu leo tollet alumnus:
In (his) den with great roaring the lion will despatch pupil.
3 4 1 5 2

Nota mathematicis genesis tua: sed grave
Known to the astrologers (is) nativity your: but (it is) tedious
2 1

tardas Exspectare colus. Morieris stamine
slow to await distaffs. You will die (your) thread
2 1

nondum Abrupto. Jam nunc obstas
not yet broken-off. Already now you-stand-in-the-way-of

et vota moraris: Jam torquet juvenem
and (his) wishes delay: now vexes the youth
2 1 4 5

longa et cervina senectus. Ociùs Archigenen
a long and stag-like old-age. quickly Archigenes
1 2 3

quære, atque eme, quod Mithridates Composuit,
seek. and buy what Mithridates compounded,

si vis aliam decerpere ficum Atque alias
if you wish another to pluck fig and other
2 1 2

tractare rosas. Medicamen habendum est,
to handle roses. A drug must be had,

Sorbere ante cibum quod debeat et pater
to swallow before food which ought both a rather
7 8 9 1 6 2 3

et rex. Monstro voluptatem egregiam, cui
and a king. I show gratification an special, to which
4 5 2 1

nulla theatra, Nulla æquare queas Prætoris
no theatres, no compare you can Prætor
3 4 5 2 1 8

pulpita lauti, Si spectes, quanto capitis
platforms of the sumptuous, if you behold, in what great of life
6 7 2

discrimine constent Inc ementa domûs, æratâ
peril stand-one-in the additions of a house, a brass-bound
1 4

multus in arcâ Fiscus, et ad vigilem ponendi
much in chest treasure, and at watchful to be placed
1 3 5 2 3 2

Castora nummi, Ex quo Mars ultor galeam
Castor money, from what (time) Mars the avenger (his) helmet
1

quoque   perdidit,   et   res   Non   potuit   servare
also   lost,   and   possessions   Not   could   protect
          5   1   2   3

suas.   Ergò   omnia   Floræ   Et   Cereris   licet
his own.   Therefore   all   of Flora   and   of Ceres   you may
  4   3   5   6   1

et   Cybeles   aulæa   relinquas: Tanto   majores
and   of Cybele   the scenic representations   leave: so much   greater
      7   4   2

humana   negotia   ludi.   An   magis   oblectant
(are) human   affairs   sports.   Do   more   delight
  2   3   1   1   5   6

animum   jactata   petauro   Corpora,   quique
the mind   projected   from the petaurum   bodies,   and (he) who
            3   4   2

solet   rectum   descendere   funem,   Quàm   tu,
is used   the tight   to descend   rope,   than   thou

Coryciâ   semper   qui   puppe   moraris   Atque
in a Corycian   always   who   bark   abidest   and
   4   2   1   5   3

habitas,   Coro   semper   tollendus   et   Austro,
dwellest,   by Corus   always   to be tossed up and down   and   by Auster,
             3   1   2

Perditus   ac   vilis   sacci   mercator   olentis;
the irreclaimable   and   vile   sack   merchant   of a stinking
                           3   1   2

Qui   gaudes   pingue   antiquæ   de   littore   Cretæ
who   rejoicest   the rich   of ancient   from   the shore   Crete
         6   1   3   2   4

Passum   et   municipes   Jovis   advexisse   lagenas?
raisin wine   and the fellow-countrymen of Jove to have brought wine-flasks?
   7   8   10   11   5   9

Hic   tamen   ancipiti   figens   vestigia   plantâ
This (rope-walker)   yet   with hazardous   fixing   (his) steps   tread
   2   1   5   3   4

Victum   illâ   mercede   parat,   brumamque
a living   by that   trade   procures,   and cold

famemque   Illâ   reste   cavet: tu   propter
and hunger   by that   rope   he avoids: you   for the sake of

mille   talenta   Et   centum   villas   temerarius.
a thousand   talents   and   a hundred   villas   (are) daring

Adspice   portus,   Et   plenum   magnis   trabibus
Behold   the ports,   and   full   of great   hulks
                            2

mare: plus   hominum   est   jam   In   pelago:
the sea: the greater (part)   of men   is   now   on   the sea:

veniet   classis,   quòcunque   vocârit   Spes   lucri,
will come   a fleet,   whatever   shall call   the hope   of gain,
  2   1   3   1   2

nec   Carpathium   Gætulaque   tantùm   Æquora
nor   the Carpathian   and Gætulian   only   seas
                                        2   1

transssiliet;   sed,   longè·   Calpe   relictâ,
will-it-bound-across;   but   far   Calpe   being left behind,
       3   1   2   4

Audiet   Herculeo   stridentem   gurgite   solem.
will hear   in the Herculean   hissing   gulf   the sun.
   3   2   4   1

Grande   operæ   pretium   est,   ut   tenso   folle
a grand   of toil,   reward   it is,   that   with distended   purse
       2   1

reverti   Indè   domum   possis,   tumidâque   superbus
to return   thence   home   you are able,   and with a swelled   proud
   3   2   4   1   2   3   1

alutâ   Oceani   monstra   et   juvenes   vidisse
money-bag   Ocean's   monsters   and   young   to have seen
   4   2   3   4   5   1

marinos.   Non   unus   mentes   agitat   furor.
mermen.   Not   one   minds   distracts   madness.
   6   3   2   1

Ille   sororis   In   manibus   vultu
That (one)   a sister's   in   arms   with the countenance
       2   1   2

Eumenidum   terretur   et   igni :   Hic   bove
of the Eumenides   is terrified   and   torch :   this (one)   an ox
     4   1   3

percusso   mugire   Agamemnona   credit   Aut
being stricken   to roar   Agamemnon   believes   or
          3   2   1

Ithacum.   Parcat   tunicis   licèt   atque
the Ithacensian.   He may spare   (his) tunics   though   and
            2

lacernis,   Curatoris   eget,   qui   navem   mercibus
(his) cloaks,   a keeper   he needs,   who   a ship   with merchandise

implet   Ad   summum   latus,   et   tabulâ   distinguitur
fills   to   the topmost   edge,   and   by-a-plank   is parted

undâ;   Quum   sit   causa   mali   tanti,
from the wave;   since   is   the motive   of hardship   so great,
                 7   1   2   3

et   discriminis   hujus,   Concisum   argentum
and   peril   of this   cut up   silver
4   6   5   8   7

in   titulos   faciesque   minutas.   Occurrunt   nubes
into   titles   and faces   small.   (There) occur   clouds
             2   1

et   fulgura.   Solvite   funem,   frumenti   dominus
and   lightnings.   "Loose   the cable,"   of the corn   the master
                     3   2

clamat   piperisque   coëmpti;   Nil   color   hic
cries   and of the pepper   bought-up;   nothing   color   this
1   2   1   2   1

cœli,   nil   fascia   nigra   minatur;   Æstivum
of the sky,   nothing   belt   the black   threatens;   It is summer-
                 2   1

tonat.   Infelix   hâc   forsitan   ipsâ   Nocte
thunder.   Unhappy wretch   on this   perhaps   very   Night
                 2   1

cadet   fractis   trabibus,   fluctuque,
he will fall   being broken   the ship's timbers,   and by the wave,
        2   1

premetur   Obrutus,   et   zonam   lævâ
will be borne down   overwhelmed,   and (his) money-belt   with his left hand
                               2

morsuque   tenebit.   Sed   cujus   votis   modò   non
and (his) teeth   will hold.   But   for whose   wishes   lately   not
     1   3

suffecerat   aurum,   Quod   Tagus,   et   rutilâ
had sufficed   the gold,   which   Tagus,   and   in saluing
   2   4   1   8

volvit   Pactolus   arenâ,   Frigida   sufficient
rolls   Pactolus   sand,   (his) cold   will suffice
  2   1   3   5

velantes   inguina   panni,   Exiguusque   cibus;
covering   groins   rags,   and scanty   food;
  2   4   1

mersâ   rate   naufragus   assem   Dum   rogat,
being sunk   [his] bark,   shipwrecked   a penny   while   he asks,
  5   4   3   7   1   2   6

et   pictâ   se   tempestate   tuetur.   Tantis
and   by a painted   himself   tempest   supports.   with so great
      3   1   2   2

parta   malis,   curâ   majore   metuque   Servantur.
(things) gotten   hardships   with care   greater   and fear   are kept.
     1   3   2   1

Misera   est   magni   custodia   census.   Dispositis
wretched   is   of a great   the guardianship   fortune.   set in order
               2   1   7

prædives   hamis   vigilare   cohortem   Servorum
the very rich   with water-buckets   to watch   (his) troop   of slaves
   1   6   8   4   5

noctu   Licinus   jubet,   attonitus   pro   Electro,
by night   Licinus   commands,   in dread alarm   for   (his) electrum,
   9   2   3

signisque   suis,   Phrygiâque   columnâ,   Atque
and his statues,   and   Phrygian   column.   and

ebore,   et   latâ   testudine.   Dolia   nudi
(his) ivory   and   massive   tortoise-shell.   The tubs   of the naked

Non   ardent   Cynici: si   fregeris,   altera
do not   burn   Cynic: if   you sh'd break (them)   another
  2   3   1

fiet   Cras   domus,   aut   eadem   plumbo
will be made   to-morrow   house,   or   the same   with lead
   2   1   3

commissa   manebit.   Sensit   Alexander,   testâ
soldered   will remain.   felt   Alexander,   tub
   2   1   2   1   4

quum   vidit   in   illâ   Magnum   habitatorem,
when   he saw   in   that   (its) great   habitant
  1   2   3

quanto   felicior   hic,   qui   Nil   cuperet,
how much happier   he,   who   nothing   des re l,

quàm   qui   totum   sibi   posceret   orbem,
than   (he) who   the whole   for himself   demanded   work,
                        3   2   1

Passurus   gestis   æquanda   pericula   rebus.
doomed-to-suffer   achieved   equivalent   perils   to the exploits.
        4   2   1   3

Nullum   numen   habes,   si   sit   prudentia: nos
no   divinity thou hast, if   there be   foresight: we

te,   Nos   facimus,   Fortuna,   Deam.   Mensura
thee, we   make,   O, Fortune, a goddess.   Measure
                                                        3

tamen   quæ   Sufficiat   censùs,   si   quis   me
yet   what   may suffice   of an income, if   any one   me
  1   2   5   4   2

consulat,   edam: In   quantum   sitis
sh'd consult, I sh'd say: Just   as much as   thirst
    1

atque   fames   et   frigora   poscunt,
and   hunger   and   cold   demand,

Quantum,   Epicure,   tibi   parvis   suffecit   in
as much as, Epicurus,   thee   (thy) little   sufficed   in
                            2   4   1   3

hortis,   Quantum   Socratici   ceperunt   antè
gardens,   as much as   the Socratic   contained   before
                                            2   3

penates.   Nunquam   aliud   Natura,   aliud
household. never   one thing   nature,   another
    1   2   4   1   6

Sapientia   dicit,   Acribus   exemplis   videor
Wisdom   says,   by too strict   examples   I seem
    5   3

te   claudere.   Misce   Ergò   aliquid   nostris
you   to hem in.   Mix   therefore something   our own
  2   1 3   2

de   moribus: effice   summam,   Bis   septem
from manners: make up   the sum,   twice   seven
  1   5   6

ordinibus   quam   lex   dignatur   Othonis.   Hæc
rows   which   the law   deems worthy of   of Otho.   this
  7   1   2   4   3   2

quoque   si   rugam   trahit,   extenditque   labellum;
also   if   a wrinkle   draws,   and extends   the lip;
  3   1   5   4

Sume   duos   Equites,   fac   tertia   quadringenta.
take   two   Knights,   make   the third   four hundred.

Si   nondum   implevi   gremium,   si   panditur
if   not yet   I have filled (your) lap,   if   it is extended

ultra,   Nec   Crœsi   fortuna   umquam,   nec
further, neither   of Crœsus   the fortune   ever,   nor
                        2   1   5   1

Persica   regna   S fficient   animo,   nec   divitiæ
the Persian   realms   will suffice (your) mind,   nor   the riches
   2   3   4   6

Narcissi,   Indulsit   Cæsar   cui   Claudius
of Narcissus,   indulges   Cæsar   whom   Claudius
            4   3   1   2

omnia   cujus   Paruit   imperiis,   uxorem
all (things) whose   he obeyed   commands,   (his) wife
   5   2   1   3

occidere   jussus.
to kill   (when) ordered.
   2   1

SATIRE XV.

ARGUMENT

After enumerating with great humour the animal and vegetable gods of the Egyptians, the author directs his powerful ridicule at their sottish and ferocious bigotry; of which he gives an atrocious and loathsome example. The conclusion of the Satire, which is a just and beautiful description of the origin of civil society, (infinitely superior to any thing that Lucretius or Horace has delivered on the subject,) founded not on natural instinct, but on princples of natural benevolence implanted by God in the breast of man, and of man alone, does honor to the genius, good sense, and enlightened morality of the author.

Quis	nescit,	Volusi	Bithynice,	qualia	demens
Who	knows not,	O Volusius	Bithynicus,	what-kind-of	infatuated
					2

Ægyptus	portenta	colat?	Crocodilon	adorat
Egypt	monsters	worships?	the Crocodile	venerates
3	1		4	3

Pars	hæc;	illa	pavet	saturam	serpentibus
part	this;	that	trembles before	gorged	with serpents
2	1			2	3

ibin.	Effigies	sacri	nitet	aurea	cercopitheci,
an Ibis.	The image	of a sacred	shines	golden	monkey,
1				2	3	1

Dimidio	magicæ	resonant	ubi	Memnone	chordæ,
from the halved	the magic	resound	where	Memnon	chords,
5	2	4	1	6	3

Atque	vetus	Thebe	centum	jacet	obruta
and	old	Thebes	with (her) hundred	lies	buried in ruins
					2

portis.	Illic	cæruleos,	hic	piscem	fluminis,
gates.	There	sea-fish,	here	a fish	of the river,
1					

illic	Oppida	tota	canem	venerantur,	nemo
there	towns	whole	a dog	worship,	no one
	2	1	4		3

Dianam.   Porrum   et   cæpe   nefas   violare,
Diana.   a leek   and   an onion (it is) impious to violate,

et   frangere   morsu.   O sanctas   gentes,   quibus
and   break   with the bite,   O holy   nations,   for whom

hæc   nascuntur   in   hortis   Numinal   Lanatis
these   grow   in   (their) gardens divinities! from wooly
         2   1

animalibus   abstinet   omnis   Mensa.   Nefas
animals   abstains   every   table.   (It is) an impiety

illic   fœtum   jugulare   capellæ: Carnibus   humanis
there   the offspring to slay of the goat: flesh   human
                                           4   3

vesci   licet.   Attonito   quum   Tale   super
to eat   it is lawful. To the amazed if   such   at
   2   1   7   1   5

cœnam   facinus   narraret   Ulixes   Alcinoo,   bilem
supper   a deed   should narrate Ulysses Alcinous, bile
   4   6   3   2   8

aut   risum   fortasse   quibusdam   Moverat,
or   laughter   perhaps   in some   he had moved,

ut   mendax   aretalogus.   In   mare   nemo   Hunc
as   a lying   babbler. "Into the sea does no one this [fellow]

abicit,   sævâ   dignum   veráque   Charybdi,
cast,   a fierce   deserving of and a true   Charybdis,
           2   1

Fingentem   immanes   Læstrygonas   atque   Cyclopas?
inventing (as he does) huge   Laestrygones   and   Cyclops?

Nam   citiùs   Scyllam,   vel   concurrentia   saxa
For   sooner   Scylla,   or   the clashing   rocks

Cyaneas,   plenos   et   tempestatibus   utres
Cyaneæ,   filled   and   with tempests   the skins
            3   1   2

Crediderim,   aut   tenui   percussum   verbere
I would credit, or with the light (to have been) struck stroke
                       3   2   4

Circes,   Et   cum   remigibus   grunnisse
of Circe,   and   with   the rowers   to have granted
   5   6   8   9   7

Elpenora   porcis.   Tam   vacui capitis   populum
Elpenor [turned into] swine. 80 empty-headed   people
   1   4   5   3

Phæaca   putavit?   Sic   aliquis   meritò   nondum
the Phaeacian has he thought?" so any one with reason not yet
   2   1

ebrius,   et   minimun   qui   De   Corcyrææâ
drunk,   and   the least   who   from   thy Corcyræan
                  3   1   5   6

temetum   duxerat   urnû: Solus   enim   hoc
strong-wine had drawn   bowl: alone   for   this
   4   2   5   1   4

Ithacus   nullo   sub   teste   canebat.   Nos
the Ithacan   no   under   witness   related.   We
2 -   7   6   8   3   1

miranda   quidem,   sed   nuper   Consule   Junio
wonderful   indeed,   but   lately   Consul   Junius [being]
4   5   6   7   10   9

    Gesta   super   calidæ   referemus   mœnia
[things] achieved above   of sultry   shall relate   the walls
3   8   11   13   2   12

Copti;   Nos   vulgi   scelus,   et
Coptos;   We of a [whole] people   the crime [shall recount] and
                             2   1

cunctis   graviora   co'hurnis.   Nam   scelus   a
than all [deeds] more atrocious tragedies.   For   the guilt from
2   1   1   13   2

Pyrrhâ,   quanquam   omnia   syrmata   volvas,
Pyrrha,   though   all   tragedies   you turn over,
3   4   5   6   7

Nullus   apud   tragicos   populus   facit.   Accipe,
no   in   the tragedians [entire] people perpetrates. Hear [then,]
8   10   11   9   12

nostro   Dira   quod   exemplum   feritas   produxerit
in our own a dire   what   an example   ferocity   produced
6   3   1   2   4   5

ævo.   Inter   finitimos   vetus   atque   antiqua
age.   Between   neighbors   an inveterate and   long-standing
7   1   4

simultas,   Immortale   odium,   et   nunquam
grudge,   an immortal   hatred,   and   a never

sanabile   vulnus   Ardet   adhuc.   Ombos   et
cureable   wound   burns   as yet,   Ombos   and
                                              2

Tentyra.   Summus   utrinque   Inde   furor
Tentyra.   the highest   on-both-sides   thence [arises] fury
3   3   2   1

vulgo,   quòd   numina   vicinorum   Odit
among-the-people, because the divinities of [its] neighbors hates
                           4   3

uterque   locus,   quum   solos   credat   habendos
each   place,   since [those] alone   it believes   sh' be held
1   2

Esse deos,   quos   ipse   colit.   Sed   tempore
[as] gods,   which   itself   worships.   But   at a period
                                                          2

festo   Alterius   populi   rapienda   occasio   cunctis
festive   of one of these peoples to be seized the occasion by all
1   4   1   5

Visa   inimicorum   primoribus   ac   ducibus,   ne
seemed (a fair one) of [their] enemies the chiefs and leaders,   lest
2   3   8   6   7

Lætum   hilaremque   diem,   ne   magnæ   gaudia
a joyous   and mirthful   day,   lest   of a grand   the delights
                                             2   1

cœnæ   Sentirent,   positis   ad   templa   et   compita
supper   they sh'd know, being placed near the temples and crossways
                              2

(21)

mensis, Pervigilique toro, quem nocte ac
(their) tables, and the over-wakeful couch, which night and

luce jacentem Septimus interdum sol invenit.
day spread the seventh sometimes sun finds.
1 2 1

Horrida sane Ægyptus: sed luxuriâ, quantùm
Savage indeed (is) Egypt: but in luxury as far as

ipse notavi, Barbara famoso non cedit
I myself have observed, the barbarous to infamous not yields
4 3 2

turba Canopo. Adde, quòd et facilis victoria
crowd Canopus. add, that also easy [is] the victory
1

de madidis, et Blæsis, atque mero titubantibus.
over (men) reeking, and stammering and with wine reeling.
2 1

Indè virorum Saltatus nigro tibicine,
on-that-side of men (is) a dancing a black (being) the piper,
2 1

qualiacunque Unguenta, et flores, multæque
of-any-sort-soever perfumes, and flowers, and many a
2 1

in fronte coronæ: Hinc jejunum odium. Sed
on the brow garland: on-this-side fasting hate. But
2 3 1

jurgia prima sonare Incipiunt animis ardentibus:
railings the first to sound they begin with minds inflamed:
6 5 4 3 1 2

hæc tuba rixæ. Dein clamore
this (is) the signal-blast of the fray. then with a clamor

pari concurritur, et vice teli Sævit
on-both-sides, it is run together, and instead of a dart rages

nuda manus: paucæ sine vulnere malæ:
the naked hand: few without a wound (are) the cheeks:

Vix cuiquam, aut nulli toto certamine
scarcely to any one or to no one in the whole contest

nasus Integer. Adspiceres jam cuncta per
(is there) a nose whole. you might see now all through
2 1

agmina vultus Dimidios, alias facies, et
the ranks faces halved, quite altered features, and

hiantia ruptis Ossa genis, plenos oculorum
protruding from torn bones cheeks, full of of eyes
2 1 2 4

sanguine pugnos. Ludere se credunt ipsi
the blood fists. to play themselves believe they themselves
3 1 5 4 3 2

tamen, et pueriles Exercere acies, quòd nulla
yet, and boyish to practice contests, because no
1 2 1

cadavera   calcent.   Et   sanè   quò   tot   rixantis
corpses   They trample.   and, forsooth, why so many of a cont. nding
                                                              2

millia   turbæ,   Si   vivant   omnes?   Ergò   acrior
thousands   crowd,   if   live   all?   Therefore   sharper
1   2   1

impetus,   et   jam   Saxa   inclinatis   per   humum
(is) the onset,   and   now   stones   inclined   along   the ground
                       8   2   3   4

quæsita   lacertis   Incipiunt   torquere,   domestica
sought   with arms   they begin   to hurl,   familiar
7   1   5   6   2

seditioni   Tela;   nec   hunc   lapidem,   quales
to sedition   weapons;   nor   such   a stone,   as
3   1

et   Turnus,   et   Ajax,   Vel   quo   Tydides
both   Turnus,   and   Ajax [hurled] or   with what·   Tydides
                                                         2

percussit   pondere   coxam   Æneæ;   sed   quem
struck   weight   the thigh   of Æneas;   but   want
3   1

valeant   emittere   dextræ,   Illis   dissimiles
are able   to cast   right-hands,   those [of theirs]   unlike
2   3   1   2   1

et   nostro   tempore   natæ.   Nam   genus   hoc
and   in our   time   born.   For   race   this
                                   2   1

vivo   jam   decrescebat   Homero.   Terra   malos
[being] alive   already   was decreasing   Homer.   the earth   bad
7   4   3   5   6   3

homines   nunc   educat   atque   pusillos.   Ergò
men   now   produces   and   puny.   Therefore
4   1   2

deus   quicunque   adspexit,   ridet,   et   odit.
d ity   whatsoever   has looked at them,   laughs at, and hates [them].

A   deverticulo   repetatur   fabula.   Postquam
from [this] digression   let be resumed   [our] story.   after
1   3   2

Subsidiis   aucti,   pars   altera   promere
by subsidies [they had been] reinforced,   party   one   to draw
                                          2   1

ferrum   Audet,   et   infestis   pugnam   instaurare
the sword   dares,   and   with deadly-aiming   the fight   to renew
           3   2

sagittis;   Terga   fugæ   celeri   præst ntibus
arrows;   [their] backs   flight   to swift   presenting
          10   12   11   9

omnibus,   instant,   Qui   vicina   colunt   umbrosæ
all   press upon,   [they] who   neighboring   inhabit   to the shady
8   7   1   4   2   5

Tentyra   palmæ.   Labitur   hic   quidam,   nimiâ
Tentyra   palm.   falls   hereupon   a certain on., in ex essivi
3   6   3   2   2

formidine   cursum   Præcipitans,   capiturque:
terror   [his] course   precipitating,   and is taken:
     2   1

astillum   in   plurima   sectum   Frusta   et particulas,
but him   into   very-many   cut   pieces   and   bits,
       2   3   1

ut   multis   mortuus   unus   Sufficeret,   totum
that   many   dead [man]   one   might suffice,   entire
     4   2   1   3

corrosis   ossibus   edit   Victrix   turba: nec
being gnawed   the (very) bones   eat   the victorious   crowd: neither
     2   1   5   3   4

ardenti   decoxit   aëno,   Aut   verubus;
in a glowing   they boiled (him)   cauldron,   or   (roasted) on spits;
       2   1

longum usque adeò   tardumque   putavit   Exspectare
so very long   and slow   they thought (it)   to wait for

focos,   contenta   cadavere   crudo.   Hic   gaudere
fires,   content   with the carcass   raw.   Here   rejoice

libet,   quòd   non   violaverit   ignem,   Quem
we may,   that   they did not   violate   fire,   which

summâ   cœli   raptum   de   parte   Prometheus
the highest   of heaven   stolen   from   part   Prometheus
   3   5   1   2   4

Donavit   terris.   Elemento   gratulor,   et   te
gave   to the earth.   the element   I congratulate,   and   you

Exsultare   reor.   Sed   qui   mordere   cadaver
(Volusius) exult   I ween.   But   who   to chew   a corpse

Sustinuit,   nil   unquam   hâc   carne   libentiùs   edit.
endured,   nothing   ever   (than) this   flesh   more willingly   ate.

Nam   scelere   in   tanto   ne   quæras,   et   dubites,
for   a crime   in   so great   do not   inquire,   and   doubt,
     3   1   2

an   Prima   voluptatem   gula   senserit.   Ultimus
whether   the first   a pleasure   gullet   felt.   Last
         3   1   2   3

autem,   Qui   stetit   absumpto   jam   toto
also,   [He] who   stood,   consumed   now   the whole
4   1   2   4   3

corpore,   ductis   Per   terram   digitis,   aliquid
body,   being drawn   along   the ground   (his) fingers,   something
2   2   3   4   1   2

de   sanguine   gustat.   Vascones,   hæc   fama
of   the blood   tastes.   The Vascones,   this   the report
3   4   1

est,   alimentis   talibus   olim   Produxère   animas:
is,   nutriments   by such   formerly   prolonged   (their) lives:
       2   1

sed   res   diversa,   sed   illic   Fortunæ   invidia
but   the case   [is] different,   but   there   of Fortune   the spite
                       3   2

est,   bellorumque   ultima,   casus   Extremi,
is,   and of wars   the last extremity,   sufferings   extreme,
1   2   1

longæ   dira   obsid'onis   egestas.   Hujus   enim,
of a long   the dire   siege   destitation.   of this   for,
3   1   4   2   3   1

quod   nunc   agitur,   miserabile   debet
which   now   is under consid ration   a-matte r-of-pity   ought
5   6   7   10   8

Exemplum   esse   cibi: sicut   modò   dicta   mihi
the example   to be   food: as   just   spoken of   by m
2   9   4   2

gens   Post   omnes   herbas,   post   cuncta
the nation   after   all   herbs,   after   all
1

animalia,   quidquid   Cogebat   vacui   ventris   furor,
animals,   whatever   compelled   of an empty   belly   the fury.
4   2   3

hostibus   ipsis   Pallorem,   ac   maciem,   et
(their) enemies   themselves   (their) paleness,   and   emaciation,   and
2

tenues   miserantibus   artus,   Membra   aliena   fame
waste d   pitying   limbs,   limbs   others'   in hunger
1   2   1

lacerabant,   esse   parati   Et   sua.   Quisnam
th y-tore-in-pieces,   to eat   ready   Ev n   their own.   Who
3   1   2

hominum   veniam   dare,   quisve   deorum   Viribus
of men   pardon   to grant,   or what   god   to en rgies
5   4   1   2   6

abnuerit   dira   atque   immania   passis,   Et
w l r tuso   dire   and   frightful (sufferings)   having endured, and
3   8   9   7

quibus   illorum   po'erant   ignoscere   manes,   Quorum
w om   of those   c'd have   forgiven   the manès,   whose
2   6   7   1   3

corporibus   vescebva ur?   Meliùs   n s   Zenonis
bodi s   th y f d on?   Best r   us   Zeno's
4   5   5   4   1

præcepta   monent,   nec   enim   omn a,   quædam
pr cep s   t ach,   not   for   all,   some (things)
2   3   3   1   4   2

Pro   vitâ   facienda   putat.   Sed   Cantaber
for-th -sake-of   life   ought to be done   h t inks.   But   Cantabrian
3   1   2   3

unde   Stoicus,   antiqui   præsertim   ætate   Metelli?
when ce   a stoic,   or old   esp cia ly   in t e age   M tellus?
1   2   3   1   2

Nunc   totus   Graias   nostrasque   habet   orb's
now   the whole   the Gr cian   and our   has   world
3   4   2

Athenas.   Gallia   caus'd'cos   docuit   facunda
Athens.   Gaul   pl ad rs   has taught   eoquent
2   5   3   1

(21*)

Britannos: De conducendo loquitur jam rhetore
the Britons (to be): about hiring talks now a rhetorician
4   4   5   3   2   6

Thule. Nobilis ille tamen populus, quem
Thule. noble that yet people, whom
1   3   2   1

diximus, et par Virtute atque fide, sed
we-have-spoken-of, and (their) equal in valor and fidelity, but

major clade Saguntus Tale quid excusat.
more [than equal] in calamity, Saguntus any such (deed) excuses.

Mæotide sævior arâ Ægyptus. Quippe illa
(than) the Mæotian more cruel altar Egypt (is). Since that
3   2   1

nefandi Taurica sacri Inventrix homines (ut
of the impious Tauric rite inventress men (supposing
3   1   2

jam, quæ carmina tradunt, Digna fide
now, what poems deliver, worthy of faith
     2   3

credas) tantùm immolat, ulterius nil Aut
you believe) only immolates, further nothing or
1   2   1

gravius cultro timet hostia. Qui
more grievous (than) the sacrificial knife fears the victim. what
     2   1

modò casus Impulit hos? quæ tanta
if nothing more calamity impelled these? what extreme
2   1

fames, infestaque vallo Arma coëgerunt
hunger, and threat'ning (their) rampart arms compelled
     1   3   2

tam detestabile monstrum Audere? Anne
so detestable a prodigy (of guilt) (them) to dare? could they
2   1

aliam, terrâ Memphitide siccâ, Invidiam
anyother, the land of Memphis (being) parched, infamy

facerent nolenti surgere Nilo? Quâ nec
bring unwilling to rise on the Nile? with which neither
     2   3   1

terribiles Cimbri nec Britones unquam,
the terrible Cimbri nor the Britons ever,

Sauromatæve truces, aut immanes Agathyrsi,
or Sarmatians fierce, or savage Agathyrsi,

Hâc sævit rabie imbelle et inutile vulgus,
with this raged madness the weak and worthless rabble,
     2   1

Parvula fictilibus solium dare vela phaselis,
puny to earthenware accustomed to give sails pinnaces,
3   5   1   2   4

Et   brevibus   pictæ   remis   incumbere   testæ.
and   the short   of (their) painted   oars   to ply   pottery-canoe.
      2   4   3   1

Nec   pœnam   sceleri   invenies,   nec   digna
Neither   a penalty   for crime   will you find,   nor   worthy
                                                        2

parabis   Supplicia   his   populis,   in   quorum
will you devise   tortures   these   peoples,   in   whose
    4   1   3

mente   pares   sunt   Et   similes   ira   atque   fames.
mind   equal   are   and   similar   anger   and   hunger.

Mollissima   corda   Humano   generi   dare   se
the softest   hearts   to the human   race   to give   herself
                                              4   3

natura   fatetur,   Quæ   lacrymas   dedit:
nature   confesses,   who   tears   has given:
  1   2

hæc   nostri   pars   optima   sensùs.
this   of our   part   (is) the best   feeling,
 1   4   3   2   5

Plorare   ergò   jubet   casum   lugentis   amici,
to bewail   therefore   she bids (us)   the misfortune of a distressful friend,

Squaloremque   rei,   pupillum   ad   jura   vocantem
and the squalor   of one accused, an orphan   to   justice   summoning

Circumscriptorem,   cujus   manantia   fletu   Ora
a defrauder,   whose   suffused   with tears   face
                         2   3   1

puellares   faciunt   incerta   capilli.   Naturæ
(his) girl-like   makes   uncertain   hair.   at natur's
     4   6   7   5

imperio   gemimus,   quum   funus   adultæ
dictate   we mourn,   when   the funeral   just-grown-up
                                                2

Virginis   occurrit.   vel   terrâ   clauditur   infans,
of a virgin   meets   (us),   or   in the earth   is enclosed   the infant,
   1

Et   minor   igne   rogi.   Quis   enim   bonus
and (one) too young   for the fire of the funeral-pile.   what   for   good (man)
                                          2   1

et   face   dignus   Arcanâ,   qualem   Cereris
and   torch   worthy of   the mystic,   such as   Ceres'
       3   1   2

vult   esse   sacerdos,   Ulla   aliena   sibi   credat
wishes (him) to be   priest.   any   foreign   to himself   deems
   2   3   1   2   4   5   1

mala?   Separat   hoc   nos   A   grege   mutorum
ills?   distinguishes   this   us   from   the herd   of dumb-beasts
  3   2   1

atque   ideo   venerabile   soli   Sortiti   ingenium,
and   therefore   the revered   we alone   having received   gift-of-intellect
                      3   1   2

divinorumque   capaces,   Atque   exercendis
and of divine things   capable,   and   for practising
      2   1   2

capiendisque   artibus   apti,   Sensum   a   cœlesti
and receiving   arts   apt,   a moral-sense   from   the celestial
    1   2   4   5

demissum   traximus   arce,   Cujus   egent
sent down   have received   citadel,   which   lack [brutes]
  5   1   6   5 1

prona   et   terram   spectantia.   Mundi   Principio
prone   and   earthward   looking.   of the world   in-the-beginning
2   4   3   2   1

indulsit   communis   conditor   illis   Tantùm
vouchsafed   the common   creator   to them   only
3   1   2   4

animas,   nobis   animum   quoque,   mutuos
the vital-principle   to us   a mind   also,   mutual
                            2

ut   nos   Affectus   petere   auxilium   et   præstare
that   us   affection   to seek   aid   and   afford [it]
1 5   3

juberet,   Dispersos   trahere   in   populum,
might urge,   the scattered   to draw   into   one people,
4   2   1

migrare   vetusto   De   nemore,   et   proavis
to migrate   the ancient   from   grove,   and by [our] forefathers
2   1   4

habitatas   linquere   silvas;   Ædificare   domos
inhabited   to abandon   the woods;   to build   houses,
3   1   2

Laribus   conjungere   nostris   Tectum
homes   to join   to our own   dwelling
5   1   4   3

aliud,   tutos   vicino   limine   somnos
another's,   safe   by a neighboring   threshold   slumbers
2   7   4   5   8

Ut   collata   daret   fiducia   protegere   armis
but mutually-imparted might assurance to cover with (our) arms
1   3   6   2

Lapsum   aut   iacente   nutantem   vulnere
having fallen   or   from a great   staggering   wound
2   3   5   4   6

civem,   Communi   dare   signa   tubâ.   defendier
a fellow-citizen, from a common to give the signals trumpet, to be defended
  1   3   1   2

isdem   Turribus,   atque   unâ   portarum   clave
by the same   fortifications,   and   by one   of the gates   key
                2   4   3

teneri.   Sed   jam   serpentum   major   concordia.
to be closed in.   But   now   of serpents   greater (is)   the accord.
1

Parcit   Cognatis   maculis   similis   fera.   Quando
Spares   kindred   spots   the similar   wild-beast.   When
3   4   5   1   2   1

leoni   Fortior   eripuit   vitam   leo?   quo   nemore
a lion's   a stronger   did take away   life   lion?   in   what wood
6   3   2   5   7   4

unquam | Exspiravit | aper | majoris | dentibus | apri?
ever | perished | a boar | of a greater | by the tusks | boar?
  | | | 2|1

Indica | tigris | agit | rabidâ | cum | tigride
The Indian | tigress | maintains | the fierce | with | tigress
 | | | 2|1

pacem | Perpetuam: | sævis | inter | se | convenit
peace | Perpetual: | to savage | among | themselves | there is agreement
 | |2|4|5|1

ursis. | Ast | homini | ferrum | letale | incude | nefandâ
bears. | But | for man | iron the-death-dealing | anvil | on-the | execrable
3| | |7|6|5|4

Produxisse | parum | est; | quum | rastra | et
to have forged | too-little | it is. | while | rakes | and
3|1|2| |3

sarcula | tantùm | Assueti | coquere, | et | marris
hoes | only | accustomed | to forge, | and with | mattocks
4|5|1|2

ac | vomere | lassi | Nescierint | primi | gladios
and | ploughshare | wearied | Knew not | the primeval | swords
 | | |3|4|5

extundere | fabri. | Adspicimus | populos, | quorum
to beat out | smiths. | We behold | peoples, | whose
4|2

non | sufficit | iræ | Occidisse | aliquem; | sed
it-does-not-suffice | anger | to have killed | anyone; | but
 |2|1

pectora, | brachia, | vultum | Crediderint | genus
breasts, | arms, | face | have believed | a kind
 | | | |2

esse | cibi. | Quid | diceret | ergò, | Vel | quo
to be | of food. | What | w'd say | then, | or | whither
1| | |1 3|4

non | fugeret, | si | nunc | hæc | monstra | videret
w'd he not | flee, | if | now | these | atrocities | he sh'd see

Pythagoras, | cunctis | animalibus | abstinuit | qui
Pythagoras, | from all | animals | abstained | who
2|2|3|4|1

Tanquam | homine, | et | ventri | indulsit | non | omne
as | from man, | and | to [his] appetite | indulged | not | every

legumen?
kind of pulse?

SATIRE XVI.

ARGUMENT.

Under a pretence of pointing out to his friend Gallus the advantages of a military life, Juvenal attacks with considerable spirit the exclusive privileges which the army had acquired or usurped, to the manifest injury of the civil part of the community.

Quis   numerare   queat   felicis   praemia,   Galle,
Who   enumerate   can [when] fortunate   the advantages, Gallus,
                                     4   1   2

Militiæ?   Nam si   subeuntur prospera   castra,
of military-service? For if   is entered   a successful camp,
        3   3   1   2

Me   pavidum   exc'piat   tironem   porta   secundo
me   a timid   may receive recruit   (its) gate under an auspicious
4   5   1   3   6   2   7

S'dere.   Plus etenim   fati   valet   hora   benigni,
star.   More for   fate   avails   an hour of benignant,
  3   6   1   4   5   2   3

Quàm   si   nos   Veneris commendet   epistola   Marti,
than   if   us   of Venus   should commend a letter   to Mars,
             4   2   3   1

Et   Samiâ   genitrix   quæ   delectatur   arenâ.
and   in the Samian   (his) mother   who   delights   sandy-shore.
      4   1   2   3

Commoda   tractemus   primùm   communia,   quorum
advantages   let-us-treat   first   common,   of which
    4   1   2   3

Haud   min'mum   illud   erit,   ne   te   pulsare
not   the least   that   will be, that not you to strike
                     3   6   5

togatus   Audeat;   immo,   etsi   pulsetur,
a civilian must dare: nay,   even though he be beaten,
    1   2   4

dissimu'et,   nec   Audeat   excussos   Prætori
he must dissemble   nor   dare   the knocked out to the praetor
                                        3

ostendere   dentes,   Et   nigram   in   facie   tumidis
to show   teeth,   and the black in the face with swellings
   1   4   2   3   4   6

livoribus   offam,   Atque   oculum   medico
livid   bruise,   and   the eye   the physician
5   1   2

nil   promittente   relictum.   Bardaïcus   judex
nothing promising   left.   a Bardaic   judge
4   3   1

datur   hæc   punire   volenti   Calceus,
is assigned these [things] to punish to [him] wishing (namely) a soldier's boot,
         3   2   1

et grandes   magna   ad   subsellia   suræ,   Legibus
and stout   the capacious at   benches   calves,   the Laws
                  3   2   4   1   2

antiquis   castrorum,   et   more   Camilli   Servato,
ancient   of the camp   and the custom of Camillus being observed,
1

miles   ne   vallum   litiget   extra,   Et   procul
(that) a soldier not   the trench   must litigate beyond,   and at a distance
             2   5   1   3   4

a   signis.   Justissima   Centurionum   Cognitio
from the standards. Most ju t [of course] of the Centurions the decision
                                                             4   3

est   igitur   de   milite;   nec   mihi   deerit   Ultio,
is   therefore   respecting the soldier; nor   will there be wanting to me revenge
1   2

si   justæ   defertur   causa   querelæ.   Tota
if   for just   be alleged   a ground   complaint.   the whole
2   4   1   3   2

cohors   tamen   est   inimica,   omnesque   manipli
cohort   yet   is [your] enemy,   and all   the maniples
3   1

Consensu   magno   efficiunt,   curabilis   ut
with unanimity great   bring-it-to-pass, to be apprehended that
2   1   4   1

sit   Vindicta   et   gravior,   quàm   injuria.
may be [your] redress   and   more grievous, than   the injury.
3   2

Dignum   erit   ergo   Declamatoris   mulino
Worthy   will it be therefore   of the declaimer   the mulish
                                      3   1

corde   Vagelli,   Quum   duo   crura   habeas,
heart   Vagellius,   when   two   legs   you have,
2

offendere   tot   caligas,   tot   Millia   clavorum.
to-run-foul-of   so many   soldier-shoes, so many   thousands   of hob-nails.

Qu's   tam   procul   absit   ab   Urbe?   Præterea
Who   so   far   can-be-absent from   the City?   Besides
            2   3   1

quis   tam   Pylades,   molem   aggeris   ultra
who [will be] such   a Pylades,   the mole   of the rampart beyond
                                                     4   3

Ut   veniat?   lacrymæ   siccentur   protenus,   et   se
as   to go?   let tears   be dried   forthwith,   and   themselves
1   2   1   6

Excusaturos   non   sollicitemus   amicos.   Da
sure-to-excuse   let us not importune   (our) friends. "Produce
5   2   3   4

testem, judex quum dixerit: audeat ille,
(your] witness," the judge when shall say: let dare that man,
                2   1

Nescio quis, pugnos qui vidit, dicere,
I know not who, the cuffs who saw, to say,
                 3   1   2

Vidi. Et credam, dignum barbam dignumque
'I saw," and I shall believe (him) worthy of the beard and wort.iy

capillis Majorum. Citiùs falsum producere
the long hair of our ancestors. More readily a false suborn
                      2   4   3

testem Contra paganum possis, quàm vera
witness against a civilian you c'd, than (one) the truth
                         1   2

loquentem Contra fortunam armati, contraque
speaking against the fortune of-the-man-at-arms, and against
1

pudorem. Præmia nunc alia, atque alia
(his) honor. Rewards now other, and other
             5   2   ·4

emolumenta notemus Sacramentorum. Convallem
emoluments let-us note of military-oaths. A valley
                1   3

ruris aviti Improbus, aut campum mihi si vicinus
rural-estate of (my) ancestral a dishonest, or a field me if neighbor
       9   8   2   10   11 5 1   3

ademit Et sacrum effodit medio de
has deprived of and the sacred has dug up the intermediate from
   4   6   2   1   5   4

limite saxum, Quod mea cum vetulo coluit
boundary stone, which my with the ancient has honored
   6   3   4   5   3

puls annua libo; Debitor aut sumptos
pulse annual offering-cake; a debtor or loaned
 2   1   6   2   1   6

pergit non reddere nummos, Vana supervacui
persists not to return money, (are) false of the useless
  3   4   5   5   3

dicens chirographa ligni: Exspectandus erit,
saying the hand-writings wood: will-have-to-be-waited-for,
 1   2   4   7

qui lites inchoet, annus Totius populi:
which litigations begins, the year of a whole people:
 2   4   3   ·1   5   6

sed tunc quoque mille · ferenda Tædia,
but then also a thousand must-be-borne tedious things,
                           4   1

mille moræ; toties subsellia tantùm
a thousand delays; so many times the benches only
      2   3

Sternuntur; jam facundo ponente lacernas
are spread [with cushions;] now the eloquent laying-aside [his] cloak
                                 2

Cædicio, et Fusco jam micturiente, parati
Cædicius, and Fuscus now making-water, (though) prepared
1

Digredimur, lentâque fori pugnamus arenâ
We part, and in the slow of the forum fight arena
2 4 1 3

Ast illis, quos arma tegunt, et balteus
But for those, whom arms cover, and the belt

ambit, Quod pla itum est ipsis, præstatur
surrounds Which pleases themselves, is fixed,
2

tempus agendi, Nec res atteritur longo
the time for pleading, nor is [their] fortune rubbed away by the long
1

sufflamine litis. Solis præterea testandi
drag-chain of litigation. alone besides of making a will
3 1 6

militibus jus, Vivo patre, datur. nam,
to soldiers the privilege (being) alive th father, is granted: for,
2 4 8 7 5 1

quæ sunt parta labore Militiæ,
w at has been earned by the toil of military-service,
3 4 5 6

placuit non esse in corpore censûs,
it-has-been-determined not is in the body of the estate,
2 8 7

Omne tenet cujus regimen pater. Ergò
the entire holds of which disposal the father. Therefore
4 3 1 5 2

Coranum, Signorum comitem, castrorumque
Coranus, of the standards an attendant, and of the camp
2 1 3 6

æra merentem, Quamvis jam tremulus,
the pay earning, although now trembling (with age),
5 4 2

captat pater. Hunc favor æquus
pays court to [his] father. Him favor equal
1 2 1

Provehit, et pulchro reddit sua dona labori.
advances, and t honorable renders its gifts labor.
4 1 2 3

Ipsius certè ducis hoc referre videtur,
himself certainly the general this to concern seems.
6 2 5 1 4 3

Ut, qui fortis erit, sit felicissimus idem,
that who brave shall be, sh'd be the most fortunate the same.
2 1

Ut læti pha'eris omnes, et torquibus
that joyous in (their) trappings all (may be), and in (their) chains

omnes.
all.

THE END.

(22)

CLASSICAL WORKS,

PUBLISHED BY CHARLES DESILVER,

1229 CHESTNUT STREET, PHILADELPHIA.

HAMILTON, LOCKE, AND CLARKE'S INTERLINEAR CLASSICS

THE WORKS

OF

P. VIRGILIUS MARO;

WITH

THE ORIGINAL TEXT REDUCED TO THE NATURAL ORDER OF CONSTRÚCTION |
AND AN

INTERLINEAR TRANSLATION,

AS NEARLY LITERAL AS THE IDIOMATIC DIFFERENCES OF THE LATIN **AND**
ENGLISH LANGUAGES WILL ALLOW.

ADAPTED TO THE SYSTEM OF CLASSICAL INSTRUCTION,

COMBINING

The Methods of Ascham, Milton, and Locke.

BY LEVI HART AND V. R. OSBORN.

In one volume, royal 12mo.. 512 pages, half turkey-morocco binding. **Price, $2.25.**

CÆSAR'S COMMENTARIES;

WITH AN

Analytical and Interlinear Translation

OF THE

FIRST FIVE BOOKS.

FOR THE USE OF SCHOOLS AND PRIVATE LEARNERS.

A New and more Correct Edition,

WITH AN

INTERLINEAR TRANSLATION

OF THE

SIXTH AND SEVENTH BOOKS,

BY THOMAS CLARK.

In one volume, royal 12mo., 435 pages, half turkey-morocco binding. **Price, $2.25.**

The plan of these works is not new. It is merely the adaptation of the expe
rience of many of the best and most inquiring minds in educational pursuits—me-
thodizing what was vague and loose. When the Latin tongue was the only language of diplomacy and scientific international communication, to acquire a
knowledge of it was considered of more importance than now. This method was
then recommended by Cardinal Wolsey, John Ascham, Latin Secretary to Queen
Elizabeth, by the best *Latin scholar and writer* of his time, John Milton, and also
by John Locke. In teaching classes by *oral dictation*, these works present advantages that no others contain.

Series of Interlinear Classics.

THE

ILIAD OF HOMER,

WITH AN

INTERLINEAR TRANSLATION.

For the Use of Schools and Private Learners,

ON THE

HAMILTONIAN SYSTEM,

AS IMPROVED BY

THOMAS CLARK,

EDITOR OF THE LATIN AND GREEK INTERLINEAR CLASSICS.

In one volume, royal 12mo, 368 pages, half turkey-morocco binding *Price,* $2.75

The first three books of this interlinear edition of the Iliad of Homer have been translated by HAMILTON; the rest, namely, the fourth, fifth, sixth, seventh, and eighth, by the editor of this American edition. These five last-mentioned books have been translated on the same plan by the editor as that on which he translated Xenophon's Anabasis — being intermediate to the plans of HAMILTON and LOCKE; — the signification of each individual word being clearly given, and so combined as to form a clear and intelligible sentence.

In preparation: *Xenophon's Memorabilia*, with Interlinear Translation by Hamilton and Clark. To be followed by School Editions of the other Classic authors on the same plan.

SERIES OF INTERLINEAR CLASSICS.

SELECTIONS

FROM THE

METAMORPHOSES AND HEROIDES

OF

PUBLIUS OVIDIUS NASO

WITH A

LITERAL AND INTERLINEAR TRANSLATION

ON THE HAMILTONIAN SYSTEM

AS IMPROVED

BY THOMAS CLARK,

Editor of the Greek and Latin Interlinear Classics.

BY GEO. WILLIAM HEILIG.

One vol. royal 12mo., half Turkey Morocco binding. Price, $2.25

THE SATIRES

OF

DECIMUS JUNIUS JUVENALIS.

WITH A LITERAL INTERLINEAR TRANSLATION

ON THE HAMILTONIAN SYSTEM

AS IMPROVED

BY THOMAS CLARK.

WITH THE LIFE OF JUVENAL,

BY WILLIAM GIFFORD, ESQ.

FOR THE USE OF SCHOOLS AND PRIVATE LEARNERS,

BY HIRAM CORSON, M.A.,

*Professor of English Literature, Rhetoric, and Oratory in the Cornell University ; Editor of
"Chaucer's Legende of Goode Women;" late Professor of Rhetoric, and of the English
Language and Literature, in St. John's College, Annapolis ; late Professor of Moral
Science, History, and Rhetoric in Girard College, Philadelphia.*

One vol. royal 12mo, half Turkey Morocco binding. Price, $2.25.

THE GOSPEL OF ST. JOHN

IN GREEK;

WITH AN INTERLINEAR AND ANALYTICAL TRANSLATION

ON THE PRINCIPLES OF

THE HAMILTONIAN SYSTEM

AS IMPROVED

BY THOMAS CLARK,

Late Editor of the Latin and Greek Interlinear Classics,

To which is appended

A CRITICAL ANNOTATION; ALSO THE AUTHORIZED ENGLISH VERSION OF THE
PROTESTANT CHURCH, AND A COMPARATIVE VIEW OF THE CATHOLIC
TRANSLATION FROM THE VULGATE, WITH HISTORICAL NOTES,

BY GEO. WILLIAM HEILIG.

One vol. royal 12mo, half Turkey Morocco binding. Price, $2.75.

(JUST PUBLISHED.)

TITUS LIVIUS.

SELECTIONS

FROM

THE FIRST FIVE BOOKS.

TOGETHER WITH THE

TWENTY-FIRST AND TWENTY-SECOND BOOKS ENTIRE.

WITH AN INTERLINEAR TRANSLATION

ON THE HAMILTONIAN SYSTEM.

The Original Text being reduced to the Natural Order of Construction,

For the Use of Schools and Private Learners.

BY REV. I. W. BIEBER.

In one volume, royal 12mo, 624 pages, half Turkey morocco binding.
Price, $2.25.

OPINIONS OF THE PRESS.

"The Satires of Decimus Junius Juvenalis, with a literal interlinear translation, by Hiram Corson, M.A." This work is one of a series of interlinear translations of the Latin Classics used in teaching the ancient languages according to the Hamiltonian system. Juvenal, in this form, has never before been published in the United States, and the present edition will be exceedingly useful to those persons who desire to become acquainted with the writings of the most bitter satirist ever known. Juvenal's description of the vices of the ancients presents a fearful spectacle of the wickedness of ancient Rome, but should be read only by advanced students. In accordance with Juvenal's doctrine, *maxima debetur puero reverentia*, "the greatest respect is due to a child," Mr. Corson has omitted the translations of the objectionable passages. — *Public Ledger, Philada.*

"The Satires of Decimus Junius Juvenalis, by Hiram Corson, M.A., Professor of English Literature, Rhetoric, and Oratory in the Cornell University." This, an interlinear edition, has Gifford's Life of the author and the sixteen Satires. The interlining runs with the text and renders translation easy to the greatest neophyte. So far as such aids are ever commendable, this is to be praised; but it is a still undecided question whether the pupil is really advanced by them, or, if undecided, the balance is against the practice. The volume is issued in a very handsome manner, and will be serviceable to teachers and to elderly gentlemen whose Latinity is a little rusty. There are no notes. Each Satire carries its lessons and argument as a brief prefix. — *N. A. and U. S. Gazette, Philada.*

Series of Interlinear Classics.

OPINIONS OF THE PRESS.

The Satires of Decimus Junius Juvenalis, with a Literal Interlinear Translation on the Hamiltonian System, by Hiram Corson, M.A., with the Life of Juvenal, by Wm. Gifford. Esq.*

The fine scholarship of Dr. Corson is an ample guaranty of the value of this translation. The order of the original has been preserved, and it is altogether the most satisfactory issue of the series of interlinear translations to which it belongs. — *The Keystone, Philada.*

Prof. Corson's interlinear translation of Juvenal has the excellence of being *au pied du lettre ;* every word has under it its exact equivalent, the difference between the Latin and English sequence being indicated by figures. Gifford's Life of Juvenal introduces the edition It is excellent for schools or private study. — *Evening Bulletin, Philada.*

To those who prefer this method of Latin study, this work is admirably adapted, for it not only presents, one beneath the other, the Latin word and the English meaning, but the order of the original has been preserved, and the order in which the words of the translation should be read, when it differs from the English order, is indicated by numerals. — *Morning Post, Philada.*

Why do not people teach Latin and Greek as they do French and German, and as it was taught in the golden age of learning? Where is the American student who, after working away half a dozen years in the classics and getting his diploma, can talk and read Latin with the ease of a German "fox" just entered at the University? It is time that this "old fogy. ism" were sent to the right about face — or rather that the real old fogyism, which had some sense in it, were revived. Meanwhile, we commend this excellent translation of " Sallust" to all enlightened teachers desirous of teaching Latin as a language, and not as a grim " discipline." — *Ladies' Journal.*

" Xenophon's Anabasis" is one of the series of Interlinear Classics, of which Virgil, Cæsar, Horace, &c., have already appeared. These interlinears are rapidly superseding every other mode of translation for scholastic purposes. The plan adopted by this translator is somewhat peculiar, being intermediate between the systems of Hamilton and Locke. The book will be found of great service to the student of the Greek language, as it removes many of the difficulties so perplexing in its study. — *Philada. Sunday Transcript.*

This interlinear edition of Cæsar is, for the first five books of the Gallic war, a revised edition of Hamilton's Cæsar, published in London. The sixth and seventh books of the Gallic war have been expressly translated for the present edition, by Thomas Clark, the American editor. Not only is this volume useful to the young, but also to those who wish to keep alive their knowledge of the Latin language. — *Baptist Fam. Magazine.*

" Xenophon's Anabasis" is here published with an interlinear translation, according to the Hamiltonian system, and we confess that we are decidedly in favor of such an easy and literal method of study, provided only that it be not undertaken or indulged in until after a tolerably correct notion of the grammar, or the construction of a dead or foreign language, shall have been first ascertained. — *Pennsylvania Inquirer.*

Like the preceding volumes, this Interlinear translation of " Xenophon's Anabasis," is intended for the use of schools and private learners, and confident we are that, by the aid of such books, the principal difficulties of translation are readily removable. — *Philada. Press.*

An excellent translation of " Xenophon's Anabasis," Greek text with English interlinear revision. The Greek type deserves special notice from its great beauty and striking legibility. The work is admirably printed on fine paper and neatly bound. — *Evening Bulletin.*

This " Interlinear translation of Xenophon's Anabasis" has been prepared with much care and learning, upon a system intermediate between those of Hamilton and Locke. To students of the Greek language such a book will be very valuable. — *Philada. Sunday Dispatch.*

The interlinear translations of " Horace and Cæsar" are evidently the result of much care, study and research, and the getting-up reflects the highest credit upon the enterprising publisher. — *Saturday Courier.*

Series of Interlinear Classics.

OPINIONS OF THE PRESS.

" Sallust," another of the series of Interlinear Classics, has just been issued from the press. It is pretty well known by this time that the quickest, most accurate and most scientific method of studying Latin or Greek is by means of interlinear translations. During the great era of classical scholarship, when Latin was learned so as to be fluently spoken, such aids were generally used. How it is that in the classes graduating at Colleges, in this country, there is seldom one single individual who can read any ordinary Latin without a dictionary, although nearly every one of them has probably devoted, on an average, one or two hours per diem to that language, for at least seven years? Such was *not* the state of scholarship in the days when beginners used literal translations. As regards the work before us, we commend it to all collegians and school-boys. It is prepared with the utmost accuracy, and is beautifully printed and bound.— *Evening Bulletin, Philada.*

We have two new volumes of the excellent series of interlinear translations of the Classics. One contains " Cicero's four orations against Catiline," with the "seven remaining orations," expressly translated for this edition by Mr. Thomas Clark, the competent American editor. This is, therefore, the most complete collection, with translations, of Cicero's finest eloquence. Another volume, translated by Hamilton, and also carefully revised, with additions, by Mr. Clark, is "Sallust — the Catiline Conspiracy and the Jugurthan War." — *Philada. Press.*

The schoolboy use of interlinear translations of the Classics has never been much favored by teachers, though the system has the sanction of common sense, and has been warmly recommended by such able and erudite men as Cardinal Wolsey, Erasmus, Roger Ascham, John Milton, John Locke, and Sydney Smith. We believe, with Sydney Smith, that this system, " the time being given, will make better scholars; and, the degree of scholarship being given, a much shorter time will be needed." — *New York Daily Times.*

Mr. Clark, the American editor, has translated the two last books of the Gallic War, expressly for the present edition of Cæsar's Commentaries — having revised that of Hamilton. He has followed the method of Locke, which has been approved by many teachers, and is a most useful innovation, superseding the former plan throughout the United States. — *New York Sun.*

Despite the acquirements of classical scholars, there are few to whom such adequate translations as these, of " Horace and Cæsar," do not frequently prove valuable, while to others they are not only invaluable, but indispensable. It would be idle to commend such works, for no one can be ignorant of their worth and importance. — *Philada. Evening Journal.*

To the student who finds a translation necessary in his classical studies, these interlinear translations of Cæsar, Horace, Virgil, &c., are very highly commended by eminent names. The students of the University will find great assistance from these works in their study of the Latin language. — *Virginia Advocate, Charlottsville, Virginia.*

A more admirable literal translation of every word in Cæsar's great work it would be impossible to meet with. It must serve as the best possible guide for the Latin student. An other volume contains a translation of the odes, satires and epistles of Horace, rendered as literally as need be. — *Daily Delta, New Orleans.*

Chas. Desilver, of this city, is publishing interlinear translations of the classics, which some of the finest minds deem the best adapted for learning languages. These volumes, " Horace and Cæsar," appear to be produced with great care, and in a style which will commend them to every student. — *Philada. Public Ledger.*

Milton, Locke, and others have recommended the method of instruction by means of interlinear translations. The appearance of this edition of " Horace" is substantial and attractive, and will prove useful to youth, and also to others engaged in the study of the Latin language. — *Baptist Fam. Magazine.*

These interlinear translations of " Cæsar and Horace" are very nicely printed. In strong handsome bindings, and will be very acceptable to teachers and students who favor this manner of teaching the Latin language. — *Boston Daily Advertiser*

MISCELLANEOUS WORKS,

PUBLISHED BY CHARLES DESILVER,
1229 CHESTNUT STREET, PHILADELPHIA.

THE BOOK
OF
DRAWING-ROOM PLAYS,
AND
EVENING AMUSEMENTS.

A COMPREHENSIVE

MANUAL OF IN-DOOR RECREATIONS:
BEING

A COLLECTION
OF
CHARADES, BURLESQUES, PROVERBS, TRAGEDIES, COMEDIES DRAMAS, FARCES, LECTURES, ETC.
ALSO,
INTELLECTUAL, ACTIVE, CATCH AND TRICK GAMES,
WITH
HINTS AND INSTRUCTIONS
Relative to the manner of "getting up" Plays, Scenes, Tableaux, etc.

BY SILAS S. STEELE,
DRAMATIST.

One volume 12mo, cloth, gilt. Price, $1.50.

Here is a book for the long winter evenings, and one that will make all merry and happy It is a collection of Plays, Farces, Lectures. Charades, Dramas, Tableaux, and other Entertainments for the use of family parties, the fireside circle, or those social gatherings among friends and neighbors, which pass away the winter evenings with so much animation and delight. It is impossible for any company to exhaust all the sources of irreproachable mirth and mutual enjoyment produced in this volume, and will be found invaluable to families, schools, social clubs, societies, etc., and as a book of reference on all matters of amusement and recreation.

OPINIONS OF THE PRESS.

This well-stocked book consists of a selection of parlor-plays, scenes from dramas, charades, burlesques, and everything where acting is required.

Very fair and often very excellent actors are found in every circle, and few persons know how much real fun can be got out of even impromptu charades until they try them. But for those who want written plays, there is no better selection than this one. — *Morning Post, Philada.*

It is one of the most comprehensive manuals of in-door recreation we have ever seen, being a collection of charades, burlesques, proverbs, tragedies, comedies, dramas, farces, and lectures, carefully arranged and adapted to private representation. In addition there are a number of games, instructions how to get up plays and tableaux, and much other kindred information. For the family, the school-room, and the seminary, this book will prove invaluable. The author has performed his task faithfully and well. — *Evening Star, Philada.*

The end sought is to accommodate lovers of private histrionics with matter that is inoffensive and at the same time amusing. To this end, plays, comedies and farces from the time of Shakspeare until now have been condensed and expurgated; several poems have been cast in dramatic form; some original plays furnished, and a quantity of miscellaneous mirth provided, fit for private entertainments. The work is very well done, and those who are arranging private theatricals will find this a convenient aid. — *N. A. and U. S. Gazette, Phila.*

STANDARD HAND-BOOK

OF

HOUSEHOLD ECONOMY FOR THE PEOPLE:

COMPRISING

Plain Directions for the Management of a Family, Servants, Lying-in Room,
Nursery, Sick-Room, Flower-Garden, Kitchen-Garden,
and Household Pets;

AND ALSO,

FOR THE PREPARATION AND ADMINISTRATION OF REMEDIES FOR DISEASE.

In one volume, royal 18mo., bound in fancy boards. Price 50 cents.

SOYER'S

STANDARD COOKERY FOR THE PEOPLE:

EMBRACING

AN ENTIRELY NEW SYSTEM OF PLAIN COOKERY AND DOMESTIC ECONOMY.

BY ALEXIS SOYER,

AUTHOR OF "THE MODERN HOUSEWIFE," ETC., ETC.

FIRST AMERICAN, FROM THE LATEST LONDON EDITION.

In one volume, royal 18mo., bound in fancy boards. Price 50 cents.

This "Cookery," by the veritable Soyer, has had an unprecedented run in England—the sales having, in a few months. reached the enormous number of 200,000 copies. It is written upon the principle of giving no directions which are not perfectly comprehensible by every reader; who can, after perusal, prepare the desired dish equally as well as could Soyer himself. Another great advantage is, that the author has not omitted the slightest article of cheap food of any description; and this, with the valuable receipts for dressing the same, has made it prove a great blessing to many, by introducing to their notice numerous articles with which they were formerly unacquainted, but which now form a large part of their daily diet.

NEW

STANDARD LETTER-WRITER

· FOR THE PEOPLE:

CONTAINING

FULL AND PRECISE DIRECTIONS FOR CONDUCTING EPISTOLARY CORRESPONDENCE

WITH

NUMEROUS SPECIMENS OF LETTERS, ADAPTED TO EVERY BUSINESS PURSUIT,
CLASS, AND GRADE OF RELATIONSHIP;   ·

MANY OF WHICH ARE

Printed in the Characters ordinarily Used in Writing.

In one royal 18mo. volume, bound in fancy boards. Price 50 cents.

105

CHARLES DESILVER,

PUBLISHER,

1229 Chestnut Street, Philadelphia,

Respectfully informs Teachers, School Committees, and the Trade generally, that all Publications may be obtained through the following named Firms:

Philadelphia: CLAXTON, REMSEN & HAFFELFINGER.
" J. B. LIPPINCOTT & CO.
" E. H. Butler & Co.
" Sower, Potts & Co.
New York: D. APPLETON & CO.
" MASON, BAKER & PRATT.
" AMERICAN NEWS CO.
" Ivison, Blakeman, Taylor & Co.
" Sheldon & Co.
"
" Leavitt & Allen Bros.
" Clarke & Maynard.
" Holt & Williams.
" Geo. R. Lockwood.
" J. W. Schermerhorn & Co.
Boston: NICHOLS & HALL.
" Lee & Shepard.
Alleghany City, Pa.: M. Spratt.
Augusta, Ga.: Thos. Richards & Son.
" " George A. Oates.
Ann Arbor, Mich.: Gilmore & Fiske.
Buffalo, N. Y.: Breed, Lent & Co.
" " Theo. Butler & Sons.
Baltimore, Md.: Cushings & Bailey.
" " Cushings & Medairy.
" " W. J. C. Dulany & Co.
" " J. Murphy & Co.
Cincinnati, O.: Wilson, Hinkle & Co.
" ROB'T CLARKE & CO.
" W. H. Moore, Sons & Co.
Cleveland, " Cobb & Bros.
" " Ingham, Clarke & Co.
Columbus, " Randall, Aston & Co.
Chicago, Ill.: W. B. Keen & Cooke.
" " JANSEN, McCLURG & CO.
" "
Columbia, S. C.: W. J. Duffie & Co.
Charleston, " J. M. Greer & Son.
" " Edward Perry & Son.
Galveston, Texas: J. E. Mason.

Hartford, Conn.: W. J. Hamersley & Co.
Indianapolis, Ind.: Bowen, Stewart & Co.
Ithaca, N. Y.: Andrus, McChain & Lyons.
" " D. F. Finch.
Louisville, Ky.: J. P. Morton & Co.
" " Sherrill, Pratt & Co.
Lansing, Mich.: J. S. Baker.
Lexington, Ky.: Purnell & Rodes.
Memphis, Tenn.: H. Wade & Co.
Montreal : Dawson Bros.
Mobile, Ala.: Manly & Co.
" " T. S. Bidgood.
Montgomery, Ala.: Joel White.
Macon, Ga.: J. M. Boardman.
" " J. W. Burke & Co.
New Haven, Conn.: H. H. Peck.
" " Sidney Babcock.
New Orleans, La.: Stevens & Seymour.
" " J. A. Gresham.
Nashville, Tenn.: W. T. Berry & Co.
Pittsburg, Pa.: S. A. Clarke & Co.
" " Kay & Co.
Quincy, Ill.: Dayton & Arthur.
Raleigh, N. C.: Williams & Lambeth.
Richmond, Va.: Woodhouse & Parham.
" " Starke & Ryland.
St. Louis, Mo.: Keith & Woods.
" " St. Louis Book & News Co
San Francisco, Cal.: A. L. BANCROFT & CO.
" " A. Roman & Co.
Savannah, Ga.: J. M. Cooper & Co.
" " H. L. Schreiner.
" " J. W. Randolph & English.
St. Paul, Minn.: Combs & Whitney.
St. John's, N. B.: J. & A. McMillan.
Toronto, C. W.: Adam, Stevenson & Co.
" " H. B. Nims & Co.
Tuscaloosa, Ala.: D. Woodruff.
Vicksburg, Miss.: H. C. Clarke.
Washington, D. C.: R. B. Mohun & Co.
Wheeling, Va.: Campbell & McDermot.

And from Booksellers generally throughout the United States and the Canadas.

DESCRIPTIVE CATALOGUES furnished on application, and any book will be sent by mail, postage paid, on receipt of the advertised price.

☞ CHARLES DESILVER has on hand, and can furnish the publications of all other Houses on the most favorable terms.

☞ Names in capitals are Special Agents.